UPON THIS ROCK

BOOK 1
FIRST CONTACT

by
David Marusek

A STACK OF FIREWOOD PRESS
FAIRBANKS

Published by A Stack of Firewood Press
An imprint of General Genius LLC
Fairbanks, Alaska

ISBN 978-0-9988633-0-6 (epub)
ISBN 978-0-9988633-1-3 (mobi)
ISBN 978-0-9988633-2-0 (softcover)
First Printing

For my sister Marie

If it turns out that God really does exist,
when you get to Heaven,
please make a case to Saint Peter
for springing me from Hell.

Characters and Glossary

Families

Bunyan

Dell — mid-50s. Evangelical pastor of the Blood of Victory Church which he keeps in his home. Preaches the pre-Tribulation Rapture. Lives on Stubborn Mountain Trail midway between the town of McHardy and the Prophecy household.

Chas — eldest of four sons. 25 years old. Navy SEAL and veteran of Iraq/ Afghanistan Wars.

Scarlett — only daughter. 13 years old. Energetic and outgoing. Sharp tongue.

Prophecy

Poppy — 79 years old. Real name Marvin Johnson. Believes in pre-millennial post-Tribulation Rapture. Desires a family of 21 children. Brings family to Alaska to sit out the Apocalypse.

Mama — 41 years old. Real name Crystal Johnson. Mother of 17 children. Currently on vacation in Heaven.

Adam — eldest born. 25 years old. A calm, capable, dependable, slightly reserved young man. Fiancé to Sue Krae.

Hosea — 2nd born. 23 years old. A warm-hearted, genuine, spiritual, not too bright man.

Proverbs — 3rd born. 21 years old. A fiery, impulsive, attractive, energetic young man. Holds the record for number of whippings received as disciplinary punishment. Victim of grievous childhood accident, he sometimes wears a leather patch on his right eye. Together with Adam and Hosea referred to as "the boys."

Sarai — 4th born. 19 years old. Eldest girl (by five minutes). A fraternal (heterozygotic) twin of Deuteronomy. Sometimes bossy. The unfortunate "twice-blessed twin of a twin."

Deuteronomy ("Deut") — 5th born. 19 years old. Sarai's twin. Very sweet, dutiful, devout, and perhaps a little naive. Beloved by all the younger siblings. Together with Sarai and II Corinthians known as "the girls."

I Corinthians ("Corny") — 6th born. 17 years old. Male. Eldest of the "middle kids." A bit of a bully.

II Corinthians ("Cora") — 7th born. 15 years old. Female. Very reliable and helpful. Dreams of an independent life.

Solomon ("Solly") — 8th born. 13 years old. Male.

Frankincense ("Frankie") — 9th born. 12 years old. Female. Identical (monozygotic) twin to Myrrh.

Myrrh — 10th born. 12 years old. Female. Twin to Frankincense.

Ithamar ("Ithy") — 11th born. 10 years old. Male. Average kid, constant companion to Uzziel.

Incense — 12th child (stillborn). Female. Considered a member of the family who resides in Heaven. A place is set for her at the table.

Uzziel ("Uzzie") — 13th born. 8 years old. Male. Eldest of the "little kids." Beloved by all. Possibly the smartest kid in the bunch.

Revelation ("Revie") — 14th born. 6 years old. Female.

Pharisees ("See Saw") — 15th born. 5 years old. Female.

Numbers ("Nummy") — 16th born. 3 years old. Male. Extremely jealous of his little brother.

Elzaphan ("Elzie") — 17th born. 18 months old. Male. The spoiled baby of the family. A little tyrant to all his siblings.

Crystal Louise Puddingpot ("Crissy Lou") — Family dog. Female German Shepherd mix. Considers herself Uzziel's dog.

Calgary — Female tabby cat.

Lawther

Rex — Mid-50s. Middle-class, Republican, small business owner of Greatland Action Sports in Wallis, Alaska. Pentecostal church elder and deacon. Honest to a fault. Good father. Pillar of community. Candidate for state office.

Cindy — 48 years old. Helpmeet to husband Rex. Homeschools kids. Volunteers in community projects.

Ginger — 19 years old. Homeschooled. Bright, fearless. Devout Christian young woman. High achiever.

Rory — 18 years old. Average student. Quit homeschooling in junior high. On high school wrestling team. Student pilot. Mechanic. Falls desperately in love with Deuteronomy.

Keagan — family dog. Male whippet.

Sulzer

Ed — 82 years old. Lives at McHardy airstrip. Paints Alaska kitsch landscapes on goldpans.

Virginia ("Ginny") — 72 years old. Also a goldpan painter. Acts as unofficial postmaster of McHardy.

Tetlin

Vera — early 40s. Beloved governor of Alaska. Losing 2008 vice-presidential candidate.

Bradd — early 40s. Snowmachine racing champion. Oil pipeline worker. "First Dude" of the state of Alaska.

Taiga ("Tye") — 20-year-old daughter.

Others

Orion Beehymer — mid-80s. Long-time McHardy area land baron. Sold house to Jace and Stubborn Mountain Mine to the Prophecy family.

Beezus — a high-ranking devil who torments Poppy Prophecy.

Agent Bertolli — special agent of the FBI.

Jeff Bridges ("Not Jeff Bridges," "NJB") — full name: Jefferson Beaumont Bridges. Poppy Prophecy's friend and business mentor. Shady background.

Kelly Cogwheel — Tea Party resident of McHardy. Owns McHardy Hotel and Saloon.

Danielle — mid-20s. French girl who visits Jace in Alaska.

Sue Krae — 22 years old. From Soldotna, Alaska. Fiancée of Adam Prophecy.

Jace Kuliak — late 20s. National Park Service Backcountry Ranger who lives year-round in McHardy. His sister Kate Kapoor, her husband Darshan, and their son Luke live in Littleton, Colorado.

Ethan Parkhurst Masterson — mid 40s. National Park Service Law Enforcement Ranger. Jace's colleague and supervisor. Extreme advocate of public wilderness.

Agent Nabor — federal special agent of the FIAS.

Ned Nellis — longtime bush pilot and owner of Nellis Air Service in Gulkana, Alaska. Runs the McHardy mail route.

Evelyn Rodgers — National Park Service superintendent stationed in Copper

Center, Alaska.

Yurek Rutz — just because.

Barbara Jean de Saul — seeker of enlightenment who lives in McHardy.

D "Beaver" Swayne — early 30s. Colonel, commander of the Alaska Liberty Force.

Glossary

ALF — Alaska Liberty Force. An Alaska-based citizen's militia under the command of Colonel D "Beaver" Swayne.

Arctic Entry — a small room adjoining the exterior door of a house, usually unheated. A place to don and store outdoor boots and garments. Also known as mudroom or wannigan.

HIS CREATIONS LLC — the Prophecy handcrafts business.

Lower 48 — the contiguous states of the United States of America. That is, the fifty states minus Alaska and Hawaii.

Outside — anywhere not in Alaska.

Shadow — the "buddy system" imposed on the Prophecy children so that no one is ever alone. Its purpose is to deny Satan opportunity for leading them astray.

The Slide — the steep hillside made of mine tailings beneath the adit to Stubborn Mountain Mine. A footpath zig-zags up it.

Sno-go, Snowmachine, Snowmobile — all terms for a motorized sled for traveling on snowy terrain.

Tired Iron — an antique snowmachine.

Touron — a disparaging term for tourist.

Up/Down Conventions Used in This Work

River, stream — Every river or stream begins at a source or sources (headwaters, glacier, lake, drainage basin) and ends at a mouth or mouths, where its water flows into another body of water. Going upstream or upriver means moving toward the source, while going downstream or downriver means moving toward the mouth.

Tunnel — An adit or mine entrance can be considered the mouth of a mine tunnel. Going up tunnel is moving away from the entrance further into the mine. Going down tunnel means moving toward the entrance from inside the mine.

Roads, trails — Traveling toward the origin of a road (or trail) is considered going up the road. Moving away from the origin is going down it. However, designating a place as an origin point is a subjective matter that can change according to each traveler's point of view.

Contents

Bolt-hole Earth   12
Mail Day   12
Trash Run   36
A Portent in the Sky   44
The Toothache   47
Looking for Love (in All the Wrong Places)   64
Cat and Woodpecker   84
NORAD of the North   108
First Contact   131
A Vial of Wrath   150
The Winged Spy   176
An Angel Falls from Heaven   202
Calling All Angels   236
The Federal Dicks   258
The Bringer of Sorrow   297
Social Media   315
Caw Caw   320

Sidebars

From time to time in the text, you will encounter prompts inviting you to read additional material. These are "sidebars," the text equivalent of the bonus material on a DVD. While these sidebars may expand your understanding and enjoyment of the story, they generally contain no information that is essential to it. Read them now, read them later, or ignore them altogether. (Actually, do read them — they're fun.)

Sidebar: Ghost Town with Footbridge   321
Sidebar: Sex on a Glacier   323
Sidebar: A Herd of Picnic Tables   334
Sidebar: Tour of the Mine   341
Sidebar: The Kitten of Our Discontent   346
Sidebar: The Man in the Skiff   347
Sidebar: A Taste of Wormwood   353
Sidebar: So He Masturbated   355
Sidebar: Raven Song   358
Acknowledgements   358
Reading List   359
Errors and Whatnot   360
Book 2   360

Bolt-hole Earth

BE1 1.0

NOT LONG AGO, in a small volume of ordinary space in the galactic south, the vacuum began to boil and seethe with non-ordinary energy.

[Following is a storyboard script for an animated prologue.]

Panel 1: A swatch of foaming, boiling space. Below it, we see the Sun and several of the planets of our solar system. In the distant background we see a wide swath of stars — The Milky Way.

Panels 2 & 3: A tiny object is expelled violently from the volume of agitated space.

Panels 4 through 6: We close in on the object. As we do, we catch glimpses of other celestial objects in the background — Saturn's rings, the asteroid belt, a NASA probe.

Panel 7: The tiny object is revealed in close-up. Three glittering spheres, like golden marbles, are combined in the shape of a chevron. The central sphere is slightly larger than the wings. One of the wings is deflated and puckered like a raisin.

Panels 8 through 11: Our point of view shifts to that of the object as it passes the Moon and approaches Earth. Earth grows larger until it fills the entire frame, which is centered on the landmass of Alaska and Canada's Yukon Territory.

Panel 12: We are hurtling straight down into a landscape of mountains, forest, ice, and snow.

Mail Day

MD1 1.0

WHEN THE SNOWFALL tapered off and the night sky cleared, moonlight flooded the land. A bull moose, or the phantom of one, lurked in thick willow brush at the edge of the field. Proverbs raised his rifle and drew a bead on it.

"Don't shoot," his brother whispered in his ear.

The two young men stood next to the toolshed across the yard from the main house. Proverbs sighted down the barrel of the rifle and leaned forward. "Why not?" he whispered back.

"It's too dark. You'll miss'im."

"I can see him fine."

"You'll wing'im."

"I will if you don't shut the heck up."

"Your language, brother."

"What about my language, brother?"

The old bull raised its heavy-antlered head to glance in the boys' direction before trundling away.

"Now see what you done."

"Me? It was you."

But the moose stopped at another clump of willow brush and resumed browsing the tender twigs. Still, Proverbs held fire.

"What's wrong?" his brother whispered.

"Quiet. I'm taking the shot."

"When? Tomorrow?"

MD2 1.0

DEUTERONOMY CARRIED THE toddler into the common room where the children sat at tables eating a breakfast of oatmeal and canned peaches. Mama was propped up in her lawn lounger with the tabby sitting on her lap.

"Begone, cat," Deuteronomy said, swiping at it with her free hand.

"Gone, cat," the toddler said, mimicking her.

The cat stretched leisurely before hopping down.

Balancing her brother on her hip, Deuteronomy draped the nursing shawl over her mother's shoulders and unbuttoned the top of her blouse. "Mama, Elzie's here for his breakfast."

Across the room, a boy shouted, "Me first," and slid off the bench. The other children tried to grab him, but he slipped through their hands and ran to Deuteronomy. "It's my turn," he bellowed, trying to push his little brother away.

"*Stop that*," Deuteronomy said. "It's Elzie's turn."

"No, it's not!" he insisted. "I'm the eldest."

"Hush. You'll wake Poppy."

The boy drummed the wood floor with his heels. "I don't care!"

"Now listen to me. Wait your turn or you won't get *any*. I mean it." She signaled for one of the middle girls to come fetch the boy. Then she set Elzaphan on Mama's lap. The toddler ducked under the shawl and went lustily to work.

Deuteronomy's own breakfast waited at the grown-ups' table, but before she could sit down, there was the sound of a gunshot outside. Everyone stopped what they were doing and looked at the door. Deuteronomy's twin came out of the kitchen wearing an oven mitt on her hand. She and Deuteronomy exchanged a glance and listened. When they were about to resume their business, there was a second shot.

"Go see what's going on," Deuteronomy told one of the middle boys. "Tell 'em Poppy is still asleep."

POPPY WAS INDEED still asleep, and the first shot only half roused him from a deep, technicolor dream of wisdom. A giant, nude, Chinese woman was squatting in a field of soybeans. Her titanic cunny was a fleshy elevator. The labial doors swooshed open, and it was his turn for a slippery ride to the top.

The second gunshot shattered the dream like glass. *What foolishness now?* He recognized the gun from its report. It was the Remington .30-06, one of the hunting rifles. He lay in his warm cocoon of comforters and blankets trying to coax the meaning from the dream before it vanished.

Too late. It was already gone.

Poppy Prophecy cracked one eyelid and saw twilight outside the window. The bed next to his own was empty and made up. Taken together, these signs meant that the hour was between 7:00ish, when the girls fetched Mama, and 9:30ish, when the winter sun rose. It would be hard to return to sleep this late in the day, but Poppy yawned and turned over to try anyway.

No dice. First the front door slammed, and someone stomped their boots on the mat. Then there was a lot of urgent-sounding jibber-jabber through the wall. Then the door slammed again. More boot stomping, more jibber-jabber. Finally, the hallway floorboards creaked, and the bedroom door inched open.

"Lord?" It was his firstborn, Adam.

"Speak."

"Uh, we have a problem."

"Wait till I get up. Then you'll have two problems."

"Yes, lord. Sorry. Uh, Proverbs killed a moose."

"Praise the Lord."

"Amen. Except he shot it in the field."

"Even better. It was delivered to our door."

"Yes, lord, except — except that today is Twosday."

"So what if it is?"

"Twosday, lord — Mail Day."

At last the fog of sleep lifted from Poppy's brain. Poaching a moose so near the house on Mail Day was not a good plan. "Hand me my britches."

Adam crept into the room and lifted his father's trousers from the chair. Poppy dug into the bib pocket and pulled out a spark plug. He squinted at it and offered it to his son. "Pull it into the trees."

"Yes, lord, except that it's a big bull, maybe the biggest I ever seen. Boone-and-Crockett big. And it's stuck in the willows."

Poppy reached into the pocket for a second spark plug. His son still seemed doubtful.

"Go on. Handle it," he barked, dismissing him.

When Adam left, Poppy sat up and swung his bony legs to the floor. He yawned and stretched and scratched. He went to the corner behind the curtain to relieve himself in the honey bucket. Because he was an old man, his juices needed time to drain, and as he waited, he combed his long grey beard with his fingers and prayed, *Thank you, Father God, for all my dullard sons.*

Poppy sniffed yesterday's shirt and put it on, tucked it into his Carhartts, and pulled up his suspenders. He took the Bible from the nightstand and slipped it into its special, tooled-leather holster on his belt. All the while he listened to the sounds coming from outside. First, the age-old Polaris fired up, and then the equally old Yamaha.

When Poppy entered the common room, everyone fell silent. The children stood up next to their tables and chorused, "Good morning, lord."

"Shut up!" he snapped. "Can't you see I'm trying to listen?" He went to the window and looked out, shielding the glass from the light of the room with his hand. He could see the sno-go headlights down in the field.

"Boy," he growled, not specifying which boy he had in mind.

"Lord?" said the thirteen-year-old, the eldest boy in the room.

"Come here."

The boy sprinted to his father's side. Poppy continued to peer out the window, and the other children took the opportunity to escape from the common room.

"Chores!" Deuteronomy whisper-shouted in their wake.

"Boy," Poppy said, "I want you to get a jug of cooking oil from the kitchen and go to the shed and fetch the chainsaw and take it and the oil down to your brothers. Do you understand?"

"Yes, lord."

"Then why are you still standing here?"

The boy flew from the room. Poppy left the window and crossed the room to the warm corner, where Mama reclined in her lounger. "Good morning, Mother," he crooned, leaning over to peck her cheek. "I hope you —" At that moment, the toddler's little head popped out from under the shawl. Startled, Poppy raised his fists in alarm and staggered backward.

"Sorry, lord," Deuteronomy said, hurrying over. She extricated the child from the shawl and refastened her mother's blouse. "I'll just get him out of the way."

But Poppy had already recrossed the room to the head table, where he sat with his back to the wall. Another girl, the youngest of the eldest girls, came out of the kitchen bearing his breakfast on a tray: four strips of crispy bacon with three scrambled eggs; fresh, hot-buttered cinnamon rolls; canned peach slices; and a mug of white coffee. The girl served him without speaking. She paused for a moment with the empty tray to see if there was anything else he required.

Outside, in the distance, the two old sleds opened their throttles with twin roars. At first it sounded like they were making headway, but first one machine stalled out and then the other.

After a few minutes, the sno-gos roared again, only to stall out once more. They were a Centurion and an Enticer, names that had nothing to do with snow, both from the unmemorable year of 1980, the year Orion Beehymer had purchased them new and brought them here to the mine. Both machines had done their time and deserved to be retired, but how was Poppy going to replace them? His third sno-go, an old Ski-Doo Skandic, was even more decrepit.

"Fetch me my boots."

Deuteronomy was the only offspring left in the room, so she went through the kitchen to the mud room to fetch her father's boots, insulated overalls, and parka.

STANDING ON THE front porch with a second mug of coffee, Poppy heard the chainsaw start up and begin to gnaw away at something. He offered a little prayer to Elder Brother Jesus to bless his sons with the good sense to deploy tarps on the snow before cutting.

Poppy climbed down the steps and followed the path to the toolshed. He heard the dog barking inside, and when he opened the door, two of his middle sons were fencing with swords made out of surveyor stakes.

The dog was the first to notice Poppy's presence. Her tail drooped, and she slunk out the door. When the boys finally looked up, they dropped their swords and hung their heads.

"Why aren't you two helping your brothers?" he asked them.

The younger boy said, "Because Adam told us to go back to the house, lord."

"Does this look like the house to you?"

"No, lord."

"How 'bout you?" he asked the older boy. "Does this look like the house to you?"

"No, lord, it don't."

"If you two can't find something useful to do with yourselves, I'll find you something. Follow me."

They followed their father around the toolshed to the little promontory overlooking the field and willow brush. Poppy was shocked by what he saw in the dawning light. What were his genius boys thinking? They had taken a stupid act — shooting an out-of-season moose right next to the yard — and made it worse. Blood splatter had turned the snow pink, and two long streaks of blood and gore crossed the field. A sawed-off moose head with enormous antlers lay nose up in the snow, glassing the sky with soulful eyes.

"You," Poppy said, pointing at one of the middle boys, "round up all the shovels you can find, and you," he said, pointing at the other, "run to the house and tell your sisters to send everyone to the field. *Now! Immediately! Everyone!* Now run, both of you." He swatted the nearest one on the back of the head as he raced by.

Before heading down to the field himself, Poppy cocked his ear toward the valley in the west and held his breath to listen.

POWDERY SNOW FLEW across the field in a miniature blizzard. Adults and children alike flung snow with shovels, raft paddles, bucket lids, and mittened hands. The bloody skid marks vanished. The pile of steaming viscera disappeared under a hill of pure white.

Poppy stood apart at the eastern edge of the field watching the western sky. When Adam shouted at him, he dropped his gaze to inspect the job. There was no telling how the disturbed snow would look from the air, but from this vantage, it looked innocent enough.

"Okay," he shouted back to Adam, "send 'em home." But as soon as he spoke, he heard the first faint sound of an engine. He began jogging back to the others, following his own tracks through the waist-deep snow. "Into the trees!" he huffed, waving his arms. "Into the trees!" The whole family retreated into the tall spruce and birch woods on the western edge of the field. The airplane would fly directly overhead, and he wondered if there was time to get everyone up to the house.

"Lord," one of his daughters said. The huddled children looked at her uneasily. It was Deuteronomy. "Lord, Sarai is sinning with her mouth."

"Deut!" her twin gasped.

"She said that if shooting a moose is such a righteous act in the Father's eyes, why do we have to hide it from the eyes of men?"

All of the little snot-noses, without actually looking at their father, keenly observed him for his reaction.

MD3 1.0

BACKCOUNTRY RANGER JACE Kuliak shined a flashlight out his kitchen window to check the thermometer that was nailed to the side of the house. The temperature had risen overnight. *Outstanding!*

He filled the thermos with black coffee, zipped up his layers of polyester and down, and went out to hitch the sled to the park service's spanking new Ski-Doo Tundra LT. It was a handsome, powerful machine, and today's assignment, a trash run to Cadigan Glacier, would put it through its paces. Forty miles each way (64 km) and a heavy load on the return trip. He gunned the engine and raced down the dark street to the trailhead.

The McHardy Creek Trail was a round-about way to get to the glacier, but Jace had a couple of things he wanted to do along the way. Besides, he'd have the trail all to himself this early in the day. Hell, he had the whole, freakin', diamond-frosted world to himself, and he didn't mind shouting out loud how sick that was. He opened the throttle as much as he dared. His headlights skittered over the frozen landscape.

After the trail crossed and recrossed the creek a dozen times, it made a sharp dogleg north and meandered up the backside of Eureka Ridge. But Jace hung south and took the Mizina cutoff.

The spur trail, narrower and much less traveled, climbed abruptly out of the glacial plain onto a high bench on the flank of Stubborn Mountain. The deep-throated beast between Jace's legs despised gravity and leaped and charged all the way up. From there, the trail hugged the side of the mountain and crossed several known avalanche chutes. But Jace flew across them without even looking up.

Soon the trail began its long descent to the river. Not wanting to miss his turnoff in the darkness, Jace eased back the throttle and paid close attention to the berm at the edge of the trail. He almost missed it anyway and had to brake hard to turn into the woods. Then he wove back and forth through the trees on a little-used track. When finally he reached the forest edge, he stopped and killed the engine. Silence rushed in to surround him.

Jace removed his helmet and retrieved the thermos. To the east, a picture postcard sunrise was unfolding, and a wall of jagged mountain pinnacles held back the pinking sky. Awesome scenery, for sure, but mere scenery was not what drew Jace to this spot, and he turned his back on it without so much as a glance.

No, he sat on the snowmobile seat facing, not east, but west where the moon still hung in a blue-black sky. He made himself comfortable, poured a steamy cup of coffee, and sparked his first spliff of the day. The snowmobile was Jace's high-performance sofa, and Alaska was his own fucking living room. He tipped back his head and exhaled two lungsful of sweet Mercury 4 in a cloud of breathcicles. *Nice.*

Before him stretched a long, straight boulevard of snow. Beneath the snow lay a private airstrip, the last six hundred yards (549 m) of which clearly encroached upon National Park Service land. A big, fat, federal case was what it was.

Beyond the airstrip lay the weathered compound of a small, defunct copper mine. Stubborn Mountain Mine had been a bit player in the great Caldecott copper discoveries of the 1910s and 20s. In those territorial days, this part of Alaska belonged to the Guggenheim Trust, whose claims at Caldecott, with ore as rich as 75% pure copper, were the most productive in the world. A century later, the played-out mines belonged to the federal government and served as a tourist destination in the heart of a national park. All of the mines, that is, except the Stubborn Mountain Mine, which belonged to a self-righteous prick who thought nothing of bulldozing public land for his airstrip.

It was still too dark to see the compound or its main house where the girl lived with her felonious father and crazy family. But two of its windows blazed brightly, and this was the sunrise he had come to behold. It was the west, and she was its sun. Arise, fair sun, and kill the envious moon, who rules a winter-weary —

Blam! Jace's dream was shattered by the crack of a rifle. He spilled coffee in his lap. He did a back flip over the snowmobile to take cover behind it, lying in the snow. All his juices ran cold.

But the shot had sounded pretty distant, upon further reflection, and it seemed unlikely that he had been its target. After a little while there was a second shot, likewise distant. It was probably only a case of sociopaths greeting the morning with gunfire. Wasn't that what sociopaths did?

Jace got up and located the spilled thermos in the snow. He couldn't find the joint. Which was a drag. Good thing he'd brought a couple of spares.

He started the Tundra and made a U-turn, leaving the headlights off until he reached the safety of the deep woods. Rejoining the Mizina spur trail, he continued on to his second destination of the day. This was Trapper's Slough, where he needed to check out the report of an illegal cabin. Someone had rebuilt a derelict structure without a permit, without so much as a howdy-do to the NPS, in whose park and preserve it allegedly stood.

MD4 1.0

THE ORIGINAL STRUCTURE had been a trapline cabin built circa 1946, long before the establishment of the park, by a disabled man named Jack (or Jaques) Dupré, who came into the country after fighting the Japanese in the Pacific. Despite a knee that did not bend, Dupré established and ran a sixty-mile (97-km) trapline loop from April Creek, along the Mizina, to its confluence with the Chitina. He trapped ermine, marten, lynx, and beaver mostly, sometimes wolves and wolverines. He built the cabin at the far end of the loop, where he and the dogs would rest overnight before running the return line.

In its heyday, Dupré's cabin had been a windowless shoebox made of unpeeled spruce logs with a dirt floor and a pole roof covered in sod. The ceiling was too low for a man to stand up in, and there was only enough floorspace to fit the little Yukon stove and army cot. But the cabin was snug on the coldest, blowiest nights, and it was all a man needed, be he wounded by war or not.

Jace, of course, had never met Dupré; few current locals had, but legend had it that he stopped overnighting in the cabin sometime in the late 1960s when he replaced his dog team with his first snowmobile, a 1967 "grey line" Ski-Daddler Power Sled. Now he could work the whole trapline in a single day. Nevertheless, he maintained the cabin throughout the 1970s for emergencies and storage. At some unknown date thereafter, Jaques Dupré left the country, traveling south, and vanishing into pre-digital obscurity. Surely by now he was dead.

Left to the elements, Dupré's little bivouac shelter fell into ruin. In this part of the world, things rotted slowly, and even after decades of exposure, only the bottom rungs of logs had melted into the moss. But the roof was stove in, and jewel-like fungi blossomed everywhere.

Then some not-yet-identified yahoos got it into their sovereign heads to blow off the park system and restore the ruins to their glory days. No, to a level even higher than their glory days. The bandit craftsmen had doubled the floorspace and raised a new, trussed roof with composite shingles in lieu of sod. They added a porch and a window. They expertly peeled, scribed, and notched new logs to replace the rotten ones.

Jace stepped on the porch to look through the window. There was no furniture or much of anything else inside. Instead of dirt, the floor was now made of rough spruce planks. Lengths of stovepipe were stacked against one wall, ready to hook up to a stove that had yet to arrive.

Above the door, the builder had nailed a polished birch plaque where it would be impossible to miss. Branded into the plaque with a soldering iron was a Bible verse. What a surprise. Isaiah 32:2. Jace dug out his iPhone to ask Siri to look it up for him, but he'd traveled too far from town for service. He'd have to look up the verse when he got home. ["Each will be like a refuge from the wind / And shelter from the storm . . .] In and of itself, the plaque did little to identify the builder, since no single park inholder seemed to have a monopoly on Bible verses. As to the level of craftsmanship, Jace knew a half dozen locals who possessed the skills necessary to pull off this renovation. Most of them decent people.

Jace trudged through deep snow around the structure to document it with his phone. A sound, like the whine of an out-of-season mosquito, that had been on Jace's verge of perception for many minutes, finally broke through to his awareness. A small airplane was approaching from down the Chitina River. Nellis, no doubt, with a week's worth of snail mail.

Ned Nellis of Nellis Air was the only reason Jace knew about this rogue construction. Peeled logs looked a lot like neon signs from the air, especially when you've flown the same weekly wilderness route year in and year out for half your life, as Nellis had.

There was no question that Jace would report the structure to his supervisor. Rogue construction in the park could not be condoned. The question was when. If he filed a report today, Masterson would be out here tomorrow to burn the place down. Literally, to burn the place down. But Jace rejected the belief that arson was the best solution to unauthorized buildings on federal lands. Especially in Alaska where ANILCA, the federal law governing public lands, made allowances for traditional use. Besides, this park had too few remote cabins for visitor use as it was. The park service should treat it as an anonymous donation from an admiring inholder and manage it, not burn it to the ground.

Screw Masterson.

So Jace would just have to sit on his report and file it next year. The open-fire burn ban would go into effect in April. The cabin would be safe then — from arson at least — until the drenching rains of October. This would give park headquarters, in far-away Copper Center, a chance to weigh in on the matter. Cooler heads usually prevailed at headquarters.

The mosquito whine grew louder, and a few minutes later Jace could see the aircraft low on the horizon. It was a green and white Cessna 206, a single-engine workhorse of the Alaska bush. Its tricycle landing gear was fitted out with skis. On Tuesdays it was the mail plane.

As Nellis flew over, he tipped his wings, and Jace waved back.

Before leaving the cabin and continuing on to the glacier and his main task of the day, Jace pried the birch plaque with its Bible reference from the lintel and tossed it like a frisbee into the frozen slough. It sliced into a snowbank and disappeared from sight. Amen.

MD5 1.0

THE GERMAN SHEPHERD stood conspicuously alone in the middle of the field sniffing at the pile of snow-buried offal. Blood was soaking through the layers of snow and turning it pink, especially around the base. The airplane was almost on top of them. Adam and Proverbs called the dog, but she wouldn't come. They yelled and whistled, but she didn't even bother to look at them. The children had cooled off after their exertion, and the smaller ones were beginning to shiver.

"She's your dog," Poppy said to one of the middle boys. "Call her off that pile."

"Yes, lord," Uzziel replied, even though it wasn't so. She wasn't *only* his dog. She was the family's dog, and she loved all of them, except for Poppy. The boy went to the edge of the forest and called, "Crissie! Crissie Lou! You come here, dog."

The dog's ears perked up — it was a voice she adored — and she trotted across the field to him. But there was something off about the way her gaggle of humans was huddling in the trees. They'd never done this before. So she held back the final few yards, no matter how urgently her favorite summoned her.

She came close enough, though, and in a heartbeat the plane roared overhead. An hour of preparation for such a meager show. But it was the effect that counted, and as the sound of the Cessna steadily diminished, Poppy knew they'd pulled it off. Ned Nellis was a good man, as men went. He professed to be a Christian, but he was not saved. That much was clear.

The older girls started shepherding the younger ones toward the house, but Poppy stopped them.

"I got something to say. Listen up."

With chattering teeth, they listened up.

"Father God loves his children," Poppy began. "He don't want to see them go hungry. That's why He led the beast to our door. That alone is proof of its divine provenance and a rebuke to the unbelievers." He looked pointedly at Sarai as he said this. "The only reason we had to hide the Father's gift from the eyes of men is because your brother was *ignorant* enough to take it *before* the mail plane went by. He could have waited till *after*. Then we wouldn't've had to *hide it*. Get it?"

He was addressing Sarai, but Proverbs answered. "I was afraid it would get away, lord."

Poppy turned to his third born. "Did I ask you to speak? Did I say I wanted to hear your lame-ass excuses?"

"No, lord."

"I didn't think so."

With her father's wrath momentarily diverted by her brother, Sarai studied her twin's face, trying to piece together what had just happened between them. But Deuteronomy was defiant.

"Your behavior," Poppy continued, "shows that you do not *believe*. Because if you *believed* in the Father's generosity to His children, you would also *believe* that He'd keep that moose hanging around long enough till we could harvest it in a normal manner."

The old man's tone changed subtly — but they all recognized it — from prosecutor to judge. "For your infidelity," he intoned, "your reckless infidelity that almost earned us a visit from federal jackals, for your dangerous lack of faith, you will receive six stripes."

The children cringed.

"I'm sorry, lord," Proverbs said.

"Sorry don't cut it, son. And for that backtalk you just earned two more stripes. That makes eight."

Proverbs groaned.

"Two more for that. Keep it up, boy."

Proverbs' eyes flashed, especially the right one, but he kept his peace, and Poppy Prophecy grunted with satisfaction. He turned toward the house before remembering he had another errant child to tune up, his twin of a twin, his eldest (by five minutes) and twice-blessed daughter, Sarai. "You," he intoned, cutting right to the judgment part, "for sinning with your mouth, shall also receive punishment."

He left it at that for now.

MD6 1.0

POPPY PROPHECY HITCHED the freight sled to the Polaris Centurion and loaded six small cartons of fulfilled orders into it. The boys had already skinned the moose and hauled the carcass to the bathhouse where they would butcher it. Adam volunteered to go into town for the mail, as he often did, but Poppy shot that idea down pretty quick.

Before he left, Poppy charged Proverbs with the task of transporting the moose head and entrails somewhere far from the house and deep in the woods where ravenous beasts could share the bounty.

Each of Poppy's three eldest boys had taken a legal bull in Ninthmonth. But two of the moose had been on the small side. The meat locker wasn't exactly bare — it still contained frozen salmon, whole chickens, rabbits, and black bear roasts — but when you have so many mouths to feed, you're always on the lookout for your next moose. How fitting, then, that Father God should send them such a large bull. It would yield them five hundred pounds (227 kg) of roasts, steaks, brisket, ribs, and hamburger, as well as tubs of lard.

The first eight miles into town on the Stubborn Mine Trail was rough in spots, but the only stretch that could be called hazardous was a blind curve around a steep bluff that the locals called Curve Canaveral. The old roadbed had collapsed there, leaving a narrow path over a sheer drop where you could launch yourself all the way to the valley floor. Especially if you didn't know it was there and came upon it too fast. Or at night.

During the day it was a nice spot to idle awhile and gawk at the Father's outrageously gorgeous handiwork: the bottomlands of the Mizina, the quarter-mile canyon, and in the hazy distance the backbone of the Chugach Mountains.

Sad to say, but even the Father's best work fades from sight after four score viewings, and Poppy Prophecy barely glanced up from the trail as he eased around the curve.

Halfway to town, Poppy passed the only other still-occupied homestead on the trail, Dell Bunyan's place. That was where the trail widened out into a single-lane gravel road. The rest of the ride in was fast and smooth. Poppy didn't even glance to see if woodsmoke was coming out of Bunyan's stack. Dell Bunyan wasn't his favorite person.

Poppy drove his tired iron through the deserted streets of McHardy to the public airstrip on the other end. McHardy didn't amount to much of a town. Only a few of the houses within its bounds were habitable. The rest had either collapsed or burned or were gracefully decomposing in place. McHardy was a town birthed in sin and killed by greed. If it was up to Poppy, he'd scrape the entire townsite clean, backfill fresh soil, and start a new town from scratch. Or better — no town.

Remarkably, it was not up to him. [see the sidebar, *Ghost Town with Footbridge* on page 321]

By the time Poppy Prophecy arrived at the airstrip, the mail plane was long gone. There was no way to know what, if anything, Nellis had seen from the air.

Poppy idled his sled alongside the Sulzer porch. Ed and Ginny Sulzer lived right next to the airstrip and served as the region's unofficial postmasters. Judging by the number of sno-gos parked in their yard and the hum of the generator, Mail Day was in full swing.

Each winter, the population of McHardy shrank to its committed core of around sixty souls. If you left out Prophecy and his family, it was closer to forty souls, half of whom were in the Sulzer living room at that moment. Poppy shuddered at the thought of so many sinners gathered in one room eating blueberry pie.

He stacked his outgoing cartons three high and two deep and carried them into the porch breezeway. He had difficulty working the screen door latch, but fortunately Ed was there to give him a hand.

"Last minute orders from Santa?" Ed said merrily. Ed's glasses were so thick and his brown eyes so big and round that you were forced to watch their every twitch and twinkle in startling close-up. And Ed was clearly baiting him. He well knew Poppy's opinion about the secular side of the holiday, but he seemed to enjoy poking at people to watch them react. And laughing when they did. Why a man would behave like that was beyond Poppy's ken, and outside his interest as well. So he dropped the cartons in a pile next to the outgoing mail sack without bothering to reply.

Along one wall of the breezeway stood a long, wooden potting bench where the Sulzers sorted the incoming mail. In the old days, the mail plane pilot would stop only long enough to toss the mail sack out of the airplane and pick up any outgoing ones. Thus, the incoming sack usually ended up on the edge of the runway where locals would paw through it to see if anything was addressed to them.

When the Sulzers arrived in 1972 to operate the remote meteorological reporting station, they took it upon themselves to end that practice. Henceforth, no one touched the mail until Ed and Ginny sorted it. And although their breezeway wasn't heated, it was dry, and the screen door was open night and day.

No one challenged the Sulzers' petty despotism, and society was improved by it. The blueberry pies started soon thereafter.

"Anyway," Ed said, "come in the house before you leave."

Poppy grunted noncommittally. He had located the Prophecy's stack of mail and was thumbing through it.

"To hear the news," Ed added.

Poppy looked up. "What news?"

"The news about the road."

"What news about the road?"

But Ed winked an enormous eye and slid back into the house. Ed Sulzer was too much an old woman. He and Prophecy were about the same age, middle to late seventies. Hard to say which one of them was the more decrepit, but only one of them was saved.

By bulk, most of the Prophecy mail was made up of fat manilla envelopes from the Alaska Lighthouse Correspondence School with lesson plans and workbooks for students from kindergarten through middle school. Expensive home heating fuel was what it was.

By density, the prize went to several small but heavy packages from Taiwan. They would contain cheap necklace chains and lapel tacks.

In between were credit card applications, direct mail coupon offers from businesses in Anchorage and Glennallen, an advert from a Fairbanks insurance agency that promised to save him fifteen percent in fifteen minutes, several glossy catalogues and magazines, *Living City* and *Guns & Ammo* among them, and a handful of belated political campaign brochures from hopeful candidates. These brochures had arrived too late to save the republic. Obama had won a second term as president. God have mercy on our homeland.

Poppy dumped the electioneering crap and advertising crap and catalogue crap into the trash barrel that Ed had kindly provided at the end of the table. One thing Poppy didn't find in his stack of mail were bills. He had none. He owed nothing to no one. Praise Elder Brother Jesus. Amen.

Another thing he didn't find was anything from NJB, his business associate in Palmer. NJB was in charge of supplying them with the fulfillment mailing labels and of forwarding sales contracts and the odd paper check that needed Poppy's endorsement. But Poppy hadn't heard from NJB in over three weeks. No emails either. Calls went straight to voice mail. It wasn't like him. NJB was one of the good guys, one of the few in this sinful world who helped his fellow man. NJB wasn't saved, however, not by a long shot, though in his case it was a damned shame.

Poppy went through the stack again, and when he shook out the magazines, two letters dropped from between their pages. One was a thick, lavender envelope addressed by hand to:

> Mr. Adam Prophecy
> Stubborn Mountain Mine
> General Delivery
> McHardy, AK 99562

It was from a Susan Krae, who lived in Soldotna and whose every written word ended in a curlicue. Adam had never spoken of a Susan Krae from Soldotna or of any girl from anyplace. Poppy sniffed the envelope. At least there was no perfume.

The other was a plain white business envelope with a Forever Liberty Bell stamp and an Anchorage postmark. It had been cancelled on the twentieth of Eleventhmonth, which meant it had taken a couple of weeks to arrive. In contrast to the lavender envelope, it was so thin it didn't seem to contain anything at all. It was addressed to him, and he recognized at once NJB's handwriting.

But when Poppy slit the envelope and peered inside, it was indeed empty. Had NJB addressed and sealed the envelope and forgotten to include any contents? Or was an empty envelope after a month of silence supposed to be some kind of message?

Then he noticed writing on the inside of the envelope itself. He tore it open and found a number with seven digits: 62-13-44-5. No word of explanation, just the number. It didn't look like an address or phone number or GPS or anything else he could think of. Illumination was deferred.

Poppy checked the envelope a final time for any other contents or marks or clues. Nada. So he tore a scrap with the number and put it into his wallet.

THE SULZER HOUSE was a grand old log structure that had been built in 1910 and added to every decade until it resembled several separate houses all jumbled together. Inside was a warren of mismatched hallways and darkened rooms that reeked of pets, cigarettes, cooking grease, and, above all, paint thinner. The main part of the house was heated by an old, cast iron wood stove in the living room. That was where grizzled men and women were congregating in puddles of shed coats, hats, and gloves.

These were the neighbors from far and wide: from the settlements of Caldecott and Larkspur Peak, from Round Lake on McHardy Road, Dan Creek, and Fourthmonth Creek. For some of these people, Mail Day was the only day they saw any reason to seek out other living people. And not necessarily to interact with them but to watch them from a safe distance while balancing styrofoam cups and pie plates on their knees. When you lived beyond the beyond, just showing up counted for a lot.

Others of them tried to burn off their cabin fever with small talk. Of these, Kelly Cogwheel led the charge. The owner/manager of the McHardy Hotel and Saloon, a husband and father, hunter, pilot, and carpenter, Cogwheel was also a community leader. And ever since the Prophecys' armed standoff with the park service a couple of summers ago, Cogwheel had treated Poppy like a celebrity. When he saw him enter the room, he waved him over to join his group. But Poppy didn't attend Mail Day to be sucked into some nudnik's orbit.

"Pastor!" Cogwheel called. "You'll want to hear this. There's proof the Democrats stole the election." But Poppy ignored him and continued to the refreshments table where he was disappointed to find the three aluminum pie tins already empty but for crumbs and lurid, blue streaks.

No big loss, actually.

Once upon a time, or so the legend went, Virginia Sulzer made world-class pies. She and Edward managed to pick enough wild blueberries in late summer on the backside of Eureka Ridge to serve real fruit pies to Mail Day guests for most of the following year. But now, several decades, spinal injuries, and six surgical procedures later, she simply scooped blueberry-infused goo out of restaurant-sized cans into box-store frozen crusts and called it pie.

Like most things in the fallen world, the idea of Virginia's Blueberry Pies far exceeded their reality. Only Father God's word can stand the acid test of reality because only His word is reality. Amen.

Poppy spied a soon-to-be-vacant seat in the corner next to the extension cord and power strip. Its current occupant, a lost-looking fellow who was successfully keeping to himself, got up to use the toilet or something. He put his half empty styrofoam cup on the seat to —what? — reserve it?

As Poppy Prophecy went to claim the seat, his way was blocked by a woman, and it took him a moment to remember who she was, Barbara Jean de Saul.

"Hey, Prophecy," Barbara Jean said. "How are you? How are all of those beautiful babies of yours?"

Barbara Jean was an unassuming woman in her mid-forties who one fine spring day three years ago abandoned her family and career as a home spa salesperson in Houston, Texas. She longed to travel to Nepal where she thought she'd be able to slow down and "figure things out." But circumstances brought her to Cordova, Alaska, instead where she learned to slime salmon and pack roe in a cannery. Three years on, she was still figuring things out. In the meantime, she rented a restored house in McHardy.

"My beautiful babies are magnifying the glory and love of their Creator," Poppy replied. "What about yours? How are *your* beautiful babies?"

Barbara Jean had three, all boys, ages five, eight, and ten the day she walked out on them and her husband.

"Just wonderful," she replied proudly. "They're growing up so smart and strong."

"How can you know that when you haven't seen them in three years?"

"Oh, I see them all the time. We Skype with their dad a couple times a week."

He hadn't thought of that. You could do that these days, even in McHardy.

Barbara Jean took his silence for confusion. "Skype is like a video chat feature on my cell phone."

"I know what it is!" Poppy snapped. "What I'm saying is *no* amount of Skype can make you a good mother."

"Oh, Mr. Prophecy," Barbara Jean said. "It's always such a pleasure to run into you. Tell Mama P hi for me, and the kiddies. I pray for you guys all the time."

POPPY PROPHECY REMOVED the styrofoam cup and draped his parka over the chair. All of the electrical outlets were in use charging phones and tablets. He had to remove one to plug in his own phone. When he turned his phone on, it went through its merry little dance of life: looking up, hooking up, and syncing up all its many indispensable services. The strong mobile signal in town was the only good thing Obama ever did.

What irked Poppy about Barbara Jean's presumption of his ignorance of the internet was how nearly right she was. Three years ago, he was a techno-ignoramus and proud of it. He'd seen plenty of computers in his time but had never touched one himself. Never felt the need. As far as he was concerned, the internet was a tool of Satan, which was why his family avoided it. But Poppy's moral compass had swung 180 degrees on the matter. What had happened to cause such a change of heart? In a word, he had met Not Jeff Bridges.

Which was why NJB's protracted silence (except for a cypher on a scrap of paper) was so vexing. What if, in those years of friendly association, NJB had actually been secretly gathering the strings of Poppy's undoing? What if he had cleaned them out? Not that the Prophecys had a fortune to their name. A couple hundred dollars was all there was when last he checked his account. So as soon as his Samsung finished plugging itself into the world, Poppy logged into his credit union. Well, it was not what he had feared. The opposite, in fact. Their online Christmas sales had been through the roof, and several brick-and-mortar vendors had paid off their balances. The current balance in his account was $4,082.76, praise Elder Brother Jesus. Praise His holy name. Amen.

POPPY PROPHECY PUT the mystery of NJB's disappearance aside and spent the next hour hunched over, oblivious to his surroundings, with his Arctic overalls draped around his knees in his phone-based office, taking care of business. The only reason he attended Mail Day was because of Ed's free electricity. When next he looked up, Dell Bunyan's melancholic face was hanging before him like the full moon in the night sky.

"Mr. Prophecy," Bunyan said with a smile that did little to brighten his expression. Maybe the muscles in his face were wired to sag that way and weren't a reliable gauge of his mood. Poppy doubted that was the case. Bunyan's muscles were all right; it was his morose soul that was showing through.

"Bunyan," Poppy replied. Bunyan offered him his cold, fat, soft hand to squeeze or shake or do something with. But Poppy had long ago stopped clasping hands with other people, unless it was to seal a deal, and he let Bunyan's hand hang in front of him until Bunyan had the good sense to put it away.

"Say, Prophecy," Bunyan went on, "I was wondering." He was always wondering about one thing or another. "We're next door neighbors. You know that you and the family are more than welcome to attend Sunday service with us." It was the same offer Bunyan made every time they met. Poppy usually replied that he would pray on it. McHardy was a town that lacked a single gas station, convenience store, laundromat, public utility, or official post office. Yet it boasted of three distinct Protestant sects. They were active even during the depopulated winter months, when the congregation of any one of them would triple or quadruple in size the moment the Prophecy family walked through its chapel doors (not that they ever would).

Unlike the picturesque log church with the log steeple on the Caldecott River, Bunyan's chapel doubled as his family's living room. Instead of stained glass windows, the walls were bedecked with musty, old bearskin rugs. There were grizzly and black bears alike, with their toothy heads still attached. These were the trophies his five sons had collected over the years. Shooting a bear seemed to be a right of passage in that household and a source of pride for its patriarch.

"I want you to stop asking me to come to your services, Bunyan," Poppy said in his best good-neighborly voice.

"I don't mean to pester you, but you said you'd pray on it, and I was wondering how that turned out."

"Well, I did pray on it. Several times in fact. And the Holy Spirit told me not to risk my children's spiritual welfare by exposing them to scriptural falsehoods."

"Falsehoods?" Bunyan said, choking on the word. "That's strong language, friend. We're likely to have disagreements of interpretation, but falsehoods? If you don't mind, please educate me. Tell me a falsehood I preach."

"You preach pre-millennial dispensationalism."

"And that's a problem?"

"It is when you preach that the Rapture comes *before* the Tribulation."

"And you don't?"

"Of course not. Anyone who thinks that the faithful will rapture out of harm's way and that only unbelievers will be left behind to suffer seven years of bloodshed and torture under the heel of the Antichrist is a complete fool. It's too easy. It's lazy, wishful thinking. The hard truth is that the souls of each of us will be forged in the fires of the greatest battle that the Earth will ever see. Only then will those who still believe in our Savior's blood be raised to glory. Otherwise, what's the point?"

Bunyan's face sagged even more. "That's certainly one point of view," he said. Tears were welling in his eyes, and the sight of them further annoyed Poppy. "Then let me run something else by you, Prophecy," Bunyan continued.

That was the pastor's MO. He'd latch on to you with some insane request and then proceed to moist-eye you into submission.

"I was wondering if some of your girls would like to come over sometime to play with Scarlett."

Without a moment of hesitation, Poppy said, "No. It's out of the question."

His neighbor didn't seem surprised. "I hear you and respect your decision," he said. By now the wells of his eyes were full to overflowing, and Poppy wanted to smack him to make him stop. What kind of character flaw was it that drove a man to snivel so?

"How about — " the man went on heedlessly. "No, before I ask, let me just tell you about her recent triumph. She took her first bear, a blond grizz. Big fella. She shot it last fall outside Cantwell and is having it tanned."

She? She who? Poppy was too busy trying not to watch the tears dripping from Bunyan's nose to pay attention to the conversation. The only she in the Bunyan household he was aware of was the wife, or late wife. She had died long before the Prophecys came to McHardy. What was her name? She had been killed in an auto accident while the family was on vacation in Hawaii. In the meantime, the five Bunyan sons had all grown up and gone off to college or war.

"It was her first kill," Bunyan went on. "I was so proud. But here's the thing. With the boys, we always had a full house to celebrate as each got his bear. Now it's just me and her. And I'm afraid I'm just too boring for her. So I was wondering . . ."

"Who are you talking about?"

"Scarlett."

"Who's Scarlett?"

"My daughter. My youngest. She's here somewhere." He blew his nose into a blueberry-stained napkin. "Anyway, it seems to me you have a girl or three about her age out there. Since you'd rather not let your girls come to my house, how about, if she wasn't a burden, I was wondering if Scarlett could come over to your place sometime to play or bake or do whatever it is that thirteen-year-old girls do. Oh, there she is." The pastor's gaze found the girl across the room standing next to the hallway door.

So that was Scarlett. A little slip of a thing in a deep burgundy dress. Unlike the Prophecy girls, who were all either blond or brunette, Scarlett had black hair. Obsidian black. It was cut short and styled in a pageboy, which was further evidence, if any more were needed, of Pastor Bunyan's unfitness to preach to others. Worse, though the girl wore a skirt, it barely reached her knees. Plus, she was wearing blue jeans under the skirt. Talk about confusing the genders. She looked like the sort of girl a father didn't want influencing his own daughters.

Across the room, Scarlett became aware of the men's attention and ducked self-consciously into the hallway.

The Holy Spirit chose that moment to whisper a name in Poppy's ear — *Mary*. Yes, that was the dead wife's name. And even though Poppy had never met the woman, he said, "I see the resemblance. She looks just like her mother."

"You think?" Bunyan said, a little surprised.

"Yes. Especially her eyes. When I saw her standing there by the door, for a moment I thought I was looking at *Mary*. For just a second I forgot that *Mary* was cruelly crushed and mangled under an automobile bumper, and I thought that she had come to Mail Day with you."

Now the floodgates opened wide, and Bunyan's tears cascaded down his cheeks.

"Too bad the Father called *Mary* home when He did," Poppy said. "After she sends all her sons off to start their own lives and finally has time to devote to her only daughter. It seems so unfair."

"I know," Bunyan blubbered. "It does."

"And the girl being at that age — twelve you said? — when she needs her mama now more than ever. I mean, she's becoming a woman. What do you know about becoming a woman?"

"Nothing! I know nothing."

Poppy stood and offered Bunyan his chair. The man all but collapsed into it, but Poppy didn't ease up on him yet. "Just think of how proud *Mary* would have been of Scarlett for getting her first grizz. What a celebration *she* would have organized." Dell Bunyan hunched forward in the chair and buried his head in his hands.

WITH BUSINESS CHORES done and Bunyan vanquished, Poppy decided it was time to leave. But first he needed to talk to Ed. The north end of the cavernous log room was the studio and the source of the paint thinner vapors. About twenty years ago, Ed had removed most of the north wall and replaced it with two, side-by-side bay windows. Each bay was crowned with a plexiglass domed skylight. A solid studio easel stood in each bay, and clamped to each easel were four, large, tin goldpans.

The northern view outside the windows was well worth Ed's effort. It was a remarkable panorama even to jaded Alaska eyes. To the east ran Eureka Ridge, the location of Caldecott and the copper bonanza. To the west were the wooded slopes of Larkspur Mountain. And in between yawned the broad Caldecott Glacier, a ribbon of ice thirty miles long (48 km) that rose twelve thousand feet (3700 m) to the snowy half-dome of Mt. Blackfriar, an extinct volcano.

The bay windows were two unblinking eyes. In one of them, Ginny slouched on a tall-backed, vinyl barstool and smoked and painted as she chatted with her guests, Barbara Jean and a couple of other McHardy biddies. Ginny's specialty was painting backgrounds with oils, and she worked on four goldpans simultaneously. Each background she painted was different, but no matter if it depicted a forested hillside or a cloudy alpine majesty or the blue-green face of recently sheered glacial ice, it came from some piece of the scene outside her window. Altogether, Ginny had an inventory of about forty good, ready-made compositions that she had been painting in all lights and all weather for decades.

When she noticed Poppy, she said, "Did the old fool tell you about the road yet?"

"He said there was news."

"Edward," she called to her husband in the other bay, "tell Father Progeny about the road."

Ed Sulzer was perched on his own barstool, smoking Kools to her Camels, and attending to his own congress of dunces. Each of the four goldpans clamped to his easel contained a finished variation of Ginny's forty stock backgrounds. It was Ed's job to add middle- and foreground elements to them. Today he was painting the same rustic log cabin in a variety of settings: in deep woods, on a high mountain bluff, in a snowy valley, next to a raging stream. The cabins usually had a twist of white woodsmoke coming out of their stack, and sometimes the windows were illuminated from within by golden lamplight. No matter what scene Ginny threw at him, Ed could drop the log cabin into it somewhere.

Ed also liked to include a man's figure in the composition. A tiny man chopping wood next to the cabin, maybe. A gold prospector on snowshoes climbing a distant ridge, a musher driving a team of huskies by moonlight.

They both signed their names to the finished pans, which sold well in gift shops around the state.

"Ed!" Ginny yelled. "Did you hear me?" She slurred a little, though Poppy didn't see any obvious booze within her reach. Maybe it was the paint thinner fumes. He felt light-headed himself.

Ed smiled at Poppy and said, "Heading to Anchorage, Prophecy?"

Poppy couldn't imagine why he would ask him that. "No, we're in till Thirdmonth. Unless . . . are you telling me the road is open?"

"DOT is plowing tomorrow."

"Why?"

"The Caldecott Lodge is reopening."

"In the winter? That's crazy."

"That's what I said, but Jack Colburn in Chitina told me so himself. They're planning to keep it open at least through the new year. It's part of some tourism study on the Northern Lights. So, I ask again, is there a bonus trip to Anchorage in the cards?"

It was a thinker. Money in the bank and no time like the present to spend it.

"Maybe. Why?"

Ed used a palette knife to point to a stack of cartons leaning against the log wall. The one drawback about cottage industry goldpans was their shipping weight. Ed and Ginny couldn't afford to buy blank pans or ship finished ones via the mail plane.

Ed said, "I need someone to drop those off in Spenard and pick up an order from Blaines." He offered Poppy a handwritten list of art supplies. "I already phoned it in, so it should be waiting for you to pick up."

Poppy didn't accept the list. "If I decide to go," he said, "the boys will come fetch your pans and your list."

Behind him, Ginny said, "How's Mama P? Any better?"

"Any better than what?" Poppy asked, turning to her.

"Is she talking?"

"Yes, ma'am. She's talking to the Savior and the saints."

"Tell her we're all praying for her."

Trash Run

TR1 1.0

WHAT KIND OF ASSHOLE, Jace Kuliak asked the rushing wind, names his daughter Deuteronomy? A girl so lovely it was hard to breathe. There wasn't even any reasonable way to shorten her name: Deuter? Deutie? Dee Dee? People in town referred to her as Deut. Rhymes with Toot, they all said like it was their original joke. They insisted that that was what her own family called her. It was parental abuse was what it was. Seriously, people, give your children normal names.

But the really weird thing was that people in town knew about this Prophecy girl two years before Jace did. How was that possible? He'd interacted with the family on several notable occasions and never laid eyes on her. If he had, he'd remember. She was that striking. You couldn't forget her in a million years.

Of course, at the time he'd been preoccupied with a French girl.

Well, forget the French girl. Forget the seasonal workers. Forget those girls in L.A. Forget Marcie from high school. Forget them all. No girl he'd ever known meant more to him than Deuteronomy Prophecy, dumb name and all.

After checking out the rogue cabin at Trapper's Slough, Jace embarked on his main mission of the day, the trash run. He tore up the Chitina River on the new Tundra snowmobile, leaving the scattered homesteads and mining claims and every trace of civilization in his wake.

Though the valley at that point was twenty miles wide (32 km), snowy mountain massifs on both sides made it feel closed in, like a canyon. If Jace continued another sixty miles east (97 km), he'd cross the Canadian border into the Kluane National Park of the Yukon. The two North American neighbors had stacked their grandest national parks up against each other at their common border, creating a combined 28,500 square miles of wilderness (74,000 sq. km), much of it permanently buried under sheets of ice. Jace was about as deep into the backcountry as a backcountry ranger could get.

Not deep enough to escape litter, however. In this case, it was a century's worth of climbing expedition trash.

With nine of the highest sixteen peaks in the U.S. located within its borders, the park (and the territory that preceded it) was a long-time favorite destination for serious mountain climbers from around the world. Current expeditions observed strict park pollution regulations: everything climbers brought in, they brought out again when they left. It wasn't always so. For generations, the standard expedition practice was to abandon whole camps in place as the climbers finished using them. They left tons and tons of airdropped equipment and supplies behind without a backward glance.

No worries. By the next climbing season, the old camp would be buried under ten feet of new snow, and a brand new base camp could take shape on virgin terrain.

And that was how the trash might have remained forever, hidden under strata of compressed snow and ice, if global warming hadn't happened. Now, many Alaska glaciers were rapidly melting, and each year a new crop of old junk sprouted from the ice like spring crocuses.

Last summer, park officials assigned Jace to a team of backcountry rangers and the park archeologist to begin remediation work on Cadigan Glacier.

Cadigan Glacier had been the site of a succession of base camps ever since the first ascent of College Peak in 1935 by the ill-fated Moore Hall Expedition. College Peak, at 14,470 ft. (4,410 m), was among the fifty highest peaks in the U.S., but it was the runt of the litter of local mountains. Its immediate neighbor, Mount Bona, at 16,421 ft. (5,005 m), ranked as the fifth highest independent peak in the United States. Yet for all its grandeur, Bona was an easy climb, a mere Alaska Grade 2, literally a walk in the park. By contrast, runty College Peak offered mountaineers a real challenge, an Alaska Grade 5, a highly technical, potentially dangerous climb. Thus it remained popular.

A helicopter dropped Jace's remediation team on Cadigan Glacier in June. Over the next few days they collected and divided climbing debris into three categories. First were objects in good enough shape and with enough historical value to be salvaged as cultural artifacts. These items they removed by air. Included were museum-grade examples of 1940s-era felt boots and wooden skis, custom-made ice axes and snow shovels, glass thermoses and rawhide snowshoes.

In the second category were objects that were too broken or worn out to be of any practical or cultural value and were constructed from decomposable material like wood, wool, or iron. These they left on the glacier to molder or rust away on their own.

Finally, there were objects deemed to be without any value whatsoever that were made from non-decomposable materials like plastic, glass, or fiberglass such as tarps, food wrappers, drink pouches, and broken ski poles. These they bundled up for winter disposal by snowmobile.

OF COURSE THEY had no future together, even if he figured out how to get past her homicidal father and brothers to ask her out. A romance was hard enough to pull off without all the loaded guns. And what about their kids, if they decided to have kids one day? Would Deut insist their kids be brought up crazy?

Kids. Jace caught himself thinking about kids again. It was happening more often lately, even before Deut had shown up. The French girl had had a kid, a son. Jace had never met him, but he was the reason Danielle was in Anchorage in the first place. She and the kid lived in a Paris suburb for most of the year, but her ex in Toulouse had custody of him for nine weeks each summer, and Danielle just found it easier to cope with her loss by leaving France altogether during that time.

Danielle spent the summer of 2009 working for a wine wholesaler who staged wine-tasting events for restaurants and liquor distributors in cities across the U.S. Meanwhile, Jace was in Anchorage attending a public hearing of the citizens' advisory commission on federal areas at the Captain Cook Hotel. After a program break, he blundered into the wrong ballroom. Winery reps from Europe, California, Australia, and Argentina were set up at tables along the walls. He saw her from across the room pouring glasses of Chardonnay for a knot of men in jackets and ties. Jace stood out in this crowd with his NPS ranger uniform. He wasn't fond of wine, but he decided he'd like to try a glass of Chardonnay. He lingered at her table, and they seemed to hit it off. Her accent floored him, and her legs made him weak. But she was on the clock, and he was wearing the wrong kind of name badge, and eventually a suit politely asked him pay the $50.00 guest fee or leave.

They met up later, and he took her to dinner at the only blues club in Alaska, and a darned good club at that, even by Danielle's refined standards. When they left Blues Central, well after 10:00 P.M., she seemed disturbed that it was still as light as day out. She invited him up to her hotel room. She was on the tenth floor with a room overlooking Cook Inlet. She quickly shut the blinds on the panoramic view and asked him to leave them shut. He said he would. In hindsight, that should have been a clue.

From the moment Danielle invited him to her room to the moment he unhooked her bra, Jace was nervous about measuring up to her sophisticated European sexual expectations. He was a meat and potatoes kind of lover. Just the basics, ma'am. Nothing too spicy or weird, thank you. But he needn't have worried; things went smoothly, and he only stumbled once, during the big reveal when her silken panties came off for the first time and she had no snatch. No, she had a snatch, only it was a completely hairless one. He'd seen plenty of bikini waxes and fancifully trimmed carpets, but nothing like this, and at first he thought there was something wrong with her, a missing gene for pubic hair or something. (He'd never heard of manscaping either.)

Fortunately, his cock wasn't confused, and he soldiered on and did his best. Also fortunately, she'd gone a long time without getting any, so meat and potatoes were fine by her, as long as the portions were generous. And they were.

Afterward, they lay in each others' arms and talked through the night. Under all the perfume and makeup, silk and nylon, and notwithstanding the nude pubes, Danielle proved to be an ordinary, lonely, single mom just trying to make her way in an uncaring world. She showed him snapshots of her little man on her phone. Jace, in turn, entertained her with tall tales about Alaska, of which she'd only seen the airport and hotel. Was she aware that Alaska was as big as the entire European Union? That the national park where he worked was the size of Switzerland and could boast having taller mountains, wilder rivers, longer glaciers, and richer oxygen?

"Some days I see more bears than I do people," he bragged.

"Bears?"

"Yes, grizzly bears! Black bears! Polar bears! It helps that I'm a man. The scent of a woman's blood can drive a bear mad. Hell, bears will chase the scent of perfume and shampoo, even deodorant." He kissed her bare breast and inhaled deeply the fragrance of her flesh. "A bear would eat you up."

Her eyes grew so wide with alarm that Jace kicked himself. Why was he talking so boneheaded stupid? He changed the topic to moose, how docile they were, and dumb, and how cute their babies.

And then, out of the blue, he invited her to visit him sometime at his little "chalet in the park."

The next day they slept in, ordered room service, and screwed leisurely until it was time for her to catch a plane. They exchanged addies, but he didn't expect to hear from her again.

JACE KULIAK'S HOUSE in McHardy wasn't exactly a "chalet." More like a Cape Cod style house that was constructed in a boomtown minute from green lumber in 1910.

About a year before meeting the French girl, Jace was at Mail Day when he overheard a couple of locals talking about Orion Beehymer's great grandnephew's car accident. Beehymer was the area's eldest old-timer. He had come to McHardy in the 1960s. His great grandnephew, who lived down in Oregon, had been texting while driving and had caused a serious traffic accident.

Beehymer volunteered to cover the boy's attorney fees and needed to sell off a town lot or two in a hurry to pay them. He'd been buying up the McHardy Monopoly board since 1971, and he owned more townsite lots than anyone else.

An impending land sale qualified as headline news in McHardy. Small subdivision lots inside the national park were rare enough, but McHardy townsite lots *never* came on the market. Jace knew what he had to do with this intel — inform his boss, the park superintendent. Despite ANILCA, the park's longterm bias was to extinguish private inholdings whenever possible. But because of the recession and budgetary constraints, the park would be unable to take advantage of the Beehymer family's bad luck in Oregon.

Not that Beehymer would have sold land to the park service in any case.

A couple of days later, Jace happened to run into the elderly land baron in person on the narrow footbridge across the Caldecott River. "Heard you're selling town lots," he said to him.

"Just the one lot, ranger."

"How much you asking?"

"How is that any of the park's business?"

"I don't suppose it is. I'm just curious, you know, as a private citizen, not as a park employee."

Beehymer looked him over. Apparently, all he'd seen of Jace before they spoke was his uniform. "I never heard of a flat hat with a pony tail. Just what kind of parkie are you anyway?"

"A backcountry ranger. We grow beards too. And yodel."

Beehymer studied him again, this time with a calculating squint. "Forget it. I'd never sell to the likes of you — whatever the likes of you are."

"I don't blame you, but I'm not in the market anyway. I was just curious how much a lot goes for in McHardy these days."

"It's a lot with a house on it."

"Really? It's got a house on it?"

"That's what I just said. And two sheds and a functioning well. The *only* functioning well on that whole block."

"So, how much you asking?"

"Fifty-six thousand US dollars, with owner financing."

Jace didn't have a handle on real estate values, but it seemed to him you couldn't buy a house anywhere for that little money, let alone a house inside the largest national park in the country. A mob of possibilities crowded his mind.

Like most of the other male rangers at Caldecott, Jace lived in the men's bunkhouse and shared sleeping quarters with five other park and concessionaire employees. This total lack of privacy had put a major crimp on his love life. This was because a national park in Alaska in the summer was an incredibly girl-rich environment. Besides the steady stream of exotic foreign girls visiting from every corner of the globe, there were the seasonal workers, including his female colleagues in grey and green. More than two hundred seasonal workers, at least half of them college girls, came up to McHardy and Caldecott each summer to bus the tables, serve the ice cream, interpret the Nature, drive the vans, row the white waters, and lead the glacier hikes. And on the mind of every college girl embarking on her Alaska adventure was the possibility of a summer romance with a tall, strapping, handsome, tree-hugging, 420-friendly, educated, gentle but firm and studly park ranger in his faux-military-style NPS uniform.

At least that was Jace's observation. The problem was finding a little love nest under the Midnight Sun to call his own. A house, his own house in the ghost town of McHardy, would solve that problem big time.

"Fifty-six thou?" Jace said, turning numbers in his head. "Sounds reasonable. So, what's wrong with it?"

"Nothin's wrong with it."

"Then how come nobody's bought it yet? There are plenty of folks wanting to buy town lots, I hear."

"Because nobody came up with the down payment yet."

"Oh, yeah? How much is the down payment?"

"Fifty-six thousand US dollars."

Jace laughed. "That's some owner financing you got there!"

"You can take it or leave it, ranger. Now, I answered your questions. Am

I free to go, or are you detaining me?"

"Show it to me."

"You said you're not in the market. Don't waste my time."

"I might be in the market after all."

"You might be, but you'd still be a ranger."

"Listen, Mr. Beehymer. I get it. You're not a fan of the park service. I'm used to that. But I'm a private citizen too, and a man, and it's my opinion that a man would have to be totally insane not to want to own a little piece of this." He waved his arms all around to take in the glacier, the volcano, the former copper mine, Larkspur Peak, Stubborn Mountain, the birds in the sky, the torrent of water under their feet, the billowing road dust, the mosquitos, the fresh odor of earth sprouting new life everywhere you looked.

Orion Beehymer stared at him.

LUCKY STRIKE LANE was located off Main Street on the south side of town. It was unpaved dirt and ended in a cul-de-sac at the McHardy Creek Trail trailhead. The house stood halfway up the block, and to get to it they passed other houses that were either boarded up, falling down, or abandoned altogether. Some had rusted-out old pickup trucks parked on rotting tires in the street out front.

Jace snorted when he first saw the house Beehymer was offering for sale. The exterior siding was falling off, exposing black tarpaper walls. Portions of the roof were covered with tattered blue tarps. What windows there were were broken. Fireweed and horsetails had conquered the yard. And one of the advertised amenities, one of two outbuildings, was a flattened pile of splintered rubble. Beehymer stood in front of the expired shed with an expression of befuddlement. When had this happened?

The front door of the house was unlocked, but Beehymer couldn't force it open more than a few inches. "Frost heave," he said by way of explanation. "Let's go 'round back."

They entered the house through the back door, and the horror show continued. The hardwood floors were so warped it would take a Mars Rover to navigate them. Paint flakes cascaded from the walls like dandruff. The ceilings all bowed in on their centers, evidence of a leaky roof. The living room ceiling sagged so much that Jace was afraid to enter in case it collapsed on him. Animal scat and not a few tiny, desiccated rodent bodies lay everywhere. The entire bedroom was full of spruce cones, the work of a hyper-enterprising squirrel. The house's only heating source was an ancient

Preway oil-drip stove. No telling if it was still operational. The walls were originally wired for electricity, but the town's power plant had gone dark in 1938. And the odor! There was mold somewhere and plenty of it.

Jace looked at Beehymer. What he wanted to say was, *You have got to be out of your skull, old man.* What he did say was, "I was looking for something a little — nicer."

"Thought you might say that. Follow me." Beehymer led Jace outside to the second, still extant shed. In contrast to the first shed or the house itself, it was of recent construction. Its paint was fresh, the roofing looked good, and the sole window was intact. Inside the shed were work benches, shelves, and bins. There was even an iron anvil in the corner. But what caught Jace's attention was the twin bed at the far end, next to a camp stove, a propane lamp, and a dish rack. Somebody had been living here.

"I let people stay here sometimes," Beehymer said. "And lookie here." He hoisted up a foam-insulated trapdoor and shined a flashlight down a large, rectangular hole in the ground that was maybe ten feet deep (3 m). "Original root cellar. Never freezes down there, no matter how cold out it gets."

Jace nodded his head. "Let me get this straight," he said, helping Beehymer lower the trapdoor. "You're asking fifty-six thousand dollars for a shed with a root cellar."

"Not at all. The town lot by itself is worth what I'm asking, maybe more. The house is a bonus to sweeten the deal. And don't forget the well. It's rare to have one here. They used dynamite to dig it."

"I'm sure the well is great. But the house is more like a giant liability than a sweetener. It's a mess of lead paint and probably asbestos insulation that needs to be torn down and safely disposed of."

"You could do that. Tear it down and build new. But let me ask you this. You ever hear of historical preservation?"

"Like what the park service is doing at Caldecott?"

"That's preservation on an industrial scale. What I'm talking about is smaller. You never wondered why folks around here aren't tearing down all these firetraps? Because they're historical, that's why. All you need to do is get the house listed on the National Register of Historical Places."

"Um, how do you do that?"

"It's a cakewalk; this whole town pre-qualifies. And not just the General Store and museum. Private residences too. Hell, even that sorry knocked-down shed out front qualifies as an historical place. Then, when you're registered, you apply to the state office of History and Archeology for a grant — up to fifty thousand dollars. I said grant, not loan. I'm talking about free money. Fifty grand. You live in this shed while you're working on the house. That little wreck of a house can pay for itself in no time, lead paint and all. That is, ranger, if you wanted to become an *inholder*." He sneered the final word.

The old coot was probably right; the lot alone at fifty-six thousand was a bargain, and it could only appreciate in value. And because he was a young man of uncommon practicality, and unlike most American men of his age, Jace Kuliak had a nest egg of CDs tucked away in his bank back in Menominee that wasn't earning any interest. He was able to put his hands on about half of Beehymer's asking price. For the rest, well, wasn't that what family was for? [see *Sex on a Glacier* on page 323]

A Portent in the Sky

PS1 1.0

A WINTER'S DAY is short at both ends, and by the time Poppy Prophecy left the Mail Day gathering at the Sulzer house it was twilight. He steered his Polaris back through the comatose town, past the boarded-up People's Museum, past the picturesque log church, across the frozen river, and out the Stubborn Mine Trail. Crybaby Bunyan and his raven-haired daughter had still been enjoying the Sulzer hospitality when he left, and their own house was dark when he passed it at Mile 8.

The trail grew narrow and rough soon thereafter, and as Poppy bounced along, he entertained thoughts of going to Anchorage. He could take Adam in the pickup, go out, load up, and be back in four or five days. They could stop in Palmer on the way and see what was going on with NJB. As he neared Curve Canaveral, he was already braking when his sno-go headlight went dim and the engine faltered and died. The machine ground to a halt.

What now? Poppy gave the engine a few pulls, but it didn't catch. He had filled the tank that morning, so he knew he had plenty of gas. It was probably a loose spark plug wire. He dismounted and lifted the engine hood to check. But his flashlight wouldn't work. *Great.* While he was patting his pockets for a butane lighter, a dizziness came over him, and his knees grew wobbly. He clutched the handlebar to steady himself as he turned around and sat down hard on the sno-go seat. He felt faint. Was he having a stroke?

The hood slammed shut and, somewhere in the darkness, a tree limb snapped and crashed to the ground. Poppy's body seemed to grow heavier by the moment, and he, too, crashed to the ground, sprawling beside the machine. Limbs and boughs were falling all around him, and he could scarcely draw breath.

With a pop, night became day. The light was brighter than the sun, so intense it cut through his shut eyelids. His arm was too heavy to move to shield his face. It took all his will power just to turn his head facedown in the snow. Even then the light was dazzling.

Pressed to the ground, he wheezed and fought for every breath. He head swam, and he passed out.

When Poppy came to, the sky was dark again, and the oppressive weight was lifted from him. He sat up and leaned against the machine as he gathered his wits. His flashlight worked fine now, and he shined it all around. The ground nearest him was littered with broken branches, and the snow was compressed, as though pressed down by a giant hand. But not far away from him the snow looked untouched. The sharp boundary between the two areas extended in a broad arc into the woods. His sno-go had stopped just inside the compressed area.

When Poppy was able, he got back on the sno-go and yanked the cord. The engine fired on the first pull, and he resumed driving around Curve Canaveral, scanning the dark valley below. When he reentered the woods, he had to go around limbs and whole trees that had fallen across the trail. He paused when he found the boundary again that ran along the forest floor. It was like a long, curved porch step of snow. No, whatever had happened was not of earthly origin. It was a miracle of the first order, a sign. It had sign written all over it. *Thank you, Elder Brother Jesus, but what does it mean?*

PS2 1.0

WHAT WITH THE freight sled loaded down with expedition trash, and despite the already broken trail, Jace's return ride to town took considerably longer than his freewheeling ride out. By the time he reached the Mizina, he was tired but not yet ready to call it a day. The mild weather was holding, and he decided to take a smoke break. He stopped where he found a jumble of driftwood poking up through the snowpack and built a fire on the riverbank.

Across the river flats, the snowy slopes of Stubborn Mountain glowed under a three-quarters moon. The mountain stood apart from its neighbors, and Jace could see it in its entirety, bottom to top. It had an iconic mountainy shape, like what you could use for a smartphone app. Click here for Mountain. It was named Stubborn because during the last Ice Age, it had blocked the unstoppable advance of the Caldecott Glacier until it forced the wall of ice to split into two channels and flow around it.

Jace jabbed his campfire with a stick, sending an armada of burning embers into an ocean of sky. The temperature was dropping, and a frozen haze obscured the stars. Jace took a final hit off his joint and flicked it into the flames.

He used the stick to trace a ridge down the ghostly mountainside to where the Prophecy compound was located. He wondered what she was up to at that very moment. Probably up to her armpits in kids and cares. Cleaning up messes. Making dinner. And speaking of dinner, it was getting to be time to head home and find some dinner of his own. He raked snow into the fire and stirred the ashes.

One of the tie-downs that secured the bundles of trash to the sled had come loose, and while he was fixing it, he heard something odd. It sounded like bacon sizzling, or soda fizzing, or maybe a hissing cat. He turned all around to find its source, even pulling back his hood to free his ears.

When Jace looked at the mountain, he saw something weird in the darkness — darker darkness. As though a triangular piece of the night sky was missing, stars and all, along with the snowy flank of Stubborn Mountain. And then the odd triangular shape lit up from within, revealing itself to be a giant cone, hollow apparently, resting on its base, and as tall as the mountain behind it.

At the same moment, a bright object, like a shooting star, entered the cone at its apex and streaked at supersonic speed straight down toward the ground. It spit out flames and sparks in all directions as it fell. But the closer it approached the ground, the slower it went, until it hardly seemed to be moving at all. The cone surface, like welder's glass, dampened the intensity of the light. And for all the pyrotechnics involved, there was no sound but the constant hissing.

Jace watched with his mouth hanging open, too awestruck to be afraid. By the time he remembered his phone, it was too late to record the event. The object — a meteor? a top-secret military weapon? an alien UFO? — had touched down, and its light was extinguished. The cone went dark as well, allowing the stars and mountain to reappear.

Holy, holy shit.

The ranger dug out his Garmin GPS and used his bearings to guesstimate those of the object. He put a pin in its location and jumped on his snowmobile.

Jace drove straight for the likely landing zone. He was forced to break new trail, and the loose snow and his heavy load bogged down his engine. So he stopped to unhitch the sled before continuing. He drove cautiously and kept a sharp eye on everything within the range of his headlights.

He'd covered about six miles when he saw something and stopped again. There was a shallow ledge in the snow, like a step about eighteen inches deep (46 cm). The snow on his side of it was pristine while the snow on the other side looked flattened and compressed. The ledge itself extended in both directions in a gentle arc as far as his flashlight could reach. Could this be the imprint of the giant cone?

Using his flashlight as a probe, Jace dismounted and poked at the air above the snow ledge. Nothing. He dropped another pin on his map and continued across the ledge.

The compressed snow covered an area that encompassed river flats, foothills, and the western flank of Stubborn Mountain. Jace searched for a couple of hours. It would have helped to know exactly what he was searching for. Would the bogey still be hot? glowing? radioactive? Was it as large as a house or small as a stone? Would it shoot laser beams at him?

Daylight would have been a big help too. So would a full belly. The temperature had continued to drop, and both he and his snowmobile were running low on fuel. Whatever the object was, it would probably keep until tomorrow. That is, unless the Prophecys saw the light from their compound and decided to check it out. That possibility alone kept him searching for another hour before finally calling it quits. He backtracked to the curved snow ledge he'd found and followed it, stopping a half-dozen times to log more GPS coordinates. If the object had landed in the center of the cone's base, as it had appeared to do, and if he could remember enough high-school geometry, he'd be able to use the GPS record to calculate its location. For now, though, he retrieved the trash sled and headed home to the chalet.

The Toothache

TT1 1.0

POPPY PROPHECY KNEW what the sign meant. Knowledge had burst upon him during the last part of his ride home. After he left the area of pressed snow and broken limbs, the Holy Spirit lit up his mind with understanding. A flash of insight. No words were uttered, just a jolt of pure knowledge: *The unbearable light in the sky was the focused attention of the Creator gazing down upon you and your family.* It meant, *Pay attention!* It was his own personal burning bush. It said that the time had come. The state plowing the road was no accident. The Lord God says, *I am pushing obstacles out of your path, my son. Take Adam with you in the pickup, yes. But also take Hosea and Proverbs in the bus. This will be your last chance to stock up on essentials. Take advantage of it.*

"Yes, Lord, I will. I will put everything I have into food and supplies."

Poppy Prophecy drove into the yard and parked the sno-go next to its mates. He deftly removed one of its spark plugs with a socket wrench that he kept in a pocket. But then, on second thought, he screwed it back in.

The little Yamaha power generator in the pump shack behind him was chugging away, and there were electric lights burning in the bathhouse. He took the sack of mail and tromped across the snowy yard.

The cur Crissie Lou loitered outside the bathhouse door and slunk away as he approached.

The boys had covered the laundry table with sheets of plywood and covered the floor with plastic tarps. Tubs of hot water were simmering on the wood stove. Roasts, ribs, and steaks lay in glistening heaps upon the table. The children, from age eight on up, were wrapping family-sized portions of Father God's bounty in butcher paper.

When Poppy stepped into the room, everyone stopped, and the younger ones chorused, "Welcome home, lord."

"We didn't lose much, lord," Hosea said, pointing a knife at a tub of oil-tainted meat. Even though they had substituted cooking oil for the chain oil, some fouling was inevitable.

Poppy ignored him, ignored all of them, and crooked a finger at Adam. Adam came around the table and followed him wordlessly out to the porch.

"Yes, lord?"

"Looks like you're about finished in there."

"Yes, lord. A little more wrapping and stacking. Then clean up. We'll let them age a couple of days before we freeze 'em."

"Good. Let Hosea handle the rest. I have something else for you to do. I want you to get the Dodge and bus ready to roll first thing in the morning."

"Lord?"

"You heard me. I'll explain at Worship. We're leaving in the morning — you, me, Hosea, and Proverbs."

"Where are we going, lord?"

"Anchorage, you fool. Where else is there to go?"

"We're going on a supply run? But the road . . ."

"Let Father God handle the road. We need to concentrate on making this trip count because it'll be our last one — ever."

"Lord?"

"Not now. You'll learn everything tonight. So stop the flapping and start the doing. The plug's already in the Polaris."

"Yes, lord." Adam turned to go, but Poppy stopped him.

"You didn't see it, did you?" It was more a statement than a question.

"See what, lord?"

"The light."

Adam shook his head.

"Didn't any of you see a bright light in the sky about an hour ago?"

"I don't think so. No one mentioned anything. Of course, we were all probably indoors."

"You'd see this light through solid walls."

POPPY PROPHECY PULLED the keyring from his belt and unlocked the solid oak door to the prayer cabin. This was a log structure that originally served as the business office for the mine. An old Meilink floor safe still squatted against the back wall.

Poppy dropped the mail bag on the desk and lit the propane lamp. Then he knelt in front of the barrel stove to build a fire. It would take hours to heat the place, but Poppy needed to come back after dinner to draw up a shopping list. A blessing though it was, four thousand dollars would not long keep his family, and he had to plan their purchases with care.

When the fire was good and started, Poppy tossed in a couple of more sticks and cranked the door shut. He emptied the bag of mail on the desk and put to one side the boxes of gold chains and tacks to take into the house. That was when he noticed the lavender envelope again. He snatched it from the pile and reopened the barrel stove door.

Poppy didn't know who this girl was, but it was obvious that she had designs on his son. The Bible said that these were not the times when women should bear children. His sons and daughters would be better off waiting out the next seven years as virgins and then go out among the survivors to find spouses. But that whole argument had made a lot more sense back when his oldest boys were still teenagers. His family had been manning the ramparts and keeping the faith for a long time, and now the oldest were adults. He had never intended for his offspring to remain celibate forever. What would be the point of that? Still, when had Adam met this girl?

Poppy closed the stove door and took the fat envelope back to the lamp light. Her name was Susan Krae, and she was from Soldotna on the Kenai Peninsula. Adam must have met her that time the family was looking for land near Homer. Poppy couldn't think of any other occasion Adam would have had to be south of Anchorage on the Kenai. But that was three years ago. How had the boy managed to keep this liaison secret for so long? Had he made Ginny Sulzer his co-conspirator, asked her to hide his letters inside the pages of his magazines? No wonder the boy was always so eager to make the mail run. It was one thing to disobey him, but lying and deceiving on top of it? Not tolerable.

All he could tell of the girl short of opening and reading her letter, something he had every right to do, and might yet do, were the six lines she had written in her own hand — the address and return address:

Mr. Adam Prophecy

It was odd to see his firstborn idiot addressed as a mister. But it showed an upbringing of respect on the girl's part. On the next line she wrote:

Stubborn Mountain Mine

Which meant that either his son had withheld from her the true nature of their mission, or that she had the good sense not to broadcast it via the U.S. post. Either way, it showed a maturity in one or the other of them that boded well.

Poppy dropped the envelope on the desk for further pondering after dinner.

TT2 1.0

THE BIG HOUSE, a long, low structure, had been the original copper mine mess hall. Successive mine owners had built upon it, and the Prophecys built upon their work, erecting two bunkroom wings on the sides of the enlarged common room.

Apparently, Sarai had dinner duty that day because she and Cora were peeling carrots and turnips next to the range. Peeling them sullenly, Poppy thought. And then he remembered he had punishment to mete out at Worship Time. What an inconvenience. But discipline must be ironclad. Especially now. *Especially now.*

Poppy continued into the common room. Next to the stove, Mama P's lawn lounger was vacant. Her blankets were folded tidily and stacked at the foot, with the cat snoozing on top of them. The babies were playing on the floor with wooden blocks and toy cars. Most of the tables were set for dinner, still hours away. One table was an assembly line for the family's handicrafts business, but only Deut and one of the middle girls were at work. All of the other busy little hands were out in the bathhouse wrapping moose. The girls stood up to greet him, but the little one's eyes were puffy from crying. She was one of his second set of twins, either Frankincense or Myrrh.

"What's wrong with her?" Poppy asked Deut.

"Nothing, lord. Growing pains."

Poppy didn't like the sound of *growing pains,* but there was nothing he could do about it. It was inevitable. How old was the girl? Twelve? Thirteen? She was one of the girls that Bunyan coveted as playmate for his daughter.

"Well, tell her to quit sniveling. I don't want to hear sniveling, and I don't want to see that ugly face. Go wash up, girl."

The girl, who well knew which twin she was, Myrrh, and that she was twelve years old, peeped, "Yes, lord," and fled the room for the kitchen.

Deut, meanwhile, distracted her father with business. She pried the small parcels from his hands and said, "These are the new tacks and chains? They finally arrived?"

"I expect they are," Poppy said. "If you're so curious, why don't you open them."

While Deut did so, Poppy examined several skeins of completed pendants hanging on delicate faux-gold chains. Deut said, "It says there's only a thousand here. Will more be coming, lord?"

"Of course," he snapped. "I ordered ten thou —" Only then did he realize what he was saying. "No." He corrected himself. "No more are coming. In fact, take these and get rid of them. Get rid of the carvings and angels and ornaments. Get rid of it all."

"I don't understand."

"We're not in this business anymore. Those days are gone. That time has come to an end."

SECOND-BORN HOSEA was the finish carpenter of the family, and third-born Proverbs was its design specialist. Together the two boys had renovated the narrow mess-hall kitchen into a more open, efficient space, albeit still powered by wood.

Skillets, pans, pots, utensils, and anything else that could be hung from a hook was hanging along the cornices of two walls. Knives of all sizes and shapes resided in a special block. And clever, movable prep tables allowed for optimal use of the limited floor space.

Sarai fed sticks of spruce into the fireboxes of the restaurant-sized range. Dinner simmered in large pots on the back burners, on hold, ready to serve in about an hour and a half. Dinner rolls were rising on trays in the warming ovens, and the water tanks were heating twenty-five gallons (95 l) of water for cleanup after the meal.

The chief puzzle in preparing dinner for the Prophecy family had to do with its timing. In the Prophecy household, dinner on six nights of the week followed Worship Time. Although the average Worship Time lasted twenty minutes, sometimes the Holy Spirit loosened Poppy's tongue, and then he shared the Word for an hour or sometimes *two* hours without pause. One night a few years ago, Poppy went on for so long that the babies were crying out loud for their supper, and he didn't even hear them, so caught up was he in the Spirit.

So Mama had come up with a plan. Hold back the trays of dinner rolls. A few minutes into Worship Time, one girl steps into the kitchen and pops them into a hot oven. For if there was one thing Mama had learned after twenty-six years of marriage to the man, it was that the yeasty aroma of baking rolls could compete even with the Holy Spirit for his attention.

Deut swept into the kitchen with a tray of dirty cups and dropped them one by one into the tub of dishwater. When she looked up, her twin sister was staring at her. Not a hostile stare, the opposite, in fact.

"Why?" Sarai said in a small voice.

"Why what?" Deut replied.

Sarai tried to speak but broke down and hid her face in her hands.

Deut was troubled to see her sister so miserable, and she almost gave in, but instead she said, "I don't see why you get to be the princess all the time. You were born five minutes ahead of me and that gives you privileges for the rest of our lives?"

Sarai shook her head, but Deut wasn't buying it. Sarai had done something really vile in the field by calling into question their father's authority in front of the little kids. Deut couldn't just stand by and let her get away with it, could she? It was for everyone's sake that she'd ratted her out.

TT4 1.0

A SOFT KNOCK on the prayer cabin door woke Poppy from his nap. How long had he been asleep? An hour at least. He felt refreshed.

"Who's there?" he said.

"Adam, lord. Dinner's ready."

"I'll be right in."

Not surprisingly, after such an active and miraculous day and after such a good nap, Poppy had an appetite. During his nap, his spirit had continued to grapple with the problems of the day, and he had come to the decision, in the interest of time, to skip the Worship Time homily and get right to the correction. Why not? Valuable spiritual lessons could be learned from witnessing the administration of just punishment.

Also, he would mete out the punishment before revealing the miracle. That way, everyone, including the punished, could cleanse their minds of distraction and be able to fully take in his good news. Father God's miracle was the message of the day, not the punishment of wrongdoers.

The creak of the porch floorboards told Poppy that his son was still outside his door.

"What?" he shouted.

"I got the vehicles ready, lord."

What was the boy going on about? Poppy sat up in the daybed and swung his stocking feet to the floor.

"Lord?"

"What is it, Adam? Why are you hectoring me?"

"Sorry, lord. Can I come in for a sec?"

In a fit of irritation, Poppy strode across the floor and unbolted the door for his son. Then he struck a match and relit the lamp and fed a couple of logs into the barrel stove. When he turned around again, Adam was standing next to the desk staring down at the lavender envelope lying there.

"What do you want?" Poppy said. He already knew what his son wanted.

"I was just wondering if any mail came for me, and I see that some has." He reached for the envelope.

"Leave it!" Poppy said, but too late. Adam was already clutching the envelope to his chest like a girl.

Poppy held out his hand for the envelope, but Adam said, "Look, lord. It's addressed to me. It's mine. I never wanted to keep this a secret, lord, I promise you, but I never found the right time to tell you. If what you say is true, and this is our last trip out, well, I guess now must be the right time. I met a girl."

"You don't say."

"I've always been an obedient son, lord, and I dedicate myself to the family totally and spend all my time preparing the keep. But if we threw the bolt tonight, I'd be in my mid-thirties the next time we open the gate, and who knows what kind of world we'll find when we come out? Am I to live my entire life a bachelor, lord? Am I never to have a wife? Or a child? Do you want no grandchildren, lord?"

Poppy said, "The Bible says there is a time to embrace, and a time to refrain from embracing. You well know which one this is."

"Yes, lord, I know, but even if we're not allowed to marry until it's all over, at least let me bring her in to live with us so that *when* it's all over she'll still be *alive* so I can marry her. How can that be against Father God's plan? She's a spirit-filled girl and godly and in complete harmony with Father God's truth. I made sure of that. If I ask her to be my wife, I believe she'll say yes. If I ask her to plight to a seven-year betrothal, she won't complain."

Struggling to hit just the right balance of filial devotion and manly independence, Adam rested his case with, "And I love her with all my heart."

All for naught. Poppy reached out his open hand again, and this time his grim-faced firstborn handed over the fat envelope dyed in the pastel color of springtime and lust. Poppy opened the stove door. If the kid had just kept his mouth shut, Poppy would have let him have the letter. Why did he have to go and challenge him like that? Do you want no grandchildren? Was that a threat?

But Poppy was no more able to destroy the letter now than before. He had followed one path for so long, it was hard to know when it was time to change course. And it was probably no accident that the letter should arrive today. It might even be part of Father God's plan. So he shut the stove door and handed Susan Krae's love letter to his son, much to his son's predictable and pitiable relief. He turned off the lamp, locked the prayer cabin door, and followed the boy who would be a man into the house.

TT5 1.0

THE PATRIARCH MOVED his chair next to the lawn lounger. It was the signal for the family to assemble and arrange themselves in a wide semicircle around their parents. Each child helped drag a bench or chair or cushions for sitting on the floor. Little ones were boosted onto laps. Adam and Hosea carried their mother in from the bedroom. Sarai and Cora stood next to the kitchen door still wearing their aprons. Crissie Lou, the dog, curled up at Uzziel's feet. Calgary, the cat, waited until Mama was installed in the lounger and then took her rightful place on her lap, where she proceeded to groom herself.

When everyone was settled, Poppy seated himself, unsnapped the holster on his belt, removed the Holy Book, kissed it, set it unopened upon his lap, and rested his ropey hands on its tattered leather cover. "Praise Father God, we're all here again," he said.

"Praise Him," they chorused. "Praise His Holy name."

"Amen," Poppy said, looking directly into the eyes of each of his congregants. "My children, and Mama, something miraculous happened today to which I was witness. Father God willing, what I saw will change the course of our lives." He paused to read their reaction. "It is my blessing to reveal it to you, but first we have some unhappy business to get out of the way. Son?"

"Yes, lord." Proverbs rose to his feet and went over to the mirror hanging on the wall. He pulled a birch switch from a quiver of switches hanging there. He slashed the air with it a few times. It made a shrill whistling sound that frightened the little ones, and Crissie Lou slunk out of the room. But Proverbs secretly winked at the children and smiled. He handed the switch to his father, pulled a chair around, leaned over it, and assumed the position.

Stenciled in red ink across the yoke of Proverbs' shirt were the words, Fair Trade 100% ORGANIC. Mama had made him the shirt when he was fifteen and midway through a particularly rebellious phase. Proverbs held the family record for most corrections. For a while he was getting two or three corrections a week, and Mama grew weary of mending and re-mending the backs of his shirts and taking out the bloodstains. So she sewed her wayward son a sackcloth shirt, the yoke and back panels of which were four layers of thick, coarse burlap. The birch switches had finally met their match. And the best part was that because prophets of old wore sackcloth, and sackcloth was mentioned in the Bible, there was little Poppy could do about it. In recent years, Proverbs loaned out the shirt to his younger brothers as the need arose, which wasn't very often. Otherwise, it was pretty much retired. Tonight he put it on for the first time in four years. It was very tight, a testament to how much he'd filled out in the meantime.

Poppy slapped the switch against his own thigh to test it. "Why is Father God punishing you, son?" he asked.

"Because I killed a moose, lord. And I'm real sorry about it."

"That's *not* why. If you're going to ask forgiveness for something, at least know what you're asking forgiveness for. Try again. Why is Father God punishing you?"

"Because I should'a waited till after Nellis flew over, but I didn't believe strong enough that the moose would hang around."

"Good. By whose authority do I raise my hand against you, son?"

"By the Father's."

"That's right. For it is written . . ." Poppy picked up the Bible and recited from memory, "'He that spareth the rod hateth his son: but he that loveth him chasteneth him betimes.'"

"Amen."

"Who loves you, son?"

"You doeth, lord."

Poppy frowned. "How many stripes did you earn today?"

"Teneth."

A ripple of suppressed giggles passed around the room at Proverbs' defiance, but one look from Poppy put an end to that. Poppy set the Bible down and raised the switch high over his head before bringing it down sharply across Proverbs' back. Proverbs flinched but made no sound. Poppy felt the flinch, and it felt genuine and not faked. The cat jumped off Mama's lap and joined the dog outside of the room.

Poppy aimed the second stripe for a tiny rent in the burlap under the coffee grower's logo. Years of patient attention to that spot had already worn through two of the four layers of sacking. Again he raised the switch and gave it his all. This time the switch snapped in two.

Poppy ordered Proverbs to fetch a replacement. The children gaped in horror, but Proverbs made goofy faces at them. He tested the second switch as he had the first with comical slashes in the air and declared it a worthy switch.

"Bring a few more while you're up," Poppy said dryly.

One stripe, two stripes, three. Four stripes, five stripes, six. Proverbs could no longer hide the pain. The children covered their faces, and the babies cried.

"Open your eyes and watch!" Poppy snarled at them. "Unless you want a taste of it too."

It wasn't until the eighth lash in about the same location that the switch drew blood. *Good.* And not until the tenth and final one that a groan escaped the boy's lips. It was a tiny groan, but it was a hard-won and satisfying one, and the only groan Proverbs was likely to give up. It was enough to assure the father that he'd gotten through to the son.

Proverbs straightened up, a little wobbly, and faced his father.

"I love you, my boy," Poppy said. He broke the switch in two and handed the pieces to Proverbs.

"I love you too, lord," Proverbs said. "Thank you for caring enough about me to keep me on the straight and narrow." One more smile for his audience of scared babies, and the boy returned to his chair. For the rest of the night he was careful not to lean against the seat back.

"Sarai, you're up."

TT6 1.0

THE ELDEST GIRL removed her spaghetti-sauce-stained apron and came forward. The children, especially the youngest, began to cry in big, wet, but silent sobs. Sarai rearranged the whipping chair and assumed the position.

"Not so fast," Poppy said. "Don't be so quick to pass sentence on yourself. Stand up, daughter."

She didn't move.

"Stand up and tell us what Father God is punishing you for."

She stood up and faced him. "Because I sinned with my mouth, lord."

"That's right. You did." Poppy slapped a new switch against his thigh, making the children jump. "But that covers a wide range of sins. To be more specific, you committed the same sin that Lucifer committed when he thought he was Father God's equal and turned the heavenly hosts against Him in rebellion. What sin is that?"

"Um, pride?" Sarai said.

"Yes, pride. You believe that Father God is weak and you are strong, when the opposite is true. And the punishment for a sin of pride is an act of humility. Here is your punishment: you will wash your parents' feet and dry them with your hair, as Mary Magdalene did for our Savior. In this way you will demonstrate the purity of your humility and obedience to the authority of your parents."

Before he even finished speaking, Sarai was heading for the kitchen.

"Come back here. Where are you going?"

"To fetch a basin of water, lord."

"No, not now. I have wondrous news to share now. Wait until after supper to wash your mama's feet. Then bring your basin out to the prayer cabin and wash mine there."

Sarai abruptly changed course and, instead of the kitchen, she went straight to the mirror and grabbed the quiver. She poured the rest of the switches into her hand and threw them across the room at her father. More of them hit her astonished siblings than her father.

"If you want to punish me, lord," she screamed, "punish me here and now. In front of everyone. Not hanging over my head like an ax. Not out in your cabin. Now!"

"Silence!" Poppy said. "It's not up to you to name your punishment."

With a shriek of frustration, Sarai stormed out of the common room, slamming the door of the girls' bunkroom behind her. Hosea glanced at Adam, and Adam shrugged his shoulders. The children watched in fear for their father's reaction. Deut asked, "Should I go bring her back, lord?"

"No, leave her. I'll deal with her later."

"But . . ." Deut said. "She's the cook tonight."

Poppy silenced her with dagger eyes.

"Yes, lord," Deut said, got up, and headed for the kitchen.

"Stop. Stay here. I want everyone to hear this."

Right on cue, the golden-crust fragrance of browning rolls washed through the room. Poppy sniffed the air, but instead of enticing him, it made him ask, "Who's in there?"

"Cora, I guess."

"Bring her out here."

"But dinner, lord."

"Shut up and listen to me! Let dinner grow cold. Let it rot! Go do what I told you, or do you want a whipping too?"

"Sorry, lord."

When Cora joined the others in the semicircle, Poppy counted heads.

"Who's missing? Someone's missing."

Deut said, "Besides Sarai, that would be Myrrh, lord. I sent her to bed because she's sick."

"That was hours ago. What kind of growing pains does she have?"

"A toothache, lord."

"Well, dab it with oil of clove! Do I have to tell you everything?"

"No, lord. We've been dabbing it all day, but it doesn't help."

"Have you prayed on it?"

"Yes, lord. All of us."

"Then it'll pass. Get her out here. She won't want to miss this."

"Yes, lord. Should I fetch Sarai too so she doesn't miss it either?"

"No! I said leave her! You're skating mighty close to the edge, daughter."

THERE WERE NO lights on in the bunkroom, but Deut was accustomed to finding her way by touch. It was easy to locate Myrrh's top bunk, just follow her little mews and moans.

"Myrrh, sweetheart, Poppy wants you out there."

"Noooo. I don't want to."

"Just for a little while. Did the Tylenol help?"

"No!"

"Well, Poppy wants to tell us about a miracle that happened to him today. Then you can come back here."

"Noooo."

Deut helped her little sister from the bunk. At the end of the room, the ghostly shape of her own twin lay on a single bed facing the wall. She was showing them her back. Not fair. Not fair. Not even a toothache is excuse enough for little Myrrh, but *Sarai* gets away with *throwing things at Poppy*. If anyone else tried that they'd be really sorry.

TT7 1.0

"I WAS SLEDDING home a few hours ago. I had just passed the Bunyan place and was coming up on the curve when an angel, an angel from the throne room of Father God, pinched my fuel line between his fingers and killed my engine."

His audience, even the older ones, leaned forward in their seats.

"Yes, an angel stopped my sno-go and then knocked me off it and pressed me down so hard I couldn't breathe. It felt as though he was trying to crush me. And he knocked down hundreds of trees all over the place and pressed down the snow for miles around." Poppy Prophecy paused to study his audience. "You don't believe me?"

"Yes, lord. We believe you," everyone shouted.

"You think that maybe I'm making this all up? Or maybe I hit my head and imagined it all? Or maybe I'm just lying to you?"

"No, lord! We don't think that!"

"You believe the days of miracles are all in the past and that angels don't visit men anymore?"

"No, lord. We don't believe that."

Adam leaped to his feet, ashen faced. "I saw it!" he exclaimed. "I thought it must have been some freak windstorm." Adam had passed through the area twice to prepare the vehicles. "All sorts of trees down. I could've used a chainsaw to get through."

"Shut up," Poppy snapped. "And sit down."

Adam did as he was told.

"There was a light too," Poppy went on. "It was no earthly light . . ." One of the middle girls sitting on cushions on the floor shifted her position a little and briefly exposed another girl who had been hiding behind her. It was Myrrh, who had just joined them. It was only a brief glimpse but enough to once again derail Poppy's account.

"You, girl, stop hiding. Show yourself."

Myrrh scooted into view. She looked absolutely wretched. She looked like she was experiencing the worst pain she had ever suffered in her life. Yet she made no noise.

"You have a toothache?" he said.

She nodded.

"Well, daughter, I believe you are learning an important lesson about this world that will guide you the rest of your life."

"What lesson, lord?"

"That our earthly bodies are not our friends but our traitors. When we're young, our bodies are the playground of Satan who uses them to tempt us from the path. And when we're old, they begin to rot before we're even dead. And all through our lives they fail us with sickness and disease. Only our heavenly bodies will be perfect."

"Yes, lord."

"I think you've probably learned the lesson enough, and the others through you. So let's all pray for Father God to drive the decay from your mouth and to restore you to good health. "Let us pray."

All together, they prayed for Myrrh's restoration and cure for the toothache. And their father used his authority to cast out the decay and whatever evil spirits were buzzing around it like flies on roadkill.

They chorused a resounding "Amen." Yet the girl's torment persisted.

"Do you believe in Father God's miracles?" Poppy asked the girl. "If your faith is weak, if you harbor any doubts in your heart, you might as well forget about it. Father God doesn't heed the prayers of doubters."

"I believe, lord."

Time would tell if that was true. He'd give it an hour. If she was still suffering, he'd pull the tooth out with a special set of pliers he kept for that purpose. It wouldn't be his first tooth extraction. You can't hope to live as sovereigns on your own land, as he and Mama had done for nearly thirty years, and to raise so many babies without picking up some basic dentistry skills along the way.

Just then Poppy received a nudge from above that gave him pause. Pliers? Why resort to the pliers when there was a real dentist plying his trade a mere one hundred thirty miles away (209 km) by road in Glennallen and when that road was being cleared tomorrow? Why not take the girl with them?

For that matter, Poppy himself had a bothersome filling in a wisdom tooth that should be looked at. And Adam wanted a wife. And NJB had left him a mysterious code. And the clincher — for the first time in a long time, he had cash dollars for gas and more.

TT8 1.0

GURGLE, GURGLE, GURGLE went their bellies. The Holy Spirit had their father by the whiskers this time. Mama's dinner-roll trick was a dud (as Mama herself was turning out to be). Deut moved the large pots away from the heat while their father communed with higher powers. Proverbs quietly retired to the boy's bunkroom. Hosea went out to the porch to break a handful of carrot-sized icicles from the eaves for his brother's back. Poor little Myrrh squirmed so much that the other children were squirming too. Meanwhile, Deut had to hang on to the two littlest babies to keep them from setting upon Mama where she lay. The center would not hold on this cartwheel much longer.

Poppy didn't notice any of this.

After a while longer, he stirred and blinked. "I have an announcement!" he bellowed, rising from his chair. He wobbled a little and clutched the seat back to regain his balance.

Hosea and Proverbs came out of the bunkroom. Proverbs was wearing a fresh shirt — and his eyepatch!

"Hear the words I speak. Tomorrow Adam will take Myrrh to see the dentist in Glennallen."

After a moment of disbelief, adults and children alike cheered.

"Not only that, I'm taking *everyone else* to the dentist too. In Wallis."

This seemed a stretch, even in god-speak, and the children doubted their ears until Poppy nailed it down. "It's a shopping run to Anchorage. It starts tomorrow. Everyone's going."

When their doubts were wiped away, the children lost their minds in celebration. Even Myrrh saw an end to her terrible trial.

"There's not a lot of time for packing," Poppy went on. "Eat your dinner quickly and then everyone pack. But pack light. We'll be buying new clothes and stuff there."

"How many nights should we prepare for, lord?" Deut asked quite sensibly.

But God the Spirit hadn't specified a time frame. Poppy still didn't know the day or the hour. That meant it was up to him to estimate how many days the Spirit would regard as reasonable for conducting the world's last shopping trip. "Let's plan to be gone ten days," he said tentatively. "And maybe we'll be blessed to wrap it up in seven."

Cora brought out the first food cart, and the children bolted for the tables without waiting for formal dismissal. And they wolfed down their food without the aid of a blessing. Poppy either didn't notice or didn't care. He gestured for the older ones to join him. To Deut he said, "Gather vaccination records and any broken eyeglasses that need to be fixed." To Hosea he said, "Give the girl a quarter tab of Percodan. Just enough to hold her till Adam gets her to the dentist." To Adam he said, "I want you to take her in the pickup as soon as the road is cleared. I'll call ahead and tell Dr. Lee it's an emergency. When they're done with her, wait for us at the Hub. You're sure to be an hour or two ahead of us." And finally he said to Deut, "Tell your sister that her punishment is on hold, not cancelled. There's nothing to help it, and she can only make it worse."

"Yes, lord. I'll tell her."

TT9 1.0

IT WAS LATE when Poppy returned to the big house from the prayer cabin with his shopping list. All was quiet. The dog was snoozing in front of the large, warm wood stove, and she silently stole away as he came over to refill it. He had to use a flashlight to get around because there was no moonlight in the windows.

Mama stirred when Poppy entered the bedroom. Either the girls hadn't properly covered her, or she had kicked away the covers, because a length of bare thigh peeked out from under her blanket.

Tired as he was, the sight of it stirred him.

He fumbled in the dark for the key to the nightstand drawer. He brought the tube of K-Y Jelly to her bed and hitched up her nightgown. She wore no panties — the easier for the girls to keep her clean without actually looking at her. He gazed at her, though, as was his right as husband and lord. He shined his flashlight at the gash of Eve between her thighs, her sweet hatchet wound of love.

"Ah, Little Mother, wherever you are, come spend some time with Papa."

Poppy undressed himself and climbed into her bed. He squeezed out a bead of jelly and spread it around inside her soft folds of flesh to prepare the way. Her eyes opened at the cold touch, and for a moment he thought she had returned to him, but it was only a reflex. She wasn't there.

He squeezed out a bit more to slather his dick, and he rubbed himself up against her. There was no change in her breathing.

He kissed her rubbery mouth. He fondled her heavy breasts. "Try," he urged her. "Just for a little while." But she remained stubbornly absent.

Poppy pinched her inner thigh — cruelly. It would leave a mark. "Feel that? That's what you get."

Nothing was happening for him either. He squeezed jelly into her palm and wrapped her hand around his dick, pumping it up and down. Her hand was as limp as he was.

"You think you're pretty clever, don't you?" He pulled her nightgown back into place and covered her with the comforter. "Things are speeding up down here, for your information, and I could use a wife again. You got a choice to make, woman, and soon."

TT10 1.0

THE MINUTE JACE got home from his trash run, shed his arctic outerwear, kicked the oil stove in the pants, and popped open a beer, he began browsing the news sites on his iPad. He couldn't have been the only one on the planet to see what looked like a tiny sun descending inside a giant cone of welder's glass. What about satellites? What about the space station?

After exhausting the news sites with no hits, he tried NASA's site, UFO and conspiracy blogs, and legit astronomy sites. Nada, nada, and nada.

The year Jace was first assigned to the park, the only phone service in McHardy and Caldecott was via a Vietnam-era radiotelephone system provided by a company out of Valdez. Lousy reception, lousy service, expensive, and unreliable. It was also totally useless for cell phones and the internet. That first season at Caldecott, Jace had been forced to go offline cold turkey for six months, and he didn't enjoy it one bit. In his backcountry postings in Lower-48 parks, he'd never been out of cell phone range for more than twenty-four or forty-eight hours at a time. Though he fell instantly in love with Alaska and the park, living offline half of the year amounted to cruel and unusual employment conditions, and he wondered if he had it in him to return to the park the following season.

Fortunately, before he had to decide, the Obama administration made the problem go away. Obama's economic stimulation plan allocated five million dollars for extending high speed voice and data service to Chitina, McHardy, Caldecott, and along much of the gravel road that connected them.

As Jace browsed for news about the strange light, he fried up a can of corned beef hash in a skillet. He scanned all the hash tags he could think of on Twitter: #meteor, #lightinthesky, #UFO, #XFiles, #alieninvasion. Billions of hits, no results.

Looking for Love (in All the Wrong Places)

LL1 1.0

THE ONLY PROPHECY woman to spend an entire morning in bed who wasn't delivering a baby or burning up with fever was Mama during the weeks before Elder Brother Jesus took her soul on a vacation. But here was Sarai, who was neither giving birth nor burning up, still in bed while the whole room churned around her.

Deut and Cora stood next to Sarai's bed and addressed her backside. Deut said, "Are you sick?" There wasn't a twitch of response from her twin, and Deut repeated the question more loudly. Then Cora leaned over the bed to feel her forehead.

Sarai brushed her hand away and said, "Leave me alone."

"Are you sick?" Deut insisted.

"Yes, no. What difference does it make?"

Deut and Cora looked at each other in puzzlement. That wasn't a typical Saria answer.

"Anyway," Sarai added, "I'm not going."

"Are you nuts?" Cora said. "Not going to town? What's wrong with you?"

"Poppy will make you go," Deut added.

"No, he won't. Somebody's got to stay behind and take care of the animals. And if I stay, Adam can leave Mama, Elzie, and Nummy. It'll be a lot easier for everybody that way."

She was correct.

LL2 1.0

IT TOOK SEVERAL round trips with all three sno-gos and sleds to haul everyone and everything sixteen miles (26 km) to the parking lot. Along the way, they were all able to see with their own eyes the angel's giant handprint in the snow. When they arrived at the parking lot, the school bus was still frozen. Its old diesel engine was especially cranky about cold starts, and the overnight temperature had returned to the minus twenties (–30s C). But they lit the interior catalytic heaters, and the children piled in and covered up with sleeping bags and blankets while they waited for it to warm up. Meanwhile Adam and Proverbs heated the oil pan under the engine block with a propane weed burner in a stovepipe. Proverbs wasn't wearing the eyepatch anymore, thank Elder Brother Jesus. Finally, after another half hour of heating, the 1958 Bluebird's engine chugged to life, and everyone cheered and offered thanks.

Then, out of the blue, Ed Sulzer showed up on his sno-go with eight large cartons of finished goldpans, which seemed strange to Poppy because he had deliberately *not* told him about their departure. There wasn't enough space in the bus for Ed's cartons, and Poppy told Ed that he'd have the boys put them in the cargo rack on top.

Ed handed him his shopping list, thanked him, and left. When Hosea began to climb up the back of the bus, Poppy told him and Proverbs to stash the goldpans in the woods instead. He pointed to a stand of cottonwoods at the end of the lot. To Hosea this seemed to be an unneighborly thing to do (besides being untruthful), and he carefully asked his father, "Then why did we tell him we'd take it to Anchorage?"

"Ed don't know it, but the time for selling trinkets to tourists is over. We do him no favor and do us a lot of wasted effort if we was to take his crap to town. We're not taking any of our own, either. Better the pans remain here. We'll return them to Ed if he wants them or find a use for them ourselves, even if we have to scrape the paint off."

When the snowplow arrived, it used the parking lot to turn around in to begin its long return trip to Chitina. But Adam jogged out to meet the operator and directed him to the back of the lot to free the idling vehicles. Soon, after a prayer and a blessing, they were off.

FIVE HOURS INTO the ten-hour trip, the bus pulled into the Hub of Alaska Maxi Mart at the edge of Glennallen. Although the town of Glennallen boasted three gas stations, the Hub's strategic location at the junction of the Glenn and Richardson Highways gave it a commanding advantage. From the Hub one could drive west to Anchorage, south to the pipeline terminus in Valdez, north to Fairbanks, or northeast to the Canadian border. The town of Glennallen had begun its life as a highway construction work camp during the Second World War, and it remained a highway town ever since. Its civic motto was, "Need Gas?" A pointless question in light of the vast distances between Glennallen and anywhere else on the map.

Adam, Solomon, and Myrrh were waiting for them in the idling pickup in the Hub parking lot. Myrrh was all smiles. She had a new filling, a new toothbrush, and a sugar-free lollipop from the treasure chest. She and Solly joined the others in the bus while Hosea joined Adam in the pickup. Before they set off again, Adam asked Poppy if he could borrow his phone.

"What for?"

"To call her and let her know we're coming, lord." He didn't have to specify who he was referring to, the girl with the lavender envelope.

"Why didn't you use the phone in the gas station while you was waiting for us?"

"Because there aren't no pay phones no more."

Reluctantly Poppy handed him his Samsung. He also gave him the DC charger; there was no cigarette lighter plug on the old school bus. "Put a charge in it."

"Yes, lord. Thank you, lord."

For the rest of the trip, the pickup would follow the bus, and as Adam and Hosea waited for the bus to get underway, Adam offered the phone to

Hosea.

"This is Poppy's phone," Hosea said incredulously.

"Yeah."

"He let you use it?"

"No, I stole it."

"Why are you giving it to me?"

"I thought maybe there was someone you wanted to call. You know, this being the end of civilization and all."

The big man's fleshy face flushed crimson, which probably meant there was indeed someone he wanted to call, but he said, "I don't know about that."

"This is no time to be shy, brother," Adam said. "When we get back, we're throwing the bolt. It's now or never."

Hosea took the phone but didn't dial right away, not even after they started driving. Adam followed the bus through town and out the other end before he said, "If you're gonna do it, do it now."

"Don't rush me. I'm rehearsing."

"I'm not rushing you, but we'll lose cell service in another few miles."

Hosea pulled a scrap of paper from his wallet and dialed. "Uh, hullo?" he said. "Is this Cherise Wannabach? . . . Yes, thank you. I'll hold." He held for about five miles. "Oh, hi, Cherise? Hi, it's Hosea . . . Hosea Prophecy . . . No, Prophecy . . . That's right. I met you a couple of years ago in Chugiak . . . Yes, fine, and you? . . . Oh . . . I'm sorry to . . . That's too bad. I'll get the family to pray for . . . I see. Actually, I'm calling because I was wondering if you'd be interested in taking a spur-of-the-moment, uh, wilderness vacation . . . No, this is not a joke . . . Prophecy. We met at your church potluck . . . Uh-huh . . . Yes . . . Brown hair, beard, tall, kinda husky . . . Yes, *lots* of brothers and sisters — that's me! . . . I know it's winter . . . To ask you to spend Christmas with us. Everyone's dying to meet you, and . . . Uh, no. No one's talking about you. It's just they'd like to . . . *Because*, that's why. Because you're a great person and . . . Yes, I could tell that from a short conversation."

Hosea looked ill. He nodded his head as he listened to the girl named Cherise go on and on. Adam nudged him and said, "Haul out the big guns."

The big guns were the Apocalypse, and Hosea did haul them out as best he could.

"Yes, the End Times," he repeated. "It's already begun . . . a safe refuge . . . inside an old copper mine. We'll be safe from the armies of the Antichrist . . ."

"Oh," Hosea said at last. "I see. No, you're right. It's not something I could . . . I mean it sounds like . . . All right, then. I'll pray for you . . . Thank you. Good-bye."

When he hung up, they rode in silence for a few miles. "She got married," Hosea said at last.

"Then why didn't she say so in the first breath?" Adam said. "Instead of dragging you through the creek like that."

"And divorced," Hosea added. "And then pregnant by another guy."

Adam wagged his head.

"Then she had an abortion."

Adam stared dully at the road ahead. Hosea handed the phone back and said, "I guess I misjudged her. But considering the alternative, I had to give her a shot. I hope you have better luck."

"Hey, thanks, brother," Adam said. He dialed a number from memory, and when someone picked up he said, "Hello, Susie Q! . . . Fine, and you? . . . Good, good. Praise Elder Brother Jesus . . . Yes, I got it yesterday. *Thanks!* . . . I'll give you three guesses . . . No . . . no . . . and close. We're just leaving Glennallen . . . That's right. Maybe a week . . . Uh, huh . . . Why don't you just *uninvite* him? . . . Tell them your plans have changed . . . That's right, just like that . . . Aces . . . Uh huh, I will . . . Father God love you too, babe. Later."

Adam broke the connection and turned on the radio, and the miles slipped by.

LL3 1.0

BUS CAMPING WAS a lot more fun in the summer than it was in December. Nevertheless, the plan was to park the bus and family in Wallis and use the pickup for shopping forays into Anchorage, another forty miles (64 km) on. There were a couple of churches Poppy could ask to park in their lot and use their toilet facilities. He wanted to call them, but he'd stupidly loaned his phone to Adam to call his girlfriend. For that matter, he could give NJB another try. Maybe he'd been out of town and now he was back. He would certainly let them camp at his place in Palmer if he was there.

NJB had come into the Prophecy orbit at a critical point in the family's mission. They'd driven up to Alaska on the promptings of the Holy Spirit (in signs and wonders and dreams of wisdom), but since they'd arrived, nothing was working out as foretold. Alaska was supposed to be this big, open country where a Christian family could lose itself and thrive unmolested by society's relentless War on Faith. Even Northern California had grown inhospitable anymore, and when the Times of Trouble came, no one in California would be safe against earthquakes, drought, fires, marauders, faggots, and pestilence.

Upon their arrival in Alaska, just inside the Alaska border on the Alcan Highway, the Prophecy bus reached a fork in the road at the tiny town of Tok. One road led south to Anchorage (civic motto: "Big Wild Weekend"), while the other led north to Fairbanks (civic motto: "Mired in Our Golden Past"). Poppy's vision had said to go north, to the past.

In Poppy's vision, Fairbanks was a God-fearing, sovereign-friendly backwater. A place of second and third chances; a place where no one pried into your business; where a large, faith-filled family could disappear into the woodwork.

At first, Alaska did seem to be the Promised Land. Mile after mile of unpeopled wilderness passed the bus windows. It looked as though you could literally stop anywhere and stake out a 160-acre (65 ha) homestead. But the federal Homestead Act and the state land disposal program had both expired a generation ago, and there was no such thing as free land. The federal and state governments and the Native corporations owned Alaska, Big Oil governed it, and no one was giving it away to the unwashed. Less than one percent of the vast territory was in private hands.

When they reached Fairbanks, instead of the small town they had expected, they found a miniature city, with all the arbitrary rules, immoral distractions, and sprawling squalor of a Los Angeles or Chicago. In midwinter, with a strong heat inversion to trap the bad air, it even smelled like Los Angeles. As to the devotion of its inhabitants, the daily newspaper, the *Fairbanks Daily News-Miner*, listed eighty-nine separate churches on its "Faith" page. That was encouraging at first, but eventually Poppy figured out that what Fairbanksans actually worshipped was dog mushing, hunting and fishing, booze and drugs, guns of all types, music of all genres, public radio and TV, hard rock gold mining, cage fighting, and the military. Only one of the churches that the family tried out — Victory Harvest Temple — was truly faith-filled. Its congregation worshipped in a WWII-era airplane hangar near the airport and welcomed the wandering family with prayers of homecoming. The Prophecys joined the church and shared in its fellowship until its young, unmarried pastor started showing too much interest in Poppy's girls.

Add to that the astonishing cost of housing and feeding a family in the

Interior of Alaska. Fairbanks sat at the tail end of the worldwide supply chain, and everything consumed there had to be hauled up from the Lower 48. Heating oil topped $4.50 per gallon, winter temperatures routinely dropped to minus forty degrees (both Fahrenheit and Celsius), raw land of any merit cost $25,000 per acre, and the soil was too poor and the climate too extreme to make truck farming practical.

One winter was all it took to sow doubts in Poppy's head about his vision. The following spring, one year after their arrival in the Great Land, the Prophecys pulled up stakes, drove south on the Parks Highway, passed unmolested through Anchorage, and continued 220 miles (357 km) down the Kenai Peninsula to the town with the spit, Homer, Alaska.

At first glance, the Homer area was a boyhood dream come true: fishing boats on dazzling blue waters, seagulls wheeling in the sky, snow-covered mountains across the bay, clams for the digging, halibut for the catching, lumps of coal that washed up daily on the public beach that you were free to gather by wheelbarrow to heat your house, richer soils, a warmer climate, and more sun than the rest of coastal Alaska. Homer was a place you could feed your family on what you grew and what you caught. Poppy's hopes ran high that this, at last, was their Promised Land.

But Homer's civic motto was "Got Cash?" If land values in Fairbanks were steep, in Homer they were astronomical. Simply put, the gilded class from the Lower 48 had discovered Homer, Alaska, and made it their own summertime playground. Their McMansion homes were sprouting up everywhere. These Outsiders traded the plagues of the South — triple-digit heat waves, civil unrest, traffic jams, crime, hurricanes, floods, drought, and wildfires — for sunny Homer days of breezy salt air, unpolluted fish, world-class kayaking and sailing on the incomparable Kachemak Bay, views to die for, a bald eagle on every lamppost, a first-rate community hospital plus medevac services, and the predominant whiteness of the population. Longtime locals, meanwhile, were drowning in inflated property taxes.

It wasn't long before the Prophecy bus was on the road again. The family spent the next year camping out across the state. Or rather, across that tiny fraction of the state that was accessible to a 1958 Bluebird school bus. They set up their little gypsy encampment in state campgrounds, on BLM land, and on vacant private lots. They stayed in one spot for a few days or weeks or until property owners or the State Troopers nudged them along.

Coming full circle, they spent their second Alaska winter in a borrowed yurt outside Tok near the Canadian border. It was a big yurt but still a tight fit. They were able to burn wood slabs from a neighboring sawmill for heat. At first the Tok community (population: 1,258) seemed to embrace the wandering Christian family. But little by little, awkward incidents and misunderstandings sprouted, and the pressure of the dense, arctic air seemed to exacerbate hard feelings on everyone's part, and by spring no one was sad to see the old, yellow bus leaving town. After all, the town's civic motto was, "Just Passing Through."

This time, unlike two years ago, when they confronted the fork in the highway, Poppy turned south toward Anchorage. He didn't know what else to do. The visions of wisdom had ceased arriving, they were near the end of their resources, and they were all pretty much discouraged. More and more of their talk turned to memories of California. Maybe California wasn't so bad after all.

That was how, in the spring of 2010, the Prophecy caravan, with the recent addition of the Dodge pickup, was encamped on a low bluff overlooking the Glenn Highway near Eagle River. It was their staging ground for trips into Anchorage. But the State Troopers, responding to several complaints, found them and gave them till sundown (about 1:00 A.M. at that time of year) to pack up and leave.

Everyone had particular duties to perform when pitching or striking camp. Everything from packing all the rolled-up tents and tarps on the cargo rack, to reorganizing the pantry, to keeping the babies from getting underfoot, to simply tying things down. When everything was stowed for blastoff, and everyone was ready to go, Hosea got into the driver seat, started the engine, and released the parking brake. With his hand on the ball of the gear shift, he turned around to look at Poppy sitting in the first row of seats. But Poppy didn't know where to tell him to drive, not even in what general direction. They'd given Alaska everything they had in them. What more did Father God want? Though it was only Fourthmonth, they knew from experience that the Alaska summers were short, and Poppy couldn't see them roughing another winter in the bus. All Poppy needed to say to Hosea was one word — California — and the caravan would turn around and head back to the Canadian border, follow the Alcan through the Yukon and British Columbia, and return to the good old US of A.

One word was all it would take, and Poppy might yet utter it, but first, why not let the Holy Spirit weigh in on the matter?

"Turn off the engine," Poppy said. Hosea shut it down, and behind them Adam shut off the Dodge. Poppy reached out his arms, and everyone held hands all around. "Oh, Heavenly Father," Poppy intoned, "look with kindness upon your vagabond family. You sent us to this marvelous land to serve You during the coming troubles. You promised us a new home and the liberty to worship You. But we have come up short. We've been struggling, Lord. The land is shut to us, and we scurry around like mice in the field.

"But don't get the wrong idea, Lord. We haven't given up yet. Not us. Not until You tell us to give up. Is that what You're telling us, Father? Is it time to pack it in and head south? Or do You want us to stick it out a while longer? We sure could use some sign from You to guide our path. In Elder Brother Jesus name, amen."

"Amen," said the family.

Poppy let go of his children's hands and said, "Now all we have to do is —" But before he could finish his sentence, there was a loud blast down on the highway below the bluff. It was followed by a *thwump, thwump, thwump* as a car rolled to a stop directly below them. They could not see the car, but they could hear the driver get out of it and slam the door.

"Ah, maaan," he moaned. "Come on, really?" The trunk popped open. A tire was dropped on the ground. It had no bounce but landed with a thud.

"You sugar-coated cunt!" the driver yelled. "You goddam piece of crap! You llama-licking whore!"

More and worse language followed, but the older children hopped up to slide shut the windows on that side of the bus. Looks of horror bounced around throughout the bus, but Poppy closed his eyes and sat quietly. He was communing with the Holy Spirit maybe, and Hosea stood up to stretch a bit before sitting back down to wait. About twenty feet ahead of the bus, a man climbed the embankment. When he reached the top and saw them parked there, he immediately came in their direction.

"Uh, lord?" Hosea said. "Here comes the blasphemer."

He came right to the bus door and knocked on the glass. He was a big, frumpy, middle-aged man with plump, sunburned cheeks and a dark, wild beard that was streaked with grey.

Hosea said, "What do I do, lord?"

Poppy opened his eyes and yawned. "Let him in, son. Looks like we have our messenger."

Hosea did a double take. "Yes, lord!" He pulled the door lever, and the man climbed three steps and looked in at all of them with as much wonder as they looked at him.

"Can I help you?" Poppy said.

"If you don't mind, friend, I could use a phone. My tire blew, my spare is flat, and my phone is dead."

"That sounds like a whole string of misfortunes."

"Naw. It's nothing a little roadside assistance can't cure. Mind if I borrow your phone?"

Poppy shrugged his shoulders. "Sorry, friend. No phone here." The man glanced around the bus, pausing at Hosea and the older girls, and Poppy added, "No phones here *at all* is what I meant to say."

The stranger sighed. "How 'bout those boys in the Dodge?"

"Nope. Them neither."

"Really? No phones? Are you sure? Wait, what am I saying? Of course you're sure. Well, there's a gas station up ahead, and it's a nice day for a walk. Sorry to bother you nice folks."

Poppy stopped him before he could leave. "We might not have phones, mister, but we know a thing or two about roadside assistance."

"You do?"

"Got to. How else am I gonna keep this show on the road?"

"You got a point."

"Boy," Poppy said to one of the middle ones. It was Uzziel. "Run tell your brothers to fix this man's tires." Uzzie squeezed around the stranger and made a dash for the pickup.

"I'm in your debt," the man said, leaning over to extend his hand. Reluctantly, Poppy shook it. "Name's Jeff Bridges, but not *that* Jeff Bridges."

Poppy was confused. "Not *which* Jeff Bridges?"

"The Hollywood actor Jeff Bridges. He and I have the same name, and I'm told that I look a bit like him and my voice sounds like his, or at least that's what people tell me. But I'm *not him.*"

The Hollywood actor Jeff Bridges? It was unlikely that Poppy, who hadn't watched a movie or looked at a TV show since 1978, was going to be able to recognize an actor's face or name. But Jeff Bridges did ring a bell. Jeff Bridges . . . Jeff Bridges. And then the Holy Spirit whispered, *Sea Hunt,* into Poppy's ear. *Sea Hunt* was an underwater adventure series Poppy had enjoyed as a young man at the dawn of broadcast television. Lloyd Bridges was the star of the show, and his two young sons, Jeff and Beau, joined him for weekly danger and excitement under the black-and-white sea.

"How's Lloyd?" Poppy said.

"If you mean Lloyd Vernet Bridges, Jr., he's dead I'm afraid, but he wasn't *my* daddy, in case you were thinking he was. Like I said, I'm not *that* Jeff Bridges. There are over five hundred Jeff Bridges on the internet, and I'm one of *those* Jeff Bridges, even though I may look like the other one."

While the man explained who he was and who he wasn't, Adam and Proverbs slid down the bluff and returned with the spare tire. Adam brought it to the bus and said, "The other one is shredded. This one has a slow leak and we can patch it."

"All it needs is to get me about ten miles without killing me," Not Jeff Bridges said.

"Don't worry, mister. Our patch jobs are as good as the tire itself." Adam rolled the spare tire back to the pickup where Proverbs was already hauling out the tools. In no time at all they patched, inflated, and mounted the tire on the man's car. He whistled his admiration and pulled out a rather fat-looking wallet.

But Poppy said, "It was a Christian act of charity. We'll take no money for it."

NJB put away his wallet and said, "Then at least let me buy dinner for you and your family. I don't know which way you all are headed, but I live just down the road in Palmer. Why don't you follow me home, and I'll treat you to a big barbecue feast. I have kosher dogs and mooseburger patties in the freezer and plenty of ice cream, chips, and beer. How 'bout it?"

LL4 1.0

NJB'S HOUSE WAS a one-story, ranch-style rambler right out of the suburbs of Cincinnati, where the builder and first owner originally came from. With vinyl siding, composite roof shingles, a lush lawn in front, and a two-car garage, it sat on an Alaska-sized lot of 7.23 acres (2.92 ha). Most of that was a mountain slope that began in his backyard.

The children spilled out of the bus, took over the yard and house, and devoured everything set before them. NJB offered them soft drinks and sports drinks, but they preferred plain tap water, and that was what they got. The more noise and commotion they made, the jollier he seemed to become. Even the newborn's hungry wails didn't seem to phase him. He confessed to Mama Prophecy that he missed having kids around the place. After the barbecue, the children took pails and baskets out back to collect cones, ferns, moss, birch bark, moose nuggets, and other raw materials for their crafts. The adults relaxed on patio chairs and talked late into the night, too late to set out on the road again.

"Tell you what," NJB said. "Why don't you stay here tonight. I have more than enough room."

Famous last words. The Prophecys parked the bus in the backyard for over a month. They had the run of the house. NJB would leave after breakfast and not return until dinnertime. Sometimes he'd be away for days. He never discussed what he did for a living, and Poppy never asked. He kept the fridge and pantry stocked with high-end food and never asked for reimbursement. He didn't bar Crissie Lou from the carpets or sofa and didn't seem to mind when the girls totally rearranged his furniture. On the contrary, he bought Crissie Lou her own dog bed and special treats, and he told the girls he loved the new furniture arrangement. He was helpful in finding Proverbs a street druggist who could sell him his Prednisone tablets by the thousand. And not once did he behave inappropriately with any of the girls or Mama.

But for all his good qualities, NJB was a deeply flawed man. His speech was still laced with obscenities, though he claimed to be cleaning it up. He drank a six-pack of beer, starting the moment he returned from work. Two whole cupboards over the fridge were devoted to bottles of hard liquor. There were *New Scientist* magazines in the bathroom; a 54-inch flatscreen TV (137 cm) in the living room and smaller ones in all the bedrooms; and a gold-plated, pot-bellied Buddha incense holder on a shelf in the hall where you couldn't help but see it (until Poppy covered it with a towel). Nevertheless, a messenger was a messenger, and Poppy was willing to cut him some slack until the message was delivered.

The inevitable, divisive crisis came one afternoon when Poppy walked in on NJB in his home office showing Corny and Proverbs how to set up Facebook accounts on his computer. Poppy waited in the doorway until Corny managed to pull his eyes from the hypnotic screen long enough to see him there. He elbowed his brother, and both boys tried to melt away. But their father had them blocked in the room, and before he let them pass, he told them to tell Adam to start packing up the family. It was time to be moving on.

"Moving on?" NJB said when he and Poppy were alone. "You found a destination to move on to?"

Poppy shook his head.

Silence filled the room. It was as if some unseen switch had been flipped and both men were listening for the rumble of distant engines. For Poppy it was just the latest stab in the back by someone he'd let through his defenses.

But NJB wasn't so willing to throw in the towel. "Uh, Prophecy," he said with a classic Jeff Bridges look of puzzlement. "I'm not sure, but I'm guessing I just did something wrong?"

"My boys, all my children, know to stay away from computers. I told them a million times. There's public computers at the library, and when they ask me if they can use them, I say no. So what do they do? They trick you into showing them. I don't blame you, Jeff. You didn't know better. But they did, and I'm very disappointed in them. I'm going to have to punish those two. Very disappointed."

"Now, hold on a minute, Prophecy. I'm not trying to tell you how to raise your kids, but what's wrong with computers? It's impossible to function nowadays without one. I didn't show them any dirty sites. I was showing them garden variety social media."

Poppy stared blankly.

"Do you know what that is? Myspace? Facebook?"

"It's new names for old vices."

NJB nodded his head. "I suppose that's one way of looking at it. I've heard that people do get addicted to Facebook. Even more get addicted to games, and I admit I showed them a couple of game sites. My apologies. I won't do it again.

"Still, if you let me put a bug in your ear, Prophecy. I'll show you what the internet could do for *you*. For your knick-knack business."

Despite himself, Poppy said, "What do you mean?"

"In a word, my friend, I mean e-commerce." He began opening a number of bookmarks on his browser. "I've been watching how you go about your business, you know. Seems like the whole family pitches in to make all those little gimcracks, some of which are really good by the way, and then the whole family pitches in to sell them at the fair, flea markets, and Christmas bazaars, right? But I'm guessing there's not enough flea markets in all of Alaska to keep the family's head above water. Am I right?"

Poppy was noncommittal.

"How'd you like to be able to sell your stuff anywhere in the world from the comfort of your easy chair?" He pushed one of the chairs to Poppy. "Come on, Prophecy, sit down and I'll show you just how all this works."

As a matter of record, Poppy Prophecy didn't sit down for anyone. It was only because he was waiting for a sign and NJB was the designated messenger of that sign that he bent the rules at all and sat in front of the Devil's TV.

TAKE A LOOK at this," NJB said. He brought up a page of search results for "praying hands figurines." Praying hands came in bronze, glass, wood, and plastic from all over the world.

"Except for one or two," NJB continued, "none of them can hold a candle to the ones your son Adam carves from birch." He opened another page of nativity sets. "And your Christmas mangers are second to none. I gotta tell you, Prophecy, you could do big business on this one site alone, and there are hundreds more just like it."

The two men stayed up all night. NJB used a couple of Adam's figurines to set up a vendor's account on Etsy. He lit the figurines with reading lamps and shot them with his phone. He wrote heartfelt product descriptions and set prices Poppy thought were way too high. He helped Poppy set up Gmail and PayPal accounts and showed him the online portal to the family's credit union. Even as they were setting things up, someone purchased a pair of praying hands.

"What do you mean?" Poppy said.

"Just what I said; you sold a figurine. Someone in —" he pointed to the monitor. "Mrs. Angela Purnell in Warwick, Rhode Island, purchased it and paid to have it shipped by second-day FedEx. That's one of the shipping options we set up. See here? All you have to do is confirm the sale, and her money goes to PayPal and from there to your savings account. Tomorrow you go to the FedEx pickup point and ship it to her. Oh, look, you just sold another. Maybe we should raise the price some more."

It took a few moments for the situation to sink in, and when it did, Poppy said, "You've got to be kidding me. This is the internet?"

APPARENTLY, THE MESSAGE Father God sent NJB to deliver involved e-commerce, the last thing in the world Poppy expected to learn from the man knocking on their bus door. But it was probably the most important message Poppy could have received at that juncture, aside from a destination. And now that the message was delivered and received with an open mind, it truly was time to move on. Fifthmonth was half over, and the Alaska winter loomed just beyond Seventhmonth. But move on where? Again Poppy called the family together in prayer, even as they packed to go. Though they were soon ready to depart, they lingered at NJB's for another week. Meanwhile, NJB helped Poppy incorporate HIS CREATIONS as an Alaska LLC. NJB took him into Anchorage to window shop for a laptop and the means to charge it in the bush. But Poppy was still reluctant to buy. It was bad enough he was learning to use a computer; how could he justify spending the last of their cash on one of them? Yet, without a computer, how could he run the business he had just set up? It was a moral dilemma, and Poppy Prophecy hated moral dilemmas.

One evening after dinner, NJB said, "Ever hear about McHardy, Alaska?"

Poppy had seen the name on a map. They'd taken the Edgerton Cutoff during their year of rambling, but they never got closer to McHardy than Denny Lake.

NJB described the town of McHardy, its community and surroundings. It sounded like the sort of unpeopled place Poppy had been searching for, especially the part about the footbridge. The following day, Poppy and Adam took the Dodge on a quick scouting trip, and a week later the family was camped out in the parking lot at the end of McHardy Road.

On the morning the caravan departed NJB's house in Palmer, NJB distributed gifts. For each of the children, from baby to adult, there was a musher's hat, all of them blue. They were sewn by a company up in Fairbanks and were good to about a thousand degrees below zero.

For Mama P there was a Nook ebook reader already loaded with several dozen Christian romances including *Redeeming Love* by Francine Rivers, *Short-Straw Bride* by Karen Witemeyer and *Love Comes Softly* by Janette Oke.

For Poppy, well, Poppy's gift was wrapped in Father's Day wrapping paper. With a wink, NJB suggested he open it later, in private. "The only thing I'm gonna tell you is it's not a computer."

It was and it wasn't a computer. It was a Samsung Galaxy smart phone that NJB had loaded with all the apps HIS CREATIONS LLC would require to operate from the middle of nowhere.

LL5 1.0

THE RHYTHM OF the road put all the passengers to sleep, including Poppy. Wallis was less than an hour away when Proverbs stomped on the brakes and the bus went into a skid. Poppy opened his eyes just in time to see the moose that Proverbs had barely avoided hitting. He clung to the rail as his son quickly brought the ungainly vehicle back under control. But instead of continuing on, Proverbs turned off the highway in Sutton.

"What's wrong?" Poppy said.

"Nothin', lord, but the road is icing up pretty bad."

Proverbs pulled into the lot of a convenience store, and the pickup rolled in behind him.

"Tell him I want my phone back."

"Yes, lord."

The boys quickly mounted heavy chains on the bus tires. Proverbs brought his father a styro cup of coffee, a local newspaper, and his phone. It began to snow in the darkness: big, wet flakes that twinkled in the sodium lights of the gas islands. It was after 6:00 P.M., and most of the headlights on the highway were coming from Anchorage. Poppy dialed NJB's number, but his call went to voicemail, and then a soulless voice said the mailbox was full. So Poppy called one of the churches in Wallis he was planning to impose his family upon. But the pastor begged off on account of they were already hosting a high-school basketball team from the bush village of Ningaluk that was in town for a tournament, and who quite filled up the fellowship hall. The other church he called rang and rang and never picked up.

Poppy sipped his coffee and browsed the newspaper by the light of the convenience store sign. It was last week's issue of Palmer's *Frontier Guardian*. Sixteen tabloid-size pages of want ads, public notices, police blotter, and opinion masquerading as news. On page three, a half-page advertisement caught Poppy's attention. It depicted a family he knew. He'd met them at the state fair last summer during the run-up to the fall election. Rex Lawther had run for State Senate from District E. And lost, apparently. The ad headline, in large brush script, read: *Thanks for Your Support*. Next to the family portrait was a graphic of an ancient scroll with tattered edges, and inscribed on the scroll was this message:

Friends

Change of Seasons Greetings!

It was a long and grueling bitterly fought election season. The votes are in, have been counted, recounted, and certified that we lost by 54 votes. With God's grace, this loss will be only a temporary setback. I will keep my website at www.rexlawtherforsenate.org, so please check it from time to time.

For now, we are blessed to turn our attention from the political season to the sacred one. May God bless you and your family as you celebrate the birth of our Savior, Jesus Christ, and anticipate the opportunities of the coming New Year.

Thank you for your prayers and encouragement. I strive to justify the faith you put in me.   —Rex Lawther

Poppy examined the photo again. It was a traditional sitting, as it should be, of Mr. Candidate in the center, surrounded by wife and kiddies. Moses would recognize that sitting. In this case, Mr. Candidate's wife was youngish, fit, and trim, and there were only two offspring, dull-looking, one of each kind, in their late teens.

The gracefully losing candidate himself was a former high school football champ who once upon a time led the East Wallis Hornets to state championship. Considerably heavier now in all his flesh, and turgid in all his juices, he gazed earnestly from the frame. Big fat face like aged soft cheese, this Rex Lawther.

Proverbs climbed into the bus and started the engine. "Might as well gas up," he said as he backed into the service island. "Know where we're spending the night, lord?"

"Yes," Poppy said, "I do."

LL6 1.0

THE LITTLE TOWN of Wallis started life as a gold miner camp on Lake Lola, forty miles by trail (64 km) northeast of Anchorage. It remained an obscure outpost, not even meriting a civic motto for seventy years. Everything changed in 1971, when the state completed the George Parks Highway. The Parks ran through Wallis on its way from Anchorage to Denali National Park and on to Fairbanks in the Interior. It quickly became the most heavily traveled highway in the state. Sleepy Wallis was suddenly on the map. It soon eclipsed neighboring Palmer and grew so rapidly that it earned not one but *two* civic mottoes, one for each direction of travel. For motorists driving south to Anchorage, Wallis was "Almost There." To those heading north, it was "Last Whiz for 200 Miles."

LL7 1.0

RORY LAWTHER WAS in the shop behind Greatland Action Sports helping Jerry, one of their mechanics, to uncrate and assemble the shipment of twenty new Arctic Cat snowmachines. He'd come over right after school and hadn't taken a break yet. None of them had. It was so close to Christmas the place was absolutely crazy. Sleds, trailers, helmets, clothes, posters — everything was flying out the showroom doors. Christmas 2012 was stacking up to be their best season since the beginning of the Great Recession.

Rory's phone trilled. It was his mom. "I can't reach your dad," she said.

"You try the office?"

"Of course I tried the office!"

She sounded a little more tense than usual.

"Find him and tell him to call me right back. No, wait. Don't hang up. Take your phone to him and put it in his hand. I'll hold."

"Is something wrong, ma?"

"No. Yes. No. Just do what I said."

Rory wiped the grease from his hands. Jerry said, "You calling it quits, chief?"

"Naw. I'll be back. I just gotta go see my dad."

"You tell your dad I need a dinner break. I get a dinner break, or else."

Halfway out the door, Rory paused to ask, "Or else what, Jer?"

"Or else I quit, and I mean it this time."

"I'll tell him."

"You do that."

In the showroom, everyone *but* his dad was waiting on customers. He asked Sadie if she'd seen him, and she shook her head without even slowing down.

George was showing Mr. Randolf a 2013 Arctic Cat Bearcat 5000XTGS, the new top-of-the-line, high performance long track. Lani Randolf, Mr. R's daughter, was in Rory's class at East Wallis High. Mr. R caught Rory's eye and waved him over.

"Yes, sir?"

"Do me a favor, Rory, and don't tell Lani about this, all right? It's a surprise."

"No, sir, I won't say a word. And nice surprise, by the way."

"Thatta boy."

When Rory went past the check out counter, Melissa said, "I'm putting together a McDonald's order. You in?"

"Yeah, thanks. A Big Mac, fries, and a coke. Get Jerry two of everything. And supersize them."

"Will do."

In the office Rex was on the phone stabbing computer keys and fumbling with files on his desk. "No, no, not B. 'E,'" he said. "'E' as in Elephant. 'O' as in . . . 'O' as in —" He covered the mouthpiece and said, "Quick, what starts with an 'O'?"

"Obama?"

"Very funny." He uncovered the phone and said, 'O' as in Okay. That's right. Elephant Okay three-one-seven-five. Say it back to me."

Rory held up his phone and showed him the display.

"Tell her I'll call her back."

"She says it's an emergency."

His dad rolled his bloodshot eyes, took the phone, and juggled the two calls together. "Who? . . . Say again? . . . That's right . . . All of them? . . . Yes, I need five complete sets ASAP . . . No, I didn't tell him . . . Well, yes, but that was *last summer* . . . Send it overnight. I know, I know, but it was your screwup in the first place. My customers are . . . what good are trailers without tongues? You tell me that! . . . Yes. Yes. That's what I'm trying to . . ."

Rory sat in the bookkeeper's chair and leaned all the way back to stare upside down at the wall of plaques and citations that his dad had collected over the years. Rotary, the Wallis Chamber of Commerce times seven, the 2009 Special O Ski Tournament (There's an O!), the Iditarod Organizing Committee, the Arctic Cat Dealership Association, and so on and so forth.

When his dad finished both calls, Rory asked him what was going on with Mom.

"Remember that family?"

"What family?"

"The one with all the kids and the bus."

Rory jerked up straight. "The Prophecys?"

"Yeah, that one. They just pulled into our drive. Seems I invited them to camp in our yard if they ever needed to."

"And they're here now?"

"According to your mother."

"All of them?"

"Looks that way. Listen, we'll deal with them later. Right now I —"

Rory was already on his feet.

"Hang on there, champ. Where do you think you're going?"

"Home."

"Are all those sleds uncrated?"

"But, Dad."

"Don't but dad me. She'll still be there when we get home."

"Sir?"

"Don't play dumb with me, son. You know who I'm referring to. You think I don't notice things?"

DEUT AND CORA carried the sleeping little ones into the living room where they laid them in a row on the carpet. Cindy Lawther hauled out spare pillows and blankets. The Lawther dog, a toy breed of some sort, sniffed them cautiously as they slept.

Out in the bus, Proverbs and Adam were setting up the bunks and curtains for the older sibs and lighting a propane heater. They discovered the cat snoozing under a sleeping bag. Calgary had somehow managed to stow away, first on the sled ride to the parking lot, and then in the bus.

"She probably had a few accomplices," Adam said.

The Dodge pulled in behind the bus in the driveway, and Hosea and Poppy got out. Proverbs said, "Let's keep the cat to ourselves for now, okay?"

"Sure thing," Adam said.

Inside the house, Cindy said, "Anything else you need? How about food? Have you girls eaten?"

"We have, thanks," Deut said. "We had a picnic on the bus."

"Why don't you sleep in the house tonight too? We have plenty more blankets."

"Thank you, but we're used to the bus."

"What about the kids if they wake up and don't know where they are?"

"They'll figure it out. Just please keep a light on and the bathroom door open."

"Yes, of course."

There was nothing left to do, but the girls lingered in the foyer. Finally, Deut said, "What about your daughter, Ginger? Isn't she at home?"

"Not right now, dear," Cindy said. "She's at a basketball game with some of her friends. But she's got a 10:30 curfew, so she'll be back soon. You can wait up for her if you want."

Neither girl could reply, so astonishing were Mrs. Lawther's words. Apparently, her daughter was allowed to go to a sporting event where boys were probably present, and she didn't have to be back till late at night.

"Yes, ma'am," Deut said finally. "We'd like that."

Cindy led them to the kitchen. "Is it my imagination, or are there a few of you missing? I seem to recall a couple of toddlers."

"Yes, ma'am. That's Elzie and Nummy. We left them at home to be with Mama."

"Then your mother is recovered?"

Deut wasn't sure how to answer. "Mama isn't sick, but she's still in Heaven visiting with Elder Brother Jesus."

"So your father never took her to a doctor to examine her?"

"No, ma'am. There's nothing wrong with her for a doctor to fix."

"You mean she's up and about and able to function normally?"

The kitchen was a large, bright, gleaming space. Deut struggled not to succumb to covetousness and envy. "No, ma'am," she said, "but we left my sister Sarai to take care of her and the babies."

Behind them in the doorway, Poppy startled everyone by saying, "Don't concern yourself about Mama." He removed his hat and parka. He'd entered the house without knocking and heard them talking in the kitchen. Even the little dog was taken by surprise. It began to growl, but Cindy picked it up and hushed it.

"Elder Brother Jesus will send her back to us soon enough," Poppy went on. "Now, if you girls have everything squared away here, it's time to head out to the bus."

"Yes, lord," the girls said. They thanked Mrs. Lawther and went out together.

"About that bed you offered," Poppy said to Mrs. Lawther, "I'm ready for it."

"Yes, of course," Cindy said. "The guest room is this way. Or would you care for something to eat or drink first? Rex said he'd be home soon, in case you wanted to see him."

"Bed."

Cat and Woodpecker

CW1 1.0

WITH WINTER SOLSTICE two weeks away, there were only about four good hours of possible daylight each day, and Jace was determined to use them searching for whatever it was he'd seen falling out of the sky. The GPS readings he'd gathered told him that the cone's imprint in the snow was about six miles wide (10 km), and he'd pinpointed its center and probable landing zone, a windswept tract of frozen bog on the river flats.

At first light on Wednesday, Jace parked the Tundra at ground zero, mapped out a search grid, and spent the afternoon walking in straight lines. He walked rather than rode because he didn't know what he was looking for and didn't want to miss anything. The object had fallen too slowly to leave a smoking crater, but there still might be scorch marks or a frozen-over melt pond.

After a cold, fruitless, five-hour slog, Jace rode home wondering if he should cover the same ground the next day, or maybe extend the grid, or move the search area to somewhere else entirely. After all, his supposition that the object fell in the center of the circle was based on appearances. The object *appeared* to fall in the center, but that may have been due to his perspective at the time of the sighting. If he had been watching from the western edge, for instance, instead of from the south, he might have seen that it fell closer to one edge or the other.

Jace spent Wednesday night surfing internet sites that offered "satellite images of your roof." You enter an address or GPS coordinates, and it returns a hybrid map/photo of your neighborhood from space. Neat, except that when he tried it using the coordinates he'd taken from the flats, the image he received was missing any indented circle in the snow. Since the circle was six miles in diameter, and the depression in the snow was eighteen inches (46 cm) deep in places, and the winter sun cast long shadows, he had expected it to have shown up. He tried again on Google Earth and got similar results.

Moving the image a little north, Jace was able to find his own roof on Lucky Strike Lane. In the front yard the old shed was still standing, the one that had been a heap of rotten wood when Beehymer showed him the property in 2010. That meant that Google Earth and the other sites he'd tried were displaying old images.

When Jace searched for real-time or near-real-time satellite images, he found a variety of sources, including the USGS Earth Now!, Landsat Image Viewer, GloVis, and EarthExplorer. These either didn't work on his iPad or had no results for his desired time and place. The closest he came was with NASA's EOSDIS Worldview. He found daytime images from Tuesday, Mail Day, hours before the event, and he went to bed confident that by morning the updated Worldview site would display Wednesday's image and that there, plain as day, would be a bullseye in the snow at 61.386472, –142.944489. Especially satisfying was the fact that he'd be able to contact NASA about his snowy crop circle using their own satellite imagery.

No such luck. On Thursday morning, though the site had been updated, a light haze obscured his whole corner of Alaska, enough to blur the image and eliminate any possible shadows.

Riding to work in Caldecott, it occurred to Jace that short of a satellite photo, an aerial photo could serve as evidence. He had decided that before he told anyone about what he had witnessed, it would be a good idea to have some kind of evidence to back up his story.

When he reached the ranger office, his senior colleague, LE Ranger Masterson, was already at his desk, pecking away at his computer keyboard. They exchanged greetings, and Jace placed a call to Nellis Air Service in Gulkana. Mrs. Nellis answered.

"I want to charter a flight-seeing ride in the park ASAP," he told her.

"You want us to pick you up in McHardy?" she replied.

"Yes."

"We'd have to charge you for Ned's flight time to and from, plus the flight-seeing itself."

"Yes, yes. When can you come?"

"Let's see," she said. "Things are slow right now, so we'd be able to get you in next Thursday, a week from today."

"Nothing sooner?"

"I suppose, if you was willing, Ned could take you on Tuesday when he delivers the mail. That'd be cheaper for you too. Are we talking about an hour or two of flying?"

"An hour would do, but it's got to be even sooner."

"Wait. Ned wants to talk to you."

The phone changed hands, and Ned Nellis said, "This Ranger Kuliak?"

"Yes. Hi, Ned."

"So, what about that trapper cabin? Was I right?"

"Yes, you were." Jace glanced at Ranger Masterson, not ten feet away. "But why don't we talk about it when I see you."

Ned said that was fine with him and that he would be in the McHardy area the following day and could maybe spare him an hour. They made pick-up arrangements, and Jace hung up.

Masterson said, "Was that official business?"

"Personal."

"One of those Asian ladies catch your eye?"

How much easier it would be if he could just level with Masterson, tell him about the falling light and snow circle. Hell, *show* him the circle. Ranger

Masterson was an opinionated SOB, but even he would have to believe his own eyes. After that, the circle's existence would become a park service matter, and with NPS resources they could get to the bottom of it. [see *A Herd of Picnic Tables* page 334]

Should he tell him or not? How would he react? Masterson was waiting for an answer to his stupid question.

"You're right. One of the Asian ladies."

Or, to be specific, one of the Japanese ladies. Ordinarily, the entire Caldecott mill town would be shuttered at this time of year. Jace's employee contract never ran beyond September or October. But this year, the park service, the state's Department of Commerce, TravelAlaska.com, and the Caldecott Glacier View Lodge concessionaire were conducting a feasibility study/pilot project for boosting Alaska's wintertime tourism. For some reason, Alaska was not a popular tourism destination during the months of December through March. Except for one demographic: young Japanese couples. Folklore in Japan promised good fortune to couples who consummated their marriage under the dancing lights of the aurora borealis. Conceiving a child under the influence of the lights was considered even more propitious. And since the Northern Lights rarely appeared over Japan, Alaska had the rare opportunity to offer "Aurora Tours" in romantic locations, such as the lodge in Caldecott. Currently there were about sixty Japanese couples booked at the "Aurororium."

JACE OPENED THE backcountry gear room to get the camera. It was a sweet, pricey Canon, with a geo-tagging feature and a variety of lenses. If he was going to go through the cost and effort of flying over the area, he needed something with more chops than the pinhole camera on his iPhone. While in the room, he noticed the metal detector and decided to borrow it too. Whatever the space artifact was, it was bound to be made of metal.

Not only that, but the park service kept a Geiger counter in its disaster kit. He found it and did a systems check. It was small enough that he could keep it in an inner pocket with his water bottle where its battery could stay warm.

AFTER DETERMINING THAT the search area was not radioactive, Jace decided to retrace his steps from the day before, this time with the metal detector. It was tedious, exhausting work. The river flats were not flat, not even under layers of snow, but bumpy, like a bunched up old carpet. And it was a lot of ground to sweep with a nine-inch (23 cm) search coil. Summer or winter, the wind always blew on the river, and he had to protect every inch of his flesh or risk frostbite.

At the end of the day, he had nothing to show for his work but tracks in the snow. On the plus side, he was getting pretty darn good at walking in straight lines over hummocky terrain while sweeping, sweeping, sweeping.

THURSDAY NIGHT MRS. Nellis called to say that a storm front was moving in that night, and that it might put the kibosh on his flight-seeing trip and, if so, did he want to reschedule? He told her no, he didn't. With the snow circle obliterated by fresh powder, what would be the point?

Sure enough, Jace awoke Friday morning to white-out conditions. Nellis called again to cancel the flight. Jace, in turn, called the ranger station and left a message saying he was maybe coming down with something and was taking a sick day. He still had the park service Tundra at home, and he raced out to the flats in the pre-dawn darkness to get in as much time as possible. He modified his search area to include a north-south band from one end of the cone base to the other. At no time did he contemplate giving up. He *knew* he saw *something* that night. He might have been high at the time, but he wasn't *that* high.

ON FRIDAY NIGHT Jace's thoroughly sensible sister Kate called from Littleton, Colorado, where she lived with her husband Darshan and son Luke. She was surprised and upset to hear that he hadn't purchased his airplane tickets yet.

"Aren't you coming?"

"I forgot. I've been busy."

"You forgot? You're kidding."

The plan had been to spend Christmas in Littleton, and there was still time to book a flight, but he said, "You know what, Kate? I think I'll stay here this year. The house needs work." Better to blame home improvement than a close encounter of the third kind.

"You're kidding," she repeated. "What'll I tell Luke? You promised to take him skiing."

"Tell him I'll come down in February. You still have snow down there in February, don't you?"

There was silence on the other end, and then, "This doesn't have anything to do with that girl, does it? The one with the big family? What's her name? Leviticus?"

"Very funny. It's Deuteronomy, and, no, this has nothing to do with her."

"You know, little brother, you can't change a person's core beliefs. I mean, you can try, but one way or the other they'll resent you for it."

"I'm not trying to change a person's core beliefs."

"Oh, no? Then have your own beliefs changed?"

"No, but so what? I'm not intolerant, you know. I could accept a partner with a different faith, if things ever came to that."

His sister snorted.

"What are you saying, Kate? That I'm a bigot?"

"No, but when it comes to religion, your mind is already made up."

"Then it may come as a shock to you that I'm a flexible person. My attitudes are adaptable. I can tolerate diversity."

"Good to hear. But tell me this, Mr. Flexible, if it's not too personal a question, have you two lovebirds actually met each other yet? Have you ever traded two words of conversation?"

CW2 1.0

WHY, YES, THEY had met. And they had traded two words of conversation, sorta. It was during the shit-storm over the airstrip.

Back in 2010, when the quarrelsome family pulled up stakes and vanished from the lot next to his house in McHardy, Jace had optimistically imagined that he was rid of them for good. But they had only moved deeper into the park, to Orion Beehymer's old mine site to act as caretakers, and soon they were making trouble again. Only this time they were the park service's headache and not Jace's. Yet he still managed to get sucked into it.

A few months after granting the Prophecys the run of his old mine, Beehymer got it into his head that now was a good time to sell off the property. So he went to the saloon of the McHardy Hotel one evening in August and bought a round for the house. Then he announced that his patented mining claim on the side of Stubborn Mountain was on the market for an asking price of one million dollars US.

Word spread, and the park superintendent in Copper Center heard about the proposed sale. Now here was a significant opportunity for the NPS. Here was a page torn from its own strategic plan. This was no mere townsite lot on offer. The Stubborn Mountain Mine property encompassed 340 acres (138 ha) was the largest parcel of private land that still remained within park boundaries (aside from Native corporation land). It was incumbent on the park service to repatriate the land and extinguish all mining rights attached to it. And there was actually a budget for doing so.

Throughout the summer and early fall, the NPS was the only potential purchaser to make a serious offer, and it looked as though Beehymer would soon accept it. But on Halloween, word came that Beehymer had just sold the mine to his on-site caretakers for his full asking price.

Needless to say, the parkies were confounded by this development. How had that hippie-dippy caretaker family with all the kids come up with that kind of dough? [see *Tour of the Mine* page 341] But however the Prophecys had managed it, the land was off the market.

Then, in November, Ned Nellis of Nellis Air sent Superintendent Rodgers a thumbdrive of Mail Day photos he'd taken from the cockpit of his Cessna. It appeared that the Prophecys had gotten the mine's ancient Caterpillar D6 bulldozer running, and that they were felling trees and dragging them to a little sawmill they'd set up. Maybe it was because Nellis was a bush pilot who was ever watchful for safe places to land in an emergency, but he said it looked to him like the Prophecys were clearing land for a private airstrip. And that the land they were clearing belonged to the park.

If true, this was a serious encroachment upon public land that had to be investigated as soon as possible. But even under the best of circumstances, survey lines on steep, forested land were hard to spot from the air. And in this case, there hadn't been a survey done or lines cleared since the original platting in 1909. So the superintendent ordered a new boundary survey to be conducted in the early spring. In the meantime, the park service went to court and served the Prophecys with a cease and desist order. Naturally, the family ignored the order and, in fact, sped up the pace of its land clearing. The park service retaliated by impounding their bulldozer in place, a heavy-handed act that infuriated them. And in April, with snow still covering the ground, Superintendent Rodgers hired a four-man, civilian survey party to locate and mark the property corners and to brush out the entire three-mile-long (5-km) property line.

In the meantime, the local community in McHardy rose up in protest against the NPS's heavy-handed enforcement against a sincere, devout Christian family that was only trying to live according to God's word. Out-of-state lands rights organizations took up the Prophecy cause and offered the family moral and legal support during its ordeal. Local pol, Kelly Cogwheel, authored a fiery retrospective of eighty years of NPS perfidy against inholders on public lands entitled, "Buy, Bully, or Burn Them Out," which was posted and reposted across the blogosphere. For months the

Christian family was the poster child for resistance to federal overreach against private citizens.

The boundary survey in April was not a success. The civilian surveyors were loaded for bear, but not for bearded, gun-toting young men who threatened them at every turn. Poppy and his boys vandalized their camp, stealing essential equipment. They spiked trees that needed to be felled. During the night they pulled up all the stakes, pins, and caps the surveyors had painstakingly set in the ground. The surveyors could make no progress and were fearful for their safety, so they quit.

JACE HAD BEEN wintering Outside while all of this was transpiring, and he returned to Caldecott in May, 2011, just in time to be assigned to the second survey party. The second party was "going in hot" with an armed escort. Superintendent Rodgers borrowed three BLM rangers for the task force, one from Montana and two from California, and three NPS rangers from other parks in Alaska. She assigned Ranger Masterson to the detail but, perhaps in light of his reputation for instability [see *The Kitten of Our Discontent* on page 346], placed one of the other Alaskans, LE Ranger Terry Swartz from Yukon-Charley, in charge. The Outside officers were trained in paramilitary operations, and the Alaska contingent possessed these skills plus extensive backcountry expertise. All of them wore body armor and carried sidearms. Their arsenal included shotguns, assault rifles, a sniper rifle, stun grenades, pepper spray, tasers, and a tear gas grenade launcher.

It was Ranger Swartz who asked Jace to join the group. Although not a law enforcement ranger, Jace was authorized to carry a shotgun in the bush for personal protection against bear attack. Swartz wanted Jace to manage the camp while the rest of them were in the field to serve as their camp cook and bull cook.

CW3 1.0

THE SECOND SURVEY attempt began in a peaceful enough manner. Early one sunny June morning, LE Ranger Swartz knocked politely on the Prophecy door. His demeanor was so deferential, his bearing so non-confrontational, and his arrival on their wilderness doorstep so unexpected that he was able to serve the patriarch with legal papers before anyone knew what was happening. Included was an injunction that restrained any member of the Prophecy family or its associates from interfering with the survey work, equipment, crew, or camp, or to approach any of the above, including NPS personnel and civilian contractors, closer than one hundred feet (30 m).

Having officially served the papers, Swartz tipped his flat hat, thanked them kindly, and took his leave of their property before they could react. Immediately thereafter, a borrowed Forest Service helicopter began ferrying material for the survey party camp to a nearby clearing on park land.

The next day, a couple of the older Prophecy boys followed the survey party around. They were armed, but they did not brandish their weapons. They recorded the crew at work with an ancient-looking camcorder, but they did so from a legal distance. There were no close encounters of the ugly kind.

The surveyors quickly reestablished the lines the first party had brushed out and set two iron and brass corner posts in fresh cement.

By the time the crew called it quits on the first day, Jace had established the campsite. He pitched tents for sleeping on high ground, set up the mess tent below, built a fire ring of stones on a dried-out creek bed, and arranged camp chairs around it.

Jace's first dinner as a newly minted camp cook consisted of heaping helpings of corned beef hash and spaghetti, with sides of corn, green beans, and mashed potatoes. There were soft drinks, coffee, and tea. A warmed-over pineapple upside down cake served as dessert.

Everyone ate; no one complained. Call it a successful culinary debut.

While the surveyors and their federal bodyguards lounged around the token campfire under the Midnight Sun, a gunshot rang out. It was the report of a high-powered rifle, and it came from the southwest, the opposite direction from the Prophecy compound. It seemed far enough away that no one was alarmed.

A little while later, there was a second gunshot, closer in and from a different direction. Rangers exchanged looks, but they mostly ignored it.

"Listen up," LE Ranger Swartz said. "Terry has something to tell us. Terry?"

Terry Thornbrus was a civil engineer in Valdez and the survey party boss. A man in his sixties, Thornbrus was still able to tramp over wild terrain all day long. He leaned forward in his camp chair and drew rectangles in the dirt with a stick.

"This here's the compound," he said, tapping his diagram, "and here's the house and outbuildings. Often for reasons of logistics, miners used to put their support buildings close to a boundary. Although this old mine site is over three hundred acres in area, the living quarters are right up against the eastern line. There's even the possibility that the main house here and the cabin here might be *over* the line. We won't know for sure till tomorrow."

When Jace heard this he felt a flush of mean-spirited elation. He knew it was petty of him, but he was thrilled to the gills by the possibility that the renegade family might lose their house. It would be karmic payback for the mountain of grief they had unloaded on him and Danielle a couple of years back on Lucky Strike Lane.

"What that means," Swartz said after Thornbrus was finished, "is that the hundred-foot buffer zone will be effectively made null and void tomorrow while we're on that end of the property unless we temporarily evict the entire family from their home. Does anyone think that's a good idea?"

Everyone glanced at Masterson, who wisely kept his head down. Meanwhile, deep in the woods, another gunshot. Swartz paused to estimate its bearings before commenting:

"There's no need to remind all of you that these people will try our resolve as professionals. They're already at it with this random gunfire. They're taunting us, testing us. They want us to lose our focus and step over the line. They might even want to be blood martyrs for their cause.

"But you know what? There'll be none of that during this mission. All we're doing is a boundary survey. This is not Ruby Ridge. There will be no gunplay on our part unless absolutely necessary. No bloodshed. In case I'm not making myself crystal clear, let me rephrase that: what we are doing here, while only a boundary survey, is under a great deal of scrutiny. Not only by the public but by our own bosses, from park and regional headquarters all the way up the chain to Secretary Salazar in DC himself.

"Successfully completing this mission in a peaceful manner will put a shine on our resumes, let me tell you, especially you young guys.

"Likewise, even one civilian casualty will kill every one of our careers. Is that plain enough?"

A lot of affirmative grunts and head nodding.

CW4 1.0

THE RANGERS TOOK shifts patrolling the cutlines throughout the night to prevent the kind of mischief that had plagued the first survey party. The random shooting continued, sometimes close in, sometimes far away. If it was meant to disturb their sleep — a kind of hectoring hillbilly psy-ops — it succeeded, and there were plenty of bleary eyes at breakfast.

On the second day, the surveyors lost a couple of chainsaw chains to tree spikes, but they were prepared for this and had brought plenty of spare chains.

During the day, Jace monitored the crew's radio chatter as he hauled water and washed dishes and tidied up the camp. Despite his duties, Jace had plenty of down time. He'd brought along his iPad but couldn't browse the internet because the mountain blocked the signal.

In the afternoon of the second day, the survey party made an unexpected discovery. A small field beneath the compound toolshed that some previous owner had cleared decades earlier for a truck garden turned out to be mostly situated on park land. The current occupants had planted a vegetable garden there and built cold frames for tomatoes and cucumbers. It would all have to be pulled up and plowed under and the land restored to its natural state. Score one for the *federales*.

The Prophecys soon evened the score.

The task force camp toilet was essentially a folding stool over a plastic trash bag behind a screen of bushes. On the evening of the second day, the chief surveyor, Terry Thornbrus, was totally monopolizing it. The others, sitting around the campfire with their dinner plates on their laps, could hear each of his juicy expulsions and gasping moans.

"Sounds like food poisoning," said one of the Alaska rangers, casting an accusatory eye in Jace's direction.

"Don't look at me," Jace said. "Everything I serve is fresh from the tin."

"It wasn't you," Scott said. "It was probably the cookies."

Scott was Thornbras' nephew, a college-bound kid from Nevada up for the summer to work for his uncle as a rodman and all-round gopher. Everyone called him "the Rodman."

"What cookies?" Ranger Swartz said.

The Rodman glanced around the campfire before answering to make sure that Ranger Masterson wasn't present. He wasn't; he was patrolling the boundaries.

"My uncle and I were working near the house today, and the front door opens and out comes two little kids in their Amish sodbuster costumes, a little boy and girl. The boy's got a pitcher of cold lemonade, and the girl's got a plate of chocolate chip cookies right out of the oven. When they offer them to us, I tell them to beat it and leave us alone, but the girl holds up her plate like this and says, It's all right, mister. It's only just cookies. I was tempted, but I told them to take their lemonade and their cookies and scram out of there before there was trouble. But . . ." The Rodman gestured to the bushes where his uncle was suffering. "He tells me, Leave 'em be. They're just little kids. They're a good Christian family just trying to survive out here, and this whole operation is overkill and an insult to liberty."

Apparently, the Rodman disagreed with his uncle's politics.

"So he accepts a full glass of lemonade and gulps it down and smacks his lips and says it's the best darn lemonade he's ever drunk. Same with the cookies. He eats two on the spot and stuffs two more in a pocket.

"The two little kids turn back to me with their sweet little faces and offer me their goodies again. I won't lie; I was about to give in and take some when Ranger Danger shows up." The Rodman paused to see if everyone knew who he was referring to.

"He comes on all official-like and runs off the kids. I mean, he seemed pretty worked up over it and used words those kids probably never heard before. I was afraid he was going to go all kitten on them, if you know what I mean, but my uncle inserts himself between him and the kids, and the kids go running back to the house crying and spilling lemonade and half their cookies on the ground. And my uncle says to Danger, Calm down, man. They're only little kids being neighborly and there's no reason to scare them like that.

"But Ranger Danger says you can't trust them, not even the kids. So my uncle picks up the fallen cookies and offers one to the ranger. Danger takes it and throws it into the woods. So my uncle takes another cookie and eats it right in front of him going, Yum, yum.

"So that's why I'm thinking it was probably the cookies. Or the lemonade."

Swartz set down his plate. "I better go see how bad it is. I might have to evacuate him to town."

One of the Outside rangers snorted. "Sounds to me like he's evacuating pretty good on his own."

CW5 1.0

ON DAY THREE, Terry Thornbras remained in camp to regain his strength. He was feeling pretty foolish, but Jace didn't try to rub it in. After Jace had washed the breakfast dishes, they made amiable small talk over a fresh pot of coffee under the screened canopy. It was another gorgeous summer day in Alaska.

Then they heard an odd radio exchange. It started with Terry's nephew:

Uh, Swartz, come in. This is the Rodman. Over.

The chief ranger replied:

This is Swartz. Go ahead. Over.

Your immediate presence is — uh — requested. Over.

Say again? Over.

There were a few drop-outs and squawks and then:

. . . that garden field. Out.

Terry Thornbras wanted to go at once to check out the situation, but his jello knees said no, and Jace told him to hold down the camp and he'd go instead. He started out but, on second thought, returned to his tent for his 870 shotgun.

Jace jogged down the survey lines, leaping over tangles of roots and stumps and approached the Prophecy compound from the west. The Rodman was lurking in the trees that bordered the encroaching field. Jace stopped next to him and asked what was going on.

"Well, as you can see, Ranger Danger is in the garden pulling up carrots."

In fact, Masterson was leaning over the mounded garden rows and pulling up leafy green vegetation by the fistful.

"And the Amish guy over there is cursing him out with plagues and lakes of fire."

Adam, it looked like, was pacing back and forth along the newly brushed-out property line. He carried a hunting rifle, but he kept it pointed at the ground as he thundered up a storm of invective. For his part, Masterson was ignoring him. His leg cannon was still in its holster on his hip. So far, not a disaster.

"How did it start?"

"A couple of girls came down from the house to water their garden, and your man over there goes postal on them and chases them away. Then the Amish dude comes out and they get into a shoutfest, which makes your man start murdering vegetables."

That sounded about right.

There was a third man involved, a balding graybeard who stood on a little promontory overlooking the field and was recording the confrontation with his phone. Behind him you could just make out the eaves of a ramshackle shed at the edge of the compound.

"Who's the old guy with the phone?"

"Him? Not a clue except that he's not a movie star."

"What?"

"He came from the house with the Amish dude, and he told me he might look like a famous movie star but he's not him."

"Not who?"

"Beats me. He says he's livestreaming to the internet so nobody better do anything stupid unless they want the whole world to see it. But that's bullshit; there's no service out here."

"I know, but eventually he'll go back to wherever he came from and upload it there. What's he got so far?"

"I don't know. Maybe twenty minutes of the Amish dude shouting and Danger pulling up the garden."

That was bad but still no disaster.

Down in the field, Masterson finished destroying a row and moved to one of the cold frames. He kicked it over and reached in for the tomato starts.

Jace said, "Let's just hope it doesn't get any worse than this."

Enter the cat.

CW6 1.0

FREE-RANGING DOMESTIC cats fared poorly in the wilderness. They were just the right size for eagles to scoop up like a take-out dinner. Owls and hawks snacked on them too, as well as foxes, wolves, and their wild cousins, the lynx. Calgary, the family's tabby, had thus far beaten the odds and survived into adulthood, despite her own fondness for the hunt. Now she was seen slinking across the cutline from yard to field, looking for something to kill. She disappeared into the brush.

Meanwhile, Masterson kicked over a second cold frame, and Jace said, "I'd better go see if I can talk some sense into him."

"Good luck with that."

Jace started across the field, but two rangers were approaching from the eastern end, and they reached him first. They were Ranger Swartz and one of the Outside rangers.

The Outside ranger was attired in full SWAT regalia, from his high-impact composite helmet to his waffle-soled combat boots. He held an AR-15 assault rifle across his bulletproof chest. In contrast to him, Swartz wore no armor and carried only a sidearm on his hip.

When Jace joined them, Swartz was telling Masterson, "It's not up to us.

It's not our problem."

"Of course it's our problem," Masterson countered. "It's our park, isn't it? If not us, who?"

"The FBI," Swartz replied. "The U.S. Marshals. But not till later, after we turn in our results and the prosecutors, courts, and lawyers all have their say. Our assignment here is the boundary survey, nothing more. We can't get ahead of ourselves. Not now when we're so close to bringing this puppy home without violence."

Masterson wasn't buying it. He bent over and yanked up another tomato plant.

Swartz shook his head in frustration. When he noticed Jace standing there, he said, "Who's watching the goddam camp?"

"Terry Thornbrus," Jace said.

Swartz looked back and forth between Jace and Masterson, and a light came on in his head. "All right, tell you what — I'm swapping out the two of you."

Masterson stood still for a moment. "Say what?"

"Masterson, you're our new camp boss. Kuliak will replace you on the line."

"Are you," Masterson asked as he bent over to throttle another tomato plant, "benching me?"

"Yes, in fact, I am. Effective immediately. Go on, get out of here. You, Kuliak, go follow the Rodman around. Where is that kid?"

"Over there." Jace pointed. "Next to the trees."

"Well, tell him to get back to work."

Just then, a screen door banged shut, and a moment later another Prophecy son came barreling across the yard. It was evil twin Hoss, the hefty second born, wielding a shotgun and a grim ugly face. The cameraman near the shed swiveled his phone around to capture his entrance.

"Oh, shit," Swartz said and hustled to intercept Hosea, with the Outside ranger right behind him. When Hosea saw the rangers, he slowed down and changed course to join Adam at the property line.

Masterson watched them go as he brushed dirt from his trousers.

Jace said, "I want you to know I didn't put him up to that."

Masterson gave him a quizzical look.

"Swartz," Jace went on. "I didn't ask Swartz to replace you."

"Oh, I know that, Kuliak. You're just an innocent bystander. What else is new?"

At the property line, Swartz and the other ranger were having an animated dialog with the Prophecy boys.

"Don't those boys run in a pack of three?" Masterson said.

"What?"

"Where's the third son of a bitch?"

Jace had no idea where Proverbs was and didn't care. He was more concerned with getting Masterson back to camp in one piece. "Come on," he said. "Let's go see the Rodman."

The Rodman stepped out from the trees, and Jace and Masterson headed his way. When they passed below the promontory, Masterson glanced up at the cameraman, who was still recording. Something about the man seemed to rub the ranger the wrong way.

"Hey, you," he called up to him, "put that phone away."

The man swung the phone to frame Masterson and Jace. "Hello, rangers," he said warmly. "Would you mind identifying yourselves and repeating what you just said."

"I said put that phone away."

"Or what?"

"Or I'll come up there and put it away for you."

The man laughed out loud. It was a jolly laugh with no hint of malice. "Well, I hope you don't do that, ranger, 'cause then I'd be filming the whole thing and catch you in the act of abridging my civil rights. You know as well as I do that the U.S. Supreme Court has ruled that photographers have First Amendment rights to record law enforcement officials performing their duties, as long as we're not trespassing or hindering or obstructing. None of which I'm doing, plainly. So please reserve your bully tactics for the peasants. Thank you."

The guy was correct about filming cops. Jace knew it, and Masterson knew it, but that still didn't make it right.

Masterson started climbing the bluff toward the man. Why did the guy have to mouth off? Was he looking for a beating? Feeling a little sick, Jace climbed up after Masterson, and when they reached the top, Masterson said, "Are you calling me a bully? Or a liar?"

"Is that what you heard me say?" The man chuckled. "I suppose you're gonna hear what you want to hear."

Masterson approached him close enough so that only the phone separated them. "Tell me this, Mr. Attorney-at-law, do you see any possible scenario in which you leave this place in possession of that phone?" He said this directly into the lens of the phone's camera.

The man said, "What I don't see is how it matters one way or the other where this phone ends up, ranger. You know I'm livestreaming all of this straight to the internet, don't you?" Then to make sure he was being understood, he added, "Say hi to your fans, Ranger Ethan Parkhurst Masterson. You and your ponytailed cousin over there are live on YouTube even as we speak."

Jace was about to call bullshit on him, but when he saw the effect the man's lie had on his partner, he held back. Masterson turned to him and said, "Can they do that now?"

"Are you serious?" Jace said. He was about to remind him that no one had cell service on this side of Stubborn Mountain, but under the circumstances wouldn't a little white lie be a better move? "Of course they can do it. They can do anything these days." He waved at the phone and said, "Hi, Kate. It's your little brother hard at work."

Big Bad Ranger Danger seemed to deflate before his eyes. Meanwhile, the confrontation at the property line was heating up, and the stranger with the phone acknowledged his victory with a satisfied grunt before turning his attention back to it. Someone down there was shouting at someone else, but it was hard to tell who was saying what. A couple more rangers had shown up, and the Prophecys were outnumbered and outgunned.

Jace sidled up next to Masterson and said, "Come on. Let's go. Swartz can handle this without us." Masterson didn't budge, and Jace went on, "So you tore up some vegetables. Big fucking deal. It'll blow over, but only if you do what you were ordered and return to camp, right now." He was tempted to add, *Besides, cook, don't you need to start prepping dinner?*

Perhaps Masterson had been working on his character flaws since being assigned to this park because he'd somehow managed to stay out of trouble till now. Perhaps he realized he'd get no more second chances. Whatever the case, he said, "To hell with it," and turned to follow Jace down the bluff.

CW7 1.0

NATURALLY, CALGARY, THE Cat Empress of Stubborn Mountain, chose that exact moment to return home from her successful hunt. She emerged from the trees and paused in the middle of the cutline for a fleeting instant to show off the trophy she carried in her jaws.

A Downy Woodpecker it was, a stout little fellow with black and white feathers and a small cap of brilliant scarlet on the crown of its knockabout head.

Masterson was stunned, and as he watched, the cat vanished into the yard. "Like hell!" he said and charged after her. By the time he remounted the bluff, she was halfway across the yard. He drew his revolver and took careful aim.

BOOM!

The magnum blast split the air and made everyone stop what they were doing and look. Whether Masterson's aim was off or whether he never intended to harm the cat, his bullet thudded in the dirt off Calgary's bow, and the shockwave was powerful enough to make her teleport away, leaving her prize behind.

Everyone watched Masterson holster his smoking Super Redhawk Alaskan revolver, watched him stride purposefully across the Prophecy yard to gather up the bird in a plastic evidence bag. Watched him return to the cameraman and present himself and the bagged bird to the whole world via YouTube.

Masterson leaned into the camera and declared, "Here's evidence of this family's total disregard both for this nation's natural treasures and for her laws."

He wagged the bag in front of the phone. "It's a violation of park regulations to allow your pet out of your control while on park land, and here's one dead reason why. Who do these people think they are?"

As if in answer, there was a faint click behind Masterson's head. "Freeze!" someone said.

Masterson dropped the bird and raised his hands. "You don't want to do this," he said, slowly turning around "This is the last thing you want to do." It was Proverbs, the third son of a bitch. He'd joined the party after all, using the toolshed as cover to sneak up on Masterson with a hunting rifle.

"Shut up!" Proverbs said. "It's my turn to talk." He wore a black leather patch on his right eye and sighted the rifle with his left.

But Proverbs wasn't the only one able to sneak around. Jace climbed the bluff and maneuvered himself behind the Prophecy boy. He pumped a shell into the chamber of his shotgun. "Drop it!" he shouted. "Drop it now!"

For a brief eternity, no one moved. Then Proverbs slowly lowered the barrel of his rifle to point it at the ground, but he did not drop it. In a flash, Masterson drew his gun on him and echoed Jace's command:

"Drop it! Drop it now!"

The rangers had the kid point blank from two directions. If he didn't drop the rifle, they would surely kill him. If he sneezed, they would surely kill him. If he so much as twitched, they would surely kill him.

About this time, Jace woke up as if from a dream to find himself standing in the sun-dappled mid-morning light of a June day in Alaska, surrounded by mountain majesties, cool forests, and babbling creeks, with the bracing scent of fresh-cut spruce on the breeze. And in his hands beat the misguided heart of a particularly obnoxious and dangerous young man who seemed hellbent on dying for the sake of fairytales and property rights. How exactly did he, Jace Kuliak, place himself in the position where he might be compelled to kill this kid? And over what? A goddam woodpecker?

Masterson cocked his cannon and said, "Last chance, freak."

Someone cleared his throat. "Still here, rangers," the cameraman said merrily. "And still livestreaming."

To Proverbs he said, "Son, I'm afraid I have to go with the rangers on this one. I know it's not fair. I know it's an insult to your faith and constitutional rights. I get that, and I agree with you, but if you don't put down that weapon right now this instant, these jackboots will use it as an excuse to blow you away."

"But you're filming, right?" Proverbs said. "Everyone will see it."

"What everyone will see is you being cut down by fire, son, and no one wants to see that."

Proverbs no longer even looked at the rangers; he was focused on the phone instead.

"What crime am I committing?" he asked the world. "I'm only just defending my family from these devils. They're the ones breaking the law. This one . . ." he nodded toward Masterson. "He was trespassing on our property. He tried to kill our cat. You saw him! He shot his gun towards the house where little kids live. He could have killed one of my brothers or sisters. No free person can stand for this kind of tyranny." Proverbs glanced up at the cameraman. "You're getting this, Uncle Jeff, right? You're showing everyone?"

"I'm getting it," the cameraman said. "Now let's call it a day and put down the gun, okay?"

The radios squawked. The sudden noise made Jace's trigger finger jerk. Good thing he'd moved it outside the trigger guard.

Masterson, what's your status? Over. It was Swartz.

Maintaining his bead on the boy, Masterson unclipped his radio and brought it to his lips. "Our status is good. We're in the middle of an inholder misunderstanding that we're attempting to resolve. Over."

Jace glanced down the property line and saw the other two Prophecy boys, disarmed, on their knees with their hands on top of their heads. The other rangers were covering them while Swartz spoke on the radio.

How can we assist? Over.

"No assistance necessary. Do not approach. I repeat, do not approach. Just stand by. Over."

Standing by. Over.

Masterson put away the radio and said, "My turn, Uncle Jeff. Your viewers should know that we came onto this man's property pursuant to a court order to conduct a land survey, nothing more. No one shot at his cat, and the woodpecker I retrieved is lawful evidence in the violation of park regulations.

"But in his haste to prejudge the situation, this young man made a poor decision and assaulted two federal officers with a deadly weapon. And for that I must arrest him and take him in. And that's what I intend to do." To Proverbs he said, "I'm arresting you one way or the other. So, with the world as my witness, this is your final warning: PUT DOWN THE FUCKING GUN!"

A pall fell over the boy's face. He licked his dry lips with a dry tongue, but he did not obey the ranger's order. One shot was all he had to his name. His hunting rifle was a bolt-action Remington, and it was doubtful that he'd be able to get off a second round. For that matter, with two guns trained on him, it was doubtful he'd get off the first.

"I am in your hands, Elder Brother Jesus," he said.

Masterson said, "Amen," and started closing on him.

Up at the house, the screen door slammed, and everyone glanced in that direction. Two young women were standing on the porch. They took each other's hand, descended the steps, and set off across the yard toward the confrontation. They began singing a hymn as they came.

"Stay back!" Masterson shouted at them, but they kept coming, swaying their long skirts in time to the hymn. Their intertwined voices floated to the men on slippered feet.

> *O sisters let's go down,*
> *Let's go down, come on down,*
> *O sisters let's go down,*
> *Down in the river to pray.*

When the young women had approached near enough, Jace recognized the brunette as one of the Prophecy girls he'd seen before, but the other one . . . Long, ash-blond hair to the small of her back, a fair complexion unsullied by the sun, a gorgeous figure, despite her pioneer costume. Both women looked terrified, but still they came.

> *O brothers let's go down,*
> *Let's go down, come on down . . .*

They crossed the yard, ignoring Masterson's repeated commands, and inserted themselves between the combatants. When they tried to disarm their brother, he resisted until the totally amazing one said, "Poppy says so," and he handed over his rifle. She kept the gun pointed at the ground as she worked the bolt, ejecting all of the cartridges, neutralizing the threat.

At some indeterminate point, Jace had also lowered his weapon, as well as his guard.

The sisters then took their brother by the arm and tried to lead him back to the house, but Masterson balked. "Oh, no you don't. I'm placing this man under arrest."

So the sisters started for the house without him, still singing, still swaying their hips in time to the music. Jace watched them go, watched her go. After a few paces she turned her head to glance back. Her eyes found his. That was the moment Jace knew he was a drowning man.

The shrill zip of plastic cuffs brought him back to Earth. Proverbs was compliant but unbowed as Masterson recited him his rights. The cameraman was telling the boy that he would follow him to town and find him a good lawyer when Ranger Swartz came up the cutline and climbed the bluff. He looked at the cuffed boy and Masterson and then turned to the cameraman.

"You Bridges?"

"That's me," the man said, turning his phone on him.

"Please follow me."

"Uh, I don't think so."

"It's all right. The excitement's over. Adam wants to talk to you."

Down the property line, Adam and Hosea were on their feet, unbound. Adam raised a hand and waved him over.

Left alone with their prisoner, the two rangers didn't speak, and Jace's mind was free to review what had happened. She had looked directly at him, hadn't she? Did she smile? It was hard to tell. Her lips were slightly turned up at the corners so that even when she wasn't smiling, her lips were. Her eyebrows were so fair and faint against her skin he didn't see them until she raised them. But why did she raise them? In alarm, of course. Did he frighten her, or was it the whole situation? The situation, dummy. It was a terribly brave thing she did, marching into an armed standoff and disarming the perp, her brother. She might have been hurt. She might have been killed.

After a little while, Swartz returned, not with Uncle Jeff but with the eldest Prophecy son, Adam. The ranger used a pair of snips to free Proverbs' hands.

"What's going on?" Masterson demanded.

"I'm releasing him into the supervision of his brother."

Masterson exploded. "Wait!" he said. "What the fuck are you doing? I arrested that man. He assaulted us."

"And now he's free to go. Go on," he said to Adam. "Get him out of here before I change my mind." Swartz blocked Masterson from interfering as Adam escorted his brother away.

"I'm happy to report," Swartz told the befuddled Masterson, "that nothing happened here today." He picked up the evidence bag from the ground, removed the tiny corpse, and flung it into the trees across the cutline.

"What are you doing?" Masterson protested. "That's evidence. We need that."

"No, we don't. Not as long as I have this." He showed Masterson Uncle Jeff's phone.

"You fool," Masterson roared. "You imbecile. You struck a loser's bargain. Don't you know that phone means nothing? He already *uploaded* everything. It's already online. It's already *out there* probably going viral as we speak, and you can't get it back."

The older ranger sighed and studied his boots. "Think, Masterson. Tell me why, in the evenings when we call our families, why do we take turns using the satellite phone? Why don't we just use our cells? Think."

"But . . ." Masterson's face clotted with anger. He glared at Jace, while Jace pretended to be someplace else.

"So, I repeat, nothing happened here today," Swartz said, "and nothing's gonna happen because I negotiated a truce. A twelve-hour accord. We're going to work through the night, and none of them will interfere. I talked to Thornbras, and he says we can finish the job if we hustle. So hustle,

Masterson. Return to camp and make dinner. After dinner, prep breakfast and then start striking camp. No one's sleeping tonight, and the helo is coming for us at noon."

CW8 1.0

IT WAS 8:00 P.M. by the time the Rodman and Jace scaled the steep slope to set the final corner and close the traverse. They carried plenty of gear, but at least they didn't need to bring the chainsaw. They soon came across a broad footpath that seemed to be headed in the same direction they were going, so they took it and climbed in silence, breathing hard under their packs. The Rodman said, "Must lead to the mine entrance." A little while later he added, "Your guy has rage issues, doesn't he? My dad's the same way. That's why I'm at my uncle's."

The footpath zigzagged up a tailings slope, and it did lead to the mine. But the entrance looked more suited to a fortress than an abandoned mine. The two men paused to stare at it.

The mine adit was an immense notch blasted into the side of the mountain. The wings of the notch spread from the entrance like giant limestone thighs. Suspended high along the wings were two fortified galleries made of heavy logs. Rifle slots along the galleries gave defenders unobstructed firing angles on any intruder. The entrance gate itself was the size of a double-wide garage door. It was constructed of heavy bridge timbers and plated with a welded patchwork of scrap iron. It looked stout enough to stop a tank, or at least to slow one down.

"Holy crap," the Rodman said. "Those prophets don't fuck around, do they?"

Jace snapped a few photos with his phone. Above the gate, wouldn't you know it, was a wooden plank with a short inscription chiseled into it: *REV 6:15.* He snapped that too. [*And the kings of the earth, and the great men, and the rich men, and the chief captains, and the mighty men, and every bondsman, and every free man, hid themselves in the dens and in the rocks of the mountains . . .*]

They continued up the slope above the mine adit. The going got rough, and they labored under their loads. They reached a wide ledge where they found a large, cast-iron grate covering a hole in the ground. A ventilation shaft for the mine. Further up the slope, near where the property boundary should be located, the Rodman found a rusty iron pipe cemented into a hole chiseled into a boulder. "This is gotta be the original post," he said. He set his pogo pole on top of it, but the instrument man, who was scoping him from down below said it was off. When the two of them finally zeroed in on the corner, it was located less than a meter from the 1909 original, which impressed the hell out of the Rodman. "They didn't even have satellites back then. How the fuck did they know where they were? Think about it."

While Jace thought about it and took in the scenery, the Rodman chipped and dug a hole for the new monument. He hammered in a pipe, anchored it with cement, and topped it with a brass marker. When he triple-checked his work, he took photos of it and repacked his gear for their descent. Jace asked him what he could tell about the location of the airstrip from their vantage point. The young man backsighted the property line with a theolodite app on his phone and said, "Let the lawsuits begin."

CW9 1.0

THEY TOOK A different route back to camp, staying above the mine adit and descending the slope on the other side. When they thought they were back on park land, the Rodman told Jace to go on ahead without him — he needed to take a dump. So Jace said he'd see him back at camp and continued on through the forest until he came to a well-traveled footpath. He took it to be the Stubborn Mountain Trail and followed it, he thought, in the direction of the NPS camp.

Instead, he came upon a small, fenced-in area. Inside were a dozen rabbit hutches. There were girls attending to them. Apparently, Jace was still on Prophecy property. He tried to withdraw quietly without being spotted, but a dog appeared out of nowhere and began to growl and bark at him with much enthusiasm.

Jace recognized her as the family dog, though he didn't know her name. She was a big dog, a German shepherd, but with a shaggy, black-and-tan coat and half-floppy ears. At the moment, though, she was mostly snarling, white teeth.

"Hey there, beautiful," Jace said softly, trying to charm her. He had a way with dogs. He loved dogs, and they usually loved him back. He hunched over to appear less threatening, meanwhile removing the canister of bear spray from his belt, just in case. He didn't have any treats or food to appease her, only the gentle and confident tone of his voice. "What a brave and fiercesome dog you are. What a champion. My, my, aren't you a sweetheart."

No good. Her hackles rose down the length of her back, and her outrage redoubled.

"Now I'm scared. Yes, I am. I'm so scared I'm going to back away a little, just like this."

A girl clucked her tongue, and the dog abruptly quit barking and dashed to her side. The girl appeared annoyed and was about to say something to the dog when she noticed Jace standing there. They stared at each other for several staggering moments.

"Oh," she said, looking away. "You're not . . . I thought . . ."

"Sorry if I . . ." he replied. "I was just . . ."

Others were coming from the direction of the hutches, and there were men's voices among them. Deuteronomy pointed in another direction, jabbing her finger for him to go, and then dashed off to intercept her family. Was she protecting him from discovery? Were they co-conspirators so soon?

Deut paused for a final, over-the-shoulder glance at him. He kinda waved. She kinda waved back.

And so, Jace's sister Kate in Littleton, Colorado, if you must know, yes, they did meet. Unforgettably so. And shortly thereafter they traded two words of conversation.

Let the wedding bells ring.

NORAD of the North

NN1 1.0

POPPY PROPHECY AWOKE in a king-sized bed, nestled in sheets and pillows that smelled like air freshener. The walls surrounding him were painted robin's-egg-blue and were smooth and unblemished. No water stains sullied the ceiling. Not one. A framed print hung on the wall opposite his bed depicting a pastoral scene with peasants and haystacks and a stone cathedral spire in the distance. On the dresser a bouquet of dried flowers sprung from a glass vase. A thermostat affixed to the wall stood by to warm or cool the room at his whim. Limitless hot and cold water awaited him in the private john just a few steps away. (The porcelain bowls emptied themselves!) On the nightstand, a lamp crouched under a tasseled shade. Poppy shut his eyes and prayed, *Heavenly Father, thank You for saving us from all this.*

Poppy could hear children shrieking somewhere in the rambling house, as well as the alien whine of a TV and feet thudding on carpet. The clock radio read 10:07 A.M. He got up.

THE BOYS WERE sitting around the kitchen table drinking coffee. "Good morning, lord," they said. "Ready for breakfast?"

"You let them watch TV?" Poppy said.

Proverbs jumped up and went out to the living room. In a moment, the television went silent.

"Where are our hosts?"

Adam replied, "The mister is at work. The missus is at a Christmas bazaar. She was surprised we didn't bring any of our own handcrafts to sell. The boy's at school, and the girl's in her bedroom with Deut and Cora."

"What are they doing in there?"

Adam shrugged. "Girl things?"

"Go make sure their door is open."

Hosea sighed and got up to comply.

The family dog ventured into the kitchen, its nails clicking on the tiles. It was a tiny, naked thing with fuzzy matchstick legs.

"It's a midget greyhound," Poppy said.

"It's called a whippet, lord. Name of Keagan."

"Well, whatever they call it, it's an abomination against Father God's plan for dogs." He enticed the dog closer with a crust of toast and then kicked it, sending it yelping from the room.

Poppy took the shopping list from a pocket and unfolded it. The plan was to hit the big box stores in Anchorage in the Dodge and to secure what they bought in the cargo racks atop the bus for the trip home. Four thousand dollars might seem like a lot of money, but their needs were great, and the troubles would last seven years. First the essentials: grains, staples, and garden seeds. Ammunition for all their various calibers. Leather tanning supplies. A Tribulation's worth of toilet paper, socks and underwear, toothpaste, and detergent. Dairy goat udder balm. The list went on. But Poppy put it away. There was important business to attend to first.

"Go start the pickup," he said. "Get your brothers."

ONLY A FEW miles of backtracking on the Glenn brought them to NJB's exit. They parked across the street from the familiar house and idled the engine while Proverbs glassed the area with binoculars.

"Something yellow's strung across the door," he said. "It's got words on it, but I can't make them out."

Adam grabbed the binoculars for a look. "That's police tape."

"What's police tape?"

"It's what cops use to mark a crime scene."

"What kind of crime does it say?"

"It doesn't say that, idiot."

Hosea said, "You notice how the neighbors have Christmas lights strung up, and Jeff doesn't?"

Proverbs said, "So?"

Poppy said, "So he hasn't been home in a while." He fished the keyring from his pocket and thumbed through the keys until he found the guest key he'd never returned. "Let's go see."

New snow on NJB's driveway was undisturbed. Though it was just after noon, the overcast day was dim enough for them to trip the porch light.

"Someone's home," Proverbs said.

"It's a motion-sensor, idiot."

Poppy unlocked the door, and they ducked under the yellow police tape to enter. (*Crime Scene — Do Not Cross*)

"Keep your gloves on," Poppy said, "and don't touch nothing you don't have to."

The furnace was working, but the thermostat was set to the forties (10s C).

Poppy shouted down the hallway. "Jeff? Are you here?" The place looked tidy enough. Not much had changed since their visit two years ago. The dining room table was set with a desiccated dinner for one: pork chops, baked potato, salad, an unopened bottle of Riesling.

It wasn't until they reached the living room that they found the crime scene. Broken lamps, overturned chairs. In the corner, a blood stain on the the charcoal grey berber carpet.

Poppy said, "Our friend may have come to harm. Let us pray for him as we continue to search."

"We will, lord," Adam said. "What are we searching for?"

Poppy removed his gloves and went through his wallet for the scrap of paper NJB had mailed him. Four numbers.

"I think we're looking for a safe."

THE FLOOR SAFE was hidden under the carpeting and several milk crates of hockey gear in the walk-in closet of the master bedroom. "Whatever happened to Jeff," Poppy said, "it wasn't a robbery. This safe wasn't that hard to find." He knelt down on creaky knees and punched in the combination. The boys jostled each other to see as he lifted the heavy door. A black nylon gym bag was jammed into the small space. Poppy tried to lift it out, but it was wedged in pretty tight. He moved aside for Hosea to help. Hosea wrenched the bag free and set it on the floor.

"I don't know, lord," Hosea said. "This don't feel right. Do you think we should be going through his stuff and all?"

Though they didn't say anything, the other two boys seemed to be thinking the same thing. NJB, whatever had happened to him, was their friend too. He had treated them right.

Poppy held up the scrap of paper with the combination. "Where do you think I got this from? Jeff sent it to me. He wanted us to find the safe. He must've known that something evil was coming his way." Poppy unzipped the bag. Inside was cash. Lots of cash.

The boys were utterly astounded.

"How much you figure there is?"

"Where d'ya think it come from?"

"Is this a miracle or what?"

It was impossible to guess how much money was in the bag. The bills seemed to be all 20s and 50s, but they weren't banded in easy-to-count bundles. Wherever they came from, it wasn't from a bank. Obviously, it was a miracle, or at least an act of divine providence.

"Close the safe," Poppy told Hosea, "and put the carpet back the way it was. Adam, take this to the truck and stay with it. Proverbs, help me stand up."

"Lord," Hosea said. "There's something else." The big man reached deep into the safe and plucked an envelope from the bottom. It was sealed and hand-addressed to a Mr. Marvin Johnson. That was the name Poppy used on his driver's license and bank accounts.

"Go, all of you," Poppy said, "and wait for me in the truck."

When Poppy was alone, he sat on the edge of NJB's neatly made-up bed and slit the envelope with his pocket knife. A single sheet of paper fell out inscribed with a single line of text: *I swear on my life that I never harmed anyone.*

It was signed Jefferson Beaumont Bridges.

Heavenly Father, what is the meaning of this?

NN2 1.0

IT WAS A girl's room with all the trimmings: posters, mirrors, make-up, and clothes. It was so much a girl's room that the Prophecy girls all hung out in it whenever they had the chance. Ginger said they were more than welcome, but Deut and Cora sent the little ones away in order to have it all to themselves.

A shelf was crammed with sports and academic trophies, another with citations and awards. There was a bumper sticker wedged into the mirror frame that said, DON'T MESS WITH HOMESCHOOLERS.

The Prophecys were homeschoolers too; that was something they had in common with Ginger. She was so pretty. And sophisticated, in a fallen-world sort of way. And nice too. She was Sarai and Deut's age, but she dressed like a girl in a magazine, which could have been intimidating but wasn't because she was so nice.

CORA WAS LYING on top of Ginger's bed and paging through a JCPenney clothes catalog with a sultry Jezebel on the cover. The bed was twice as wide as any of theirs, and Ginger didn't have to share it with a sister. Cora sighed and said, "Don't you wish we lived here?"

"Oh, I don't know," Deut said. "I like it fine at home."

"I do too, but I'll never have my own room at home."

"You will when you get married."

"No, I won't. I'll have to share it with my husband."

Deut was sitting at the desk where a laptop computer vied for space with stacks of books and college catalogs. There was a framed photo of Ginger in a ski jacket posing with other girls and boys. They were all pretty, especially the boys, and they were all laughing as though someone had just told a funny joke. There was nothing wrong with having friends and telling jokes.

Deut had found a Bible on Ginger's bookshelf and taken it down without Cora noticing. She sat with her back to her little sister-shadow while she searched it for verses her father often quoted.

Just then the door flew open without a knock and Ginger breezed into the room and went straight to the closet. In less than a blink, the JCPenney catalog and Bible were out of sight.

"Hey there," Ginger said. "How're things?" She rooted in the far recesses of the closet and emerged with two pairs of insulated ski pants.

"Things are great," Deut said. "Thank you for letting us be here."

"Don't mention it. You're my guests. Oh, and hey, Rory says he's taking the kids to the sledding hill."

Deut said, "Who's Rory?"

"My little brother. You met him."

"Oh, right, Rory."

"Anyway, he wants to know if you two'd like to come along. I even have extra ski pants if you need 'em." She laid the pants on the bed next to Cora.

A silent test of wills arose between the sisters. Then, Cora, the apparent loser, whined, "But I *want* to go."

"Want, want," Deut said. "The Devil's middle name is want."

"Fiiine."

"Whoa," Ginger said. She wasn't sure what she had just witnessed. "If Cora wants to go sledding, what's wrong with that?"

The question flummoxed the Prophecy girls. The fallen world had different rules. How to explain?

"There's nothing wrong with it."

"Then, why can't she go and you stay here, if that's what you both want?"

"We can't," Cora said. "We have to stick together."

"Why?"

"It's our buddy system," Deut said. "Like when you go swimming with a buddy."

"Okay," Ginger replied, sitting on the edge of the bed. "I get it for when you're swimming, but why do you need a buddy when you're at home?"

"Are you kidding? The home is Satan's favorite hunting ground. You let your guard down when you're at home, and you're most vulnerable where you feel the safest. This is how we look out for each other."

"I see," Ginger said, though she didn't really. "Well, if Cora wants to go with the others, I guess I could be your buddy here. Does that work?"

Such an idea! — to have this stranger as a buddy? Satan would have a picnic. It was bad enough with Cora as it was. Meanwhile, Cora willfully took Deut's silence for approval and grabbed the pink pair of ski pants.

AFTER CORA LEFT, Ginger began changing into a sweatshirt and jeans. Deut turned her back when she realized what she was doing. "I see you're homeschooled," she said, taking a stab at small talk. "So are we."

"That's what I hear."

"But if I lived in a town and had the chance to go to a real school, there's no way I wouldn't go there."

"I didn't like homeschooling at the beginning," Ginger said, "but I participate in a lot of extracurricular activities, so I don't feel like I'm missing out. And believe me, I don't miss the whole high school drama machine."

"Do your parents force you?"

"They took Rory and me out of middle school. In high school Rory wanted to go back, and they let him. But by then I decided I liked homeschooling better." Before Deut knew it, Ginger was heading for the door. "You want something to drink?" she said.

Deut managed to say no thanks, but Ginger left too quickly for Deut to go on to explain that buddy shadowing didn't work like that. You couldn't just up and leave your buddy alone. Deut should have gotten up and followed Ginger to the kitchen, but the house was quiet, her brothers and Poppy were gone, and so she stayed where she was, *alone*, with a purloined Bible hidden on her lap. Could Satan have an easier target?

DEUT TRACKED THE words with her finger. "Stop de . . . deprive . . . depriving one another ex . . . except by agree . . . ment. Stop depriving one another except by agreement." No, whatever that meant, it wasn't what she was looking for. Where was it? She was in the right book, 1 Corinthians, but the verse she sought was proving elusive. And the wording sounded odd.

The next thing Deut knew, Ginger was standing behind her and reading over her shoulder. Blame it on the wall-to-wall carpeting that sucked the sound from your footsteps. "I have the Bible on my computer if you want to use it," Ginger said.

Startled, Deut jumped up to return the Bible to the bookshelf. "I'm sorry," she said.

"For what? Borrowing my Bible? You're welcome to borrow any of my books, especially my Bible. Actually, I'm a little surprised you didn't bring your own with you."

"I don't have a Bible."

"Really? Why not?"

"Because the apostle Paul says that only men can read the Bible and only after they're married."

Ginger blinked. "I never saw that one. Do you know the verse? I'm pretty sure everyone is *supposed* to read Scripture, including women." She took the seat at the desk and woke up her laptop. "Actually, we can probably find the verse ourselves." If there was such a verse. She browsed to the Biblehub.com site. "What should we use for keywords?"

Deut drew a blank.

"You know, keywords," Ginger said helpfully. "Let's start with 'woman.'" She typed the word into a search field and hit Enter. *Woman* appeared over four thousand times in the Bible. She skimmed the links out loud: "'She shall be called woman . . .' 'A woman of excellence . . .' Oh, look, here's one from your namesake book."

"My what?"

"You know, the Book of Deuteronomy."

Ginger moused over and clicked a button. The display was replaced by another screen from which she read, "Deuteronomy 22:5 'A woman shall not wear man's clothing, nor shall a man put on a woman's clothing; for whoever does these things is an abomination to the Lord your God.' No, not even close."

Out of politeness, Deut refrained from pointing out that Ginger was wearing pants. Instead, she said, "What is this? What are you doing?"

"Uh, this is similar to the Strong's Concordance," Ginger said, "only it's online, and in English."

Another blank look.

"A concordance. You know, like a cross-referenced index of all the words in different versions of the Bible. Type in any word, and it'll list the verses that contain that word."

"Oh," Deut said, "a concordance. Of course." Instead of pretending she knew what Ginger was talking about (pretending wasn't exactly lying), Deut knew that she should be fleeing the room. Different versions of the Bible? What was she talking about? Her "buddy," instead of fortifying her against Satan's wiles, was leading her to Hell with a keyboard.

Ginger sifted through the results and tried other keywords. She did find the bit about women not speaking in churches, but nothing about women not reading Scripture. [1 Corinthians 14:34–35 "The women are to keep silent in the churches; for they are not permitted to speak. . . If they desire to learn anything, let them ask their own husbands at home; for it is improper for a woman to speak in church."]

"I don't know what to tell you," Ginger said when she exhausted all the keywords she could think of. "I could ask my dad."

The look of horror on Deut's face made her add, "Or not. You're welcome to continue looking yourself." She stood up to offer Deut the chair.

Temptations were swarming like bats in a cave. "Thank you," Deut said, "but we're not supposed to touch a computer."

"Of course you're not," Ginger said.

"What do you mean by that?"

Ginger checked herself. "Nothing, except I have an idea. Wait here. I have to get something."

She hurried from the room, and returned a moment later with a small, flat object. "It's Rory's. I'm sure he won't mind if you borrow it."

"What is it?"

"His tablet." She switched it on. "It's a tablet, not a computer." She tapped the screen a few times with her finger. "But it can take you to the same places where computers go. See?" She passed the tablet to Deut. "I'm very interested in what you learn about this verse of yours. It affects all of us, you know, if it exists. And if it doesn't exist, you should know that too."

WHEN THE OTHERS were asleep, Deut pulled out Rory's tablet to continue her research into why her sister should be special in their father's eyes and not her. They were both twins of a twin, after all. She couldn't find the verse he was always quoting or indeed any verse about a twin of a twin. In fact, if you believed the concordance, the word "twin" only showed up nine times in the whole Bible, and most of those were in reference to Elder Brother Jesus' disciple, Thomas, who was a twin. Esau and Jacob were the twin sons of Isaac, and Solomon compared twins to lambs, teeth, and a woman's breasts. Other than that, nothing. No twins of twins, a verse her father used constantly to shower favors on Sarai and not her. All of which confirmed what Deut had been suspecting all along — Satan had loosed false Bibles upon the fallen world to confound the faithful. No wonder Poppy kept their only copy on his belt.

So there was no point in searching the concordance any further. But the tablet itself was a marvel and a joy to explore. It had books, magazines, television shows, movies, shopping, games, and much more packed into its slim sandwich of metal and glass. She even took a selfie — by accident — a moonlit self-portrait in her nightgown with her hair loose around her shoulders, her lips parted just so, and a little wrinkle of thought troubling her brow. At first she didn't recognize herself, and when she did, it was all she could do not to succumb to the sin of pride. She was pretty!

It was hard to keep the tablet a secret from her sisters, but she didn't want to explain the difference between a computer and a tablet if she didn't have to. She didn't want to return it either until it was time to go back home. But after a couple of days, it quit working.

"I'm sorry," she said to Ginger's brother. "I must have accidentally broke it. I'll pay for it. How much does it cost?"

Rory was looking right at her but didn't seem to hear a word she said, and she had to repeat herself.

"Don't worry about it," he said finally. "It just needs a charge. It's fine."

He smiled funny. He was a funny boy.

NN3 1.0

POPPY WAS PUTTING on his coat when the whippet Keagan came through the dog door. Poppy aimed a kick at it, but the dog escaped untouched.

"Mr. Prophecy!" Rory said. He had witnessed the whole thing from the hallway. "Why are you kicking my dog?"

"That's no way to talk to me," Poppy said, going out the door. "Have more respect, boy."

"Never do that again, Mr. Prophecy," Rory said. "Am I making myself clear?" But Poppy was already safely out of earshot.

NN4 1.0

POPPY WAS RETURNING to Wallis on the Parks Highway from Houston where he'd gone to check out used acetylene welding tools he'd found on Craigslist. The money donation from NJB — more than $250,000 in rumpled bills — greatly expanded the quantities and variety of end-time supplies that they could afford to purchase. He'd sent the boys to Anchorage with a revised shopping list. Ten 55-gallon drums of various fuels, a back-up generator, deep-cycle storage batteries and control boxes, spare lead battery acid, LED headlamps, lots and lots of AA and AAA batteries, 100-hour candles, hand tools for everything from woodwork to home surgery, antibiotics and pain meds, Proverbs' special prescription, a new pair of chainsaws and replacement chains and parts, a pair of hand-cranked radios — the list went on for eight handwritten pages.

"Rent a U-Haul truck to carry everything in," he told Adam, "and avoid the red flags."

"Lord?"

"They won't rent vehicles to just anyone, you know. You have to pay with a credit card, not cash."

"Then how'm I gonna pay?"

"With this." Poppy handed him his Chase Sapphire card. Poppy didn't believe in credit cards. They were another diabolical scam of Jewish bankers for skimming wealth from ordinary folks. But he couldn't run his e-commerce business without one.

"Another red flag," he went on. "They'll ask you where you plan to drive their truck. If you tell them you're driving the McHardy Road, they'll say it falls outside their operational zone or some bullshit and won't rent you the truck. So tell them you're driving it up to Fairbanks by way of Glennallen."

Adam said, "You want me to lie to them, lord?"

"Lying to the Devil is not lying, son."

Poppy bought the welding tools with cash but couldn't fit the tanks into the borrowed car. The boys would have to return for them with the pickup. The car was a 2010 Toyota Camry he'd borrowed from the Lawther girl. What was her name? Gina? Gerri? No, it was Ginger. Ginger Lawther. What kind of a name was Ginger? (Not to mention the boy's name — Rory.) Still, Ginger was a fine-looking girl. Maybe a little too headstrong. Nice hair, nice smile. She was the same age as his elder set of twins and might make a match for Proverbs. The boy certainly seemed to think so. She looked physically strong, which would be critical to surviving the next few years. And she had wide hips, the better to bear children with, especially when there would be no doctor or midwife around except him.

In the negative column was the fact that this Ginger had been coddled too much. She was soft and weak inside and would buckle in the first crisis.

Poppy passed the frontage road to the Best Western Motel. That was significant because it was also the road to Lake Lola and the governor's house. The governor of Alaska spent very little time in the state capital of Juneau. (civic motto: "Where the Hell is Vera?") She hated the weather there, always raining or snowing, always gloomy. She had no patience for petty politicians. She detested the moldy old governor's mansion. Her first official act upon becoming governor was to fire the cook. Before the first year of her term had passed, she abandoned the mansion and Juneau altogether in favor of Bradd's home-cooked meals in their sunny, spacious house on Lake Lola.

For his part, Poppy had always ignored politics and politicians. During his decades of residency in California, he'd have been hard-pressed to name the current governor in Sacramento. He never voted. Elections were a sham. Who cared who made it into office if the price of victory was sucking up to Satan?

But everything changed two years ago when the Alaska governor's energy rebate program, combined with the annual Permanent Fund Dividend payment, made it possible for the Prophecy family to purchase the Stubborn Mountain Mine. All credit for this miracle went to Father God, of course, but He had worked it through this Vera Tetlin person. Until then, Poppy hadn't even been aware that the Alaska governor was a woman, let alone a born-again Christian.

Poppy's curiosity was aroused enough for him to order her memoir, *An American Maverick,* from Amazon. Not only was it the first book he purchased online, it was the first book he purchased *ever.* When it arrived, he retired to his prayer cabin to give it his full attention. He read the book cover to cover three times. He had never studied a book, other than the Bible, so thoroughly. [read a chapter, "The Man in the Skiff" on page 347]

Clearly, Vera Tetlin was Father God's special gift to the world even before the world even knew her name. From her days as champion high school athlete to her first political struggle against the entrenched crypto-Jew mayor of Wallis, Tetlin was confounding the enemies of the Lord. At every crossroads of her life, she turned to Father God for guidance. She was a mom, a world-class leader, and an anointed prayer warrior. Amazing. And stunningly beautiful to boot. Her memoir included dozens of color snapshots of her and her family.

At last Poppy had found his true soulmate. His blossoming love for Vera Tetlin was tender and pure and more fervent than his love even for Mama P, who had given him a peck of babies. He and Mama P were yoked together in the task of raising children for the kingdom, while his (future) union with Vera was a spiritual one by which they would further the Creator's plan for the world. For the first time in a long time, Poppy had a crush.

When Poppy finished absorbing Tetlin's memoir, he passed it to Mama P and instructed her to read it very carefully. For all her many flaws, Mama P rarely disobeyed him (openly) or questioned his authority (directly). When he assigned her the book and patiently explained why it was so important, she said, "Should I tell Adam to move another bed into our bedroom?"

"No," he said, taking her question at face value. "That might be confusing for the children. No, I think it's probably best if we build her her own little house."

"Yes, lord, that would probably be best. But what about her husband? Where will poor Bradd Tetlin sleep?"

What about Bradd indeed. During his three readings of Tetlin's book, Poppy had skimmed over the parts about her husband, who was just a bit player in his wife's saga. He was a village boy from western Alaska, of mixed Native/white heritage, a part-time commercial fisherman, a winning sno-go racing champion, and North Slope oil line laborer. The "First Dude" wasn't even baptized in the spirit, let alone saved. He and Vera were so unequally yoked it was a wonder they weren't pulling their matrimonial sled around in circles.

Yet Bradd was clearly part of the picture. In her memoir, Vera mentioned him on every other page. A reporter once asked her about a rumor going around that she'd been seen stepping out on Bradd with an Anchorage dentist. Her response: "Cheat on Bradd? Are you serious? Bradd's a hunk. Have you seen Bradd?"

Bradd was the fly in the ointment, a puzzle and a problem, one that the Holy Spirit didn't clear up for Poppy until the following pre-holiday craft season. The children were busily building up their stock of angels, ornaments, and nativity sets. One day Poppy was inspecting their work when he noticed that all the carved birch figurines of Joseph were smaller than the Virgin Marys. They looked ridiculous, and he told the carvers to throw them in the stove and start over. But Uzzie lifted his sweet, freckled face and said, "Behold, lord, Joseph is a smaller saint."

How true! How wise! During the Annunciation, when the Holy Spirit impregnated the virgin with the Father's seed, It saw that Mary would need a human stand-in for a husband. Otherwise, sanctimonious Pharisees would accuse her of fornication and stone her to death.

Enter Joe the Carpenter.

That was who Bradd was, a Joseph to Vera's Mary.

POPPY SLOWED THE Camry as he came to the Best Western access road intersection. If he wanted to meet Vera Tetlin in person, all he had to do was turn right, drive less than a mile to the lake, and take a left on the shore road. The Tetlin place would be the second house on the right. He'd knock firmly on her door, and she would answer it herself. He wouldn't have to say a word because, even though they'd never met, she would instantly recognize him for who he was, her preordained partner. She'd say something like, "So there y'are. 'Bout time you showed up, mister." And she'd give him one of her trademark winks.

Poppy didn't turn off the highway. He didn't knock on her door. Even now, as close to the End Times as it was, it was best to leave the time and place of their first meeting to Him. Otherwise he'd be showing the same lack of faith that led Proverbs to shoot the moose.

"SO, WHAT BRINGS you out of the woods this time of year?" Rex said. It was the first time the two families had managed to sit down together for a meal. They filled the table and spilled over onto folding chairs and TV trays. Cindy had prepared her old standby for feeding small armies — spaghetti. "Kinda late in the year for a supply run, isn't it?"

The children kept their little mouths shut while everyone waited for Poppy to thoroughly chew and swallow his mouthful of noodles and take a sip of water before replying, "Toothache."

"Oh, I heard you all kept Dr. Higgins busy this week. Did he get you squared away?"

Poppy grunted.

Cindy and Ginger asked who wanted seconds, and Deut and Cora jumped up to assist, but Cindy said, "Sit, sit. You're our guests."

Ginger added, "And don't forget there's cake and jello for dessert."

When Ginger served Proverbs seconds, he smiled disarmingly and said, "Not to sell my sisters short, but this might be the best spaghetti I ever ate in my life."

Ginger laughed. "It's from Ragu. We can't claim any credit for it."

"I don't know who Ragu is, but you'd do well to copy down her recipe when she's not looking."

Rex said, "Got plans for church tomorrow? We'd be pleased to welcome you to ours."

Poppy said, "What church is that?"

"The Wallis New Hope."

Cindy added, "Rex is a deacon there."

"Never heard of it."

"We've been around awhile. Three hundred or so members. We're strictly Bible-based."

Rory got up to refill everyone's glasses, starting with Deut's. There were 2-liter bottles of soda chilling in the fridge, but the Prophecys seemed to prefer plain, room-temperature tap water.

"Thank you," Deut said.

"Don't mention it, Deuteronomy."

"Which translation?" Poppy said.

"Well, we keep copies of the King James under the seats, but some folks prefer their own NASBs, and we don't mind. Most any version will get the job done."

"Most any version will certainly *not* get the job done," Poppy said.

"I used to think that too, frankly, but then I tried my hand at teaching Bible study to teen-agers, and I gotta tell you, Prophecy, that with all the firmaments, girded loins, smiting, vouchsafing, and come to passing, I was spending more time *defining* words than *teaching* the Word." He smiled at his own wordplay. "The English language has changed a lot since the sixteenth century, and —"

"What's *that?*" Poppy said, cutting Lawther off. He pointed at something on little Pharisees' lap. "Show it to me!"

The five year old cringed. She held up a small plastic action figure and dared not to look at her father.

Deut said, "It's a doll, lord."

"Then why is it blue? Drop it. Drop it this instant."

See-Saw dropped the toy as though it were scalding hot. "I'm sorry, lord," she said, on the verge of tears. "I won't do it again. I promise."

Ginger exchanged a glance with her mother. Adam and his brothers picked at their food. Rex seemed dumbfounded. Rory set his fork down, smiled at Deut, and picked up the action figure from the floor.

"It's blue because it's a Na'vi, Mr. Prophecy." He brought it over to him for a closer look. "The Na'vi are an alien species from the moon Pandora. It's from the movie *Avatar*. I don't know if you've had a chance to see it, but the —"

Poppy took a swipe at the figurine in Rory's hand and sent it flying across the room. "Shut up, boy, and never shove that demon idol in my face again. You hear me?"

"Easy there, Prophecy," Rex said, finding his tongue. "My son meant no harm. It's just a toy from a movie."

"You teach your children to play with demon dolls and call it harmless? Is that what you preach in this church of yours, *Deacon* Lawther?"

Rex chose his words carefully. "Like my son says, it's a blue alien from outer space, not a demon. There is no demon worship here."

"Oh, no? The *Bible* says there's no such thing as space aliens."

Rex winced. "The Bible says a lot of things about a lot of things, but I'm pretty sure it has no opinion on aliens one way or the other."

"Maybe not *your* Bible, but the King James is pretty clear on the matter."

Rex sat back in his chair. He consulted his wife with a look, then got up from the table. "I'll go fetch a KJV, and maybe you'd be so kind as to show me the verse. I'm always glad to learn new things."

"No need," Poppy said, unsnapping the Bible holster on his belt. "I carry my own." He drew his book and set it on the table.

The rest of the meal became somewhat strained as Poppy searched for the verse. Conversations sputtered. Flirtations choked. Dessert flopped. Cindy went into the kitchen to make coffee, and Deut excused the children from the room. The adults stayed on, and still Poppy searched, flipping pages in the old book with barely concealed frustration.

"If you have a keyword," Ginger offered, "I could do an online search." Poppy ignored her completely. "In *all* translations," she added. Her father warned her off with a frown.

The boys started discussing their day of shopping. A twenty-foot (6 m) U-Haul truck was parked on the street in front of the house. There was still room inside to fill, and they still had money to spend. One of the things they had purchased was a brand new Arctic Cat sno-go, still in its shipping crate. Although Lawther was the local Arctic Cat dealer, they had purchased it in Anchorage rather than from him. They'd never even discussed it with him. Rex decided not to bring the matter up; what good would it do?

There would be no shopping the next day, for it was the Lord's Day, a day of worship and rest. But not for Adam, who had received permission to drive the pickup to Soldotna to "help a friend move out of her apartment." Hosea volunteered to come along and help. Meanwhile, Proverbs was wondering if Ginger wanted to go ice skating with him at the new sports center (thanks but not really), and Rory was wondering if Deut would enjoy a movie at the cineplex (thanks but not possible).

Rex kept glancing at his watch. "I gotta head back to the shop," he said at last. "Tonight's a big night, and I've been away too long as it is. When you find the verse, just leave me a note, and I'll look it up when I get back." He stood up and nodded at Rory to accompany him.

"Here it is," Poppy announced. "For some reason I thought it was in Jeremiah, but it's actually in Romans. Chapter 8, verse 22." He marked the place with his finger while he checked to see if he had everyone's attention.

"'For we know that the whole creation groaneth and travaileth in pain together until now.'" He shut the book with a satisfied thump and fixed Rex with a challenging look. But Rex was slow to understand, and Poppy continued, "Let me explain it to you, deacon. Before Adam's sin, there was no death, and man was without fault. But the woman led man into sin, and death entered the world. Not only our world but all worlds everywhere. That's what this passage says." He tapped the book with a heavy finger. "'The *whole creation* groaneth' under the weight of Adam's transgression. That means that if there are people with souls on other planets, they too are part of His creation and they too die because of Adam. And in the final days — which are upon us — their planets will burn. And yet, since they are not children of Adam, they cannot be saved. For the Bible says that Elder Brother Jesus was the *second Adam,* not the second blue man, not the second space alien."

"Hmm," Rex said, "you make a point, Prophecy. Do you mind?" He took Poppy's Bible and reopened it. "Romans 8:22 you say?"

Poppy addressed the young people. "Space aliens, flying saucers, vampires, zombies, and werewolves are all inventions of Satan to spread demon worship in the world." He looked at Rory. "Tell me, boy, is your God a just God?"

"Yessir, He is!"

"Then why would He create a race of blue men to suffer eternal damnation and give them no means of salvation?"

"I don't know."

"He wouldn't. It would go against everything we know about the Father. That's how we know there are no space aliens."

LATER THAT NIGHT, as Rex and Rory were returning from the store, Rex said, "Before you go to bed tonight, I want you to gather up all your Star Trek and Star Wars memorabilia. The Doctor Who and Futurama posters and stuff too."

"But those are *science fiction,* Dad. It's not like they're *Harry Potter* or *Twilight* with all the dark magic and all."

"I know, son, but Prophecy makes a good argument. I'm a little embarrassed that I didn't see it myself."

"But, *Dad.*"

"I'll discuss the whole thing with Bishop Thornby, but in the meantime, it's probably a good idea to keep that stuff out in the garage."

NN6 1.0

FIRSTDAY WAS A day for unfinished business. Poppy idled the Camry in front of the Palmer police station. No matter what kind of hurt NJB had gotten himself into, the Prophecys owed him a lot. The least Poppy could do in return was to learn what had happened to him.

Still, Poppy despised the police in all their many shapes and forms, from meter maids to FBI agents, and everything in between. He'd found in his long and eventful life that the best defense against their bullying ways was to avoid them whenever possible. And so, despite his desire to learn about the bloodletting in NJB's house, he slipped the car into gear and drove to his next destination, the Palmer post office.

Poppy's business, HIS CREATIONS LLC, kept a post office box there that NJB checked for him on a regular basis. Although most of Poppy's business was conducted online, a sizable portion of his customer base was elderly and unplugged and still preferred to use old-fashioned paper order forms and personal checks.

Poppy's drawer-sized postal box was full to overflowing, another sign of NJB's prolonged absence. A pink card on top of the pile directed him to call at the parcel pickup window to collect even more. He did so, though it meant standing in line, and he despised standing in line about as much as he despised the cops. He gathered all of his mail and carried it to one of the tables next to a tall trash bin.

The envelopes contained checks and completed order forms. Some orders were for praying hands and other carvings, but most were for nativity sets and tree ornaments. While it was too late to fulfill new orders, it would be a shame to waste the payments. So he set about opening the envelopes, plucking out the checks, and tossing the remainder into the trash bin. Slit, pluck, toss. Slit, pluck, toss. He fell into the rhythm of the job. It was as mindless as shelling peas. The checks were stacking up, and they'd be able to add another three or four thousand dollars to their shopping spree.

One envelope contained neither check nor order form but a folded sheet of paper. Thinking it was a letter, he unfolded it and got a nasty surprise. No letter, it was a photocopy of what at first glance appeared to be an artsy, black-and-white photograph. It was taken in a studio against a fabric backdrop and was lighted for dramatic effect. The subjects were two completely naked men, one embracing the other from behind, the swollen shaft of his penis swallowed up in the rear end of the other. The man in back was a young black man and was no one Poppy knew. The shocker was the other man. It was unmistakably his friend and benefactor — Not Jeff Bridges — leering into the camera's eye.

"My sweet God!" Poppy exclaimed. Other post office patrons turned to look at him. He flipped the sheet of paper over, but there was nothing on the other side. The envelope was addressed to: Postal Patron, Palmer, AK

99645. The return address had been left blank.

After scooping up his stack of checks, Poppy stormed back to the pick-up window, cut to the front of the line, slammed the offending image on the metal counter, and demanded, "What in damnation is this?"

The postal employee, a bored-looking man in his 50s, glanced at the sheet of paper and said, "It looks pretty obvious to me what that is. Now, if you don't mind, there's a line ahead of you."

"Who sent this to me?" Poppy roared.

The employee simply lowered the metal shutter, closing the window. Poppy's fury exploded, and he hammered on the shutter with his hands. Other patrons backed away and left the building. When Poppy's arms grew tired, he marched down the aisle of postal boxes and headed to the retail lobby. Before he got there, another postal employee came out to intercept him. It was a small woman whose name badge identified her as the postmaster.

She disarmed Poppy with a look of concern and said, "May I help you, sir? I understand you received one of those horrid letters."

"I received this!" he bellowed, waving the offending photocopy in her face.

She retreated a step. "Rest assured that you weren't the only one. Every postal patron in Wallis and Palmer received one of those. They caused a big stink about a month ago when they started showing up. But it was legitimate mail, and we had to deliver it, even though we got many complaints. There was nothing we could do but warn people. You must have been out of town and missed that."

"Who sent it to me?"

"We don't know that yet. The postmarks on the envelopes say they originated in several small towns outside Topeka, Kansas. But rest assured, the FBI is looking into the matter. Especially after . . . "

Poppy felt a chill. "Especially after what?"

Poppy could see that he was frightening the woman, so he took a breath and tried lowering his voice. "My anger is a just and righteous anger, ma'am, but I apologize for unleashing it upon you, for I know it's not your fault." He wadded up the flyer and stuffed it into his coat pocket. "It's ugly business is what it is, and it took me off guard is all. I don't get into town too often, so it came as a nasty surprise. And now that I've seen the obscenity, I can never *unsee* it, if you know what I mean. I grieve for the innocence of any child who accidentally got a look at it."

The postmaster began nodding her head in agreement.

"So I feel I must at least learn the circumstances of the matter, if you would be so kind as to explain it to me. Who are those men? What has become of them?"

"Well, that young man is — was — the pharmacist at the Palmer One-Care Clinic" the postmaster said. "But he disappeared some two months ago. It caused a stir, but he was having problems at home, and he apparently told all his friends he wished he lived anywhere but Palmer. So folks figured he just left town without telling anyone. The other fellow is a local businessman. He also disappeared, shortly after that letter started showing up in everyone's mail. The police suspect foul play, but they're keeping tight-lipped about the whole investigation. The FBI came in to determine if there is any connection between the letter and the disappearances. That's all anybody knows about it."

Poppy thanked her for her trouble, retrieved the remainder of his mail, and returned to the car. *I swear on my life I never harmed anyone.*

NN7 1.0

IT WAS NEAR midnight when Rex returned from Greatland Action Sports, but Cindy and Ginger were still up and waiting for him in the kitchen. Their guests were all bedded down for the night. Rex sat at the kitchen table with a weary grunt and said, "What's up?"

Ginger glanced at her mother before launching into it. "They're leaving tomorrow, and Deut was saying how nice it would be if I visited them. I'd like to do that, spend the holidays with them."

"Where? In McHardy?"

"Yes, at their mine."

This was not a request Rex had anticipated, and he glanced at Cindy, who said, "I already told her I don't think it's a very good idea."

"Why not?" Ginger said. "I've lived in Alaska my whole life, but I've seen so little of it. Tourists see more of Alaska than I do. This is my last chance to experience real bush life before I leave for college. And I want to do it."

Rex was about to reply, but she wasn't finished. "Besides, I like her. I like Deut. We could be friends, I think, and she doesn't have *any* friends in the whole world. I mean, she has plenty of brothers and sisters, that's for sure, but there's no one else our age lives out there. I mean, except her twin, but I get the idea that they don't get on too well. Do you have any idea what that must be like? And their 'lord' prohibits TVs, radios, books, computers —

everything. So it's not like she can even have online friends."

This daughter of his always surprised Rex with the things she came up with. But this one was a stretch.

"And you're good with that?" he said. "You can unplug yourself for a few weeks?"

"I don't see why not. Anyway, I'll go on the bus with them and just stay till after New Year's. I can get back out to Glennallen on the mail plane or a charter. And Rory says he'll drive to Glennallen to pick me up. I already asked him. So, can I go?"

"Actually," Rex said, "I'm tending to agree with your mother on this. While I'd be curious to see the results of that experiment — you offline for weeks — what happens when Mr. Prophecy orders you to start calling him lord? Think you can do that?"

"He won't," she said breezily. "He hasn't asked me once or asked Rory either to call him that."

"Not here, maybe, but under his own roof?"

"The question, Dad, is whether or not you and Mom raised a responsible person or not. Have I ever let you two down? Have I ever gotten into something I couldn't handle? If you can't trust me to take care of myself in McHardy, Alaska, how are you ever going to trust me in North Carolina next year? I might as well forget about going to college."

The girl had a point. She usually did.

NN8 1.0

THE SHOPPING WAS done, the money mostly spent, and the Prophecys were returning to Stubborn Keep, never to emerge again. At least not on this Earth.

Sue Krae, Adam's betrothed, stayed overnight at a Wallis motel. Poppy went over there to interview her and pass judgment on the match. He asked her questions about everything from her relationship with her parents and the finer points of her faith to the kinds of skills and assets she'd be bringing to her new family. Her answers seemed forthright and respectful, and it was obvious that she was in love with Adam. Poppy asked her if she was forced to choose between her own life and the welfare of her new family, which would she choose?

The welfare of her new family, of course.

On the other hand, she was a coarse-looking woman with a slight whiff of trailer trash about her. Still, on such short notice and all, she was about the best Adam could hope for. So Poppy blessed the match and asked her to join them in the keep.

Afterward, Poppy pulled the Camry into the spacious Fred Meyer parking lot. He disentangled a shopping cart from the rack and rolled it into the bright, cavernous store to the pharmacy.

The Fred Meyer department store chain was a wonder, really. One-stop shopping had to be the crowning achievement of a materialistic society. You, the almighty consumer, could roll your cart down spacious boulevards lined on both sides and stacked to the ceiling with everything from paint to yoghurt, bullets to band-aids. You simply tipped whatever you desired into your sturdy wire basket on wheels.

In reality, there were no Aisles of Plenty. Fred Meyer was an illusion. It had no more substance than a public fountain. Shut off the water and all you had left was an empty basin.

Alaska had no large-scale agriculture of its own to lean on in times of disruption. Nearly everything Alaskans ate came up from the Lower 48. Alaska had no large-scale industry either (besides Big Oil and Government), and it imported every mass-produced item that Alaskans used. Everything. Alaskans were voluntary hostages to long, vulnerable supply chains of 18-wheelers, ocean barges and freighters, and no one seemed to notice or care.

People were sure to begin caring very soon when the supply chains were permanently broken by an inconvenient Apocalypse, and six hundred thousand residents all discovered at the same time that they couldn't buy food anymore.

Poppy scanned the faces around him as he pushed his cart. Future looters all.

In the pharmacy alcove, there were lines of shoppers at the cash registers. To stand in a line anywhere was galling enough for Poppy, but to stand in line in Alaska was doubly so. Reluctantly, Poppy joined the shortest one.

You could still find physicians in Alaska who were sympathetic to the bush lifestyle and had no qualms writing scripts for one's bush medicine chest. The Lawther's family doctor was one such physician, and he had written Poppy scripts for Amoxicillin, 800 mg ibuprofen, and a ninety-day supply of prednisone for Proverbs.

Ninety pills weren't much. Even if Proverbs could return in ninety days for a refill, Poppy doubted that this pharmacy would still be here. The pharmacy was sure to be the first target. Either the pharmacy or the firearms department. Or the liquor store.

Fortunately, Proverbs reconnected with a street pharmacist NJB had found him and managed to acquire three factory-sealed jars containing one thousand prednisone tablets each. That should tide him over.

After the looters had armed themselves, liquored up, and raided the pharmacy, they would tackle the canned goods, bottled water, and bulk food. They'd clear out the clothes and shoe departments. They'd haul off all the electronics though there'd be no way to use them once the electricity failed. The looters wouldn't stop until every shelf in the store was picked clean. A lot of them would spill their own blood in the mad rush and some would meet their Maker in these very aisles.

After placing his order, Poppy had forty-five minutes to kill before he could pick it up, and he wandered the store with his cart looking for anything else he may have left off the supply list. Condoms, for one. Tobacco for another.

Today, the future mob was pushing shopping carts around, planning dinner, and yakking on their phones. He pitied them even as he made his farewell tour of this whole, exploitative, delusional, intoxicating way of life.

In the corner of his eye, Poppy saw a woman rush by in a red and white track suit. He paid her no mind, but he saw her again a little while later in the frozen desserts aisle. A crowd of other shoppers was making a fuss over her. She had opened a freezer case, and frosty air was spilling out. He made a detour to avoid the scene except that he heard a man shout, "Give 'em hell, Vera," followed by cheers and applause.

Vera?

Poppy immediately backtracked. Abandoning his cart in the cheese aisle, he elbowed his way through the crowd.

There she was, with her hair in a bun and a huge pair of glasses framing her handsome face. The Barracuda of God. The anointed one. She was lovelier in person than any photo could capture. The common people of Fred Meyerland were loving her, and she was right there loving them back — with local gossip and pointed wisecracks.

Poppy grew faint. It was finally happening. Father God had brought them together at last.

How generous she was with her admirers, pressing their flesh, signing autographs, making slow progress toward the distant check-out lanes.

Finally, she raised her voice above the hubbub and announced, "It's a thrill to see you all, but Bradd's waiting for me in the car, and he won't be happy if this melts before I get there." She held up a quart container of

Gambardella's Double Dare Chocolate gelato.

People laughed and made way for her. But Poppy held his ground, and in a moment he was standing face to face with the governor. She gave him a quick once over, from the bald spot on his fuzzy head to the frayed cuffs of his oil-stained Carhartts trousers.

"Why, if it isn't Sourdough Sam," she quipped and held out her hand. "Hi, I'm Vera. It's always a pleasure to meet an old-timey Alaskan."

Poppy took her hand and held it gently in his own. He could barely breathe. He was never one to be so starstruck, and she almost pulled away before he managed to say, "NORAD of the North."

"Say again?"

"NORAD of the North, governor. A fortress within a mighty mountain where you will be safe from the greatest armies. I am Poppy Prophecy from McHardy, and me and my family have shelter there for you. Soon the seven angels will pour out their vials of wrath, and the beast will roam the land, and when they do, remember our meeting here today and know that you are welcome at Stubborn Mountain Keep. That is my oath to you. Stubborn Mountain Keep near McHardy, remember it."

The rabble around them tittered in embarrassment at his oath making, but not the Woman. No, Vera met his gaze directly and took his measure.

"Thanks," she said matter-of-factly. "I'll keep that in mind."

And then she was gone.

First Contact

FC1 1.0

ON TUESDAY MORNING when Jace awoke in his warm bed, the first thing that crossed his mind was that it wasn't too late to buy a ticket to Colorado. He didn't have to give up his search, just interrupt it for a while. He'd been scouring the flats for a week now without any results. He knew that he'd seen something unearthly there. The snow circle, though it had been erased by wind and weather, was proof enough. But for all he knew, maybe nothing ever touched the ground except a pressure wave. The falling fireball itself might have burned up so completely that it left behind only dust and ash floating on the breeze.

On top of that, the weather forecast said a cold wave was moving in, the first bonafide cold snap of the season.

Jace made the decision over coffee. He would hit it hard today, even skipping Mail Day, and if he didn't find anything, he'd buy tickets tonight and head to the Anchorage airport tomorrow. With the decision out of the way, Jace packed a lunch, gathered his gear, and set out for another day of grid-walking.

FC2 1.0

THE CARAVAN WAS ready to depart at 9:00 A.M., record time for the Prophecy family. Poppy and Proverbs would drive the bus, Hosea and Corny the pickup, and Adam and Sue Krae the U-Haul truck.

Uzziel would ride along in the truck to serve as Adam and Sue's chaperone shadow. Though what a little kid could do if the adults decided to sin or what a sin of that sort might even look like was a puzzle to the boy.

So far, family members had caught only glimpses of Sue, their future in-law. She seemed nice enough, though she didn't smile much. And she didn't look like the rest of them. That is, her features were angular and bony, not rounded and angelic. But Adam was smitten with her, and he smiled and joked around a lot when he was with her.

They started the engines and offered a prayer for a safe journey. Only Cindy Lawther was there to see them off. Ginger waved at her mother from a bus window. The U-Haul left first. Proverbs put the bus into gear to follow, but suddenly all the children were clamoring for him to stop. Calgary, the stowaway cat, was missing. Where was Calgary? They couldn't leave without Calgary.

It turned out that no one had seen the tabby for several days, though no one had noted her absence either. After a quick search of bus, house, and yard, Poppy declared the feline lost and ordered Proverbs to drive on. The children were appalled, but no one dared challenge his decision. Cindy said she'd take care of the cat when it returned, but that did little to reassure the children. And so the journey, which had seemed so promising only moments before, started with tears and grief.

Poppy was suffering his own loss. He had been mostly successful in banishing his former friend from his thoughts, especially after the encounter with Vera Tetlin, which he replayed in his mind in all its tiniest details. But when they passed the exit to NJB's neighborhood, the image of his friend engaged in sinful deviance came rushing back to him and filled him with revulsion and anger. Revulsion so deep and anger so bitter that not even

NJB's quarter-million-dollar endowment to the family could absolve him of his betrayal. *I swear on my life I never harmed anyone.* How could that be true when he saw the photo with his own eyes? Photos don't lie.

A COUPLE OF hours into the trip, while Poppy was taking a turn at the wheel, Proverbs went to the back of the bus to see if Ginger was comfortable. She and Deut were sharing a seat and talking nonstop. Proverbs gave Deut a hard look and asked her to go make the kids lunch. She replied that she'd already made their lunch, or didn't he remember the two sandwiches he himself had swallowed? He told her in that case she should make them a snack and not talk back to her elder. But when Deut got up to comply, Ginger went with her saying she wanted to help, leaving Proverbs by himself.

It was midafternoon when they reached Chitina but already dark. The place was deader than usual, and the caravan blew through town and didn't stop until it had crossed the Copper River bridge. They pulled over below the steep slope that marked Mile 0 of the McHardy Road. This stretch of road had once been the steepest gradient along the old copper mine railway. Today, a large, orange state highway sign stood on the shoulder of the gravel road and warned:

TRAVEL BEYOND THIS
POINT NOT RECOMMENDED

If that weren't enough, an even larger sign beneath it read:

IF YOU MUST USE THIS ROAD
Expect Extreme Cold/Heavy Snow
Carry Cold Weather Survival Gear
Tell Someone Where You Are Going

While the vehicles idled, the men gathered in the headlights to assess the driving conditions. The temperature was minus twenty-five degrees (–32 C), about average for that time of year, though it was forecast to drop overnight. A few inches of new snow had fallen since their trip out. They decided to put tire chains on the bus and U-Haul truck. From that point on they'd be crawling along. Sometimes it took longer to travel the final fifty-nine miles than the first three hundred.

The rattling, choppy ride rocked the tired passengers to sleep, and they slept as familiar landmarks passed in the the darkness: the collapsed trestle, the one-lane bridge, the drunken forest. They slept for three hours until they reached Milepost 33 where the caravan came to a halt in front of the first road glacier.

Here McHardy Road crossed a region of bogs and muskeg that never froze completely. Water flowed under the ice and flooded the roadway, freezing in layers and building up thick sheets of glare ice. Worse, the ice sheets weren't level but tilted with the natural downward slope of the countryside. Not even tire chains could keep vehicles from sliding sideways off the road. The snowplow had squared things off, but that was a week ago, and a new glacier had formed in the meantime.

The boys chained up the four-wheel-drive Dodge, and Adam took it across first. *No problem.*

The U-Haul was next. Hosea was the one with the hot hand at glacier driving, and he took the wheel of the ungainly truck. Proverbs and Corny spread a bag of sand on the road before him. Hosea eased the engine into gear and crept across the glacier.

Despite the tire chains, despite the sand, the truck slipped sideways as it moved forward, but Hosea kept the front end pointed uphill and sort of crab-walked it across. When he got to the other side, everyone cheered.

Hosea crossed back on foot for the bus. When he got behind the wheel, the children were bouncing in their seats. He bellowed at them to settle down and scowled at them in the mirror until they did. He threw the stick into the lowest granny gear and inched the bus forward. The sand helped, and though he slipped sideways, he managed to keep the unwieldy vehicle pointed in the right direction. And he might have made it across if he hadn't hit a patch of slush. The front right tire broke through it and sank to its axle.

The boys were prepared for this. They unhooked two stout wooden planks that were affixed to the sides of the bus. They used one plank as a base for jacking up the front end of the bus high enough to ram the second plank under the tire, bridging the gap. Meanwhile, Adam positioned the pickup at the other end of the glacier, chocked its wheels, and walked the winch cable across to the bus. When all was ready, they winched and powered the bus to solid ground. The children cheered again, and Hosea stood up to take a bow.

Ginger was astonished by the whole operation. "That was amazing," she said when they were moving again.

"You think so?" Deut replied. "There's three more glaciers ahead just like that one."

FC3 1.0

THEY PULLED INTO the parking lot at the end of the world just after midnight. They parked the three vehicles side by side and silenced the engines. The drivers got out to stretch their legs. It had gotten really cold out, as forecast, and they were exhausted. They pulled their hoods up and buried their hands in their pockets.

"Get to work," Poppy shouted from the bus doorway. He checked the spark plugs with a flashlight before tossing them out one by one. "Polaris, Yamaha, Skandic."

The Skandic refused to start, period, so they were down to two sno-gos and sleds. Deut and Cora put See-Saw, Revie, Uzzie, and Ginger in one sled and Ithy, Frankie, Myrrh, and Solly in the other and buried them all under blankets and sleeping bags. Cora rode behind Adam on the sno-go, and Deut rode behind Proverbs. And off they went.

Poppy and the others waited in the bus. Adam had loaded the U-Haul so that the perishables and freeze-sensitive cargo were easy to access, and it made no sense to unload anything until the sleds returned.

Hosea lit the bus's propane heater, and they sat wearily around it. There would be no sleep tonight for any of them, except maybe for Sue who was looking a little overwhelmed.

Hosea asked his father, "So when we get everything unloaded, lord, who's going to return the truck back to Anchorage?"

Poppy said, "No one."

"The rental truck, lord. We can't just keep it."

"This is the Apocalypse, son. If they want their truck back so bad, let them come out here and get it themselves. If they can."

The sno-gos returned in record time. They couldn't have traveled all the way home and back so quickly, and Poppy wondered if there had been trouble on the trail. But the sleds were empty. They had obviously dropped the children off somewhere, but where? Adam and Proverbs let the machines idle and joined the others in the bus. Adam seemed a little nervous as he explained the situation to Poppy.

"Deut said the children were getting cold and we should stop at the Bunyan's place to warm them up. I didn't want to put anyone at risk, so we did that, and while they're warming up, we thought we'd quick grab another load."

"What? That's foolishness," Poppy said. "They'll all be asleep when — What happens when you — Oh, never mind. Who's this coming here?"

Another sno-go had arrived in the parking lot.

"It's Chas Bunyan, lord," Adam said. "Dell's son." He pulled the lever to open the bus door, and the young man bounded up the steps. "You remember Chas, lord? You met him two summers ago. He's home on leave and wanted to help out."

Chas removed his face mask, revealing a large, open smile. He took off a glove and offered Poppy his hand. Poppy marveled at how Father God had brought this boy home at this exact time to help the Bunyan family survive the troubles. Crybaby Pastor Bunyan must be doing something right after all.

"We appreciate the help," Poppy said. "Pull around to the back of the U-Haul. The rest of you, out! Let's get this started."

They loaded the sleds: six cases of 24-dozen eggs, two hundred cases of canned meat and vegetables, ten 5-gallon buckets of latex-based paint, three hundred cartons of batteries, assorted electronics, shampoo and liquid soap by the gallon, medications and liquids of one sort or another, ball point pens, glue. Anything that could be ruined by freezing. They left enough room in one of the sleds for Sue. And they were off. This time Poppy ordered them to keep going all the way home.

AGAIN THEY RETURNED too soon, again with empty sleds. Adam apologized and said it was too cold for Sue who wasn't used to this kind of weather.

"So you dropped our things in the Bunyan yard to freeze?"

"No, lord. Pastor Bunyan said we could use their mudroom. Won't freeze in there, he says, and we can store it there until we can get to it. That's actually not a bad —"

"Idiot! You want to load and unload everything twice? You call that a good idea?" Poppy was inclined to say a good deal more, but, in fact, it was too cold to stand around jawing. So they loaded up the three sleds again, and this time Poppy rode in with Chas. He ordered Adam and Proverbs to go all the way home with their loads, no excuses this time, and to let Mama P and Sarai know they were coming. He'd be right behind them with Chas after he'd had a word or two with Deut.

At the Bunyan place, Poppy's body was so stiff with cold that he couldn't lift himself from the sno-go seat, and Chas discreetly and silently helped him until he was steady on his feet.

Chas said simply, "Cold." He wasn't a gabber.

They walked up the steps and into the mud room. Two sled loads of goods were stacked on the floor at the far end, leaving enough space for the rest of their perishables. It was well below freezing there.

"Maybe in most years this room won't freeze," Poppy said. "But tonight . . ."

"You might be right, sir," Chas replied. He picked cartons off the floor and stacked them on the benches against the house logs where they'd be warmer. "We'll get to them tonight or put them in the house. Don't worry; I won't let them freeze."

Inside, the house was dark and hushed. A single oil lamp burned in the chapel, otherwise known as the rug room. Eight bear rugs, made from the hides of local black or brown brutes, had been removed from their hooks on the walls and laid out as sleeping mats on the floor. The smallest six children were sleeping two to a bear. Even Deut was sleeping on a bear. When Poppy looked into the chapel, the Holy Spirit spoke to him and said, *Your girls will need spouses too.*

Poppy was still getting used to the idea of his sons finding wives and hadn't given a thought to the girls. He stole a glance at Chas.

Just then, Dell Bunyan moused into the chapel and drew Poppy and Chas to the kitchen. The remains of an impromptu meal covered the table and counters. The Bunyans had not only taken in Poppy's family but fed it too.

"I guess you met my son," Dell said. Saying even that much was enough to dampen his eyes. "He's a Navy SEAL; I don't know if I ever had the chance to tell you. He's seen action in Iraq, Afghanistan, the Gulf of Iran, and other places I'm not authorized to disclose." Tears began to leak down his cheeks.

At the sight, Poppy ground his teeth in suppressed rage.

Whether or not Chas would make a good son-in-law was unknown, but if the two families were joined in holy matrimony, Dell would become part of the family too, and Poppy didn't think he could handle that.

"Why don't you sit yourself here next to the stove, Mr. P," Chas said, ushering him to the kitchen table. "I told Scarlett to make up a guest room for you. But first Dad'll get you something warm to eat. Won't you, Dad?"

"You bet I will."

"Thanks, but I can't stay," Poppy said. "Too much work to do."

"Don't worry about that, sir," Chas said. "I can take it from here. If I leave now, I can catch up with Adam and Proverbs."

FC4 1.0

ENOUGH WAS ENOUGH. Late in the afternoon Jace called it quits and turned the Ski-Doo toward the Mizina spur trail and home. He'd given it his best shot; there was nothing more he could do. His sister Kate would be pleasantly surprised to see him. After months of cooking for himself, Jace was looking forward to her Christmas ham and cherry pie. Which reminded him — he needed to buy Christmas gifts along the way. Which further reminded him — he needed to winterize his house on Lucky Strike before departing. There was no sense in heating it while he was gone, and since it lacked water pipes, sink traps, and toilet tanks, he wouldn't have to worry about major freeze damage. But there were still things he needed to do, like emptying the kitchen slop bucket and moving all of his canned goods to the root cellar. The root cellar under the shed had proven to be a boon, just as Orion Beehymer had claimed when he first showed Jace the property. Summer and winter, it maintained a constant 38 degrees (3 C), the perfect temperature for beer, eggs, milk, fresh fish, and meat. It was as good as a 480 cu. ft. (14 cu. m) refrigerator.

So Jace's mind was elsewhere when he first spotted the light in the distance, and it took him by surprise. He stopped his snowmobile and consulted the GPS. The light appeared to be within his search area, and at first he supposed it came from snowmobile headlights. Someone had discovered all of his grid tracks in the snow and was investigating. But the light didn't move and didn't look like headlights. He stood on top of his seat and opened his helmet for a better view. The light shimmered a little, was rosy at its center, and radiated pale violet streaks around the edges. No, not headlights.

Then what?

Jace's heart began to pound.

FC5 1.0

FOR ALL THE time and effort Jace had spent chasing the tiger, he'd neglected to plan for what he'd do once he caught it. He pulled the Ski-Doo to within a dozen yards of the source of the strange light and stopped. A slender, glowing, translucent stalk appeared to have sprouted from the snow. It was taller than he, maybe eight or ten feet high (2.4–3.0 m), and it was crowned with a tulip-shaped bell. The bell threw off enough pinkish light to illuminate the entire area, but it wasn't too bright to look at directly.

Jace let the engine idle and climbed off the snowmobile. He knew where he was, at ground zero, the center of the snow circle and origin point of his search grid. He'd been right all along. This was it. Whatever it was, this was what he'd seen fall out of the sky.

Jace wanted to get a closer look at the odd lamppost and took a few cautious steps toward it. A child of *Star Trek*, he understood the profound importance, incredible fortune, and unforeseen dangers of the first contact between two intelligent species. A stupid blunder on his part could doom humankind to years of intergalactic warfare. A positive first impression, on the other hand, could launch a new era of innovation and discovery for both civilizations. He extended his arms out from his sides to show he carried no weapons. "Greetings," he said in a friendly, confident voice. "On behalf of the National Park Service, allow me to welcome you to planet Earth." He lowered his arms slowly and added, "I mean you no harm."

As Jace waited for a reaction or response of some sort from the tulip person, an incredible wave of fatigue washed over him. He felt like he'd been going non-stop for days. He shook it off and took another step closer. "Do you understand my language? I am a human being. What are you?"

The glassy stem appeared too delicate to support its own weight, let alone its tulip corolla. It tapered from about the thickness of his pinkie at the top to that of a spaghetti noodle at the ground where it disappeared in the snow. A gust of air should bring the whole thing down.

When Jace was confident that the lamppost was not trying to communicate with him, at least not on any channel he could receive, he took another step closer.

Maybe the thing wasn't a life form at all but a robotic probe, one of billions sown across the galaxy as part of a deep-space inventory of planets and solar systems that were ripe for exploitation. Maybe it was already transmitting data back to its Death Star, and he would be the alien race's first glimpse of an Earthling. What would inhabitants of Tulipia make of a creature with a high-impact plastic head and puffy nylon skin? If it was a probe, at least it hadn't vaporized him yet, as the ones on the ice world of Hoth were known to do.

Another possibility crossed Jace's mind. What if this oversized flower was neither person nor probe but the fruiting body of some kind of spacefaring, planet-eating, invasive species, the cosmic equivalent of elodea or bird vetch? Maybe, instead of welcoming it in the name of Earth he should be bashing it to pieces with a wrench before it could spread.

Not his call. Let NASA do that. Now that he had indisputable proof positive of a close encounter of the freaky kind, Jace would not hesitate to call in the experts with his discovery.

"I'm going now," he said. "I'll be back, with *scientists*." He turned and trudged to the snowmobile. Although only a few steps away, it felt like a long journey reaching it. Long enough for him to realize that he didn't actually have any more proof than he'd had before. Who would believe a story about tulip probes? He needed some kind of solid evidence. So he lifted the seat cushion of the snowmobile and grabbed the Canon camera he had borrowed from the backcountry gear room. He had to remove his outer mitten to operate the tiny buttons. Tulip person was probably impressed. *They can remove parts of their body at will! And reattach them!*

"I'm going to take your picture now," Jace said. "Your photograph. Photos aren't dangerous, and this won't hurt a bit. I promise."

The camera wouldn't turn on; the battery was completely dead. No mystery there. He'd left it out in the cold for days, and the battery was simply frozen. But he still had his iPhone. He always kept it buried deep in an inner pocket where it stayed nice and warm. So he unzipped and unsnapped and reached into his parka. *They can open their skin to reach inside their bodies!*

His phone was dead too. There wasn't even enough juice to display the lock screen. This was harder to explain than the camera; he'd charged it up at the ranger station yesterday and hadn't used it since.

Jace sat hard on the snowmobile seat. He needed to think. He needed to map out his next move. He reached into his parka again and retrieved his water bottle. He fumbled while opening it and dropped the cap in the snow. No matter, he drained the bottle and was still thirsty. His heart was fluttering in his chest.

The snowmobile engine, which had been idling unobtrusively, sputtered a few times, backfired, and died. The fuel needle was pegged at Empty. Another puzzle — he'd topped off the tank that morning.

Jace always carried three gallons of spare gas in a jerry jug, but when he checked the jug, it too was empty.

That was a problem because he was about twenty-four miles (39 km) from town. Ordinarily, he could hike twenty-four miles with ease. Once he'd hiked two hundred miles (322 km) of the Iditarod Trail in six days. But that was when he was in good form. Right now, Jace wasn't even sure he had a mile left in him. Why was he so tired?

He slouched on the seat and worried away at his plan. He might have even drowsed a bit. If this were a movie, he and everyone in the theater would be yelling at the schmuck on the screen to *Get off the snowmobile and run for your life!*

"I hear you," he said, jerking awake. He struggled to his feet. He would leave the snowmobile, leave the scene. It was good advice. Thank you, studio audience.

The first step was stupid difficult, and the second was just as bad, but by the third step he'd built up a shambling momentum that he was able to maintain, and he kept going. The further he retreated from the lamppost, the clearer his thoughts became. But physically he was still shot, and he stumbled on and didn't look back.

Once outside the reach of the alien light, it was too dark to see. Only the barest sliver of moon hung in the sky. He removed his helmet, letting it drop in the snow, and cinched up his insulated hood into a face tunnel. He figured his flashlight would be dead, but he tried it anyway. It was dead. He continued on by starlight, picking out the trail by the faintest of shadows in the snow.

After a very long time, another hard-packed track crossed the one he was on. He looked up to see where he was and realized that it was the track he had made the day of his trash run. It led to the trapline cabin that he had investigated. He could stop there and recover. And the Bunyan place was not much further. At least it was closer than town.

FC6 1.0

WHAT WAS HE thinking? Jace had known there was no stove in the trapline cabin, but when he arrived, he was surprised not to find one. For the last hour he had followed the odor of boiled cabbage on the breeze and had lived out a whole fantasy in which the cabin was finished and occupied and welcoming. It wasn't. It was empty and unfinished and cold. He sat on a sawhorse in the dark. With his flashlight and headlamp dead and his iPhone dead, he sought to illuminate the cabin with the little stub of plumber's candle that he always carried in his cargo pocket. But he couldn't find it. For that matter, his Bic lighter was empty too.

What Jace wouldn't give for some junk food around now. Warm, cheesy, juicy meat. He would ravage a Big Mac this instant if he could, even though the Big Mac said no a thousand times and begged for him to stop.

Oh, Mister Ranger, spare me. Spare me my secret sauce. Spare me my greasy virtue.

No! I will not spare you!

He did keep a few emergency energy bars in a pocket. He hadn't been able to find them while he was walking, but he turned out his pocket now and found two empty Clif Bar wrappers. They were still sealed, and when he tore one open with his teeth, all he found inside was a pinch of dust.

Impressive. The energy thief could eat a Clif Bar through its wrapper. Forget NASA; he needed the Army. He needed the Marines.

JACE WAS RELUCTANT to completely trust his senses, but the temperature seemed to have dropped off a cliff, as it had been forecast to do. He didn't have the spare energy to dig out his camp thermometer to check. Just say it had gotten cold and leave it at that. It was better to concentrate on the task at hand which was one thing and one thing only — making it to the Bunyan house alive. Nothing else mattered. Anything that distracted him from attaining this goal was inherently evil and must be resisted. Anything furthering this goal was good and must be trusted. Life could be simple when it hung from a thread.

Whoever had renovated the cabin had used the Trapper's Slough Trail to bring in material. This trail joined the Stubborn Mine Trail four or so miles away. Six miles further was the Bunyan place. About ten miles all told (16 km). Ten miles. He could do ten more miles. He had ten miles in him. He launched himself up the trail.

ALTHOUGH JACE WAS half-asleep and ready to drop, he didn't feel the cold. That was because when he had first come north, he put together a set of winter gear that could handle anything the Alaska winter could dish out. For parka and overalls he went with a brand that competitive dog mushers wore on the trail, Apocalypse Design. It was made in a little shop in Fairbanks by a guy named Dick and his team of needle monkeys.

Jace's boots were Eiger Polars made by Baffin. They were rated to minus 148 degrees (−100 C). Unlike other shin-high snowmobile boots, they crossed over well for hiking, as he was proving to himself one tired step after another. All in all, he was glad he'd spent the money.

If anything, Jace was feeling a little too tropical, even at his snail's pace, and he was tempted to open his parka to cool off a bit. You didn't want to sweat in your gear if you could help it. It fouled the insulation and left you chilled when you stopped moving. But Jace wondered if he was really overheated or just imagining it? Delusions at sixty below (−51 C) could be deadly. Nevertheless, Jace unzipped his parka halfway down his chest and opened the flaps. He still felt warm. Which senses do you trust, the ones telling you it's *really* cold out, or the ones telling you you're roasting? He unzipped a little more.

When Jace left the flats and entered the forest, the starlight turned the trail into a dark corridor in which the walls were only slightly darker than the floor. As long as he stayed equidistant from the walls, he was bound to be on the hard pack. Tack too close to either side and he'd stumble into deep snow. He'd lost the trail twice already but had been able to find it again both times. Otherwise, the corridor walls never changed, and he might as well be hiking in place on a slightly inclined treadmill. Until it curved, that is, and then he knew for sure he was still making progress. Constant Progress was a good thing and his Prime Directive.

People did just that, undress before they froze to death. The EMT trainers at the academy had covered it. He'd seen the photos. The clothes neatly folded and stacked in the snow. Next to them the nude victim curled up in a snowbank, like they crawled into a warm bed. What was going on in their heads so that their last act in life was not only undressing in the cold but taking the time to fold their clothes? Whatever train of thought that takes you to that place is a train you never want to board, and Jace swore an oath to himself then and there that if he ever saw that train coming down the tracks he would let it go by. You don't want to be one of those people, Jace, the dumb fucks lying blue-cheeks-up in a snowbank.

After a little while, Jace was feeling chilled, and so he zipped up again. See? His senses were working fine, thank you very much.

Just then, a yellow cab pulled up alongside him, and the driver leaned out the window to size him up before zooming away in a cloud of French fries. It made him laugh out loud. So, things had gotten to the point of full-on hallucinations. That was a welcome sign. Jace had experience with hallucinations. Hallucinations were harmless. They could be good fun. It was the delusions you had to watch out for. It was the delusions that could kill you.

JACE HEARD THE approaching snowmobiles before he saw their headlights poking through the trees. He couldn't imagine who would be out riding after midnight in this cold on this trail, but he would be most grateful for a lift. Also to warn them not to go down to the river flats.

The machines passed from left to right without coming any closer.

At first he took them for another hallucination, like all the baby turtles on the trail he'd been forced to step over for the last hour.

Then he realized that they weren't on the same trail as he. They were on the Stubborn Mine Trail, and he was nearing the intersection. He also knew who the riders were, the Prophecys, home from wherever they had been.

Reaching the main trail forced Jace to reconsider his decision to turn left to the Bunyan place. At the intersection, the Bunyans were still about six miles away, three times further than the Prophecy place. If he turned right, he could be at the Prophecy door in an hour or so. The question was — would they be willing to put aside their hatred of parkies and flat hats long enough to let him in, or, as was more likely, would they be content to watch him freeze to death on their porch? (She would be there. Would she plead his case?) If they did help him, they'd want to know what he was doing out here on foot after midnight in this cold, and the last thing he wanted was for that family of all families on the planet to learn about the alien artifact. Yet, regrettably, his tracks in the snow would lead them directly to the prize, and there was nothing he could do about it. On the other hand, if they messed with the artifact, as he had, it might kill them, and wouldn't that be a fucking shame?

Jace decided to deal with the artifact later. If he remained at the Y in the trail much longer, he'd freeze in place. So he turned left and plodded on to the Bunyans.

FC7 1.0

SOME TIME AND many baby turtles later, Jace heard the snowmobiles again, this time approaching him from behind. They sounded real enough, and he wanted to jump off the trail and hide in the trees until they went by, but he just didn't have enough spark left in him to do so. A pulse of anger flooded his weary brain, and he wished he was carrying a gun.

Of course, if the tulip had been able to eat his Clif Bars through the wrappers and slurp his gas from the tank, what chance was there that bullets would have any gunpowder left in them?

Rumbling, gaseous, blinding: the snowmobiles nipped at his heals. Men were shouting at him, but he continued slogging up the middle of the trail. Finally, one of the machines roared past him in the loose snow. It regained the trail in front of him and stopped. Now he was boxed in, and he stopped too.

"Who is it?" the man behind him shouted over the engine noise.

"It's the ranger," replied the one in front. The man was wearing a hood and thermal mask in lieu of a helmet, but Jace recognized the voice as belonging to the youngest of the three. Proverbs was his stupid name. The other one was Adam. Any man who names his firstborn Adam must have a God complex.

"Which ranger?"

"The one lives in town."

"What's wrong with him?"

"I don't know."

"Well, *ask* him."

"Hey, Ranger Rick, how're things?"

Jace tried to reply, but his jaw wouldn't work and all that came out were mumbles.

"What he say?"

"I don't know. Hey, ranger, you okay?"

What Jace wanted to do was to ask for a lift to the Bunyan place.

"Well?"

"He looks half-froze."

While the interlopers were discussing his situation, Jace saw that the freight sled blocking his way was empty. Moreover, it was pointed in the right direction. It looked real enough, and so, without over-thinking matters, he climbed aboard and lay down. Christ, it felt good getting off his feet. Wake me up when we reach Kalamazoo.

Jace's trip was short-lived. One of the men was pulling his feet.

"What're you doing?" the other one said. "He needs help."

"That don't mean we have to be the ones to help him."

"Of course it does. The Samaritan finds an injured man on the side of the road."

"This ain't Samaria. You heard Poppy. It's the Apocalypse. The center don't hold no more."

Proverbs dragged Jace off the sled and into the snow by the side of the trail. Adam didn't help, but he didn't intervene either. Jace tried to get to his feet but couldn't manage it until Adam helped him up. When Jace was standing on his own, Adam said, "There you go, Ranger Rick. This is how we found you, and this is how we'll leave you. Good luck now. You're free to go. And as you do, never forget that as long as you draw breath, it's never too late to pray for forgiveness and save your soul."

The brothers returned to their idling sno-gos, but they didn't leave right away because another sno-go was approaching them from the direction of the Bunyan place. The boys waited until they could identify the driver, and then they dismounted again, and Adam returned to Jace, who was standing where they'd left him. "Looks like it's your lucky day," Adam said as he lowered Jace back into the sled.

A strange face hovered above. "Is he conscious?" someone said, blinding

Jace with a light. "Why don't we trade rigs. I'll take him home and get him warmed up." He bent closer and sniffed Jace's breath. "Hello, ranger," he said in a loud voice. "I'm Chas Bunyan, Dell's son. Just lay back now and hang in there, and we'll go to my dad's place. All right?"

FC8 1.0

IN THE FAR recesses of the rug room, cloaked in darkness, Deut sat up and for a moment didn't know where she was. Some sound had awakened her, and there were voices coming from the other end of the room. Two men, Chas and the pastor, were helping a third man take off his parka. They sat him down in an armchair near the wood stove and removed his boots and leggings.

It was the ranger.

The cute one.

Was he hurt?

The pastor left the room and returned a few minutes later with a china mug. Chas helped the ranger sit up and sip from it. The pastor left again and returned with a saucepan, which he used to refill the mug. Then he gathered up the ranger's things.

The children sleeping on bear-rug islands surrounding Deut made hushed sleeping sounds in the darkness. Deut was too far away to hear what the Bunyans were saying, but the ranger seemed to be sick or something. The pastor and Chas left the room, left the ranger alone with his mug of soup.

It crossed Deut's mind that it might be improper for her to be staring at a man the way she was staring at the ranger, but she found that she couldn't turn away. When her father entered the room, she ducked down, though surely he couldn't see her in the dark. He loitered in front of the ranger for several moments, not saying anything.

When her father left, Deut got up and tip-toed across the room. The ranger was asleep. The china mug had fallen from his hands and spilled what looked like cocoa on the wood floor. Deut crept closer. She came so close that if he happened to open his eyes he couldn't help but see her. She wasn't very presentable. She was wearing the same old clothes she'd worn all day in the bus, and her hair was a mess.

But he wasn't a pretty picture either. There was a week's worth of stubble on his cheeks and chin. His long brown hair was spiking out in all directions. His eyelashes were matted with melted ice. And there was a cocoa mustache above his upper lip, which she had to admit was kinda cute. She crept a little closer.

What made some men handsome and others ordinary? People always said her brothers were handsome, especially Adam and Proverbs, but she couldn't see it. They looked so ordinary to her. Mama, before she went to Heaven, had told her that Father God makes some people attractive to other people so they knew who He wanted them to marry. But the last person in the whole world she would be free to marry was a flat hat. So why was he so disturbingly beautiful?

He had a nice nose, straight, narrow, and with a chisel tip. His eyes — she'd never seen his eyes up close, and now they were shut. She didn't know what color they were, but she guessed brown. Her own were blue. His voice she had heard on only one occasion, and then he'd only spoken a few words. But it was enough to tell her that his voice was warm and melodic. His skin was darker than any of her brothers'. Certainly darker than her own. With a racing heart, she extended her arm to place her wrist next to his. What a contrast in size and color. She almost wished he did open those eyes of his and see their hands so close together. What would he think about that? What would he say?

A sound in the hall alerted her to someone's approach. She darted across the room to her rug, barely avoiding the sleeping lumps along the way.

FC9 1.0

POPPY WAS NODDING off at the kitchen table. He roused himself when he heard a sno-go enter the Bunyan yard. He opened the kitchen door and waved at the rider, who turned out to be Adam. Adam pulled up next to the back porch. He was driving Bunyan's machine. He came inside and shut the door.

"Is the ranger here, lord?"

"Yeah. Dell's boy drug him in. What happened out there?"

"Not sure, but Proverbs found something you should see."

"What is it?"

Chas came into the kitchen just then. He greeted Adam and said, "I'm almost ready to go out again."

"Thanks," Adam said. "We still have a lot to move."

Chas turned to Poppy. "Well, we got the guest room set up for you. Any time you're ready . . . Oh, I hope you don't mind. We're putting Ranger Kuliak in there too. It's a king-sized bed, so I hope you're okay with that."

Poppy snorted. "I never slept with a man yet, and I don't plan on starting now."

"In that case, I'm sure we can find—"

"Don't bother. I don't plan on sleeping until the work is done and then sleeping in my own bed."

Poppy climbed back into his arctic gear and joined Adam outside. They left the Bunyan rig next to the kitchen porch and retrieved their own from the front yard.

"You were telling me something," he said to Adam.

"Yes, lord. The parkies are up to something out on the flats since we were gone."

"What is it?"

"Not sure, lord, but we should maybe check it out." He helped his father into the sled and covered him with sleeping bags. "It's out by Proverbs' cabin."

FC10 1.0

ADAM IDLED THE old Polaris next to the renovated trapline cabin. He switched on his headlamp and led his father to the top of a little rise overlooking the valley. "Look over there."

Below them lay an ocean of darkness, and upon it sat a little island of brilliant light. Adam handed his father binoculars, but they didn't help much.

"What do you think it is?"

"I don't know, lord. A work camp of some sort?"

"How far would you say?"

"Two, two and a half miles."

As they watched, the light dimmed and faded to black.

"Can you find it?"

"We can follow the ranger's trail." Adam tilted his head to illuminate Jace's tracks in the snow.

"Then let's go see what those federal dicks are up to."

"Now, lord?"

Poppy returned to the sno-go. "Now."

FC11 1.0

THE HEADLIGHT CAUGHT something shiny in the snow alongside the trail, and Adam stopped the sled next to it. It was a rider's helmet, abandoned or lost.

They continued on without speaking and soon came to an area where multiple sets of tracks, both human and machine, crisscrossed the trail in an orderly pattern. Adam pointed them out to Poppy without slowing down. Finally, they came to the ranger's abandoned sno-go, and they stopped. They knew it was the ranger's sled because it had a decal emblazoned on its side with the despicable arrowhead logo of the National Park Service.

"Warm enough, lord?" Adam said, helping him off the seat.

The old man ignored the question and went to work inspecting the area with a flashlight. "They're looking for something," he said, illuminating the labyrinth of tracks. "Must be pretty important."

"Lord," Adam called. "Over here."

"What is it?"

"I . . . don't know."

It was a wonder that Adam had found the thing in the darkness at all, so thin and insubstantial it seemed. It resembled a tall glass reed. No ordinary glass either because, Adam confessed, he had accidentally stumbled into it.

"And it didn't break?"

"No, lord. It's stronger than it looks."

With their flashlight and headlamp they picked out purple threads embedded in the glass, like tiny, spinning pinwheels. Poppy shined his light along its length to the bell at the top.

"What do you think it is, lord?" Adam said.

"One way to find out." Poppy reached under his parka for the socket wrench he always carried in his bib pocket.

"What are you doing, lord?" Adam said. "Don't break it."

"Have faith, boy. You didn't break it when you ran into it, did you?" He handed his son the wrench. "Here, hit it."

Adam accepted the wrench but only lightly tapped the delicate-looking object with it.

"I said hit it, boy. Give it all you got."

"Yes, lord." Adam hesitated but swung the wrench and delivered a good smack. The object clanged but did not shatter.

"Harder!"

Adam swung again with no more effect.

"Honestly, you swing like an old woman." Poppy took the wrench and delivered the heavenly object a resounding blow. The impact stung his hand through his glove, and the wrench flew out of his grasp. It landed in the snow and was buried.

While Adam searched for the wrench, Poppy pushed the snow away from around the bottom of the object. It was rooted in solid ice.

"We need to dig it out," he said.

"Why don't we wait for daylight? We could bring tools with us. And besides, there's still freight to move tonight, and it's cold."

"We can't wait. The rangers already found it. It's too important to let the government have it."

They used a screwdriver and hammer from the sno-go tool kit to chip the ice away. Every few inches they dug, they tried pushing the object over. It was strong enough to take their combined weight. Eventually, they felt something give, and they rocked it back and forth until it came free from the ground.

A Vial of Wrath

VW1 1.0

JACE WAS TRYING to piece things together. He was in a strange bed in a strange room in his underwear. A nice room, to be sure, with embroidered pillowcases and wall-to-wall carpeting. The last thing he remembered of the night before was confronting the Prophecy boys on the trail. Had they brought him to their place after all? No, this couldn't be their ramshackle house.

His clothes were draped over the back of a chair. He was getting out of bed, feeling more tired than he ever had in his life, when the door opened and a young man looked in. "Good, you're up," the man said. "Breakfast is ready." He looked Jace over and added, "You okay? Need any help?"

"No, I'm good, uh . . ."

"Chas Bunyan," Chas said. "Dell's my dad. I'm home from the Navy. You might be a little confused. I think you might have got a little hypoglycemic last night on the trail. Are you diabetic?"

"No."

"I wasn't sure. Anyway, breakfast is on the table. There's a toilet down the hall. Get dressed and come on out to the kitchen."

ON HIS WAY to the kitchen, Jace peeked into the rug room. No one there but dead bears and a lynx or two.

Flapjacks, sausages, scrambled eggs, canned peaches, and coffee. Seconds, thirds, another percolated pot of coffee — there was no bottom to Jace's appetite.

Chas joined him at the table, but all he had was coffee.

"Thank you," Jace said, "for taking me in."

"Don't mention it. I'm only glad we caught you in time."

"We?"

"Adam and Proverbs had you loaded in a sled. I brought you here and poured sugary cocoa into you. That seemed to perk you up."

Jace remembered something about a sled, but it was hard to fathom the boys actually helping him. "You're in the Navy?"

"Yeah, I'm a SEAL."

Jace's estimation of the man rose. He seemed — level-headed — like his father but without all the religious hooey. He seemed — trustworthy.

"By the way, ranger — "

"Call me Jace."

"By the way, Jace, I'm curious. What were you doing out there on foot?"

Jace wondered if he should confide his secret to this man. After all, they were both uniformed agents of the same Uncle Sam. Until that moment he hadn't given much thought as to how to proceed. There was no question that he needed experts to take charge of the alien artifact. But maybe not the military. Anyone who ever watched sci-fi films knew that the military's first impulse was to smash whatever it didn't understand, not study it.

"I was doing some field work on the Mizina," Jace said, "and my machine quit. It's a long walk back."

"I'll say. But don't you guys have backup or something?"

"Well, I filed a trip plan," Jace lied, "but Masterson wouldn't come looking for me unless I failed to show up this morning. Which reminds me, I'd better call in. Do you have phone service out here?"

"We're on the edge, and it's spotty. But at these temps it's usually pretty good." Chas rose from the table. "I'll get my phone. And then I'll take you out to fetch your snowmachine."

"Not necessary. Masterson will do it. About time he started earning his keep."

"Masterson, eh?"

"Yeah, our LE Ranger."

"I've heard about that one."

"Better hide your kittens."

They both got a chuckle out of that.

WHEN JACE REACHED Masterson on Chas' cell and told him about his mechanical problems, Masterson said, "Leave it where it is. Weather's supposed to warm up in a few days. We'll get it then. I'm up to my tits in Nips right now. Ask Dell to bring you in."

"I think we should get it now."

"What's the rush? Sounds like it's not going anywhere."

"The Prophecys know it's out there."

"The Prophecys left for Anchorage."

"I know that, but they returned last night. They saw me on foot on the trail, so they're bound to figure out my ride was crippled. You want to give them time to go out and put a bullet through the engine block?"

It was a shame to use the Prophecy card, but it was effective, and after a drawn-out pause, Masterson said, "I'll be there in an hour. I'll bring tools."

"Bring gas too."

"You ran outta gas? That's your so-called mechanical problem? You got high and forgot to fill up before you left?"

"No and no. Bring a come-along too and about a hundred feet of tow rope."

"Just what kind of mechanical trouble you have anyway?"

"And binoculars. Bring binoculars. And a camera with a telephoto lens if you have one."

VW2 1.0

DAWN LIGHT TRICKLED through the frosted window of the prayer cabin. The sound of sno-gos entering the yard awakened Poppy. He lingered under the warm heap of comforters trying to remember why he had chosen to sleep in the prayer cabin instead of the house where it was warm. The boys had continued to work through the night transferring their critical supplies from the rental truck, and it sounded like they were still at it. He remembered telling Adam to build a fire in his stove, but it must have gone out hours ago, leaving none of its heat behind.

Poppy heard multiple voices in the yard, laughter, bickering. He braved the bitter cold of the cabin to scrape ice from the window and look out. His children were home, but it wasn't his sons who had brought them. The Bunyans had, the pastor and his daughter, Scarlett. The old crybaby had finally gotten the playdate for his kid he'd been angling for at Mail Day.

There was only one thing for Poppy to do — restart the fire and go back to sleep until the Bunyans left. But when he searched the floor for his slippers, his foot bumped into something, and it all came flooding back: the strange light on the flats, the tracks in the snow, the heavenly object they had brought here so he could pray over it. It was nearly as long as the cabin itself. He reached for his trousers and unsnapped the Bible holster. If this thing was what he thought it was, he'd surely find mention of it in Revelation.

VW3 1.0

IF ANYTHING, SARAI had grown bossier while they were away. "See-Saw, you bunk with Cora, and Revie bunks with Frankie."

"Nuh-uh," Cora said. "No way. Let her bunk with Myrrh. I'm the elder, and I'm not sharing my bed."

"Not fair," Myrrh said.

"Not fair," echoed her twin.

Sarai threw up her hands. "Fair? You want to talk about what's fair in this house?" She told Deut to deal with them and stalked out of the bunkroom. The girls all turned to Deut.

"It's only for a little while," she said. "Ginger's only here for a couple of weeks, and Adam will figure out something for Sue."

"It's okay," said See-Saw, the littlest girl. "Can I sleep with you?"

"Sure," Deut said. "You and me, sister." She turned to Cora, but Cora was fifteen years old and dreamed of having her own bedroom to herself. So she looked at the twins.

"*Fine*," Frankie said. "We'll take turns. Revie can sleep with me one night and with Myrrh the next. *Satisfied?*"

"Thank you," Deut said. "I'm glad you're all being so helpful. Elder Brother Jesus must be smiling."

The girls went back to unpacking their little travel bags but stopped to watch when their guests came in. Ginger had a carry-on bag and a duffel, while Sue wheeled in two large suitcases. She set them in the middle of the room and scanned the beds. "Which one's mine?" she said.

"This one," Deut replied, patting See-Saw's bunk. "As soon as we get the sheets changed."

"Don't you have a top bunk," Sue said. "I don't like bottom bunks."

Revie's bed was also a lower bunk. "*Fine,*" Frankie repeated. "I'll trade her."

"Thanks," Sue said. "In the meantime, I'll take a shower. After yesterday, I'm pretty rank."

The girls giggled. "We don't have a shower," Myrrh said. "We have a bathhouse."

"But bath day isn't until Sixthday," Frankie added.

"Oh?"

Deut said, "Cora will show you how to get a basin of warm water in the kitchen."

Cora sighed theatrically and headed for the door. "Follow me."

Deut called after her, "Thank you, Cora."

Ginger, meanwhile, was wandering around the room holding up her cell phone. "I can't seem to find a signal," she said.

Deut said, "That's because the mountain is in the way."

"Then how do I call my parents?"

"You can't, unless you ride into town."

The twins covered their mouths, and Frankie said, "I'm sure Proverbs will take you, Miss Ginger, if you ask him."

Ginger snorted. "I'm sure he would, but I'd rather drive myself. I've been handling snowmachines since I was six, you know. My dad sells them."

VW4 1.0

WHILE WAITING FOR Ranger Masterson to take him out to ground zero, Jace rehearsed in his mind how the recovery should go down. He had chosen to reveal his find to his colleague rather than to Chas, he supposed, because Masterson was the devil he knew. Given Masterson's views on the mission of public land management, upon seeing the alien artifact, his overriding concern would be for containment. Keep a lid on it. Keep the situation from becoming a media stampede and harming the wild nature of the park. Masterson would work with him.

So when Masterson showed up and again asked Jace what had happened to his snowmobile, Jace shrugged and said, "See for yourself." It was early afternoon; they had a couple hours of daylight left. They hopped on

Masterson's machine and took the outbound Stubborn Mountain Trail to the Trapper's Slough Trail.

This was Jace's plan: about a hundred feet (30 m) before they reached ground zero, Jace would tap Masterson on the shoulder to stop. Then Jace would pop the lens caps off the binoculars and hand them to him saying:

> *I was across the river last week when I saw a tiny sun float down to Earth inside a giant cone of welder's glass. I mapped out a search grid covering the probable impact point and spent the last week walking the area with a metal detector. I was about to call off the search last night when I saw a weird light here. I checked it out and found that thing . . .*

He would point at the thing, whose tulip top should be visible in the daylight above the scrubby, snow-covered brush.

> *I didn't understand the danger and got too close to it, and it stole all of my physical energy. It stole the gas from my tank, too, and the juice from my batteries, and the butane from my lighter. I was lucky to make it back at all.*

Then, using the tow line and come-along, they would ratchet his snowmobile out of the danger zone. Then they would document the artifact with photos and videos from a safe distance. Then they would go back to the office and put in a call to NASA. One alien-spouting ranger was crazy. Two alien-spouting rangers, one of them a licensed peace officer, with photos and GPS coordinates would . . . should . . .

So Jace got on the back of Masterson's snowmobile, and they left the Bunyan place. What he had failed to factor in was how Masterson would react when he saw the renovated trapline cabin along the way. Jace had forgotten that the trail to the artifact led right past it.

Masterson brought the snowmobile to a sudden halt. "What the fuck," he said and dismounted. Jace's tracks to the cabin were still clearly visible, as well as an adjoining set on top of them. Masterson looked in the cabin window with his headlamp and went inside. Jace stayed with the machine and waited.

When Masterson returned, he was clearly furious, and Jace said, "Let's discuss this later, okay? You probably have some questions, but believe me, this cabin isn't the main event. I swear to you, there's something way more important up ahead. And dangerous."

Masterson took control of himself and got back on the snowmobile without comment. They continued down the trail. Jace saw at once that the Prophecys, or someone on a snowmobile, had already followed his tracks to the artifact. When they came upon his discarded helmet, Masterson stopped for him to retrieve it.

Jace braced himself for the scene he would witness just ahead: one or more bodies at the foot of the alien lamppost, all life sucked out of them. The near certainty that they would be Prophecy bodies did little to lessen the horror (but he refused to feel guilty for their misfortune).

When they passed into the search zone with the checkerboard of tracks, Masterson pointed at them and shouted over his shoulder, "What the hell?"

"Keep going," Jace shouted back.

When they were still a hundred feet from ground zero, Jace tapped Masterson's shoulder as planned and opened the binoculars. Masterson braked the snowmobile and took in the scene.

"Mind telling me what the fuck is going on out here?"

Jace couldn't see the lamppost from where they had stopped, so he dismounted. "Follow me. All will be revealed."

Jace approached ground zero cautiously, like a hunter, expecting to see the tulip looming over the treeless landscape at any moment. So he was surprised to come upon his Ski-Doo parked where he'd left it, the camera still resting on the seat, and no tulip, no lamppost, no Prophecy bodies in sight. He hurried to the spot and found the hole and ice chips.

"They took it!" he wailed. "They fucking took it!"

Next to him, Masterson regarded the hole. "I'm still waiting," he said, "for any of this to make one shred of sense."

"Okay, okay," Jace said. "This might sound crazy."

"That's a given."

"I was across the river last week when I saw a tiny sun float to Earth inside a giant cone of welder's glass . . ."

VW5 1.0

DELL BUNYAN AND his daughter left. The girls got their city guests squared away. The toddlers were warned to be on their best behavior and to stay away from the towering pile of supplies stacked in the middle of the common room. And no one was allowed near the boys' bunkroom where the older boys and Corny were sleeping off their exhausting day and night of driving and hauling.

Poppy never came in from the prayer cabin for breakfast. He was probably sleeping in too.

The boys dragged themselves out of bed in time for lunch. Sue stuck close by Adam's side, and Deut instructed Ginger in the finer points of cooking on a wood-fired range.

The children stared with open mouths as Sue massaged Adam's shoulders. Adam arched his back like their missing cat and said, "I'd let you do that for hours, but it's getting late, and we haven't accomplished anything yet today. Ithy, how cold is it outside?"

The boy pulled a chair next to the window to check the outdoor thermometer.

"Forty-two below (–41C)," he announced.

"Oh, good," Adam said. "It's warmed up some."

Hosea and Proverbs both looked at Adam, who sighed and said, "I don't want to hear it."

Proverbs spoke anyway, "I thought the whole point of getting this stuff in was so we could leave the rest in the truck till things warmed up."

"And besides," Hosea added, "the sno-gos both need some attention. We gotta repair the Yamaha track as it is."

Adam rose and paced the room as he pondered the situation. At last he said, "Proverbs, you work on the Yamaha. Hosea, start figuring out what part of this pile needs to go to the storeroom first. Hasn't Poppy come in at all?"

Sarai said, "No."

Adam went to the window and scraped ice so he could see the prayer cabin. "At least he's up." There was smoke coming from the stack. "We can use the plastic sleds to move stuff up to the keep. If he comes in and we're all sitting on our hands . . ."

He left the thought unfinished, and Sue said, "Surely, you deserve a day off after all that work."

Adam smiled at her. "Doesn't work that way around here, babe." He fetched his parka from a peg next to the door. "I'll just go see what his plans for the day are. Sarai, quick make me up a tray for him. Meantime, you boys get a load started."

POPPY DIDN'T ANSWER Adam's repeated knock. The door wasn't bolted, so Adam opened it a crack and said, "It's me, lord." When there still was no response, he opened it a bit more and peeked in. His father was seated at his desk, reading the Bible. He was dressed for the outdoors — boots, parka, hat — and Adam could see his breath in the frosty air. The thing, the bizarre object they had wrested from the ice, lay on the floor where they had left it last night. Adam brought the tray inside and bumped the door shut with his hip.

"It's warmer in the house, lord," he said, placing the tray on the desk next to the open Bible. He went to reload the stove, but the firebox was already full, and the flames roared and cackled. Yet, Adam could feel little heat coming out. Damp wood maybe. He shut the cast-iron door and cranked the handle tight. Made sure the intake and damper were open and clear.

"I came to see what you're doing out here," he told his father. Poppy continued to ignore him. "And to let you know we'll wait till it warms up a bit before hauling in the rest of the supplies. Instead, we'll start moving the perishables up to the keep."

Poppy's head snapped up. "Did you tell anyone?"

Adam looked at the object at his feet. "No, lord. You told me not to."

"Well, don't. I have so much to learn about it first." He did a double take when he saw the lunch tray lying next to his elbow. He picked up the moose roast sandwich and began to eat. "I think I know what it is," he said between bites. "That terrible light I witnessed? A falling star. If it was, then this is the trumpet that belongs to one of two herald angels. Either the Third Angel or the Fifth Angel, in Revelation. The Third Angel poisons a third of the waters of Earth, and the Fifth Angel holds the key to the bottomless pit of Hell. [see *A Taste of Wormwood* on page 353]

"But I'm not finished studying it, and I don't want you talking about it."

"No, lord, I won't," Adam said. "Anyway, like I said, we'll need the key to the gate."

The dozens of keys on Poppy's keyring came in all shapes and sizes. He unthreaded an old brass key and dropped it into Adam's hand. In turn, Adam gave him a spark plug.

"Where's the other?"

"Um," Adam said. "Proverbs must still have it."

THE TOBOGGANS WERE of the molded-plastic variety you could buy at Fred Meyer. They were toys meant for fun on sledding hills, not tools for hauling freight in the extreme cold. One trip up the tailings slide was enough to reduce two of them to a handful of colorful plastic shards.

So Adam suspended all non-essential outdoor chores. Instead, he and Hosea assigned the middle boys to tasks within the keep, of which there were varied and many. Sue went along to learn and help.

The house was mostly empty in midafternoon when Poppy surprised Sarai by slamming the front door and bellowing, "Gather round! Gather round!"

Sarai came out of the kitchen. See-Saw came out of the girls' room with Nummy and Elzie.

Poppy surveyed his small audience and said, "Where is everyone?"

Sarai said, "Some in the keep. Some in the toolshed. Some in the bathhouse."

"Round them up! Everyone. I have important news!"

Sarai sent See-Saw to the outbuildings to round everyone up and to tell Cora to go up to the keep. Poppy visited the kitchen and poured himself a cup of coffee while he waited. The common room filled with voices, and when everyone returned from the keep, Sarai came into the kitchen to inform him. Poppy couldn't decide whether she was being surly or sullen with him, but either way he didn't like it. However, now was not the time.

Poppy crossed the common room to the corner where he usually presided over Worship Time. He leaned over Mama P and crooned, "Wake up, Mother. You won't want to miss this." She didn't stir or open her eyes. "Soon, Mother," he whispered. "Soon you will have to decide."

When his congregation settled around him, Poppy cleared his throat and intoned, "You have borne witness to the glory of the Father. You have seen His handprint in the snow where He pressed me down and deprived me of breath."

"Yes, lord, we have," chorused the children.

"You have borne witness to —" Poppy broke off and said, "Where's Proverbs?"

Adam sighed and said, "I told him he could take Ginger to the Bunyans', lord."

"Why? Did she have enough of us already?"

"I don't think so, lord. She said she wanted to phone her parents to let them know she arrived safe."

"And that couldn't wait until Mail Day?"

"Mail Day was yesterday, lord. She would'a had to wait a whole week."

"And when does Proverbs intend to return?"

"Soon," Adam said. "Anytime now."

Poppy was not pleased, and Cora chose that moment to add a bit of information of her own. "She's got her own phone, lord."

"What was that?"

"A cell phone," Cora said. "Ginger Lawther brought a cell phone with her."

Now Poppy was even less pleased. He looked at Sue and startled her with a direct question. "You have a phone too?"

"Uh, yes," Sue said. "I do."

"Yes, *lord.*"

"Excuse me?"

"You will address me as lord."

Sue glanced around at the others and hesitated only a moment. "Yes, lord, I do have a cell."

Poppy extended an open palm. She reached into her jeans pocket and surrendered her phone to him.

"And another thing," Poppy went on. "From now on you will dress like a woman, not a man."

Sue glanced at the girls in the room, all of them in long skirts.

"I'm sorry, lord. I didn't know."

"Don't fret over it, daughter. You'll learn our ways soon enough. In case you need 'em, there's dresses in all sizes in the storeroom. Sarai will show you where."

"Thank you, lord."

"Now, daughter," Poppy went on, "Adam tells me you are a faith-filled young woman, but I'll bet you didn't expect to come here to witness miracles."

"No, lord, I didn't. What miracles?"

"On the night before we came to town, our Heavenly Father revealed to me a terrible light in the sky and a pressure that all but suffocated me.

"But what I didn't know then was that something fell to Earth from Heaven on that same night. Something precious and perfect."

"What was it, lord?" the smaller children clamored to know.

"It was something that an angel in Heaven lost on Earth."

Amid their cries of amazement, the children shouted, "What was it, lord?"

Adam squeezed Sue's hand and they joined the chorus. "What was it, lord?"

"It was something the federal devils tried to steal while we were away."

Gasps. "What was it, lord!"

"They were the same devils that stole our garden patch and airstrip.

"Last night, while your brothers were busy moving this great pile of provisions, the flat hats tried to steal what the angel had lost, but Elder Brother Jesus smacked them down with His mighty hand."

Small mouths hung open.

"Elder Brother Jesus struck the ranger's sno-go who was trying to steal from the angel and forced him to walk all the way back home with his ponytail tucked 'tween his legs."

Deut looked up. Ponytail?

"So now," Poppy continued, "who wants to see a wonder that was wrought in the forges of Heaven?"

"We do! We do!"

"Who wants to proclaim all glory to the Almighty?"

"We do! We do!"

"Then turn on the lights, and I will fetch it for you."

The winter sun was gone, but the girls had lit only one of the propane lamps in the common room. Cora dashed to light the other two. Poppy stepped outside and left the door hanging open. Dense air flowed over the threshold in a river of fog. A minute later he reemerged carrying a long, sparkly object. When he held it over his head for all to see, it threw off rainbow shards of light.

Everyone cried out in wonder, even Adam who had discovered it, and Cora said, "What is it, lord?"

"It's what it looks like. It's a herald's trumpet. An angel's lips touched it just last week when one of the seven seals was broken and a vial of wrath poured out.

"Which angel and which seal I don't know yet, but I will continue to study and pray until the Holy Spirit reveals the answers to me.

"I don't know why the angel came to drop his trumpet, but it proves one thing beyond a shadow of doubt, something we already knew, that the Last Days are upon us. After all, that was why we went to town for our final supply run, wasn't it? That was why we encouraged your brothers to invite their betrothed to join us in our keep."

Sue squeezed Adam's hand. *Betrothed?*

Frankie said, "Why is the trumpet so long, lord?"

"It might seem long to us, child, but angels are not puny creatures like we are. They're more like giants. In fact, before the Flood, when angels sometimes married human women, their children were a race of giant s called the Nephilim. But Father God didn't approve of his angels marrying human women, and He let their children drown in the Flood. Not even giants could tread the floodwaters for forty days and forty nights."

The children hung on every word.

Sarai said, "What makes you think it's from Heaven, lord? It just looks like glittery glass to me."

No one understood why their sister was always challenging their father. The congregation grew quiet and studied its feet.

But Poppy seemed not at all bothered. "It does look like glass, don't it?" he said merrily. "I'll give you that. It probably *is* glass, but glass made in Heaven, not our corrupted kind here on Earth. How do I know this? Watch, I'll show you."

Poppy stepped between the ceiling-high pile of supplies and the large wood stove. The stove had been fashioned from the firebox of a steam engine boiler, and it dominated the common room with its plate-iron immensity. Poppy grasped the trumpet like a long bat and wound himself up for a swing.

"Don't break it, Poppy!" See-Saw shrieked, and the other children took up her plea. "Don't break it, Poppy!"

But he only grinned at them and swung the glass trumpet in a shimmering arc. It struck the side of the stove with a resounding *thwanng* that reverberated in their ears. The congregation sang out cheers and praise, but the dog slunk out of the room.

"Again," the children cried. "Again."

Poppy struck the stove again and again to the same effect. He called Hosea forward to take a swing. At first Hosea, running his fingers along the instrument's delicate throat, held back, much as Adam had with the wrench, and barely tapped the stove. Adam jeered him, and he took another swing, this time with all his bulk. *Thwannnnng* sang the trumpet, jolting his hands.

"Blow it," Cora urged, and the others chanted, "Blow it. Blow it."

Poppy hushed them with a look. The party was abruptly over. "I would sound the trumpet if I could," he said gravely. "Archangel Michael might hear the blast and fly down to fetch it, and we would all get to meet an angel. But look here, the mouthpiece is stoppered by this golden marble."

The end of the trumpet didn't seem shaped for human lips, and it was indeed plugged by a small golden ball. Poppy tried to pry it out with a dinner knife, but it was jammed in too tight.

"It prevents air from passing," he explained. "It's some part of the mystery I haven't ironed out yet. Tonight we will all pray for knowledge."

VW7 1.0

IN THE COMMON room, few of the wall logs were left bare. A traffic jam of hooks, shelves, and cubbies spread across every wall and stored everything from dishes and hand towels to weapons, tools, fiddles, and tambourines. Poppy circumambulated the room twice looking for the perfect spot to display the family's new treasure. The trumpet should have a place of honor; it should have an entire wall to itself. But it would take a lot of reshuffling to make that happen.

The sound of approaching sno-gos interrupted Poppy's task. It should have been his wayward son and his son's betrothed, gone now for hours without permission or chaperone. But there were two engines pulling into the yard, and neither of them sounded like the family's Polaris.

Poppy handed the trumpet to a boy and told him to take it to the bunkroom. The children in the common room put aside their games. Footsteps crossed the porch. The dog sniffed under the door. There was an authoritative knock, as if with bare knuckles, once, twice, three times.

Poppy gestured for everyone to vacate the common room. They stampeded either to the kitchen or one of the bunk rooms where they crouched at the doorways to watch.

When Poppy opened the front door, there were two rangers standing there. He didn't offer to let them in, though frigid air flooded into the house.

"What do you want?"

The taller of the pair, the law enforcement ranger, spoke, "Was that you or a member of your household that rebuilt the trapline cabin in Trapper's Slough?"

"Come again?"

The ranger repeated his question.

"Where's Trapper's Slough?"

The ranger scowled and got right to the point. "The cabin on Trapper's

Slough and all of its improvements and chattel are solely the property of the National Park Service, which alone has the authority to maintain it and regulate its use. Is that clear?"

"Is what clear?"

"Use of the Trapper's Slough park service cabin requires a reservation. You can obtain a reservation application at the park information office in Caldecott during normal business hours, which won't resume until April 8, 2013. Or you can register on our website. Is that clear, sir?"

The other ranger, Ranger Rick, was attempting to peer around Poppy into the room, and Poppy half shut the door to block him.

"I said, is that clear, sir?" said the first ranger.

"Is what clear?"

"Any unauthorized use of that cabin is considered trespassing and a violation of federal regulations, and violators *will* be prosecuted to the full extent of the law. Is *that* clear, sir?"

Poppy met the ranger's simmering gaze and said, "What's clear to me, Ranger Danger, is your intolerance for Christian people who are only trying to live the way Father God told them to live and your hatred of *His* law."

He tried to shut the door, but Ranger Rick blocked it with his boot. "We're not finished, sir," he said. "You are in possession of National Park Service property."

"I am?"

"Yes, sir, and I demand you return it at once."

"You do, do you? You *demand*? Do you also demand the sun to rise in the morning and the stars to twinkle at night?"

The ranger turned to his partner and said, "See? I told you he has it." He turned back to Poppy and said, "Return it at once."

"Return what?"

"Don't play games with me, sir. You know what I'm talking about. The artifact that you dug out of the ice down by the Mizina. It's the property of the park service, and under the Antiquities Act it's a federal crime to remove it."

"And you'll persecute me to the full extent of the law. I already know that."

"I'll obtain a search warrant and search your property."

Even while attempting to intimidate Poppy with the law, the young ranger's eyes continued to search the room behind him. Then he asked an odd question. "Anyone here sick with fatigue and weakness?"

Was that some kind of threat? "Go get your search warrant," Poppy said. "It won't do you no good since I didn't find any ar-ti-fack. Now the two of you better get yourselves off my property while you still can." With that he swung the heavy door shut.

The children returned to the common room, their excitement stoked by this latest run-in with the federal devils.

Poppy waited until he heard the rangers' sno-gos fire up and leave the yard. Then he said, "Fetch me my coat."

Sadly, the house was no place to keep the herald's trumpet.

VW8 1.0

THE MACHINE ROOM on the first level of the keep had once served as a steam-driven manufactory for the modest copper mine. Today, rotting leather belts hung from rusted pulleys. Gargantuan iron gears meshed with shafts and wheels of forgotten purpose. Two coal-fed boilers sat under air shaft chimneys that were blasted from solid rock. Along one stone wall of the chamber stood a row of stout, wooden workbenches. Their tops were gouged and grease-infused from decades of rough service.

Upon one of these workbenches Poppy reverentially placed the trumpet. He became mesmerized by its shimmering reflection in the lamplight. He longed to keep it forever, a keepsake of Heaven, but he knew he must try to return it. And the most straightforward way of doing that, as the children had guessed, would be to remove the little ball from the mouthpiece and sound it. He imagined himself standing at the entrance to the keep, raising the long instrument to his lips, pointing its bell toward the heavens, filling his lungs with pure Arctic air, and blowing. Before long, Michael and Gabriel would glide down on feathery wings and hover overhead. With a knowing smile, Poppy would hoist the glass trumpet in the air with one hand and the golden marble with the other and say, *Lose something, boys?*

Wouldn't that be something?

He already knew the trumpet was indestructible, so when he put it in the vice, he squeezed the jaws extra tight without fear of damaging it. He used a variety of tools to try to tap, pry, or heat the marble loose. Nothing doing; it was stuck good.

Poppy lost track of time in his efforts, and long after his belly began to complain, he heard someone's footsteps in the tunnel. It was his wayward son.

"Family's waiting dinner on you, lord," Proverbs said. "They sent me out here to . . ." He broke off when he saw the trumpet. "It's true!" he said, turning his head to shine his headlamp along its sparkly length.

"Of course it's true. You think your father's a liar?"

"Never, lord. What I thought was that Adam and the others were playing me for the fool. I mean, an angel's trumpet? You don't see one of those every day, do you?"

"I don't guess you do. Tell me, boy, how are those stripes on your back healing up?"

Proverbs grimaced and offered his father the spark plug. "I wanted to apologize for that, lord. There's no excuse; it's all my fault. Ginger was desperate to call her folks to let 'em know she was okay. She said they'd worry themselves sick if she didn't call and she wanted to drive there herself. I wanted to get your permission, but you hadn't come out of the prayer cabin, and yesterday was such a hard day on everybody, and I didn't want to disturb you in case you was sleeping or praying, and, well, I wanted to show Ginger I could take care of her in case, you know, she ever decided to like me.

"I know you love me, lord, and how you never want to, you know, spoileth me, but I was hoping you could make a tiny exception this time?"

Poppy puffed himself up with righteousness. "And let you slide without an accounting?"

"No, lord. I done wrong. I know I must be punished. All I'm asking is for maybe you can find another way to punish me that won't, you know, scare her away before she has a chance to get to know us.

"Like maybe give me my licks here." He showed Poppy the three birch switches he'd brought with him.

For a solid moment or two, Poppy felt genuine pity for his son. His resolve to raise him up right almost crumbled on the spot. "If it was a simple phone call, that would'a been one thing," he said, "but you were gone all afternoon, boy."

Proverbs shrugged. "What could I do, lord? They needed some help moving some solar panels. Chas is building an extension to the house, and Dell's got a pulled muscle in his back, or so he says. After all they done to help us last night, I couldn't just refuse, could I? I asked myself what you would say, and I heard you tellin' me to help 'em. Was I wrong?

"And that girl of theirs — Scarlett? She glommed onto Ginger like shit on a log, and it was all I could do to separate them. Believe me, lord, I tried."

Poppy said, "I do believe you. But I'm not hearing anything to change my mind."

"Yes, lord, I understand."

Poppy picked up his lantern. "And as far as scaring her off goes, if she can't bear to watch the loving administration of just punishment, then maybe she's not the right kind of girl for us in the first place." He turned and headed for the tunnel.

"Yes, lord. I can see that. I guess Chas is a better match for her anyway."

Poppy stopped abruptly. "What did you say? Is the Bunyan boy interested in her?"

"I can't say that he is, lord, but she sure took to *him*."

That was a problem. Poppy approved of Chas, what little he'd seen of him, and he thought a match with Deut might be favorable. But if Chas paired up with Ginger, it would eliminate two possible Prophecy matches in one stroke.

"Tell you what," he said. "I'll pray on it."

"Thank you, lord."

"Now let's go. We don't want the babies to go hungry."

"Yes, lord, except I gotta ask you — you blow the trumpet yet?"

"Can't. There's a marble lodged in it."

"That's what I heard."

"It's in there good, and it's not coming out."

"Did you try blowing it out?"

"Don't talk stupid, son. I just told you, it's plugged up so you can't blow it."

"I meant from the other end. Wait." Proverbs went to another part of the chamber where decades worth of worn-out machinery was collected in bins and piles and returned with a short length of rubber hose. He jammed one end into the bell end of the instrument as far as it would go. Taking a couple of deep breaths, he blew into the hose. His cheeks bulged. His face turned red.

With a pop, the marble detached from the trumpet and flew across the chamber, bouncing like a pinball against the discarded machinery. "There," Proverbs said, catching his breath. "That's how it's done."

Poppy was amazed. Why hadn't he thought of that?

"Blow it, lord," Proverbs said. "Let's hear the sound of the throne room."

Poppy was as eager as his son, and he loosened the vice and lifted the trumpet. Without the marble, it weighed next to nothing. The end resembled a pipe fitting more than a mouthpiece, but that didn't stop him from trying to wrap his lips around it.

He blew. Nothing came out the bell but old man's breath. No resounding blast. No call to war.

"Here, let me try," Proverbs said, putting his hands on the instrument. "I've blown a bugle before. You have to shape your lips."

"No!" Poppy said, wrenching the trumpet from his son's grasp. He filled his lungs and tried again.

Ffffffp.

"That's better, lord. You're getting the hang of it. Do it again."

Another deep breath made Poppy lightheaded, and before he could blow, his fingers started to tingle.

"What's happening?" Proverbs said. "The trumpet . . ."

The glass was turning dull and cloudy, and it broke apart in Poppy's hands. The pieces fell to the stone floor in sizzling heaps of sand. The sand continued to disintegrate until all there was left was a thin layer of dust.

Poppy gasped. He groaned. He grew faint.

VW9 1.0

WHEN THEY RETURNED to the big house, Proverbs kept his head down and tried to make himself invisible.

Everyone was still talking about the angel's trumpet, and the little ones begged Poppy to show it to them again. When he refused, they said, "But Ginger hasn't seen it, lord."

"Whose fault is that?" he snapped. He dragged a chair to the warm corner, signaling that it was time for worship.

Ginger approached Proverbs. "Did you see it?"

Proverbs nodded and went to sit alone on the outermost ring of siblings. Ginger hadn't expected that and was pleased. Maybe he was capable of taking a hint after all. She pulled a chair and sat next to Deut.

Worship Time was brief that evening, and the homily got straight to the point: Never get ahead of yourself.

Poppy did not open by welcoming the newcomers to their home. He did not lead his family in a prayer of thanksgiving for the success of their supply run to Anchorage or for the unexpected gift of cash from NJB, which filled so many of their corporal needs. He didn't mention the trumpet once. Instead, he read from Obadiah:

> *Though thou exalt thyself as the eagle, and*
> *though thou set thy nest among the stars,*
> *thence I will bring you down, saith the Lord.*

Before Poppy could raise his terrible visage to glower at his family, Ginger's bright, young voice piped up.

"What verse is that, Mr. Prophecy?" Ginger had her own Bible open on her lap. It was the same one Deut had looked at in Ginger's bedroom in Wallis, a small volume with a cheery blue cloth cover.

"Obadiah is only two pages long," Poppy replied. "Maybe they left it out of your Bible."

"No, it's here. Oh, here it is, fourth verse."

Poppy waited in silence until she looked up at him. He said, "I understand you brought a cell phone into my house."

"Uh, yes, I did."

"Only Mama and I have phones in this house. It's a rule. I should'a told you to leave it behind in Wallis."

"I didn't know."

"It's my fault for not telling you, but no harm done. Kindly give it to me." He held out his hand."

Ginger froze. She was clearly undecided what to do.

"You'll get it back when you leave," he added.

"But . . . but it's how I communicate with my family."

"Don't worry about that. We'll call them every Twosday when we go in for the mail."

Still she hesitated.

Poppy said, "Sue has already given up hers."

Sue nodded in confirmation.

At last, Ginger rose and handed him the phone saying, "It's not like there's service out here anyway."

"Thank you."

"You're welcome."

"You're welcome — what?"

Ginger knew the answer to this question. She had anticipated it and decided on a proper response before leaving Wallis.

"You're welcome, Mr. Prophecy."

Poppy shook his head. "Close, but no prize. You can address any man as Mr., but the head of your household, however temporary, you address as 'lord.'"

"I don't believe that's true. What do you base it on?"

If the whole conversation were not dangerous enough already, Ginger's challenge to debate their father made the room hold its breath. But Poppy merely raised the Book from his lap in response.

"On this," he said.

"Actually," Ginger said, "I don't think so."

Little Myrrh began to cry.

"You don't think so?" Poppy said mildly. "That should put the saints at ease. Let me toss your question back at you. What do you base *your* opinion on?"

Ginger sighed. Pity that it should come to this on her first day here, but there was no avoiding it, and maybe it was for the best. If she caved now, her entire visit would be miserable. Besides, she had rehearsed in her mind for this very confrontation. So she raised her own Bible, mimicking him, and said, "Likewise, of course."

"Go on."

All eyes went to Ginger, standing there in defiance of the Truth and the Law. When she spoke, she was addressing the girls in the house as much as their lord.

"The word 'lord' appears in the Bible, no matter *which* translation you use, more than 6,700 times. That's a lot for any word in Scripture. But every time it's used, it clearly refers either to the Lord God or to the Lord Jesus Christ." She thumbed through the book, stopping at random pages and found an example on nearly every page: "Then the Lord God said . . ." "I am the Lord, the God of your father Abraham . . ." " . . . offering before the Lord." "For you know the grace of our Lord Jesus Christ . . ."

"Clearly," she concluded, "the Bible reserves the term 'lord' for God and does not condone its use for earthly men." She closed her Book, sat down, and balanced it on her blue-jeans-clad knees. She took pains to stifle any urge toward Pride.

All attention turned to Poppy, who had listened calmly throughout Ginger's argument.

"There's a reason why children in his house do not read the Word without guidance, my newest daughter, and you just reminded us of why. I, myself, never bothered to count how many times the Holy Spirit uses 'lord' in His book, but clearly — as you say — clearly you have built your foundation on sand. It would take only one exception to undermine your whole argument. And here is that exception."

Poppy turned the pages of his Bible but stopped and closed it. "I have a better idea. Since you brought up the subject of Bible translations, I will show you the proof using your own false Bible." He returned his own Bible to its holster on his belt and snapped it shut. He extended his hand and said, "If you don't mind."

Ginger, looking less certain than a moment before, went forward to hand him her Bible.

He took it and said, "Stay here so you can see with your own eyes and be instructed."

Poppy weighed the book in his hand, thumbed through its pages, sniffed it, then turned to a chapter in the Book of Genesis and read:

> Now Rachel had taken the household idols and put them in the camel's saddle, and she sat on them. And Laban felt through all the tent but did not find them.
>
> She said to her father, 'Let not my lord be angry that I cannot rise before you, for the manner of women is upon me.' So he searched but did not find the household idols." (Gen 31:34, 35)

Poppy leaned toward her, pointing at the word in question with his stubby index finger. Ginger stared in disbelief, as though he had just conjured up the impossible. She went to her chair, but returned for her Bible.

"You'll get it back," Poppy said, tucking the book under his arm, "along with your phone when you leave." He glanced at her legs and added, "And your manly clothes. My daughters will loan you womanly clothes to wear while you are here."

Ginger still had some fight left in her. "This is ridiculous," she said. "It's the *Bible*. It's *mine*, and I want it back."

"Return to your seat and shut your mouth," Poppy said, paraphrasing Paul's message to the women of Corinth.

Ginger was stunned. She didn't know what to do. And while she was still off balance, Poppy concluded Worship Time with a final thought.

"Therefore, our Lord Father God tells us in Obadiah, fourth verse, not to put our own selves up on a pedestal, or He'll be obliged to knock us down. Let us give thanks, amen."

"Amen!" echoed the household. The little ones stampeded to the tables and tucked in their napkins.

Poppy did not stay for dinner but told Deut to make him a tray and to bring it to the prayer cabin. He had a long evening's worth of study ahead of him.

He left the house marveling at the cleverness of the Holy Spirit. Obadiah's text had not only served to knock him off his own high horse in regards to blowing the angel's trumpet, but it knocked that uppity girl down a few pegs as well. Only time would tell if she learned her lesson.

VW10 1.0

IN THE MORNING, Poppy returned to the machine room with an LED lantern, their most powerful flashlight, and a broom from the kitchen. First he examined the rock floor where the trumpet had disintegrated, but it was impossible to distinguish heavenly dust from decades worth of rock dust. So he swept it all up and deposited it in an empty cardboard carton to be stored securely. Some of the dust sparkled as it floated in the air.

Then he proceeded to the vast graveyard of obsolete machinery in the chamber and began searching for the golden marble. He got down on his ancient knees to check under the rusting hulks. He searched the entire chamber but couldn't find it. He grew so weary of bending down and standing up that he had to take rest breaks. His lantern and flashlight, bright when he had started, were gradually losing their charge. They needed fresh batteries, and, frankly, so did he. *Give me strength, Lord, to see things through to the end.*

Poppy left the keep, and as he was climbing down the tailings slide, Adam arrived at the bottom on a sno-go pulling a freight sled. The weather had warmed overnight into the twenties below (–29 C) and their temperamental Skandic was running again. So, while Proverbs was assembling their new Arctic Cat sno-go on the parking lot, Adam, Hosea, and Corny resumed transferring supplies from the rental truck.

They had to leave the supplies at the foot of the slide, however, because the switchback turns were too sharp for sno-gos to negotiate. The final lift would have to be done by hand with toboggans.

At the bottom, Poppy watched his son unload the sled. Adam grew nervous and said, "Is the trumpet okay, lord? Proverbs claims that . . ."

Poppy waited to hear what Proverbs was claiming. He hadn't instructed Proverbs to keep the matter secret; and he was curious. But Adam changed the subject, telling him how positive Sue's first impressions were of their household.

"I only wish you didn't call her my betrothed, you know, before I got a chance to pop the question myself. It made things . . . awkward, lord."

"Listen," Poppy said, cutting him off. "I want you to head out to where we chiseled the trumpet out of the ice. Collect the ice chips in a plastic bag and bring them to me."

"Yes, lord. I'll do that this afternoon."

"No, do it now."

"Yes, lord, except if I wait till Proverbs gets the new sno-go up and running, we can keep three sleds on the trail and —"

"Now. I said now."

VW11 1.0

POPPY WAS STUDYING in the prayer cabin when Adam returned with the bag of ice chips. Poppy poured them into a coffee mug and set the mug next to the wood stove. He figured that some of the chips must have been in direct contact with the golden marble.

An hour later, he sniffed the meltwater. There was no odor, and the liquid was colorless and clear, like ordinary water. So he wetted a finger and tasted it. It tasted like meltwater with no hint or trace of wormwood. Praise Father God.

Still, the test results wouldn't be final till he repeated it with the actual fallen star. Which continued to elude him in the machine room.

VW12 1.0

AFTER A MEAL and a nap, Poppy returned to the slide. Although he was still strong, he was old, and he loathed having to climb to the keep more than once a day. Plus, the fatigue he had experienced earlier in the day hadn't lifted completely, despite the meal and nap.

The middle boys were already hauling supplies up the slide on their remaining plastic toboggans. Even burdened with heavy loads, they passed Poppy twice by the time he reached the top.

At the gate, he collared two of them, Ithy and Uzzie, and told them to follow him. They all donned hardhats and hiked the tunnel to the machine room.

An hour later, Uzzie found the golden marble. Being the smaller of the two boys, he had crawled under the wreck of the carriage of a steam-powered drill. The drill sprawled in pieces against the south wall of the chamber, directly below a large ventilation shaft.

"I still can't reach it," he yelled.

"Go fetch your brother the broom," Poppy told Ithy.

The ventilation shafts handled the air exchange for the entire first level when the gate was shut. The system relied on natural convection to move the air up the twenty-foot (6 m) shaft. Poppy zipped his coat against the draft and yelled into the chamber behind him, "What's taking you so long?"

Ithy returned with the broom and passed it to his brother under the machine.

"Got it!" Uzzie said, and a wobbly golden marble rolled into the open. Ithy gaped at it.

"Are you stupid?" Poppy asked him. "Bring it here."

Ithy grunted as he picked up the marble. "It's heavy," he said, "and look — it's got ears."

Poppy took the marble and was surprised that his boy was right; the marble was heavy, two or three times heavier than an equal amount of lead. He had't noticed its weight while it was still attached to the trumpet. And it did have ear-like flaps, soft and pliable. Like they might have been their own marbles once upon a time but lost their innards. They must have been hidden inside the trumpet mouthpiece.

"Will it explode?" Uzzie said, crawling out from under the machine and dusting himself off.

Poppy was about to criticize the whole notion of an explosion but checked himself. For all he knew, the marble might explode at that. He smiled at the boy, the smartest brat in the brood. With his innocent question, he had hinted where his father could keep such a valuable and mysterious bauble — in the powder room.

Poppy dismissed the boys. "Now git, the both of you, back to your chores." But as they fled the machine room, he called Uzzie back. "Before you go, fetch me some water from the cistern." He took a glass jar from a shelf and tipped its collection of metal washers into another jar of bolts. "Here, use this. Rinse it out good first."

Poppy set the heavy marble on a workbench and turned on a lantern to get a good look at it. He leaned over to sniff it. Was that a hint of brimstone he smelled? He went to a far shelf to retrieve a tray laden with old padlocks. There were dozens of them, and they came in all sizes. The newest were Master locks dating from the middle of the 20th century. The oldest were heavy, old brass antiques with skeleton keys. Paper tags told where in the mine each lock had been used, but the ink on the tags had faded away. Poppy selected a relatively modern, case-hardened Master lock and threaded its keys onto his already overburdened keyring. He wrapped the marble in a rag to make it easier to carry. Then he leaned over and picked up the carton of trumpet dust.

The powder room was located on the same level as the machine room but deeper inside the mountain. Poppy carried his burden only so far as the ramp intersection, where he waited for the boy. Soon Uzzie's footsteps echoed in the darkness above, and a moment later his headlamp lit up the ramp.

"Here, lord," he said, handing his father the jar of spring water.

"No, you carry it. And that box. Follow me."

With the boy in tow, Poppy continued up the first-level tunnel. They passed the mess room, where miners had once taken their meal and breaks. Beyond it, the powder room marked the spot where the tunnel began to narrow. The initial copper vein had petered out there, and the miners had shifted their attention to the second level.

The powder room was a small space no larger than a walk-in closet, and it was fitted with an extra-stout timber door. A wooden crate that once held blasting caps sat on a shelf. Poppy put the carton of dust next to it. He set the Mason jar on its own shelf and dropped the golden marble into it. The marble looked enormous in the water.

"What is that thing, lord?" Uzzie said.

That was a good question, and Poppy was impressed that the boy should ask it. Pity that Poppy didn't have an answer yet.

"It was what was plugging up the trumpet so we couldn't blow it," he said. "What do *you* think it is?"

"Is the trumpet destroyed? Did Proverbs break it?"

"Nobody broke it. It just went away."

"Went away where?"

"Here." Poppy tapped the carton with his finger. "What's left of it."

When they left, Poppy padlocked the door.

VW13 1.0

BACK IN THE machine room, a few particles of floating dust wafted up the ventilation shaft and were deposited in the snow alongside the metal grating on the mountainside.

The Winged Spy

WS1 1.0

THE RAVEN WAS a large, fit male, as big as a small dog and twice as clever. There was a routine to its days as it searched for food, and it knew every scrap heap for miles around. When not scavenging, it often sat on the top of spruce trees or utility poles and cawed or chortled at the passing scene below.

One day while making its rounds, the raven spied something shiny on the side of a mountain. It detoured to take a closer look. The thing glittered in the sunlight in a most appealing way. After watching it from a stone ledge for a while, the bird glided down and landed not far from it. It was a sparkly flower, and the raven hopped closer to examine it, first with one eye and then with the other. Finally, it hopped right up next to it and seized it in its pliers-like beak.

But its beak stuck to the thing and the raven couldn't let go. The bird struggled to break free, but only for a short while, as warm, gentle oblivion bubbled through its frisky mind.

THE RAVEN WADDLED about drunkenly with outstretched wings. To the red fox, observing from a snowy lair, the bird was injured and easy prey. The fox stalked it and pounced upon it. It seized the bird by the neck and gave it a terrific shake. But instead of feathers and flesh, the fox got only a mouthful of smoke and ashes. It abruptly abandoned its kill and fled down the mountainside.

THE FIRST FEW times the raven attempted to fly, it pitched forward and plowed into the snow. But it didn't give up, and with each attempt it gained better control over its many competing parts. When it did achieve flight, it didn't remain airborne for long but crashed, sometimes spectacularly. After each catastrophe, the bird was obliged to remain still awhile as its parts coalesced.

THE RAVEN FLEW far and wide. It circled the mostly vacant town and outlying camps and cabins. It loitered wherever it found living creatures to observe. It visited dump sites and fuel tanks. It spread its wings and climbed high into the sky to take in great swaths of countryside. It flew east as far as the Canadian border and Mt. Logan, south to the Bagley Ice Field, north to the Alcan Highway, and west to the Copper River and Glennallen. In all, it surveyed ten thousand square miles of territory (25,900 sq. km) that surrounded its point of origin.

UP AND DOWN, up and down, all the livelong day. The middle boys and their surviving plastic toboggans moved supplies, cordwood, and lumber up to the keep. Adam told the boys that they were at the age when hard work outdoors built solid muscles and deep lungs that would serve them for the rest of their lives. Proverbs told the boys that so much pulling would stretch their arms down to their knees and that they would become knuckle-draggers and unfit for human wives.

When Uzzie and Ithy were pulling their toboggans past the grove of trees at the base of the slide, Crissy Lou started barking at a raven perched atop a spruce tree.

"What's her problem?" Ithy said.

"I don't know," Uzzie replied. He crouched and called the dog to him. She came, but she would not be soothed, and when the bird took flight, she tore herself from Uzzie's grasp, berserk with rage.

Ithy said, "She don't like that ol' crow, it looks like."

"She don't," Uzzie agreed.

COOKING; BAKING; DISHES; sweeping; mopping; dusting; childcare; homeschooling — though Ginger didn't see much education going on — mending; doing everything for Mama P, including bathing, dressing, and feeding her; burning trash in an outdoor incinerator; making up beds; tending the rabbits and chickens. All this and so much more was considered girls' work. Add the fact that there was no electricity or running water to simplify things, and bush living was nowhere near as romantic as Ginger had imagined.

And it wasn't as if the boys' work was any easier. Besides their relentless roles as family sherpas on the slide, the four middle boys (1 Corinthians, Solomon, Ithamar, and Uzziel) hauled water from the pump house to the kitchen. They kept the various wood bins full of firewood. They were in charge of emptying and cleaning all the honey buckets — a task that required constant reminding. Whenever a rabbit needed to be slaughtered, it was usually a boy who did the deed. In the spring, they and the elder boys tilled the garden, and they did most of the weeding and harvesting. They painted whatever needed to be painted, kept the footpaths clear of snow, and skinned the spruce poles needed for construction. Most of their chores took place outdoors, no matter the weather.

By far, the most onerous of the girls' chores, in Ginger's opinion, was doing the laundry. The large family generated a mountain of it every day, and a daily load or two had to be done (except on the Lord's Day) just to keep up.

Fortunately, the Prophecy family owned a washing machine — of sorts. It was a gasoline-powered Maytag model from the 1930s that Hosea had found rusting away in one of the sheds when the family first moved in. He replaced the engine with a new Kohler and added a hand crank to the rubber clothes wringer on top.

The bathhouse, not far from the big house, doubled as the family laundromat. Today the task fell to Deut and her shadow, Cora. Ginger helped out, carrying basket after basket of dirty laundry from the house. She helped lay the hose from the pump house and filled metal buckets on top of the barrel stove with water.

A big raven sat on the roof ridge of the toolshed watching them, and each time Ginger went by, she spoke to it. "I'll bet you're glad you don't have to wear clothes, Mr. Raven." The bird ruffled its shiny black feathers as if in sympathy. When Crissy Lou followed the boys home for lunch, she barked at the raven until it flew away.

The girls rolled the washing machine out to the little bathhouse porch and loaded it with steamy water and a load of laundry. Deut locked its casters and pull-started the engine. The old contraption, with belts and pulleys, chugged like a steam locomotive.

The girls retreated indoors to pull yesterday's washing from a spiderweb of clotheslines to sort and fold, all the while supervising the little kids who were taking their baths.

After the washing machine had churned for ten minutes or so, Deut killed the engine and drained the tub right off the porch. The family's laundry had already built up its own little glacier. They refilled the tub with cold water for a rinse cycle. Finally, after draining the rinse water, they wheeled the machine back indoors to crank the load, piece by piece, through the wringer and hang it up.

Then they did the next load.

At one point, the little girls in one of the bathtub stalls were getting a bit rambunctious, and Deut, who was up to her elbows in sudsy water, asked Ginger to go in and "speak to them." When Ginger pulled the curtain aside, she was surprised to see three little girls bathing in a tub while wearing their undergarments. Words failed her. The giggling girls interrupted their game to watch her. It took Ginger a moment to find her adult voice and say, "Your sister says no more horsing around in here. Got it?"

"Yes, Auntie Ginger," they replied sweetly. "We'll be good."

Ginger closed the curtain more confused than ever, and not just about the odd bathing fashion. When had she become their auntie?

WS2 1.0

THERE WAS A thump, the sound of a melon hitting the floor, followed by shrieking. The girls rushed to the common room. Elzaphan, who had been nursing, now sat on the floor holding his head and raging at his older brother, Numbers, who was climbing on top of Mama P to take his place at the catatonic teat.

"Nummy!" Sarai scolded. "You have to wait your turn."

"No, I don't!"

"Oh, Numbers, don't defy me. You know you can't win."

Sarai picked up the boy, who kicked and punched at her, and when she placed him on his feet, he ran to the bunkroom. Sue, meanwhile, gathered Elzie in her arms to soothe him, and in a little while he stopped crying.

"You're good with him," Sarai said.

"Three baby brothers. What can I say?"

Sarai laughed. "Only three? Lucky you."

"Three's plenty." Sue placed Elzaphan on Mama P and lifted the nursing shawl for him. "By the way," she said, "isn't Nummy a little old to still be nursing?"

"Another couple of months, and then we're cutting him off."

"I mean, he's hardly a baby anymore, and he eats everything on his plate. How old is he?"

"He'll be three in a couple of months, and then we're cutting him off."

"I see," Sue said, not sure that she did.

WS3 1.0

THE RAVEN WAITED on the fortified gallery above the open gate for the boys to drop their loads of firewood and begin their slog back down the tailings slide. When the way was clear, the bird flew into the mouth of the keep and threaded its way through the dark tunnel to the door of the powder room. It examined the padlock and gave it several tentative pecks with its beak. Nothing doing — the barrier was more than it could handle. So it turned around and flew back through the tunnel to the gate and away.

WS4 1.0

THE TWO RANGERS had stayed out of each other's way since their visit to the flats. They kept themselves busy completing the end-of-season checklist for shuttering the mill town. The Japanese aurora-watchers left by bus on Friday (with a half dozen lucky new blastocysts on board), and manager Gonzales and crew were winterizing the lodge in preparation for their own departure on Sunday. At end of shift on Saturday, Masterson asked Jace to meet him at his house that evening to discuss his annual employee evaluation. Technically, that was after hours, but Jace didn't bother to object, in case that caused his evaluation to be worse than it was already bound to be.

Due to his rank, the park service had assigned Masterson one of the restored single-family houses in Caldecott as his residence. There was a row of them north of the power plant on the lane that led to the glacier. Masterson's house had originally belonged to the mine's timekeeper. In an era before computers, keeping track of the labors of over three thousand men was both an arduous and a prestigious occupation. Masterson hated the house — it was like living in a museum — but the alternative was staying in the mens' bunkhouse, which he hated even more.

When Jace arrived that evening, there was a 6 kW Generac generator running on the front porch. They had already mothballed the big Caterpillar diesel rig that electrified the entire town, and Masterson's home oil stove needed electricity to operate. Jace knocked on the door and waited. He knocked again, and when no one answered, he simply went in.

Masterson was slumped in an armchair in the old-timey parlor with his feet propped up on a suitcase. An empty bottle of single-malt whiskey lay on the floor. The ranger was wearing jeans and a Cal sweatshirt, and Jace couldn't recall another time seeing him out of his starched green and grays. Masterson looked up, thoroughly shit-faced, when Jace entered.

"Come in," he said, "and make yourshelf at home." He tried to get up, but abandoned the project. "Shit anywhere."

There was only one other seat, a straight-backed dining room chair. An internet radio station was playing on a docked iPod.

"Drink?" Masterson said. But when he spotted his bottle on the floor, he said, "There's beer in the cooler. Get me one while you're up. Or if you're holding, go ahead and smoke it. I don't care."

Nice try.

"I don't know why you keep insisting I do drugs," Jace said. "Have you ever seen me high?"

Masterson laughed. "Based on your job performance, you're either high all the time or a cretin. Take your pick."

The cooler was on the back porch, about twenty feet from the drop off to the glacier. There was no ice in the cooler, but at these temperatures none was needed. In fact, the cooler was for keeping the beer from freezing solid. Jace brought back two cans of Coors.

"So, you staying over this winter?" Masterson said.

"Looks that way. You?"

"They want me at headquarters after New Year's. Terrence is going off contract."

That about wrapped up the smalltalk. They sipped beer slushies and listened to Beethoven, or Mozart, or somebody — Jace wasn't really into classical music.

"I like you," Masterson said. "I didn't think I would, but I do. You're solid enough, in your own millennial dipshit way."

"Thanks."

"I mean it. That's why, as your reporting officer, I don't want to fuck you over too much. But I gotta tell them *something*. You know? So, I'll give you another chance to set the record straight. What were you doing out there for a week on the government's dime using government property? And don't — *don't* — tell me about your alien abduction crap again, or so help me, I'll arrest you."

Jace had anticipated the question, but despite thinking about it for three solid days, he hadn't come up with a better story than the truth. No further satellite updates had revealed the snow circle, his google searches came up dry, and it was unlikely the Prophecys would voluntarily give up the only real evidence anytime soon. All he had was the truth and his word.

"I know it's hard to believe. I wouldn't believe it myself if I didn't see it."

"Bullshit! I know you were searching for something, Kuliak. I know you borrowed the metal detector. I know you wanted to charter a flight with Nellis. Just tell me what you were looking for. A drug drop gone wrong? A body? Explosives? A weapons cache? I promise I'll protect you as much as I can, but you gotta come clean."

"That's crazy talk. I'm no criminal."

"How is it any crazier than a giant talking tulip? What about human trafficking? Are you smuggling in illegals?"

"I never said the tulip talked."

"Well, at least we got that straightened out. Scratch the talking tulip."

The two rangers went back to sipping beer. Jace wondered if the discussion was over and how it had gone. Could he leave yet? Masterson was as morose and withdrawn as he'd ever seen him, not to mention drunk. When Jace finished his beer, he crushed the can and looked around for somewhere to toss it.

When Masterson spoke, his voice was choked with emotion. "I've done some pretty lame crap in my day, and I'm not proud of it. But one thing I never did and never would do is walk into a school with an assault rifle a week before Christmas and blow away twenty-six little angels."

What the hell? Jace asked Masterson to explain himself, but the ranger buried his head in his hands and wept. He gestured for Jace to leave him, to go away, and Jace did so, gladly.

WS5 1.0

ON SIXTHDAY NIGHT, the temperature dropped again, and the Lord's Day broke clear and cold. There would be no work done on this day, aside from the mostly female labor of getting everyone fed, the dishes cleaned, and taking care of Mama P. But neither would there be any additional time spent in prayer than the usual evening Worship Time.

"What about church?" Sue asked. She sat at the grown-ups' table having a breakfast of corn mush and moose gravy. Poppy wasn't present, and the children at the kiddie tables were all amped up.

"Hain't no churches around here worth calling a church," Proverbs said. He had worn his eyepatch to breakfast. It was the first time Ginger had seen it, and she thought he wore it as a joke.

"Hain't there now, matey?" she said and immediately regretted it. She'd meant it to be funny, what with the pirate eyepatch and all, but "matey" sounded uncomfortably close to "mate," and she didn't want to give him any ideas. Fortunately, no one seemed to have heard her joke, least of all

Proverbs.

"What about the Bunyans' church?" Sue said. "They told us they hold services in the rug room on Sundays. Dell's a pastor."

Proverbs said, "Pastor Dell teaches falsehoods."

"That's terrible. What kind of falsehoods?"

Proverbs began to reply, but Adam raised his hand. "Leave this to me, brother."

Proverbs nodded and gave him the floor.

Adam took a sip of coffee before beginning. "Among his other errors, Pastor Bunyan preaches that the Rapture comes *before* the Tribulation."

"Well, duh," Sue said. "Wait. Are you saying it doesn't?"

"No, it doesn't. A true reading of Scripture says that the righteous will suffer the End Times right alongside the damned. That's why we came to the mountain. That's why we built the keep." Then Adam waved his hand dismissively. "But enough theology for now. My brother has brought it to my attention that we've been so caught up with work this week that we've been neglecting you ladies. So we thought it would be fun if we went on a picnic this afternoon, just the four of us."

"A picnic?" Sue said, surprised. "In this weather?"

"What weather? It's only minus ten (–23 C) out. Practically springtime. Besides, it don't have to be an outdoor picnic. We bought a Yukon stove in Anchorage for Proverbs' new cabin, and this would be a good time to install it. Then we can get a nice fire going in there and heat the place up for our picnic. How does that sound? We get out of this madhouse for a few hours, see a little countryside."

"Sounds like fun," Sue said, "but is that the same cabin the rangers were talking about the other day?"

Ginger said, "What rangers?"

"You missed them," Sue said. "You and Verbs were gone to the Bunyans' when these two forest rangers came to the door complaining about a cabin someone built on park land."

Proverbs said, "The parkies might think it's their cabin and their land, but those times are gone, and it's a little late to be knocking on our door over it."

Ginger said, "What's that supposed to mean?"

"It means, in case you've been sleepwalking lately, that the Tribulation has already begun. We're already in the End Times."

Adam rested a hand on his brother's shoulder. "We can talk about all that if that's what the girls want," he said, "but let's talk at the picnic, not here. Sue, are you in?"

"Definitely."

"Ginger?"

"Sure. It does sound like fun. Deut, you'll come too?"

Deut, who had been quietly sitting out the whole conversation, said, "Huh?"

"Want to go with us on a picnic?"

Proverbs said, "There's only room for us four."

"Nonsense," Ginger said. "We can use a sled."

"I *said* there's only room for us." Proverbs' good eye flashed with annoyance.

His attitude wasn't very inviting. "Thanks," Ginger said, "but count me out. Maybe next time."

Proverbs abruptly pushed away from the table and left the common room. The little ones all fell silent and watched him go.

DEUT AND GINGER stood side by side in matching floral-print aprons at the large galvanized sink where they rinsed the breakfast dishes.

"You know what I'd really like to do today?" Ginger said.

"Obviously, not go on a picnic."

Ginger laughed. "No, really, I'd like to go up and check out this mountain keep of yours. I've been hearing about it all week, and I'm really curious."

Deut thought about it a moment. "We might do that. I'll ask Poppy."

"You need permission?"

"Maybe. It's always a good idea to ask."

"But Sue goes up there all the time."

"Not really. She only goes when Adam or Hosea takes her. You could ask Proverbs to take you up there."

"I'm asking you."

WS6 1.0

"HOW'S THIS NOT working on the Lord's Day?" Ginger asked reasonably. They were loading two plastic toboggans with cordwood at the foot of the slide. "Hauling wood up the side of a mountain should qualify as work, it seems to me."

"We're climbing up there anyways," Deut replied. "We might as well bring a load up with us. Why go up empty handed? Besides, I don't see it as work so much as doing a kindness for my brothers. One less load for them. Besides," she added, "like Mama always said, we're Christians, not Jews."

Ginger was a little shocked. That sounded a bit bigoted, though she wasn't sure how. "What's that supposed to mean?"

Deut tugged the tow rope, breaking the toboggan free from the snow, and began the long climb. Ginger followed suit.

"It means that we're Prophecys, not Pharisees, and our sheep are ever falling into pits."

Ginger laughed out loud. "Oh."

IF IT WASN'T work, it was a good approximation. Both girls had unzipped their parkas and vests by the time they reached the mine adit at the top. Ginger stood between the two cliff faces and gawked at the defensive log galleries overhead with their sniper slots. She stood before the armored gate and gawked some more.

"It's on account of we may have to keep people out," Deut said.

"Oh, I get that," Ginger said. "I just didn't expect it. It's so, you know, *Game of Thrones*. I didn't expect to see something like this. That's all.

"*Game of Thrones?*"

"Yeah, you know, the cable TV series. Oh, you wouldn't have seen it. It's a show about a war for a medieval kingdom with dragons and demons. You'd hate it, but your keep could be one of their sets."

Unsure of what Ginger meant by that, Deut opened the sally door and they went in.

They each chose a hardhat from a peg on the wall and switched on the headlamps. The tunnel, hewn from solid rock, was also gawk-worthy, as was the machine room. Ginger saw Instagrams everywhere she looked, if only she had her phone. They stopped when they reached the ramp intersection.

Ginger turned her light all around. "Why do I suddenly get the feeling that someone's watching us?"

"You mean besides Elder Brother Jesus?"

As they climbed the ramp, Ginger said, "What's the deal with the eyepatch anyway? I mean, it's none of my business, but is his eye injured or something?"

"No, not his eye."

"Then what?"

"When my brother was seven years old, a mule that we had at the time kicked him in the head. I was too little to remember any of this, but they say his brain swelled up and the doctor said he would probably die.

"But we all prayed for him day and night, and he didn't die. But later he told me he wished he did because he had these grievous headaches all the time. He couldn't sleep or eat, or study his lessons, or even be around people. He started acting out so bad the sheriff wanted to lock him up. Poppy wouldn't let that happen. We prayed and prayed for years, but Father God didn't see fit to heal him. Mama took him to a bunch of doctors all over California, and they all had their cures, but nothing ever worked for him.

"Until this one faith-filled doctor outside Sacramento who gave him a pill that helped a lot.

"And when he turned into a teenager, the bad spells mostly went away. And now he only has 'em when he gets really stressed out. I guess all this running around we've been doing and trumpets from Heaven and all brought it on."

"And the eyepatch?"

"When he has a spell, his right eyelid doesn't blink on its own. He doesn't notice it until his eye gets so totally dried out it gets sick. The patch just keeps the lid down so it stays moist."

"And that cabin they're going to for the picnic? Adam said it belonged to him."

"Oh, that's just a fallen-down old shack we found. He and Hosea fixed it up, so when things get really bad, Proverbs can go out there to be alone for a few days. When he's suffering so bad he can get pretty mean and not nice to be around."

Deut must have thought she'd revealed too much because she added, "My brother takes a little getting used to, but he's a good man down deep."

"I'm sure he is," Ginger said, "but I still wouldn't have gone on the picnic."

"Why not?"

"No offense against your brother, but he's not my type, and I don't particularly like Sue, so why spend an entire afternoon with them?"

It was Deut's turn to be confused. "Did you change your mind . . . ? About wanting to marry him?"

"What? Marry your brother? Whatever gave you that idea?"

"Then why are you here?"

"Because *you* asked me to come. I came here to get to know *you*. And your family, and learn about life in the bush and all."

Deut didn't reply, and when they reached the top of the ramp, she stumbled and Ginger almost walked into her.

"Are you all right?" Ginger said. "Are you crying?"

"No, I'm not," Deut said. "I'm okay."

THEY ENTERED THE large, arched opening to the cottage chamber. In their headlamps stood one of the weirdest sights Ginger had ever seen: a two-story wood-frame farmhouse, with a gabled roof and wrap-around porch, the kind you'd see in a Kansas wheat field. Only, they weren't in Kansas but in a ginormous cavern inside a mountain.

"There aren't any windows!"

"Who needs windows when it never gets light out?"

There weren't any shingles or rain gutters either because it never rained. And no paint, lawn, or driveway.

"It's got plenty of insulation," Deut went on. "Hosea says if we wear sweaters, then all of our body heat will be enough to keep it warm. He says the cookstove might drive us outdoors."

"Out into a sea of darkness."

"I know. It'll take some getting used to. It'll be like living inside a refrigerator with the light turned off and the door shut for seven years."

"About that," Ginger said, trying to sound matter-of-fact. "Your brother says the Tribulation has already begun. What does he mean by that?"

"Exactly what he said."

"He believes we're in the Apocalypse?"

"We all do."

"Um, and you're okay with that?"

Deut laughed. "Like I get a vote?"

Their headlamps picked out a trail of small stones on the limestone floor. It led off into the darkness on their right.

"That goes to the woodpile," Deut said. "We have about a hundred cords split and stacked so far."

"How do you know it's begun? The Tribulation."

"Because of the signs. The handprint in the snow. The angel's trumpet."

Ginger had still been in Wallis when Father God knocked Poppy off his snowmachine, and she had been at the Bunyans' house with Proverbs when Poppy showed them the heavenly trumpet, and by the time she had returned and heard about it, some angel had come to reclaim it or something. But not before everyone but her had seen it. She was the only one not to have seen any of the signs.

Not that Ginger Lawther was a skeptic. She believed she was living in the Final Days. She even believed that the Apocalypse might occur during her lifetime. But despite everything she believed, it was another matter altogether to believe that the end times had already begun.

"But wouldn't, like, the whole world know it if the Apocalypse had begun?"

"I'm sure the outside world is finding out even now."

"Good," Ginger said. Here was something they could test. "Do you have a radio? We could listen to the news."

There was a radio, two radios, in fact. They were of the variety of civil disaster radios that could automatically receive tornado and hurricane alerts and be charged with a hand crank or solar panel. But Deut didn't know where Poppy kept them, and she didn't really want to ask.

Inside the cottage, the walls were framed but not yet covered. Only half of the second story floor had been laid. Hand tools and saw horses lay about where they'd last been used.

"We'll have more room than we ever did," Deut said. "Not as much as you're used to maybe, but . . ." She had intended to say, *but you'll get used to it.* However, if Ginger wasn't interested in marrying Proverbs, there was no way Poppy would allow her to stay with them on her own. He'd toss her out the gate and lock it behind her, even if it meant death by starvation or by wild beasts. They didn't have enough stores to feed the whole hungry world. That was why you prepared yourself for the worst. That was why the whole family worked at it so hard. They could have simply prayed for Father God's protection, but prayer without action only got you so far.

They walked through the future kitchen. "The plan is to take apart the range in the big house and move it here piece by piece."

Maybe Ginger would fall in love with Hosea, or even with Corny, and then she could stay. Maybe that was Father God's plan. Deut prayed that it was so. She couldn't bear the thought of losing her first friend in the whole world.

Behind the back porch was another trail of stones leading further into the dark chamber.

"Where does that one go?" Ginger said.

"To Sue's house, or future house."

"Sue gets her own house?"

"It'll be her and Adam's house once they get married, but till then it'll be Sue's."

"What about you? Are they going to build you a house too?"

Deut laughed. "When the time comes, I'm sure they will. Adam says a village could fit into this one cavern."

"You have anyone in mind yet?"

"In mind for what?"

"For when the time comes."

Deut blushed so fiercely that she lit up the entire cavern in pink. Or at least that was how it felt.

Ginger said, "I'll take that for a yes."

WS7 1.0

DEUT AND GINGER were gone about two hours on their tour, and when they returned, the entire household was turned upside down.

Sarai had gone to bed with a headache (something only she had the power to get away with) and left twelve-year-old Frankie and Myrrh in charge of the kitchen.

The tweens had managed to serve lunch but neglected to clean up afterward. And instead of prepping for dinner, they spent their energies baking a cake.

The middle boys fled the house after lunch, along with the dog, and no one remembered to feed the common room stove.

Mama P, who had not been moved for hours, lay soaked in her own urine, while Nummy sat on her and worried her breasts raw.

Revie and See-Saw were closeted in the girl's room, and baby Elzie tottered about the cooling house in a soiled diaper.

To make matters worse, Poppy came in from the prayer cabin to witness all of this before Deut had a chance to set things right.

"I said you could visit the keep, not spend the whole afternoon there," he said.

"Yes, lord," Deut replied, "but I didn't know Sarai was going to —"

Poppy cut her off. "I'm talking to you, not your sister."

"Yes, lord. Sorry, lord."

Poppy cast a sour glance at Ginger. "I hear you turned down the chance to go on a picnic."

"Yes," Ginger said. "I wasn't up for it."

"I wasn't up for it — what?" Poppy said.

So here it was, the final showdown. Ginger had spent the last few days since her humiliation over Bible verses dreading this inevitable moment. Now it was happening. Now she had to decide what kind of woman she was, one who stood her ground or one who knuckled under.

On the one hand, addressing the old goat as lord was a small thing; it meant little in the big picture; it was a minor annoyance.

On the other hand, where did this temporary guardian of hers get off demanding more from her than her own, faith-filled father? And for that matter, who had put her in charge of reforming this bizarre family? Who had made her the Prophecy girls' champion? No one, that was who.

Poppy was not a tall man, and his bushy beard made him look a bit gnomish. Ginger stood nose to nose with him, but he seemed so much more powerful, substantial, commanding. So she stood a little taller and met his rheumy old gaze, and said, "I wasn't up for it, Mr. Prophecy."

A tiny gasp escaped from Deut, but Poppy didn't seem upset. If anything, he seemed relieved.

"Maybe you'd feel more comfortable staying with the Bunyans," he said, "until you return home."

"Actually, Mr. Prophecy, I'd rather stay here, if you don't mind. I like it here. I like being your guest. But there are things that a host just can't expect their guests to go along with, and this is one of them for me. So, I understand if you decide to send me away, but until then I'm eager to stay. Maybe we can come up with some kind of compromise we can both live with. How about Pastor Prophecy? Reverend Prophecy? Or just plain sir? I could call you sir. I wasn't up for it, sir. How's that?"

Poppy wondered what seven years locked up in a cave with such a hellion would do to his nerves. He shook his head and said, "I'll pray on it." Maybe she was sent to test his patience. If it weren't for Proverbs, she'd be on the next plane out.

WS8 1.0

OVER THE LAST twenty years, anytime Poppy bothered to tune into the mainstream news, which wasn't often, there were reports of disasters, droughts, floods, jihad, massacres, terrorism, plague, and so on and so forth all over the globe. Was it possible, against such a pervasive and unrelenting backdrop of doom, that the Apocalypse had begun but that no one had noticed?

According to Revelation, when the Fifth Angel unlocked the bottomless pit, clouds of black smoke would spew forth, so thick that they would block out the sun. And from the smoke would spring a swarm of stinging locusts that would attack not green things, as ordinary swarms of locusts did, but people who were not marked with God's seal on their foreheads. Surely, if some part of the planet was buried under bilious black smoke, if killer locusts were loosed upon the population, news would leak out, no matter how strenuously the media and government tried to bury it.

On Firstday morning, Poppy awoke with a desire to catch up on current events. Ordinarily, he'd wait until Twosday and log in on his Samsung at Mail Day. But if he went to the Sulzers' this week, Ed would no doubt badger him for his art supplies. And then he'd want to know why his precious souvenir goldpans were dumped in the woods next to the parking lot. There would be a confrontation, a scene, hard feelings, needless hassle. Better to let Ed stew about it until even he saw the writing on the wall.

So when Poppy turned the key of the new Arctic Cat, he had a different destination in mind. There was a McHardy snowbird named Yurek Rutz who kept a nice, out-of-the-way cabin on the outskirts of town. He arrived each year in Sixthmonth to spend the summer fly-fishing and drinking whiskey under the Midnight Sun. He usually left in Ninthmonth for points south, well before the first snow.

Yurek Rutz was not saved, and since he was not likely to ever return to McHardy in this life, it was only a matter of time before his cabin would be considered abandoned and all of his goods forfeit. It would be prudent then, and not at all larcenous, for Poppy to get a jump on future scavengers and claim first pickings. In the meantime, he could take advantage of the cabin's excellent cell reception.

As expected, the snow on the trail leading to Rutz's cabin was undisturbed. A lone raven witnessed Poppy removing the bear shutters from its windows. Rutz kept a good supply of seasoned wood about the place, and Poppy quickly built a hot fire in the old Jøtul stove. While he waited for the place to warm up, he gathered what supplies and equipment he deemed useful and loaded them into his sled.

Yurek Rutz had a lot of nice stuff, including a new Yamaha 1200-watt portable generator and a set of deep-cycle storage batteries. They would come in handy.

Then Poppy pulled Rutz's ratty old armchair in front of the stove and sat down to browse on his Samsung Galaxy.

The headlines were unremarkable. Obama is in Connecticut speaking to survivors of yet another school shooting. The Syrian vice president deplores the continuing civil unrest in his country. House Speaker John Boehner tearfully agrees to tax millionaires. Venezuela's Chavez has cancer. Italy's Berlusconi is engaged to a teen-ager. Duchess Kate Middleton is recovering from morning sickness.

In other words, remain calm, nothing is happening here, and if something was happening, we wouldn't tell you anyway. The only story Poppy could find that had anything to do with reality, albeit a twisted version of it, was about the handwringing over the so-called Maya Apocalypse. According to pagan superstition, the ancient Mexican civilization was supposed to have predicted that the world would end that Fifthday, only four days away.

That gave Poppy pause. He'd heard about the Maya calendar, of course, but had always dismissed its doomsday prediction as demonic fear mongering. Now, however, he saw that the timing could be no accident. It made sense that Satan would want to distract the unsaved populations from preparing for the real Apocalypse with a phony one. Clever.

As Poppy browsed and pondered, he became gradually aware of a sound outside the window. He ignored it at first. It was the call of some forest creature. A lynx or a bird of some sort. Not loud. Not far away. He looked out the window but couldn't spot its source in the woods surrounding the cabin. It sounded forlorn and frightened, like a baby animal bleating for its parent. A bunny trapped in a snare, maybe. A baby fox separated from its litter mates.

At some point, the sound ceased, and Poppy didn't notice its absence until it started up again. This time it was more clearly a human voice, the voice of a child, in fact. *Help me pleeease.* The hair stood up on the nape of Poppy's neck.

He jumped to his feet. Could it be one of his own? He was miles from home. Could one of his kids have followed him? Impossible. He pulled on his hat and gloves and dashed out the door. On the porch he stopped to get a bearing, but the cry had ceased again.

Poppy cupped his hands and shouted into the woods, "Where are you?"

Nothing.

He tried again. "Where are you?"

Poppeeeeee, came the voice. Poppy's heart lurched. It *was* one of his, and he even knew which one — Uzziel — his irascible eight year old, his pride, his favorite.

Poppy leaped off the porch and waded through waist-high snow to the forest edge. "I'm coming, child," he shouted. "Where are you?"

No reply.

"Tell me where you are, boy. Poppy's coming." He was out of breath by the time he reached the trees, but once under the forest canopy, the snow cover wasn't as deep.

I'm coldeeeee.

It came from behind a large spruce tree, and Poppy charged ahead. But when he reached the tree, there was no one there.

"Uzzie, where are you?" He cocked his head, focusing on every sound. "Poppy's here. Where are you?"

Help meeeeee.

There, that way. Poppy corrected his course and slogged deeper into the woods. He spotted snowshoe rabbit tracks and fox tracks, but nothing human. He called again and again, but nothing more came from his son. Had the boy succumbed to the cold? Had he been dragged off by a wild beast? Poppy looked for blood on the snow. He dashed this way and that until he was out of breath. But the only tracks he found were his own. He searched until he had to stop. He was spent. He was getting old after all and was no longer the superman of his youth. If only Adam were here, or Proverbs, or, for that matter, Uzzie's worthless dog.

Sobered by the cold, Poppy made his way back to the Rutz cabin. The fire had died down, but before he could reload the stove, he noticed glass shards on the table and floor. One of the windows had been shattered during his absence as though someone had thrown a brick through it.

He searched the floor and found no brick or rock, but he did find his phone, or pieces of it. He had left his phone on the table when he went out. Now the display was smashed and the case broken open and tossed aside. The electronic innards were missing. He searched all about the cabin but failed to locate them.

Poppy turned up some duct tape and a piece of cardboard that he used to patch the broken windowpane. Lying in the snow just outside the window was a single black feather. Ordinarily, he wouldn't have noticed it, but there was nothing ordinary about any of this, so he went outside to investigate. But by the time he waded around the side of the cabin, the feather was gone.

Poppy's whole soul shuddered.

"Keep the phone, Satan," he said. "I don't need it no more. You are proof enough."

WHEN POPPY ARRIVED home, he summoned everyone together for an emergency meeting. The middle girls were dispatched to fetch their brothers from the slide and keep. Poppy counted heads as they arrived. Uzzie was one of the last to show up, and Poppy whispered a prayer of thanksgiving when he saw him. For once he was even happy to see the dog.

When the family, Adam's betrothed, and their obstinate guest were all assembled, Poppy quickly told them about his frightening encounter. "I was beguiled by a demon," he concluded and drew from his pocket pieces of his phone. The children all leaned forward to see. "It has begun. Demons are loose on the land. Let us pray."

Worship Time had come early, and the family never prayed so fervently as they did that afternoon.

When they said their last amen, Adam asked, "What now, lord?"

"We double our efforts. Move the rest of the supplies. Finish the cottage so we can move in. And in the meantime . . ." He paused, deep in thought.

"Lord?"

"In the meantime," he repeated, "we secure what we have. Bring me a jug of oil."

Ithy, closest to the kitchen, ran to fetch it.

"As the eldest-born," Poppy told Adam, "you stay here to hold down the house. Sing hymns, pray, make such a righteous racket no devil or demon would dare to creep in. You, you, and you," he said, pointing at girls and boys alike, "and you, you and you." Elder, middle, and little. "We're going up to purify the keep."

Ithy returned with a gallon bottle of Wesson Oil and handed it to his father. Poppy swished the cooking oil around in the plastic jug for a moment before returning it to the boy. "Don't we have any olive oil?"

Without a word, Sarai took the jug from Ithy and went to the kitchen.

THE SPIRITUAL WARRIORS gathered inside the gate and passed around hardhats.

"For where two or three are gathered together in my name, there am I in the midst of them," Poppy recited, quoting Matthew. "How many of us are gathered in His name here?"

"Seven," Uzzie answered. Poppy, Hosea, Deut, Corny, See-Saw, Nummy, and himself.

"Seven," Poppy affirmed. "Does anyone know what that means?"

Uzzie replied, "That Elder Brother Jesus is here with us?"

"That's right. Elder Brother Jesus is here with us, so don't nobody be afraid. Say praise Him."

"Praise Him," everyone said.

"Praise His holy name."

"Praise His holy name."

"Now this is what we're gonna do. We plan on spending the next seven years locked in this chill, damp sanctuary. Though we can learn to live with the chill and the damp, we'll never survive the demons. That's why we got to chase them out now and lock the gate against them. And the way we do that is by anointing all the chamber entrances. Now the demons might put up a fight, so I want everyone to hold hands and think of Elder Brother Jesus as we go."

The children walked hand in hand behind Poppy up the length of the tunnel, up the ramps to the highest level. They sang hymns as they went, and when they came to the cistern chamber, they filed in and stood on the rocky ledge overlooking the still, black pool.

"This is our fountain of waters," Poppy proclaimed. "It will slake our thirst, help prepare our meals, and cleanse our home and bodies. Say amen."

"Amen."

"With the power given all believers by the one true Father God, His Son Jesus Christ, and the Holy Spirit, I command all devils to leave at once." He raised his voice. "I cast thee out! I cast out thee demons and all unclean spirits! Begone! Say amen."

"Amen."

"Now where is that bottle of oil?"

Deut handed him the pint bottle of extra-virgin, cold-pressed, Italian olive oil. He spilled a little of it on his fingers and dribbled it over the cistern chamber threshold.

They proceeded from chamber to chamber on all three levels, naming the purpose of each space, casting out unclean spirits, and anointing the entrances to seal them.

When they got to the powder room on the first level, Poppy pulled out his keyring and opened the heavy door. He shined a light on the shelf where he'd left the golden marble. It was still there, sitting in the Mason jar of spring water. He took the jar down from the shelf and showed it to the children, who pressed forward to see. "This little ball is what the angel left behind when he fetched the trumpet."

Deut said, "What is it, lord?"

"It's a fallen star, I think, but I'm not sure which one." Poppy sniffed the water in the jar. It didn't smell bad, so he dipped his fingers in and brought them to his lips. The water tasted fine, not bitter at all. That ruled out the Third Angel and the star called Wormwood. He plucked the marble from the water and held it out for all to see. "Or maybe it's the key to the bottomless pit of Hell. I still have to pray on it."

Deut's eyes grew wide. "Can I hold it?"

"I don't know, can you? It's heavy." He dropped it into her hand and let her pass it around to the others. It was too heavy for See-Saw, and Nummy was too afraid to touch it.

Poppy placed the marble on a shelf by itself before closing and padlocking the door.

"In the name of the Father, Son, and Holy Ghost, I take dominion over any evil spirit tied to the heavenly orb, whatever it is. Begone devils and demons. I cast thee out! Say amen."

"Amen."

They continued to the entrance, casting out spirits as they went. When Poppy anointed the fortified gate itself, they were done, and they walked down the tailings slide in silence. The little ones were spent, and Deut carried Nummy on her hip. They could hear the rest of the family singing a hymn as they approached the house.

Together, they cleansed the big house of evil spirits from one end to the other. They paid special attention to the places where they prepared their food and where they lay their heads. Poppy anointed every exterior door and window so that they were safe and secure. They praised their Savior and sat down to dinner.

"IS THE TRUMPET still there?" Ginger whispered. The girls' bunkroom was asleep, and Ginger crouched on the cold floor next to Deut's bed.

"No, I told you; the angel already took it," Deut whispered back, yawning.

"Did you *see* the angel?"

"No, but I saw what he left behind. It looked like a little golden robin's egg." When Ginger didn't ask anything more, Deut went on, "I wish Poppy let you come. I know how hard all of this must be to accept without seeing any of it. But it's real. You have to believe me."

"I do believe you, but I'm not so sure about your dad. This anointing the house tonight just because he broke his phone? Lots of people break their phones."

"You misunderstood him. Poppy didn't break it."

"You really think Satan broke his phone?"

"There was no one else there."

"So he says."

Deut propped herself up on her elbow. "Are you calling my father a liar?"

"No, Deut. Believe me, I'm not. But I'm not willing to just take his word for it that an angel left him a little golden robin's egg or that demons are interested in smart phones. I need a little more than his word to go on."

"Do you think maybe if . . ." She left the thought unfinished.

"If what?"

"Nothing."

"Tell me."

"No offense, but do you think that if you wasn't so contrary and started showing him the respect he's due, maybe he'd take you along next time, and then you'd see for yourself?"

Contrary? Was standing up for herself being contrary?

WS10 1.0

ELZAPHAN AND NUMBERS were at it again. This time Sue caught them in the act. Elzaphan was nursing, and Numbers was trying to push him off their mother.

"Stop that!" Sue shouted. "Numbers! That's not allowed."

Deut and Ginger hurried out of the kitchen. "What's going on?" Deut said.

"I've got it," Sue replied. "It's just the Numster acting out again."

"Nummy, come here. I have some soup in the kitchen for you."

"No!" the little boy screamed. "I don't want *soup!* I hate *soup!*"

"Oh, come look," Sue said, leaning over Mama P. "This isn't good."

Deut strode across the room. "What is it? What's wrong?"

"Mama P's tits are red and raw. And look, the left one is bleeding."

Deut stopped in her tracks and looked away. "Oh," she said. "Is it bad? What should we do?"

"Not so bad. Bring me something to clean them with, and some balm and a band-aid."

Deut went off to fetch what was needed, and Ginger joined Sue at the lawn lounger. "Come, Elzie," she said. "Let's give your mama a little break."

"No!" the little prince shouted, imitating his brother. He tried to glom back on to the injured breast. Sue lifted him off and set him on the floor next to Numbers.

"Listen to me, both of you," Sue said in a stern voice. "*No teeth.* You hurt your mommy with your sharp little teeth. Do you hear me?"

Shock at such treatment was written across their greedy little faces.

"Go with Auntie Ginger and have some soup in the kitchen. Both of you. *Now! March!*" She spun them around and gave them each a little swat on the bottom to get them moving. Ginger took their hands and led them away, bawling. When she returned to the common room, Sue was attending to Mama P's breast while Deut stood next to her not watching.

"I've read the Good Book twice," Sue was saying, "from Genesis to Revelations, and I can tell you honestly, there's nothing like that anywhere in it. A verse like that I think I'd remember."

"Nevertheless," Deut insisted, "it's there."

"What?" Ginger said.

Sue replied, "They seem to believe that there's a biblical edict that you're not allowed to wean a kid completely until they turn three. I never heard of such a thing. Have you?"

Ginger said, "No, but breastfeeding was a sort of natural birth control in the olden times. It helped them to space out their kids. I never saw it in the Bible though."

"Natural birth control?" Sue snorted. "We see how well *that* works."

Her comment stung, though Deut wasn't sure why.

"Anyway," Ginger went on, "I'm afraid I have to agree with Sue on this one. There are some crazy dietary rules in the Old Testament, but I never saw such a verse about how long you have to breastfeed either."

"And yet it exists," Deut said.

Sue threw up her hands. "How would you know that?" She snapped.

"Your father keeps the only Bible in the house locked up on his belt, and from what I can tell, you can't read anyway."

Deut flushed with shame. She looked at Ginger in horror, swiveled around, and strode from the room. Ginger began to follow her, but Sue said, "Hmmm."

"What?"

Sue had pulled up Mama P's long skirt and was sniffing her crotch area. "Smells like a funk factory down here. Help me turn her on her side."

The two women turned the older one, and Ginger said, "What are you looking for?"

"Here, see it? Her tailbone is inflamed. I'm surprised she doesn't have full-blown bedsores by now."

"Oh," Ginger said, leaning over to see.

"What say you and me take Mama P out to the bathhouse today and give her a real bath, hmmm?"

WS11 1.0

ON MONDAY EVENING after work, Jace was installing the wood stove he had purchased from Kelly Cogwheel to replace his old Preway oil-drip. It was a smart move if for no other reason than the outrageous cost of heating oil (over $10/gal by the time you got it over the footbridge) and the easy availability of firewood.

The stove was an old Blaze King, a model from the 1980s, manufactured before the EPA started rating wood stoves for PM2.5 pollution. Inefficient but reliable.

The end of December was probably not the ideal time to swap out a heating source while you were using it, considering how fast the house could freeze at forty below, but it was doable if you had all your ducks in a row. It was during the preparation phase, before he turned off the Preway, when the two stoves were sitting side by side in his living room when Jace first flashed on the idea of keeping both stoves in service. Why not? All it would take would be an elbow joint and a Tee to hook the Blaze King into the Preway stack. The stack was new; his cousin and he had replaced the original stovepipe with brand new six-inch metalbestos.

Jace figured he could set the oil stove regulator to its lowest drip rate. This would keep some minimal heat on in the house even when he was away for hours at a time. Also, on those nights when the temperature dipped below fifty below (−46 C), both stoves in action could actually prevent his thin-skinned house from freezing.

While Jace worked on the stove, he listened to streaming radio on his phone, NPR's "All Things Considered." His usually flawless internet connection had a case of the hiccups that evening. The link kept breaking and rebuffering until the distraction was so annoying he shut it off. The news stories were mostly about Sandy Hook anyway, and how much of that could you listen to?

Later, when he quit for the night and logged into Facebook on his iPad, the connection was slower than a dial-up modem, so slow that his profile page never even managed to load completely. After a frustrating half hour, he logged off and wondered what he should do until it was time for bed.

Before that moment, Jace hadn't given much thought to how it must have been to spend an entire winter in McHardy in the days before the internet. What would you do with yourself? What did the pioneers do? Play cribbage? Even cribbage needed a second player.

Jace did have about five hundred books on his iPad, along with about a dozen of his favorite movies. But how many times could you watch *The Matrix*? Really?

He decided to conserve his batteries and shut off both phone and tablet. With the ranger office closed and the power plant shuttered, he would have to come up with an alternate means of charging them.

Fortunately, for tonight at least, he had a reliable backup entertainment system — a carton of old paperbacks he'd borrowed from the Sulzers. It was pretty amazing, but not surprising, how many moldy old books you could find in remote Alaska towns like McHardy. Most of Sulzer's were paperback Westerns, sci-fi, forgotten bestsellers, and literary classics, many lacking covers, that dated back to the 1960s and 70s. Their pages were yellow and their glue binding brittle. Everyone in town older than fifty seemed to have a carton or two of them tucked away in an attic or shed, and people were happy to lend, borrow, or trade.

Jace reached into Sulzer's stash and pulled one out at random. It was called *Computer War* by someone named Mack Reynolds and was published in 1967. Instinctively, he reached for the iPad to check out the author on Wikipedia and was brought up short — battery life, wonky internet. He'd have to look it up later.

Anyway, *Computer War* not only had its original cover, it had two. The back cover was printed upside down and seemed to be for an entirely different book — *Death is a Dream* by E. C. Tubb. A printing error? Apparently not, for each half of the book contained a separate short novel, upside down from each other, that met in the middle. Not an error, then, but a marketing gimmick. How clever they were back in the pre-Amazon days.

E. C. Tubb was a more familiar name to Jace; he had died not long ago at the age of ninety, and NPR had done an obit on him that Jace remembered listening to. One of the original paperback hacks, Tubb had more than one hundred forty novels to his credit and probably ten million short stories.

Jace flipped the dual book over several times trying to decide which story to read. Some unidentifiable brown liquid in the uncertain past had soaked through the center of the book from page 97 on the *Computer* side to page 134 on the *Death* side, and one book corner bore the tooth marks of an inquisitive rodent. All of which showed that pre-digital books could be interesting in and of themselves.

He went with the *Computer War* side and jumped in:

> *Tilly Trice looked up at his entrance into her shop. She winked perkily and blew him a kiss, but didn't get up from her work.*
>
> *She was, he told himself all over again, the most unlikely young woman a powerful and wealthy governmental head could ever expect to make himself a fool over. She was tiny. Her figure could hardly have been less, being that of a teen-age boy, rather than one of the current TriDi sex symbols. Her face was pert rather than pretty, not to speak of beautiful . . . .*

Powerful and wealthy governmental head? Uh-huh. The figure of a teen-age boy? Hmmm. As to making oneself a fool over an unlikely woman, the hero of this book and Jace Kuliak were on the same brown-stained page. Jace's own mismatched sweetheart had a very feminine figure, but what future was there in falling in love with a Jesus freak? Even if she fell for him too, would she be willing to leave the family madrasah? Who knew? Maybe she would. Maybe she was dying to be rescued from the family cult and was only waiting for someone like him to come along and steal her away. Not that that would be ideal. He didn't want a woman who needed to be rescued. He wanted a self-assured, empowered, independent partner. A modern girl, in other words. Not someone who prostrated herself before an imaginary sky god and believed that evolution was "only a theory." Why was he so hung up on her? What was wrong with him (besides the fact that he chose to live in a place inhabited by more porcupines than girls)? Was it just the power of infatuation? Those eyes, those hips, that smile — that had blinded him? If he could just spend even one afternoon with her, his bubble would burst, and he would be cured. He was sure of it. Love was so frackin' strange.

After reading the entire halfling book by lamplight, Jace went to bed. He wasn't the least bit sleepy, but he didn't have anything else to do. [see *So He Masturbated* on page 355]

An Angel Falls from Heaven

AF1 1.0

THE NEXT DAY, the internet and phone service were still spotty. Ranger Masterson told Jace that he'd already called it in — after several disconnects — and talked to an IT guy at Valley Communications in Valdez. "They're working on it. The whole Copper Valley is affected. Someone's sucking up all the bandwidth, but they can't pin down who, or how. A phantom IP of some sort."

Though browsing at the ranger office was next to impossible, Jace did receive his email, including a letter from NASA. It was in response to an inquiry he'd made when he was trying to find satellite imagery of the snow circle. In his inquiry, Jace had been careful to sound as non-delusional as possible, but apparently he used the wrong keywords and triggered a canned response intended for the wingnut crowd.

> *Dear Space Enthusiast:*
>
> *Thank you for your recent post regarding doomsday prophecies currently circulating on the internet. Like you, many people have contacted our agency to ask if there is any scientific basis to the rumor that the world will end later this month.*
>
> *We hasten to assure you there is no factual basis in science for such a rumor and that our planet will still be around for the coming New Year.*
>
> *The source of much of the latest round of doomsday anxiety can be attributed to a misunderstanding of Maya mythology.*
>
> *The Maya was a Mesoamerican civilization that flourished over an extensive region of southern Mexico, Guatemala, and Belize from the second millennium BC to the sixteenth-century Spanish colonization*

of the Americas. The Mayas were noted for their art, architecture, fully developed written language, and remarkably accurate calendar. This calendar was used not only for the mundane task of tracking day-to-day affairs but to explain Maya mythological concepts and history. And it is the misinterpretation of this calendar, specifically the Maya Long Count Calendar, that underlies many doomsday scenarios.

According to the Maya Long Count Calendar, a "world age" is 5,126 years long and is divided into thirteen b'ak'tuns, each lasting 394 years. The current world age is nearing its end. In fact, it ends later this month on what our calendar (the Gregorian calendar) labels as December 21, 2012, the winter solstice.

It's important to keep in mind that the end of a world age is not the same thing as the end of the world itself. No Maya, Aztec, or other Mesoamerican tradition or prophecy suggested any global upheavals on this date, let alone total global destruction. It was simply a marker where one age ended and a new one began. In that sense, you could think of December 21 as similar to December 31, New Year's Eve, and celebrate it accordingly with fireworks and champagne.

On a related matter, there is no factual basis to the belief that a rogue planet called Planet X or Nibiru (or Nemesis, Hercolubus, Sedna, Eris, or Tyche) will collide with Earth. If a planet was approaching Earth on a course that would cause it to strike Earth sometime in the next few months, it would already be visible in the sky. It would appear larger than the moon and easily be seen with the naked eye. In fact, astronomers would probably have years of advanced warning before any such event. And there would be no way for any government to conceal it.

Therefore, there is no cause for alarm, and NASA sincerely urges the public to enjoy the holiday season free of any apocalyptic angst or fear whatsoever.

From all of us at NASA, we wish you a happy and prosperous New World Age on December 22, 2012.

Masterson was reading the monitor over Jace's shoulder. He'd been doing a lot of that lately. "Is that what this is all about? You're out on the flats marking a landing zone for the mothership?"

"Caught me," Jace said.

WHILE ADAM AND Corny hammered away in the cottage chamber, Hosea and Proverbs ferried up loads of building material in the mining cart. It was heavy work, and even in the chilly tunnels, big-bodied Hosea was sweating. When he paused to wipe his forehead, he heard something odd on the first level and called for Proverbs to wait up.

"What?" Proverbs said.

"Quiet. Listen."

They stood still and listened.

"I don't hear anything," Proverbs said.

"It sounds like someone humming. Don't you hear it?"

"No. It's probably just a draft in the tunnels."

"It sounds like a woman humming."

"Maybe one of the girls."

"What would a girl be doing in the keep?"

"I don't know. Why don't you ask her when we're finished." Proverbs readjusted his eyepatch and went back to work.

They continued with their task, but on the next load, the sound returned, and this time Proverbs heard it too.

They left the cart and walked up the tunnel. When they reached the old break room, they paused to shine their lights all around inside. Four long tables filled most of the space. A wooden counter ran along one side. There was a rusted sink at one end with a wooden slop bucket under the drain. Antique light bulbs hung from wires strung along the stone ceiling. Everything lay under a thirty-year accumulation of dust.

They heard the sound again coming from further up the tunnel. It was definitely a female voice, and she was half-singing, half-humming a choir hymn of some sort.

"What's a girl doing singing in the tunnels?" Proverbs said.

"You got me, brother."

They followed the voice to the powder room door.

"Who does that sound like?" Proverbs asked.

"I don't know."

"Ginger?"

"I don't think so."

"Sue?"

"Beats me. The question is, how did she get in there?"

"Well, obviously," Proverbs said, pointing at the iron hasp on which hung a padlock, "someone locked her in. Poppy probably, except that this is where he put the angel's marble."

The singing/humming continued without interruption, and Hosea raised his hand to knock. "I don't like this," he said. He knocked three times and said loudly, "Who's in there?"

The singing stopped.

"Whoever it is, hang tight. We're going to find the key and open the door." To Proverbs he said, "You stay here and keep her company. I'll be right back."

"You're crazy," Proverbs said. "I'm not staying here by myself."

"What's wrong, brother? You scared?"

"No."

"Well, you won't be alone. She's here too, and just think how scared she must be locked up in a tiny room."

"She didn't sound scared. She was *singing*."

"If it was up to you, we'd'a never found her in the first place."

"What's that supposed to mean?"

"You didn't even hear her. I had to tell you *twice* I heard something."

"So what? Maybe your hearing is better than mine. Big deal."

"Just stay here till I get back. I'm the elder of you, and you have to obey me." Raising his voice, Hosea addressed the girl again. "Don't be scared, miss. My brother will stay here to keep you company."

Hosea trundled down the tunnel to the gate where he paused to put on his parka. Someone behind him said, "What if he locked her up?"

It made Hosea jump and knock his shin against the bench. Proverbs had followed him out. "Don't do that! Don't sneak up on a body. Why didn't you stay there like I told you?"

Proverbs' good eye burned with excitement. "What if it's Ginger, and Poppy locked her up as punishment for something?"

"Well, seeing how he has all the keys, that would be a logical deduction, but I think he would'a told us."

They hiked down the slide with sore backs and sore legs and went first to the big house. Poppy wasn't there, but there was smoke in the prayer cabin stack, so they went there and Hosea rapped lightly on the door.

"Who is it?"

"Uh, Hosea, lord, and, uh, Proverbs."

"Why aren't you two working?"

"Because we have something to tell you, lord."

"And it takes two of you to tell it?"

Hosea gave his brother a dirty look. "Uh, lord," he said to the door, "there's a girl locked up in the powder room."

"Say again."

"A *girl*, lord, locked in the powder room."

"What girl?"

"We don't know, lord. She wouldn't talk to us."

"Where is she?"

"In the powder room, lord."

"I'm busy, son, and I don't have time for your bullshitting around."

"It's not bullshit, lord."

Proverbs added, "I heard her too, lord."

There were footfalls inside, and a moment later the door swung open to reveal the old man in a robe and stocking feet. His beard was sprinkled with cookie crumbs. He blocked the doorway with his belly to prevent them from entering and said, "Boys, I'm in no mood for your foolishness. There can't be a girl in the powder room because there's a lock on the door with only two keys, and I have both of them right here." He showed them his keyring. "Now get back to work and leave me alone."

"Yes, lord, but —" Hosea said.

Poppy was shutting the door when a raven, perched in a nearby spruce tree, took off into the air. Poppy watched it fly away. "Wait till I get dressed," he said.

THE GIRL WAS singing "Saved by the Blood of the Crucified One" in a rich mezzo-soprano. It was not the voice of anyone in the family. Moreover, a brilliant light shined around the edges of the powder room door.

"Wasn't no light before," Hosea whispered.

"Silence!" Poppy hissed. He put his ear next to the door and listened intently. The voice had a Midwestern twang to it, and though he couldn't place it, he was sure it wasn't the child's voice he'd heard in the woods. Naturally, a demon could imitate any voice it chose, but a demon probably couldn't utter the words:

A child of the Father, joint heir with the Son,
Saved by the blood of the Crucified One!

without gagging on them. So he located the key on his keyring and slipped it into the lock. "Stand back," he urged his sons as he removed his Bible from its holster. Clutching it before him like a shield, he opened the door. A blinding light spilled into the tunnel.

"About time," said the voice. "I was beginning to wonder if I'd come to the right place."

Poppy covered his eyes and peeked through his fingers. He saw a face, a giant face that completely filled the doorway. Actually, it was a giant face plus the cleavage of two enormous, snowy breasts.

"Who are you?" Poppy demanded.

"I am Martha of the Seraphim in the First Rank of the Ninth Order of Archangels. And don't bark at me, mortal."

Poppy's eyes adjusted to the light, and he lowered the Bible. He could see her hands now too, also huge, but mostly he saw the tops of her ginormous breasts. She appeared to be resting on her elbows and knees in the cramped space, pressed against the wall and ceiling of the powder room.

"You're an angel?"

"Isn't that what I just said? Now, step aside and allow me to get out of here."

Poppy moved away from the door. His sons, he noticed, had already retreated down the tunnel halfway to the break room. As the angel squeezed through the doorway, her shoulder got hung up on the jamb. She sucked in her breath and muttered something in an ancient-sounding tongue. Carefully, she backed up and tried again.

Out at last, the radiance of her person lit the tunnel in both directions. She tried to stand up, but the tunnel at that spot was only eight feet high (2.4 m), and she was forced to crouch, with her shoulders and upper back pressing against the ceiling.

The boys, meanwhile, fell to their knees. To them the angel said, "Arise, sons of Abraham. It is unseemly for men to kneel before angels. I am not a deity but only the servant of the Almighty." To Poppy she added, "It is I who should bow to thee, O favored servant of God."

Even Poppy was taken back by this pronouncement, but only a little.

"On further reflection," the angel Martha continued, "it appears I am already bowing." She rapped the rocky ceiling with her massive knuckles.

"Prithee, let us remove ourselves to a more commodious den."

"Yes, of course," Poppy said, still reeling from the encounter. "We can go to the machine room. Or even closer to the break room. Follow me." Poppy set off down the tunnel, but the angel called him back.

"I pray thee return and carry the key for me. Now that I have found it, I dare not let it out of my sight again."

"The key?" Poppy said. "I don't understand."

"I believe you do understand, Master Prophecy. I am the Fifth Angel."

AF3 1.0

THE FIFTH ANGEL lit up the break room chamber with her high-wattage aura. Her lustrous mahogany hair was gathered into a bun on top of her head, with a halo surrounding it like a ring toss.

The golden marble seemed even heavier than before, and Poppy had difficulty carrying it all the way to the break room by himself. With so much mass in such a small volume, the little sphere felt more pointed than round in his hand. Hosea offered to help, and Poppy gladly handed it off to his son. Hosea set it carefully on one of the lunch tables. The old wood creaked under the load.

The angel's robe was a loose garment of shimmering white linen cinched at the waist with a splendrous green sash. When she spoke, her body glowed so brightly that her robe all but disappeared, and the boys averted their eyes.

Not so Poppy. He coolly compared the angel's attributes to those of earthly women. Her breasts, pendulous by anyone's standard, had no nipples. Like Eve, she possessed no belly button. Surprisingly, she also seemed to lack a snatch. Her nether regions were as smooth and unslotted as a child's baby doll. It made Poppy wonder how, if male angels were likewise so poorly endowed, they had managed to impregnate human women before the Flood. This was a question for later study.

The angel's legs and haunches were stout and muscled, like those of athletes depicted in ancient statuary. She had the biceps of a weightlifter, as well as the thick neck and broad shoulders. The better for supporting wings, he supposed. Her only softening feature, besides her breasts, were her warm, brown eyes.

Then it struck him who she reminded him of, the governor of Alaska, Vera Tetlin. Once he noticed the resemblance, it was inescapable. They could be cousins.

"You say you are the Fifth Angel as recorded in Revelation," Poppy said. "And that the marble is the key to the bottomless pit of Hell."

"Verily."

"How is that possible? The Bible says nothing about the Fifth Angel fumbling her trumpet and key."

"Truly, it does not," she replied. "Nor does it say that she didn't drop them, does it?"

"No, it doesn't, but it seems like an important detail, and I can't imagine the Apostle John leaving something like that out."

Those warm, brown eyes grew suddenly cold and flinty. "Are you saying you know better than the Holy Spirit what to record and what to leave out? Are you second-guessing His disciple John?" She stood tall and seemed to fill the room.

"No, no," Poppy hastened to say. "Not at all. But it's a fair question, it seems to me."

Martha's radiance dimmed a little, and her shoulders slumped. "Be at peace, my friend. You are right, it is a fair question, and one that deserves to be answered. I shall not let my bruised honor prevent me from doing so. In a word, I was clumsy, and my sturdy arm was buffeted by sin."

"You committed a sin?"

"No, not I. Angels have only sinned the once when my brother, Lucifer, and his legions tried to topple the Creator from His throne. For which treachery they were cast out of Heaven before the dawn of time. No, it was Man's sin, or sins, billions of them each moment in this wicked world, that disrupts the harmony of Heaven, makes the Almighty weep, and His servants clumsy and dull-witted.

"On Earth, you have a concept called the 'fog of war,' yes? This calamity also afflicts the Heavenly host; sin is Satan's weapon, and sinners are his unwitting allies. That is the reason why the Final Battle takes place on Earth, for nowhere else in creation does Satan stand a chance of prevailing."

The angel's sturdy feet were shod in Roman-style sandals, with leather bindings that wound around her ankles and calves like snakes. Her feet left no prints on the dusty floor. Odd, for she seemed to be a physical being. And for that matter, why hadn't she carried the "key" herself?

"Or," Poppy said, "you are an impostor, a devil in disguise to trick us."

"Have you so little faith in your own righteousness, Master Prophecy? I can see with my eyes that you have cleansed this fortress of all devils and demons and sealed its portals with the juice of the olive. To heavenly eyes, this anointing shines brighter than the fires of pitch and brimstone that rage in Hell, and it marks this place as sanctified to the Lord of Heaven. It was the sign I needed to locate the missing key. Do not doubt your God-given powers, Master Prophecy, for Heaven will have sore need of them in the coming days and weeks. If I am to fulfill the Word as prophesied, I too will have need of the one called Prophecy and of his noble sons."

Poppy and the boys exchanged a glance. "What need," Poppy said, "do you, an archangel of Father God, have of me and my sons?"

"The bottomless pit must be opened and the locusts and stinging scorpions released to torment evil men as written in Revelation. Otherwise, the opening salvo of the final battle will be botched, and Satan will gain the upper hand.

"Until the pit is opened, the sixth angel cannot sound her trumpet that will loose the four Angels of Death who are bound in the River Euphrates to accomplish their bloody assignment of slaying the third part of men.

"Until the pit is opened, the war cannot proceed, God's victory cannot be proclaimed, and the New Earth cannot be founded. Lucifer and his followers lack the power to defeat Almighty God, but they can delay His will for millennia."

All of this sounded plausible, but Poppy remained uneasy. "If you are Father God's warrior assigned by Him to unlock the pit, why can't you do it yourself? Why do you need the help of mortals?"

"I will show you why, although it fills you with revulsion and me with shame." Until then, the angel had not turned her back to the men. Now she did so and extended her six wings. Her two main wings, her snowy-white instruments of flight, were withered, crippled things. One ended in a twisted, little knob. The other was scorched along its length, its fine bones broken, and its fabric of feathers ripped to shreds.

The four small trim wings were wrenched from their sockets and plucked, like chicken wings from the grocery store.

"Sin!" she exclaimed, carefully folding and extending her damaged wings. "Behold the power of sin over angels." She turned to them again. "Pray for me, Prophecys. Prayer is a balm that helps me heal. But I am too badly damaged and won't heal in time to unlock the pit by myself. I need your prayers, yes, and I need your help even more.

"I must send up a beacon of light to rally the angels. My comrades must arrive before Satan's horde, or all hope will be lost. But I am in no shape to summon them myself. Will you help?"

The sight of her injuries was shocking, but her naked plea for help was even more.

"A beacon?" Poppy Prophecy said. "What sort of beacon?"

"A flare," replied Martha, the self-proclaimed Fifth Angel. "Similar to the flare an injured hunter might shoot skyward to summon his rescuers. In this case, the flare's brilliance will escape the bounds of Earth and be seen from the Throne Room."

"If it's so bright, won't Hell see it too?"

"Verily, Hell will. Thus shall my flare serve as the starting gun for a desperate race. The fleetest of my comrades and enemies will strive to arrive first. We must prepare ourselves for the situation in which our side is the runner up."

"Wait a minute. What if I don't want my family's refuge to become your battleground?"

"What can I say, Master Prophecy? My key fell into your back yard, but no one made you pick it up. You are the one who brought it here. Here is where I found it. Here is where it remains."

Why was the angel so comely? Why did she resemble the Alaska governor? *Dear Holy Spirit, feel free to clue me in at any time.*

"And if I refuse to help? What then?"

The angel seemed puzzled by his question, as if refusing were even an option. "God has granted mortal men the burden of free will, so I suppose you may well refuse," she said in an even voice. "In that case, the forces of Satan will surely arrive first, whether or not I launch a flare, and though this sanctified fortress may hold fast against them for a while, without relief from Heaven it cannot withstand them indefinitely. The gate will be breached, I will be overwhelmed, you and your offspring will be slaughtered, and the key to the pit will be lost forever."

"If it's the key they want," Poppy said, "I could remove it from the keep myself and take it somewhere far away from here."

"You could, and by doing so betray the Father's trust in you. Do you imagine He has led you to this place and endowed you with the cash needed to possess it and to stock it — all for your own private sanctuary and nothing else?"

Well, to be honest, yes. Until that moment, that was exactly what Poppy had imagined. And the scope of the angel's sudden revelation left his head spinning.

"When do you need my decision?"

"Go, supplicate the Father for guidance, but keep in mind that each hour that passes, the enemy approacheth."

AF4 1.0

THE VERY IDEA of angels looking down on the roof of their house thrilled the children, but not as much as the fact that there was an actual angel at that very moment inside their keep and that it had spoken to their father and Hosea and Proverbs. The little ones kept glancing back at their brothers in wonder even as their father spoke. The heavenly trumpet was old news compared to this latest miracle.

"Can we see it?" Frankie begged, and the rest of them took up her plea.

"Silence!" Poppy said. "The angel didn't come here for your amusement. There's a war on, and we have very little time to prepare. The angel says an army of devils will attack us within a week. Are we ready? No, we're not."

He succeeded in spoiling the mood. The children's excitement gave way to anxiety, and they held each others' hands. Deut took Ginger's hand in hers, and Ginger let her do it though she didn't believe a word Poppy was saying.

Poppy turned to Adam, who sat in the back, arm-in-arm with Sue. "How close are we to moving into the keep?" he asked him.

"Well, lord," Adam replied, "the cottage won't be finished, but I reckon we can sleep rough till it is. We have most of the major supplies in but only about half of the lumber and cordwood. And then there's all the stuff we want to take from the house."

Poppy said, "I know we all been working extra hard lately, but we need to work even harder. Every boy, down to you . . ." he pointed at Uzzie, "drop whatever you're doing to help Adam. You girls will take over the boys' chores. The older girls will start packing things to take to the keep. Get the essentials first."

Ginger caught Proverbs watching her from across the room. He was still wearing the eyepatch, and Ginger wanted to apologize for her insensitive remark the other day. But his brooding manner was making her uncomfortable.

"No one is to go outdoors without a shadow," Poppy continued. "That means *no one*. Keep this in mind: between here and the keep, a whole army of demons is skulking around looking for someone to jump into. Don't give them the chance. Pray out loud. Sing His glory. Repeat His holy name again and again. Remember, prayer is our best defense against unclean spirits."

"Speaking of defense, I want you older boys to be armed at all times. Corny, you too."

"Me too?" said Ithy.

Poppy looked at Adam, and Adam nodded.

"You too, and Uzzie, but only with .22s. I want you boys to shoot down every raven you see hanging around. I know that at least one of 'em is a demon. Don't take any chances — shoot 'em all."

"Excuse me, sir," Ginger said, raising her hand. She hadn't intended to speak, but this was taking things too far. "Ravens are protected birds in Alaska. You can't just go around shooting them."

Poppy gave the girl a hard look. He was *this* close to packing her off to town. "Leave us," he said.

"Sir?"

"Go to the girls' room until we're finished here."

Ginger harrumphed. Banished. She supposed it could be worse. She smiled at Deut as she got up. She went to the bunkroom as ordered, but she stood just inside the doorway to eavesdrop.

"Any questions?" Poppy asked his congregation.

"What about when we're asleep, lord?" little Myrrh said. "Will the demons bother us then?"

"No, we're safe inside the house. Remember how we anointed it after chasing all the evil ones out? This is a sanctified place. Don't worry. Just don't go outside unless you have to, and if you do, go with someone and pray the whole time."

Poppy looked around for more questions. Finding none, he said, "Then it's time for dinner. I won't stay. I have to go pray. I have a really big decision to make.

"Which reminds me. Sarai still owes Father God a punishment. Now would be a good time to settle your debt, daughter. So after you eat, I want you to bring a basin of water out to the prayer cabin. Understand?"

Everyone looked at Sarai, who sat alone and didn't seem to be paying attention.

"I'm talking to you, girl."

Sarai lifted her head and met his gaze.

"Wash your mother's feet first, then come out to wash mine. We can't have any lingering sin befouling this house. Got it?"

He waited — everyone waited — until she nodded.

AF5 1.0

THE HUMANS LOCKED the gate when they finished work for the day. The raven flew to one of the narrow sniper slots overlooking the mine adit. The bird squeezed inside the gallery and hopped along the floor to the entrance area. From there it flew through utter darkness to the break room where it alighted on the wooden table next to the sphere. Except for the sphere, the room appeared to be unoccupied. The raven leaned over the sphere and pecked at it, but its beak left no mark.

Wait till I soften it, the angel said.

The bird, endowed with legacy reflexes, startled and leaped into the air. But it landed again and settled, searching all around for the source of the communication.

Now. Try it again.

This time the surface of the sphere was pliable, and the raven was able to peel away a tiny strip of it with the tip of its beak. The bird dropped the shiny strip on the table, where it sizzled and condensed into a tiny ball the size of a mustard seed.

When the seed had cooled, the raven seized it in its beak and without so much as a squawk of farewell flew down the tunnel

OF THE DOZENS of ancient volcanos in the Wrangell-St. Elias Mountain Range, only one was considered still active, though dormant. Its last eruption had occurred in 1930, and even that was little more than the release of gasses. This was Mt. Wrangell (14,163 ft. or 4,317 m), looming over the Copper River Valley. It did occasionally belch ash and sulfurous clouds from three fumarolic vents on Mt. Bonasso, a 13,009 ft (3,965 m) cinder cone that sat like a wart on its northwestern flank. The fumaroles led, after many twists and turns, to the massive magma chamber deep inside the mountain.

The raven landed next to the largest of the fumaroles. Snow surrounding the vent had been melted, leaving a bare ring of fractured basalt. Hot, poisonous gasses ruffled the bird's feathers as it hopped into the breach.

The raven didn't get far. The large opening at the surface quickly narrowed, and after advancing only a few yards, the bird encountered an immense rock blocking its way. The rock was too large for the bird to hop over, and the space was too confined for it to spread its wings.

So the raven backed out and tried the two smaller vents. Both proved equally impassable. The bird's avian architecture, while ideal for covering long distances in the atmosphere, was the wrong kind for burrowing underground.

With the seed still clamped in its beak, the raven climbed into the air and circled over the volcano, before turning south and continuing to its secondary destination. Needle Peak was a mountain bordering the Bagley Ice Field but still within the park. The bird alighted on a granite ledge above an exposed seam of coal that it had logged during its initial survey of the region. There were gaps in the seam where large chunks of coal had broken off and fallen away. Into one of these cavities the raven dropped the golden seed.

The seed rattled down the crevice and out of sight.

The raven waited in the icy wind until a trickle of smoke began to escape from the cavity. The trickle quickly grew into a smoky cloud leaking from cracks and seams all along the cliff face. When black smoke began to spout from multiple coal veins, the bird launched itself from the ledge and headed for home.

AF6 1.0

DURING COLD MONTHS, when the stove in the common room ran out of fuel in the middle of the night, the entire house cooled down. Sleeping girls and boys snuggled deeper into their downy cocoons, and no one seemed to notice the chill. Except maybe the dog whose water dish in the kitchen sometimes formed a skin of ice.

Something awakened Ginger. The sound of the front door closing perhaps. It was Sarai in the shadows, returning from her punishment in the prayer cabin. So late? Ginger had asked Deut about this punishment, and Deut recounted her twin's transgression before their trip to Wallis. Without, however, including her own part in the event or her simmering resentment over the special-daughter status her sister enjoyed with their father.

"But washing feet?" Ginger had said. "That's so, I don't know, odd."

"It's the right punishment for the sin," Deut replied, confident in the biblical basis of her argument. "Sarai committed a sin of pride. Our Savior washed the feet of his disciples as an act of humility. What better remedy for pride?"

Lying in bed, Ginger listened to Sarai preparing to retire, and she drifted back to sleep. But her bladder, once awakened, refused to settle down until she emptied it. Eventually, despite the frigid room, Ginger surrendered to necessity and slipped her feet onto the cold, cold floor.

With an LED candle to light her way, Ginger padded silently past the beds and bunks of sleeping girls to the corner where the honey bucket was kept. When she pulled aside the curtain, she was startled to find someone already there, seated on the bucket. It was Sarai.

"Oh, I'm sorry —" Ginger began, but Sarai shushed her.

"Don't tell," Sarai whispered. "Please don't tell."

"Don't tell what?"

Then Ginger saw Sarai's bare thigh, a rare sighting in this house, and a knife. Blood trickled from a short notch Sarai had carved into her own flesh. She held a baby diaper under it to sop up the blood. Before Sarai was able to lower the hem of her nightgown, Ginger saw two more notches next to the fresh one, older and scarred over.

"Swear you won't tell. Swear!"

IT SEEMED THAT Ginger was Sarai's friend now. Sarai had exchanged no more than a dozen words with their guest since she'd arrived, and now suddenly they spent every minute together, whispering like sisters. When Deut asked Ginger to help her sort out the linen closet for their move, Ginger begged off saying she wanted to help Sarai that day.

It was unfair, typical, and the story of Duet's life. Evil thoughts coursed through her mind — jealousy, self-pity, anger — but she throttled them back because they were unchristian and unloving and because they would make her soul an easy path for Satan to invade their home. And she, at least, took the safety of the household seriously. Sarai might steal away the only friend she ever had, but that was no reason to wallow in sin.

AF7 1.0

THE COTTAGE CHAMBER was mostly dry. Except for a few spots where water dripped from the limestone ceiling, it would never rain there. So there was no reason to cover the firewood. Nor was there any compelling reason to stack it in neat piles. Yet that was how Hosea chose to store it, and since he was in charge of the firewood, that was how he insisted it be done. So far he had about fifty two-cord stacks lined up in rows of ten.

"Five rows times ten in a row times two cords to a stack," he told Adam, "makes one hundred cords. This way, we'll be able to see how fast we go through it and whether we need to ration it."

"Oh, for pity sake," Adam replied. "We're in a race against the devil. You heard Poppy. You saw the angel. Just dump it now and arrange it later."

Hosea relented. His brother was right. It was a small thing. What counted now was just getting the wood in. He'd have seven years to stack it. But when he played his light over the existing stacks, there were gaps in the ranks. He couldn't believe it. A pile was missing here, another pile there.

"What the frick!" he said.

"Your mouth, brother."

"Look, there are whole double-cords missing."

"What?"

"There should be piles there, there, and there."

"Maybe you missed those spots."

Hosea gave his brother a withering look. "I didn't leave any gaps. Why should I leave gaps?"

"Maybe someone moved them."

"Who? Where to? *Why?* They could just ask me for wood. They didn't have to pull stacks apart I already built. And who's burned through that much wood in the last couple of days?"

No one had. Adam and Hosea explored the gaps. The cordwood was gone, not even a splinter or piece of bark was left behind, only a thick layer of dust on the rock floor. It was a mystery, but there was no time to sort it out just then.

AF8 1.0

DEUT HADN'T MEANT to eavesdrop. She was busy collecting cast-off mittens and scarfs in the arctic entry that adjoined the kitchen. When Sarai and Ginger came into the kitchen to start prepping dinner, Deut's first impulse was to storm through the kitchen, head held high, impervious to Ginger's treachery. If they said anything to her at all, she'd just say, "Sorry, but I'm busy," and not look back.

But Deut was anything but impervious. There was a big gaping hole in her heart where her friend had been. She hated Ginger. She hated her with all her might.

The two girls in the kitchen spoke in low voices and paused each time one of the little ones came in to ask for this or that. Their tone sounded serious, but the arctic entry door was mostly shut and Deut couldn't make out the words. Which was fine. Except, once she'd straightened out the arctic entry, what was she to do? Put on her own coat and go outside and around to the front door? Otherwise, they'd know she had been eavesdropping.

Then the door swung completely open, and Deut's heart stopped. But it was only Crissy Lou, who had come through the kitchen searching for something. Uzzie probably. The dog wagged her tail when she saw Deut lurking there, and Deut pulled her all the way in so she wouldn't give her presence away.

With the door now open, Deut could hear everything, and the first thing she heard astonished her.

"Please don't," her sister was saying, urging, begging. "They'll sic the state on us. That's not what I want. That's not why I told you."

"You told me," Ginger replied, not unkindly, "because I saw what you were doing to yourself."

Then her sister began to cry, and Deut's first impulse was to rush out there to her defense. But she held back and continued to eavesdrop.

"I'm sorry," Ginger went on. "But when the Troopers come out here to arrest him, Child Services won't be far behind, and there's nothing I can do about it. That's just the way it is. Especially with your mother sick and all."

"Mama isn't sick," Sarai insisted, "and my brothers and sisters shouldn't be split up because of something he done. I'd rather die before that."

"Maybe they won't be split up," Ginger said. "We have a big house. I'm sure my parents will take you in until we figure things out."

"All of us? We make a crowd of people, you know."

"I know! Well, the three oldest are adults and can do what they want, even stay here, but we have a big church in Wallis with plenty of good people there who can help out. We'll figure something out so you can all stay together. I *promise*. The big question is how do I get to town."

"Aren't your parents picking you up?"

"My brother, in Gulkana, but that's still a couple weeks away, and I don't think I can last that long here. And besides, what are the chances that your *lord* will want another *foot bath* before then?"

"Stop it!" Sarai pleaded.

"I swear, I'll shoot him myself before I allow that to happen."

Deut's sister was crying hard now, and Deut couldn't make out anything else she said. For that matter, she couldn't make out anything she'd already heard. None of it made sense. It was gibberish. What were they talking about? Arrest him? Him who? Poppy? Adam? Proverbs? And for what?

DEUT WAS SO shaken up, she had to talk to someone. But who? Not Poppy; she didn't dare. He'd probably punish them all (though the idea of Poppy whipping Ginger with a willow switch did hold some appeal). Not her brothers. What could they do but tell Poppy?

So Deut told the only person she dared, Mama, while she brushed her hair in the warm corner.

"What gives her the right to judge us?" Deut asked. There was so much noise and commotion swirling around the common room that she could talk in a normal voice without the danger of being overheard. "Just because people don't wash other people's feet in her church doesn't mean it's not biblical. I mean, Mary Magdalen washed Elder Brother Jesus' feet, didn't she? And dried them with her *hair*. The pope in Rome washes Catholic feet, don't he? But according to Miss Busybody it's child abuse. Call in the highway patrol. Haul Poppy off to prison. Put the rest of us in foster care. Put you in —"

Whether or not her mother was paying attention was hard to tell. She did seem to wince when Deut's hairbrush struck a knot. That meant some part of her was present, right?

"You must tell Elder Brother Jesus, Mama. Someone's got to stop her before she ruins everything."

Mama P made no promises.

AF9 1.0

"AREN'T YOU A clever little striver," the angel said. "You've come up with your own song." [see *Raven Song* on page 358]

The raven stood on the table pecking at the golden marble and pulling off a half-dozen strips of its foil-skin. Each strip shrank into a tiny seed, which the raven swallowed and stored in its crop.

"Hurry, my pet, deliver these and come back for more before the boneheads lock me up again. And please don't get too smart for your own good. At least not yet."

THE RAVEN FLEW far and wide. It regurgitated its payload seed by seed over mountain peaks, glaciers, remote woods, riverbanks, deep gullies — anywhere humans were unlikely to venture or look anytime soon. Everywhere the bird stopped, tulips began to sprout. Let the tulips bloom.

AF10 1.0

"I PRAYED UP a storm," Poppy said. "I've been on my knees for forty-eight hours straight."

Angel Martha slouched against the wooden table as though too weary to stand up straight. Her stubby wing was still horribly misshapen, perhaps worse than before. And her angelic radiance had dimmed.

"I am glad to hear it, son of Abraham. With prayer comes clarity. Tell me what you have decided."

"I have decided to help you."

"It gladdens my heart to hear this, though it comes as no surprise. I knew that your love of the Father surmounts all other affairs of your life."

"Maybe it does, but the decision didn't come easy. You know, Martha, I have taken the name Prophecy, but I'm no prophet. I just try to keep myself open to the whispers of the Holy Spirit. I used to think the Holy Spirit led us to this place to shield my family from the devastation of the End Times. I said, Let the armies of the Antichrist do their worst. Let them scorch the Earth. Let them slaughter everyone in their path. We would be safe in our keep.

"And I must confess, I was puffed up with all we accomplished here. But now I see how blind I was. Father God didn't lead us here to sit out Armageddon on our asses. I know this now, and I accept it, though I still fear for the lives of my babies. Yet, when Father God calls, who can resist?"

Martha bowed her head. A tear, a liquid diamond, ran down her cheek. "Praise Him," she said.

"Praise Him. Amen." Poppy pulled a rag from his pocket and blew his nose. "So, tell me, Martha," he continued, "how do I shoot off this emergency flare of yours?"

"Pull either flap from the key, but do not hold onto it. Pull it off and let it go. As soon as it comes free, drop it."

As Uzzie had discovered in the machine room, the otherwise perfect sphere had two flaps. Poppy grasped one of them and pulled. It was softer than before, and it came away easily from the golden marble. Although he let it go immediately, it grew so hot so quickly it singed his fingertips, and he put them in his mouth.

The liberated flap danced around the tabletop for a few moments, like a drop of water on a hot skillet. And when it settled, it was a tiny ball, the size of a pea. It sat in a little dimple of scorched wood.

"Now what?"

Angel Martha laid out the steps Poppy was to follow. They weren't complicated. He was to take the tiny sphere to a remote, forested area of his choosing and drop it on the ground. That was all there was to it, except that once he dropped the sphere, he was to leave the area as fast as he could.

"And you must do it tonight," Martha concluded. "There's no more time to lose. You must accomplish this mission tonight, or not at all."

"Tonight is good."

AF11 1.0

THE SKIS HAD been discarded behind an outlying shed, along with lumber scraps and empty paint cans. A decades-old trash midden.

The skis were of an ancient Nordic style, made from laminated wood. The varnish had chipped off eons ago, and the leather bindings were missing, eaten by voles.

"I don't know about this," Ginger said. "Don't you have anything newer?"

"We don't have skis because none of us ever learned how to ski," Sarai said. "We never learned in California."

"I suppose I could make them work," Ginger said. "I'll have to make new bindings of some sort and ski poles." But when she found a large crack at the curved tip of one of them, she tossed the skis back into the refuse pile. "On second thought, I'll just walk."

"It's sixteen miles to town," Sarai said.

"I only need to get to the Bunyans'. They'll help me."

Sarai wasn't fond of the idea of the Bunyans involved in her family's affairs. "Eight miles then, but in this cold?"

"It's not that cold or that far." Big words coming from a Wallis girl who drove her Camry everywhere she went. Also, her home in Wallis was near the Gulf of Alaska where it never got really cold, not like it did here on Stubborn Mountain.

"You could drive a sno-go," Sarai said. "I know where Poppy keeps spare spark plugs. They're in the safe in the prayer cabin, and I know the combination. I seen him open it once."

"Why didn't you say so?"

"'Cause he keeps the cabin door locked when he's not there. But I thought maybe if he wants me again . . ."

"No! I already told you. That'll never happen again."

"But it's not like it's a sin, is it? The prophets of old did it. He read me the verses. And on account of Mama —"

"It *is* a sin. It's rape. It's incest, for heaven sake. You are a *victim*, Sarai. Unless we turn your father in to the authorities, Cora or Frankie or Myrrh will be his next victim. Is that what you want?"

"No, of course not. But he wouldn't touch them anyway. I am the special daughter, the one Father God gave him for his ease and comfort. Not even my twin. Just me."

"Will you please get that out of your head. *There's no such thing as a special daughter.* He made that up." And before Sarai could disagree, Ginger added, "No matter what verses he *pretends* to read you, it's a lie."

They retraced their steps in the snow in silence. At the edge of the yard, Sarai stopped abruptly.

"What is it?" Ginger said.

"Only just my brother."

Like she had only one. Ginger scanned the yard and at first didn't see anyone there. "Which brother?" Then she saw a man pointing a rifle at them. "What the —"

A blast shattered the afternoon stillness, and bits of black feathers rained down upon their heads. A black shape fell from the tree next to them into the snow where it thrashed on the ground.

Proverbs jogged across the yard, and Ginger demanded, "What did you do?"

"I saved your soul is what I did," he said, grabbing her arm and drawing her toward the house. "Let's get you back inside."

"Don't touch me!" Ginger shouted, throwing off his hand. "That was a bird! Birds are not demons! Birds are God's creatures, you freak!"

Sarai stepped between them. "Don't speak to my brother that way."

But Ginger was too wound up to stop. "I'm going to report what he did. You hear me, creep? Ravens are protected. And that moose you poached? Oh, yes, I know all about the moose. You think I don't? You can't just go around killing everything you see and get away with it."

Proverbs reeled under the attack, but Ginger wasn't finished. "What do you think?" she said, her voice so tight it squeaked. "That killing things is sexy? That you'll attract girls that way? Well, I've got news for you, Romeo — it's not the least bit attractive. It's repulsive. You're repulsive. You make me want to vomit."

Proverbs stood there, taking it, rubbing his eye under the patch. When her fury was spent, he said, "We kill moose to feed ourselves."

But Ginger wasn't listening. She turned abruptly and set off across the yard to the house. Brother and sister watched her go. Finally, Proverbs said, "She wants to turn me in to Fish and Game?"

"I think so."

"Stupid bitch."

"Proverbs! Language!"

"I'm sorry, but she is." He expelled the cartridge from his rifle and chambered a new round before continuing toward the tree.

"Where are you going?"

"I gotta make sure I killed the damned thing."

"Your tongue, brother."

"It *is* damned. It's a demon, ain't it? That's the very meaning of damned." An unexpected smile flashed across his face. "Go on, say it. It feels good, and this is the one time you can say it."

"Damned thing," Sarai said, trying it out.

"See?"

"Damned thing," she repeated, following him around the tree. *"Damned thing! Damned thing! Damned thing!"*

"Whoa there, sister. Don't wear it out. Did you see where the demon fell?"

She pointed, and Proverbs began to wade through the snow to the spot. But before he was halfway there, there was an explosion of snow, and the black bird powered into the sky on supercharged wings. Proverbs brought up his rifle and snapped off another round, but the damned thing was gone. They watched the sky, shaken by the demon's resilience.

They walked back to the house together. "The problem is," Sarai said, "we all seen wonders, just like now, but she hasn't. I seen the trumpet. The rest of you seen that plus the handprint. You and Adam and Hosea seen the angel. We don't need no convincing, but she does. Her faith isn't as strong as ours."

"So? What can I do about it? You saw the way she hates me."

"Show us the angel."

Proverbs grunted. "Poppy says no."

"I know he does, but it's either that or you can forget about her. I thought you wanted her for a wife. You want her to stay, don't you? Not leave and rat you out to Fish and Game."

"I can't just take you up there."

POPPY WAS SAFELY settled into his prayer cabin. His curtain was open. He was propped up in the daybed, reading, the Bible it looked like.

They ran into Corny and Ithy loading toboggans with supplies at the bottom of the slide. Corny wore a Ruger .22 pistol on his belt, and Ithy had a rifle slung over his shoulder. The boys stared at Ginger, but before either of them had a chance to say anything, Proverbs told them to mind their own business.

"Or what?" Corny said. "You calling the shots now, brother? That eyepatch make you the boss? You know Poppy doesn't want her in the keep."

Sarai got into the boy's face. "Knock it off."

"Or what?" Corny repeated. "Now I gotta take orders from a girl?"

"No, you don't, but let me ask you something; have *you* seen the angel?" She turned to Ithy. "How about you?"

Neither boy could meet her gaze.

"That's what I thought. Poppy told you to stay away from the angel too, didn't he? But you decided for yourselves to go behind his back, and now you want to tell us what to do?"

The two middle boys made excuses about getting back to work, and Proverbs asked where Adam and Hosea were working.

"Adam's in the cottage. Hosea's in the storeroom."

AS THE TWO girls and Proverbs made their way to the break room, the illumination in the tunnel increased gradually. Near the ramp intersection, the tunnel was so bright they could turn off their headlamps.

Proverbs stopped at the ramp and said, "You two go on. I'll stay here in case anyone comes down. You can't miss the angel because of — you know — her light. And also 'cause she's like ten feet tall."

"Her?" Ginger said. "The angel is a her?"

"Yeah. Her name is Martha."

"Interesting."

PROVERBS WASN'T KIDDING about the light. The doorway to the break room blazed like the sun. But as they approached it, the brilliance dimmed to a tolerable level, and a musical voice came from within. "Welcome, daughter of Abraham."

The girls stepped through the doorway and were overwhelmed by the very sight of her, the size of her, her beauty, the heavenly light emanating from her flesh, and her air of mastery.

Sarai began to cry on the spot. Ginger was dumbfounded. It was real!

Ginger had been so sure of Poppy's lunacy, but here was something she could not explain away.

The angel tipped her head toward Sarai, and her glowing halo struck sparks on the rocky ceiling. "Hail, special daughter of the prophet, who knows the Father's commands and faithfully embraces them."

"Me?" Sarai said. "Father God knows about me?"

"Of course He does," Martha said. Her smile was so glorious it filled the girl's heart. "The Father knows thee and heaps praise and blessings upon thy head."

Sarai became dizzy and had to sit down on a bench.

"The Father would only ask that thou cease punishing thy flesh, for thy earthly form is a gift He has given thee, and it must not be unduly spoiled."

"I'll stop," Sarai sobbed. "I'm sorry."

"Wait a minute," Ginger said. Despite her utter amazement, she felt compelled to speak. "Are you seriously telling her it's okay with God what her father does to her?"

The angel turned to Ginger with a look of disgust. "What accursed imp do we have here?"

"Uh, this is my friend, Ginger," Sarai said.

The angel pointed at Ginger's chest. "Your friend has acquired unwelcome company."

"Excuse me?" Ginger said, examining herself. "What's that supposed to mean?"

"Leave us, fiend. You've seen what you came to see. Remove your filthy presence from this sanctuary."

Sarai said uncertainly, "You want us to go, angel?"

"No, not thee, cherished one. Only her. I pray thee stay and favor me with the joy of thy company. And I pray thee resist thy false friend's lies. She can only do thee harm and lead thy soul to grief. Prithee stay away from her."

"You're right," Ginger said. "I have seen what I came to see. I'll go now. Come on, Sarai. Let's get out of here." Ginger went to the doorway. "Are you coming?"

Sarai was plainly torn. "But the angel wants me to stay."

"Of course she does," Ginger said, returning to grab Sarai's arm.

Sarai continued to gaze at Martha even as Ginger pulled her away. "Thank you, angel," she said. "I can't tell you how much this means to me what you said about me. You've given me back . . . my whole life. Thank you. Thank you."

"Thy life was always thine own," the angel said. "Thy father is a holy man."

"No, he's not!" Ginger said. "He's a child molester and a rapist."

"Begone, imp," Martha commanded. The angel grew so bright that Ginger had to cover her eyes. But not Sarai. "Cherished one," Martha said to Sarai, "I see thy brother standing guard several steps away. Prithee ask him to summon thy father to speak with me."

"Yes, angel," Sarai said. "I will."

BAGS AND BASKETS of dirty laundry awaited Sarai in the arctic entry, courtesy of Deut. Proverbs volunteered to help her move the laundry to the bathhouse. But when Ginger offered to pitch in as well, Sarai told her she didn't need her help anymore.

Ginger said, "You don't believe what that thing said, do you?"

"How can you see a real-life angel and call her a *thing*?"

"Because whatever she is, she's no angel. Angels don't lie, and all she told were lies."

"You really are possessed, aren't you?"

"Whatever," Ginger said and went into the kitchen.

As Proverbs and Sarai carried loads of laundry across the yard, Proverbs said, "What was that all about?"

"Nothing."

"You told her she was possessed. That don't sound like nothing."

"I'm not sure that's what the angel meant, but she told me to stay away from her."

"The angel told you to stay clear of Ginger?"

"Yes."

"Great," Proverbs said. "I defy Poppy's orders and take you guys to the angel, and what do I get out of it? A possessed girlfriend. Thanks a lot."

Inside the bathhouse, Sarai hummed a little tune while lighting the barrel stove. Proverbs laid the hose from the pump house and offered to load the washing machine. But Sarai said, "I'll take it from here. Don't you have to go tell Poppy? The angel wants to talk to him."

"Yeah, but what am I going to say when he finds out I took you girls up there?"

"It'll be all right," Sarai said. She looked happier than Proverbs had ever seen her. "Just tell Poppy that his special daughter is blessed in the Father's eyes. I'm a good person, brother. The angel says so."

AF12 1.0

POPPY STARED AT the steep, switchback trail above and sighed. This was his second climb of the day.

"Are you all right, lord," Proverbs said. "Do you need to sit down?"

"Don't be stupid. I'm fine. You go on ahead. Tell Adam to wait for me at the ramp."

"Can you make it on your own?"

"Go. Just go."

THEY WERE ALL waiting for him at the ramp: Adam, Hosea, Proverbs, Corny, Solly, Ithy, and Uzzie, all the older and middle boys.

"No, no, this isn't what I told you at all," Poppy said. "Adam goes with me. The rest of you get back to work. Armageddon won't wait for you to stand around scratching your butt."

"GREETINGS, SONS OF Abraham," Martha said as they entered. "Be of good cheer." Her radiance was dialed down to a modest level, and she looked weaker than the last time Poppy visited.

"Is there some change of plans?" Poppy said. He turned to Adam. "I haven't told you yet, but I decided to shoot off Martha's flare."

"Praise Him."

"Praise His holy name. Amen. Tonight."

"Tonight, lord?"

"We do it tonight, unless Martha has a change of plans."

"No," Martha said. "No change of plans, though we may have to adjust them."

"Why? What happened?"

"This sanctuary is only secure because it is off the traveled pathways of the world. Indeed, neither Satan nor the Antichrist know we are here. They have consulted sorcerers and witches and dispatched spies to every land, but we are as yet invisible to them. This wilderness has served us well. Our isolation is our greatest defense, and —"

"Excuse me, archangel," Adam said, "but I gotta ask. Who is the

Antichrist? Have we heard of him?"

"Adam!" Poppy said. "Don't interrupt."

"Peace, Master Prophecy. Your first-born asks a worthy question. Verily, you have heard his name, and it should come as no surprise. The Antichrist is Black Obama."

"I knew it!" Adam said. "I knew it!"

"You and every Christian alive," Poppy said. "Now shut up unless you're spoken to."

"Yes, lord."

"Go on, angel. What were you saying?"

"Before I continue, call in your third son. He lurks just outside trying to eavesdrop."

"What? Proverbs? Are you out there? Sorry, Martha. I will tan the boy's hide for this."

"Pray, spare him the rod this once, Master Prophecy. He too needs to hear what I must say."

Proverbs came in, head down, and took a place next to his brother.

Martha continued. "I received a visit today from a demon."

Poppy was aghast. "Here? In the keep? How?"

"Peace, Master Prophecy. Yes, here, in this very chamber. It was a smug little spirit, but do not be concerned about your defenses. The keep is secure; the anointing holds. This demon entered while riding a mortal soul, and olive oil is useless against mortals." Martha glanced at Proverbs, who cringed under her gaze.

"Mortal?" Poppy said. "One of mine? Who?"

"The girl who goes by the name of a common spice."

"A common spice?"

Adam said, "I think she means Ginger, lord."

"Yes, Ginger Lawther," the angel said. "It's her demon. It's ridden her for years. She doesn't even know it's within her. It's always trying to tempt her with vice. It's constantly planting 'good ideas' in her head that are anything but good. Ideas about the place of women in the church, the meaning of Bible verses, the limits of modesty and chastity. Are you familiar with any of this?"

"Yes!" Poppy said. "I seen it first hand! Yet I brought her into my home. What have I done?"

"Worry not. You have done your job as a parent well, and thus far your household has mostly resisted the demon's urgings."

"Only mostly?"

"Peace, Poppa. Your children are true. It is but a petty demon, no more than an imp. It has no mind of its own, only an implacable thirst to despoil innocence and lead God's people astray." Again the angel poked Proverbs with a glance.

"Thus far, the demon is not in direct contact with Satan or any devil; its status is too paltry. It would be like a private in an army calling upon a general. It's not done. Otherwise, Satan would already know the location of the key.

"This demon has put a false idea in Ginger's mind that your son, Proverbs, is a criminal."

Poppy turned to his son. "What did you do now?"

Proverbs froze. "I . . . uh . . . I . . ."

Martha said, "You already know his transgression, Master Prophecy, and have already punished him for it. He killed a beast on the Antichrist's land to put its meat on your children's plate. Now Ginger Lawther proposes to punish him again by informing the game wardens. They will come to remove him to the city, where he will be lost with its other inhabitants under the sword of the enemy.

"Yet, as bad as that is, the situation is more dire. While here, the imp beheld the key lying on the table. It would have tried to snatch it away if I had not intervened. It knew it was no match for me, even in my desperate state, and withdrew. But since leaving here, it has called for help from among its kind, and in the last hour several more demons have come to ride the poor girl's soul. Right now I see . . ." Martha turned to the southwest, as though peering through solid rock. "I see not one by seven demons riding her."

"Seven?" This was too much. Poppy looked for a place to sit down, and Adam pulled one of the dusty benches over to him.

"Verily, seven, and several of them enjoy higher ranks than the original imp."

"Where is she now? In my house? Near my children?"

Martha gazed at the rock wall again. Poppy looked too, but all he saw was fractured limestone.

"She is in the kitchen of your dwelling helping Deuteronomy prepare dinner. But fear not; they are not speaking. A rift has opened between them, and your second daughter has closed her mind to Ginger's influence."

"Praise Father God," Poppy said. Deut had always been the dreamy one.

Good that she had acquired some sense.

"It is your first daughter, your special daughter, who is at risk," the angel went on. "Ginger has nearly convinced her to help her leave this place in secret."

"Sarai?"

"Yes, but I spoke to Sarai today and have turned her soul back to the light of the Father's love."

This was news to Poppy. "They were both up here? Ginger *and* Sarai?"

"Verily." For a third time the angel accused Proverbs with a glance, and this time the boy cracked.

"I did it, lord," he said. "I brought them up here. It's on me. I wish I never done it."

"That's not all you'll wish when I'm through with you."

"Master Prophecy," the angel said, "punish him for his transgressions tomorrow. Today's business is more urgent. Though frustrated in her attempt to flee, Ginger hasn't given up trying. Even now she is scheming to learn the secret code to the strongbox in your prayer cottage."

"My safe? She wants to rob us?"

"I think not. She wants the gap sticks you keep there."

Poppy looked to Adam for an explanation.

"I think she means spark plugs, lord."

"Yes, spark plugs," Martha said. "Forgive me my ignorance of human tools. Ginger wants a spark plug to flee by sled to summon the civil authorities to come take Proverbs away. And the demons within her are already clamoring for their superiors' attention. Once they succeed, word will go up the chain to Satan, their Dark Lord. Thus the mortal girl represents a threat on both planes, the higher and earthly realms. Satan will assemble an army of fallen angels against us, while Black Obama will dispatch his thugs to flush you out of hiding. Any chink in your armor will give him the opening he needs to destroy you."

"No!" Poppy said. "We've worked too hard to be taken down by a spoiled girl. I've got to stop her." He rose from the bench but sat down again. "The question is how? She can't stay in the house with those demons near the children. That's unthinkable. I've got to separate her, but where? I don't want demons here in the keep either."

Proverbs said, "I'll take her to my cabin, lord."

"And leave her there alone?"

"Uh, no. I guess I'll have to stay with her."

Poppy laughed out loud. "You, a lusty girl, and seven demons alone in a cabin. What could possibly go wrong?"

"Then I'll take Sue along as shadow."

"And deprive me of two workers when I need everyone's help? No, that won't do." After giving it some thought, he continued, "The only solution I can see would be to take her out to the woods and shoot her."

"Lord!" Proverbs said, alarmed. "I know you don't mean that."

Poppy looked at him without speaking.

"But, lord, that would be murder. You're not seriously . . . Murder is a sin."

The angel said, "To kill an enemy during time of war is not murder."

"But still . . ." Proverbs said, groping for an argument to use. "She's not our enemy; she's my betrothed. You can't just kill her. I won't let you."

Adam cleared his throat. "Lord, what if we *cast out* the demons? Then she could stay in the house." He looked at the angel for confirmation. "Wouldn't that take care of everything, Angel Martha?"

Martha shook her head. "If only that were true, but purging the girl would be no more effective than slaying her. The displaced demons would still be able to raise the alarm, and they would badger the other children looking for a new soul to ride. You would end up with three or four children in thrall to Satan instead of just one. The same would happen if you killed the girl; the homeless demons would seek out new souls to torment while they summoned Satan's army."

"See?" Proverbs said to his father. "Murdering Ginger is not the answer."

"Then what do we do, Martha?" Poppy said. "What do you suggest?"

The angel closed her eyes a moment to think. She looked exhausted. "Any solution requires us to stop both the girl and her passengers at the same time. I believe I know how to accomplish that."

"Tell me," Poppy said.

"The same anointing that keeps unclean spirits out of this keep can keep them in as well. Anoint the cell again where you found me and bring her there. The demons will be trapped. Both girl and demons will be your prisoners until the angels arrive."

DESPITE BEING THE warmest room in the house, the atmosphere in the kitchen was downright chilly when Adam arrived for Ginger. Though four girls were busy preparing dinner, there was none of the usual banter, and all of them stopped what they were doing when Adam entered.

He looked at Ginger and said, "I hear you were up to see the angel today."

"I was up to the keep, but I didn't see any angel."

That was an answer Adam hadn't expected. "Well, she says she saw you."

"If you mean the devil in the mine, then, yes, I did see her today."

Frankie dropped a baking sheet that clattered to the floor.

"That's odd," Adam went on. "She said the same thing about you. Anyway, Poppy wants to talk to you."

"Where? In his cabin? Tell him I don't wash old men's feet."

Deut shooed Frankie and Myrrh to the common room, but she herself remained at the stove.

Adam watched the middle girls leave. "No, up in the keep, and he didn't say anything about punishing you. He just wants to talk."

"Then he can come here and talk to me in the house."

"Why?" Adam said. "Why do you always have to be so contrary? He's the lord of this house. Treat him with some respect, can't you?"

Ginger said, "I've had enough of his kind of hospitality, Adam. I want to go to the Bunyans'. Today."

"That's what he wants to talk to you about. So don't worry. And he can't come down here because then he'll just have to climb back up there, and three times in one day is too much for his legs. So give him a break already. Okay?"

Ginger took off her apron and hung it on a peg. "I'll go, but I won't be alone in the same room with him."

"No one's asking you to."

Ginger paused at the door. "Where's my shadow? Shouldn't I have a shadow?"

"Oh, for pity sake, girl. We're only going up to the keep."

ANGEL MARTHA CROUCHED under the low ceiling watching the preparations. Hosea was sawing a food tray slot in the heavy door. Ithy was setting up an army cot and camping heater. Uzzie was clamping a toilet seat to a plastic bucket.

Proverbs wasn't helping. He sat against the tunnel wall and held his head in his hands. When he heard Ginger and Adam approaching from down the tunnel, he pulled himself to his feet and went to meet them.

"What's wrong with you?" Ginger said. "You look awful."

"Nothing," he replied. "Only just a little headache."

"Did he hit you?"

"What? Who?"

"Did your father hit you for bringing me to see that *thing*?" She jabbed her chin in Martha's direction.

"No, of course not."

"What's all this going on?"

"I'm sorry," Proverbs said. "It's for your own protection."

Ginger didn't like the sound of that, so she spun around and started back down the tunnel. But Adam seized her by one arm and Proverbs by the other, and they led her to the powder room. They stopped in front of Martha, who regarded the girl with naked hostility.

"This is your doing," Ginger said. "You look good, but you're the serpent, not me."

"Hello, Rath," the angel replied cooly. "It appears you have found reinforcements since we last met."

"My name is Ginger, not Rath."

"The girl's name is Ginger. Your name is Rath. Besides you I also see Zorn, Box, Puck, and Tork in there. Plus two more imps whose names are hidden from me."

"Liar!" Ginger shouted. "Godless liar!" She turned to Proverbs. "Let me go. Can't you see?It's a trick. I'm not the evil one. That *thing* is."

Next to the powder room, Poppy said, "We're ready. Bring her."

The boys backed away from the doorway as Adam and Proverbs dragged Ginger — biting, kicking, and clawing — and roughly pushed her through. Hosea quickly slammed the door, and Poppy slapped on the padlock. Ginger battered the door with fists and feet and screamed oaths and curses through the food slot.

"Do not be alarmed by the ferocity of her protests," Martha told them. "It is the custom of demons to howl when they are frustrated. Make haste now and anoint the portal, Master Prophecy, before any of them can escape."

Poppy sprinkled olive oil on the door and prayed, "I block this doorway against any evil spirit, in Elder Brother Jesus name. No evil spirit may pass in or out. Amen."

"Amen," chimed the others.

"That should do it," Martha said. "Well done."

Poppy's shoulders slumped with fatigue. He screwed the cap back on the oil bottle and sighed. "Come on, boys," he said. "We need to prepare for tonight."

But as they shuffled down the tunnel, Ginger, in a remarkably calm and measured voice, spoke through the slot. "Wait. *Please.*"

"Ignore her," Martha said. "It's only more deceit."

"I want to talk to Proverbs," Ginger said, and added, "I want to talk to my betrothed."

That got everyone's attention, especially Proverbs'.

"Forget it," Poppy said. "A demon will say anything."

"Proverbs!" Ginger called from the slot. "I *need* you. *Please!*"

Proverbs said, "I'll just see what she wants, lord."

"Ten stripes and counting, son."

"That's not fair, lord. You can't punish me for this. You heard her; she wants to be my wife. When all of this is over and done, the demons will be gone from her, but she'll still be here. How can she love me then if I don't stand by her now?"

The boy had a point. Wives had a knack for keeping old wounds fresh. Poppy shook his head. "All right, but don't get close enough so she can touch you."

"I won't, lord. Thank you, lord."

Proverbs squatted at the slot. Ginger's eyes were steady and clear. "I'm sorry," he said again. "This is only for a little while. You'll see it's necessary when you're yourself again."

"Listen," she said. "I was angry. I didn't mean what I said. I'd never report you to Fish and Game. I know you only killed that moose to help feed your family. Heck, I've been eating it too. What kind of a hypocrite would that make me if I reported you?"

"I'm glad to hear that, Ginger, but it's not why we have to lock you up."

"I know. Come closer. I want to whisper something in your ear."

That raised Proverbs' guard. Was this Ginger or a demon speaking?

"*Please.* I don't want that creature to hear me. See how she's watching us?"

Proverbs inched closer to the slot and offered his ear, ready to pull it back in an instant.

"I have to give her credit," Ginger whispered. "She *looks* impressive. Clearly, she's supernatural. I never thought I'd see a supernatural creature while I was still alive. But that doesn't mean she's an angel."

Ginger's warm breath tickled Proverbs' ear. Her close proximity and breathy voice were more intimate than any interaction he'd ever had with a girl. He couldn't help the stirring in his jeans, and he struggled to follow the conversation.

"If she's not an angel, then what?" he said.

"I don't know for sure, but the way she lies about me makes me think she's a devil. I don't know what else she could be, but I know she's no angel."

"How can you be so sure?"

"Well, for one, because there's no such thing as a girl angel."

Proverbs did a double take. "Don't be ridiculous. I've seen pictures of girl angels my whole life. There's probably more girl angels than there are boy angels."

"No, there's not. Don't you see? Those pictures you've seen are from an artist's imagination. They're from Hollywood and Hallmark Cards, not from the Bible."

Proverbs pulled back a little. "I don't think that's true."

"It *is* true. We learned it in Bible study. I've read the Bible, Proverbs, from beginning to end. Have you? All you have to go on is what your father tells you. Go to Pastor Bunyan; he'll tell you I'm right."

"But Pastor Bunyan —"

"I know, I know. Pastor Bunyan preaches falsehoods. But this isn't about the timing of the Rapture. If he says there are girl angels, tell him to show you the verse. Tell him to use a King James Bible. Not *read* you the verse like your dad does, but *show* you the verse so you can read it yourself. He can't do it because the verse doesn't exist." She thought to ask, "You can read, can't you?"

"Of course I can read. You think I'm ignorant?"

"I didn't say you were. I was just asking if you can read, and you can, so it's perfect. Go to Pastor Bunyan. That's all I ask. *And get me out of here.* I'll *die* in here if you don't."

THE BOYS WENT on ahead while Martha kept Poppy at the entrance to the break room. "I pray the Creator guides and protects you on your mission tonight," she told him. "Know that while you are gone, I will protect the key to the bottomless pit with my very existence. But if we are attacked, I may be separated from it in the heat of battle. Better that the key not be out in plain view."

They both glanced at it lying on the table.

"Where should I hide it?"

"You cannot hide it from spirits, holy or evil. We can see its light from great distances. You need only hide it from the Antichrist."

"Then I'll lock it up in the armory."

"Nay. Obama's men will surely search out your weapons. The armory is one place they are certain to find."

"Then where?"

"I see a tunnel two levels above us that leads to a deep, subterranean lake. Drop it in the lake. It'll be safe there."

"In the cistern?" Poppy shook his head. "Not there, angel."

"It's a formidable hiding place."

"Maybe, maybe not."

Calling All Angels

CA1 1.0

"HUBBLE TROUBLE" WAS the headline. Jace wondered why news editors were so fond of rhyming or punning headlines. Was it compensation for their failure at real writing?

He browsed the rest of the page. "Obama addresses Sandy Hook Massacre." That was the tragedy that Masterson had been so upset over.

Internet service was still dial-up-modem slow. Jace couldn't stream content, but he was able to use a news aggregator, as long as there were no embedded videos or tons of photos.

Jace's food supply was on his mind. Before Caldecott Lodge manager Elmer Gonzales had departed for points south, Jace had struck a deal to purchase the lodge's leftover canned and bottled goods, a mixed case of booze, coffee, teas, and condiments. It was a win-win because the lodge had no freeze-free storage, and it saved Jace a supply run to Anchorage. Elmer also leased him the lodge's sole snowmobile for the winter, since Jace would lose access to the park service's machine.

Heating fuel. Installing the wood stove had taken the pressure off his fuel supply. What remained in the 300-gallon (1136 l) tank behind the house would probably stretch till spring. But now he had to start cutting and hauling firewood. So he would need a chainsaw, splitting maul, chimney brush, and whatnot.

> *Early this morning, the aging, beloved Hubble Space telescope went offline. Engineers at the White Sands, NM, ground station managed to bring it back an hour later, but, according to a spokesperson, the telescope stopped responding to operational instructions from ground control at that time.*

> *Meanwhile, Hubble did continue to transmit data via tracking and relay satellites. Officials at the Space Telescope Science Institute in Baltimore, MD, where Hubble data is translated and disseminated, said the telescope appeared trained on a portion of space located in the galactic south, or below the plane of the Milky Way galaxy in which the Earth resides.*

> *Chief scientist Malcolm R. Peabody at the Goddard Space Flight Center in Greenbelt, MD, has speculated on whether the soon-to-be-retired instrument was the target of terrestrial cyberattack or the victim of the harsh conditions of space. "A micrometeoroid might have taken out its attitudinal controls," he told reporters. "On the other hand, a cyberattack would take sophisticated knowledge of the Hubble systems to pull off. And for what purpose?"*

> *Whatever the cause of Hubble's troubles, with the end of the space shuttle program, NASA is unable to launch a repair mission, even if such a mission was deemed practical. The James Webb Space Telescope is slated to replace the Hubble later in this decade, at which time NASA plans to send up an unmanned spacecraft to assist Hubble in reentry for a safe and final crash landing in the Pacific Ocean.*

> *In the meantime, ground-and-space-based telescopes will attempt to take up the slack during Hubble's absence.*

The story caught Jace's attention because it was the first curious space-related news story since his own curious adventure. Though he failed to see how the two things could be related.

CA2 1.0

POPPY HAD JUST the spot in mind to fire off the angel's flare, a wooded ravine on the other side of the Mizina about seven miles from home. It was close enough but off the mail plane's flight path.

Today was the twenty-first day of Twelfthmonth, winter solstice, the longest night of the year. A half moon hung in a cloudless sky. The temperature had dropped again to minus thirty (–34 C). Poppy was in the lead, breaking trail with their new Arctic Cat Bearcat. Adam and Hosea followed on the old Polaris and Yamaha. Poppy carried the angel's golden pea in a small, leather poke so that he wouldn't lose it.

After they crossed the frozen Mizina, they climbed the bluff on the other side and threaded their way through a dark forest. After several miles they came to a long, broad ravine and descended to its bottom where Poppy stopped.

"Better leave them idling," Adam shouted. He and Hosea stomped their feet and swung their arms to get their blood moving.

"See somewhere you like, lord?" Hosea said. He untied the shovel he had brought along.

"It don't matter," Poppy replied. "Just dig till you hit dirt."

Hosea dug in the snow under a large spruce until the shovel struck the frozen ground. Poppy opened the poke and spilled the pea into the hole.

"Now what?" Adam said. "We leave?"

"Not yet. I want to see what happens."

"But you said the angel said —"

"Don't argue with me, boy. I know what the angel said. Go, sit on your sno-gos if you want, but I'm going to watch."

Adam looked at Hosea, and Hosea shrugged. While they waited, the Northern Lights came out and waved like a milky green banner in the starry sky. They passed around a thermos of tomato soup that Deut had packed for them.

"Anything happening, lord?" Adam said. His father ignored the question.

Hosea asked Adam, "Did the angel say how long this would take?"

"No. She just said to hightail it outta here as soon as we dropped it."

"Go!" Poppy shouted. "Go home, you cowards. I'm tired of listening to you." That shut the complainers up, but it *was* cold, and Poppy's toes were already numb. He prayed to Father God to let whatever was supposed to happen with the pea happen already, but still they waited.

It was Poppy's habit to never let logic interfere with the tenets of his faith, but something about this whole exercise in the snowy woods refused to sit right in his mind. That is, if Father God was omniscient, which He was, and routinely heard Poppy's and everybody else's silent prayers day and night, which He did, then why did the angel need to send up any kind of flare to alert Heaven? Couldn't Father God simply tell the angels where Martha and the key to the pit were located? For that matter, how could the key or anything else become lost to Father God? And if Father God was all powerful, why was there any need for a final battle at all? It would be more of a massacre than a legit battle, wouldn't it? Did it mean that sin was more powerful than Father God? Was Satan an actual contender to the throne? Poppy became lost in his thoughts and stopped paying attention to the hole in the snow.

Hosea, the one blessed with exceptional hearing, cocked his head and said, "What's that?"

"What's what?" Adam said.

"That noise, like a crackling sound. Like when you pour soda pop into a glass full of ice."

Neither Poppy nor Adam heard anything. Poppy shined his flashlight all around inside the snow hole. The heavy pea wasn't visible, but there didn't seem to be anything happening down there.

Hosea said, "Turn off the engines and you'll hear it."

Adam said, "No thanks. Leave 'em running."

"It's getting louder. Don't you hear it?"

Poppy said, "You're just listening to your belly, son. Either shut up or go home."

"Yes, lord."

Adam said, "Why don't we all go home, lord? We can come back in the morning to see if anything happened."

After some thought, Poppy agreed. "Maybe you're right. If it's a flare they can see in Heaven, we should be able to see it from the house."

They returned to their machines. Hosea's was the one in the rear, the old Yamaha Enticer, and when the big man sat on it, the snow under it slumped, and Hosea and his ride dropped about a foot. Hosea tried to drive out of the little dip, but his engine died. It restarted with one pull on the cord, but it lacked the power to move forward. Meanwhile, the other riders disappeared up the trail.

The sizzling sound had grown loud enough to drown out the engine noise, and fear gripped Hosea's mind. *I need some help here, Lord,* he prayed. All around him the trees started to rattle and shed the snow load in their branches. They leaned this way and that, and a large one near him came crashing to the ground.

That got the boy's attention. Hosea climbed halfway off the seat and pushed with one foot while gunning the engine. His boot sank into icy slush, but he managed to advance a few feet. Another couple of pushes and he was free. More trees were falling, one of them right across his path. He had to detour around it, and the machine bogged down in the loose snow. He was able to regain the trail, but even at full throttle the engine labored without accelerating. And then it just quit moving at all.

The icy slush had frozen on the rails, he figured, and was preventing the track from sliding along it. So he climbed off, lifted the seat, and dug out the tool kit. He put his ample weight against the machine and tipped it over, intending to chip the ice away with a screwdriver. All around him, trees were reeling drunkenly, and large patches of snow on the ground slumped into pools of sizzling slush.

To Hosea's surprise and incomprehension, there was no ice buildup fouling the undercarriage of his sno-go. There wasn't much of a track left either. All the lugs and studs were missing — gone — and the metal links and bolts were stretched and misshapen. He poked at them with his screwdriver. Case-hardened steel was as pliable as warm taffy. Amazing.

A tree crashed several yards away and whipped him with its branches. He jumped back in alarm. More trees were falling all around, so he abandoned the machine and began to jog up the trail.

Hosea had never been much of a jogger, and jogging in snow took more effort than he could maintain. He huffed and puffed and ran for his life.

Through the grace of Father God, Hosea managed to pull ahead of the sizzling snow. He didn't stop until his lungs gave out. He paused only long enough to catch his breath before resuming his flight. When he began to believe that he might make it to safety, one of his boots came off.

They were pac boots, the kind that laced up to mid-shin. Not the sort of boot to fall off on its own. It lay in the snow, and Hosea resisted the impulse to pick it up. He shined a light on it and was horrified to see that it too was melting. Both the rubber sole and leather upper were in pieces. And the felt inner liner was splayed open like the pelt of a small animal. It was the boot that had been immersed in the slush while he was pushing the sno-go.

Hosea abandoned the boot and continued on. In no time at all, his entire foot went numb, but he didn't dare stop until an ugly thought crossed his mind — what about his stocking? If whatever was in the slushy water was able to dissolve metal, rubber, cowhide, and felt, what chance did a cotton sock have against it? And what about his foot? It was so numb it might be melting away at that very instant and he wouldn't even know. So he stopped long enough to lift his leg and inspect his foot with the flashlight. The grey stocking had a red toe and heel, and it looked intact. But he wasn't taking any chances, and he pulled it off and tossed it into the trees. It hadn't been doing him much good anyway because his foot below the ankle was a solid block of wood.

Hosea hobbled on.

A HEADLIGHT BOUNCED on the trail ahead. Adam had doubled back to check on him. He made a U-turn and stopped next to him.

"Where's your machine? What happened to your foot?"

"Not now," Hosea said, hopping on the seat behind him. "Go! Go! Go!"

"But your foot."

Hosea reached around his brother's waist and twisted the throttle. The machine lurched forward, and Adam grabbed the handlebars to control it. They raced up the trail. Or labored up the trail. The old Polaris was a gutsy machine with three cylinders, but any sno-go labored under Hosea's weight. With both of them on it, the engine whined in protest.

After about a mile, Adam stopped and hopped off the seat. He helped Hosea to stand up long enough to get to the storage compartment. He knelt in the snow and placed his brother's foot on his lap. The skin was yellow and waxy-looking. Adam opened a foil blanket and wrapped it around the foot. Then he shucked off his heavy parka to remove his down vest. He wrapped the vest around his brother's foil-covered foot and fastened it with duct tape.

"What happened?" he said as he placed Hosea's bundled foot on the running board. "Where's your machine? Where's your boot?"

"Melted. Gone."

"Say again?"

POPPY STOOD AT the ridgeline and watched the ravine below through binoculars. Something was happening down there. Not a whole lot, but something. Sparkling blue lines crisscrossed the ravine from one ridge top to the other. Other lines, red and orange ones, stretched from the ground up to a central pole that was located above where he'd dropped the angel's pea.

Something was happening there, but what?

A single sno-go was climbing the ridge, coughing and misfiring, and when it drew near he saw that both boys were riding it.

Adam pulled behind the Bearcat and killed the engine.

"What's that I smell?" Poppy said as he continued to watch the ravine.

"Rubber belt, lord," Adam said. "We're too heavy for it. We need to use your machine."

"Where's the other?"

"On the trail. Hosea says it melted and fell apart. Same with his boot. I gotta get him home quick, or he could lose some toes." Adam helped Hosea transfer himself to the new sno-go. "All right if we borrow the Cat, lord?"

"No, it's not all right. I'm riding it. Ride your own."

"I don't think this one will go much further with two of us on it."

"You should'a thought about that sooner."

"His foot is frozen, lord. He could lose it."

Finally, Poppy lowered the binoculars and looked at his son's wrapped-up foot. "What's wrong with your foot, boy?"

"It's frozen, lord."

"Where's your boot?"

"Melted, lord."

Poppy turned back to the ravine. The bright, colorful threads were surmounting the ridge lines and spilling over into neighboring ravines. The ones closest to them looked to be about a mile away.

"What's happening down there?" he asked the boys.

"I don't know, lord," Hosea said. "All the trees started to rattle, and then they fell over. The snow is melting, and so is everything else."

"What do you mean 'melting'?"

"Melting, lord, like hot wax."

Poppy didn't want to be left alone out there with a crippled sno-go, but neither was he ready to leave. Adam was probably right, though: he needed the new machine to make it home with Hosea. Hosea was just too fat. He'd been fat ever since he was a baby, and no amount of praying, fasting, or dieting had made any lasting difference. It was a puzzle Poppy had never been able to solve. None of his other children were fat. Obesity didn't run in his family, or in Mama P's. It must be the boy's own doing, a character flaw or a cross to bear.

"Sit opposite each other. Adam, put your brother's naked foot on you belly against your naked skin under all your clothes. Warm it up with your body heat. Understand?"

"Yes, lord."

AFTER AN HOUR or so, the expansion of the threads had stopped, and the number of blue ones had multiplied exponentially. The central pole — in his mind he called it a pillar — was so interconnected with them that it appeared to be a solid object.

Behind Poppy, the Polaris suspension squeaked as his boys shivered. They had pulled the two sno-gos side by side. Adam had complained fiercely when he received his brother's ice-cold foot against his stomach. Much later, Hosea had gasped and moaned as feeling returned to his foot. Now the boys were silent, except for the squeaking.

Binoculars were no longer necessary. An irregularly shaped circle of lights stretched out beneath them, and the central pillar had risen two or three hundred feet (60 – 90 m) into the night sky.

"How much longer, lord?" Adam said.

The question wasn't worthy of an answer. How should he know how much longer it would take?

So Adam asked another question. "What are we going to do with Ginger? We can't keep her locked up forever. What do we do when it's time for her to go home?"

Poppy said, "We can chase the demons out of her, but we can't change her stubborn heart. She's no good to us or Proverbs. When this is over, we'll send her back to Wallis. We're better off without her."

"Won't she tell the Troopers about what we done to her?"

"Let her. We'll be in the keep by then, and they'll have plenty of other death and general anarchy to deal with without coming out here to bother us."

HOSEA COCKED HIS ear in the direction of the lake of lights. "It's changing," he said.

Poppy said, "I can hear it."

The sizzling sound had become a distant drone. Now it acquired a beat, an oscillating pulse, maybe one beat per second.

Soon the tangled threads themselves began to pulsate. Beads of light seemed to run along their length from ground to pillar. The pillar brightened a little. All the reds and greens were gone. It was all blue.

Then — nothing. The threads all went dark, and the blue pillar gradually faded to black. Whatever was supposed to happen had happened. Or not.

Hosea said, "That's it?"

Adam said, "Did it work?"

Poppy had no answers for them.

CA3 1.0

AFTER DINNER, JACE went outside to pee off the back porch because at minus thirty-three (–36 C), even the outhouse was a journey too far.

The sky was clear, and the aurora was out. One of the joys of a lack of indoor plumbing was the number of opportunities each day one had for standing outdoors and gazing up at the stars.

Jace thought he saw a blue flash on the southern horizon. He continued to watch the spot for as long as he could stand it before the cold drove him back indoors. The flash didn't repeat. Maybe it was his imagination.

CA4 1.0

GOVERNOR VERA TETLIN was finishing up a live *Night Desk* interview on MSFOX from her home studio in Wallis when the satellite feed went kablooey. Lines, stars, frozen pixels, then a screen of color bars. Bradd, her camera operator and station engineer, leaped into action to troubleshoot the failure. He had built the studio for her and knew every switch, cable, and fuse in the place. He went from camera to control board to electrical panel, while she remained in her chair under the video lights. The feed returned a half minute later, but by then the network had moved on to the next segment.

"Sunspots, probably," Bradd said as he cut the lights and shut down the equipment. "I'll run a diagnostic tomorrow."

"I have a teleconference with Juneau first thing."

"All right. I'll do it tonight after dinner." He went to the doorway to the house. "Coming?"

"NORAD's inside a mountain, isn't it?"

"Used to be, Cheyenne Mountain in Colorado, but they moved it."

"It was part of the Army?"

"Air Force. It was a strategic command center during the Cold War. They designed it to withstand a nuclear blast. Why do you ask?"

Vera got up and accompanied her husband to the house.

"I was just wondering. Some old coot said he was living inside a mountain near McHardy."

After Vera changed into sweats and let down her hair, she sat at the kitchen counter and watched Bradd preparing dinner.

"Tell me," she said, "how easy would it be for them to cut us off?"

"For who to cut us off what?"

"For whoever, for whatever reason, to cut all communication to and from Alaska."

"Not a clue."

"I want to find out. Call someone. Call Swayne tomorrow and have him come over."

THE FOLLOWING AFTERNOON, Colonel Swayne appeared at their door. He was wearing his ALF uniform, he explained, because he had just come from a meeting with his senior officers. The uniform was of his own design, a forest-green, button-down cotton shirt tucked into a loose pair of forest-green dungarees. There were no insignia except for an embroidered patch on one shoulder that depicted a rearing, roaring grizzly bear encircled by the words ALASKA LIBERTY FORCE.

To Vera, it resembled the uniform a Forest Service janitor might be required to wear, except for the patch. Also, it made Swayne look even more ridiculously boyish than he already did.

Yet Colonel "Beaver" D. Swayne did command, by his own count, over three thousand loyal sovereign patriots. Patriots who, it seemed to Vera, were in need of a civilian commander-in-chief.

They sipped cold beer in the living room overlooking the lake. They were feeling each other out with small talk. It was a job interview in which each party was looking to hire the other. Impressed by what they saw, they quickly got down to business.

"Beaver, I have a security question for ya."

"Shoot, governor."

"If Obama wanted to, how hard would it be to cut Alaska communications off from the rest of the world?"

Swayne didn't even have to think about it; his answer was instantaneous: "Not hard at all. They just demonstrated last night how easy it would be."

Bradd said, "Last night?"

"Yeah, it's why I called an emergency meeting today. Around 8:00 P.M.

last night, someone cut the feeds of the entire Landsat system for about a half hour."

Vera and Bradd looked at him with blank expressions, and he continued, "The Landsat are the non-military satellites that continuously record images and data of the Earth from space. There's been seven of 'em since the 1970s, two of which are currently in service. Landsat 8 is supposed to launch in February, making it three satellites up there at the same time. A record, I think."

Vera said, "What does that have to do with communication?"

"On the surface, nothing. But think about it. If you wanted to do something you didn't want us to know about, like, I don't know, move a shock force of troops from Point A to Point B, it would be very helpful to have a kill switch to disable all civilian Earth observatory stations, wouldn't it?"

"I see," Vera said.

Bradd said, "But couldn't it have been a technical glitch, a sunspot or something?"

"Sure, except that the Landsat system incorporates independent receiving stations all over the world, and according to my inside sources on the internet, they all went offline at the same time. That's a helluva glitch.

"Look at it this way," Swayne went on. "Last night's action might'a been a proof of concept. If you can cripple the Landsat, you could also take out the telecom satellites, GPS, weather satellites — the works. Alaska relies on about eight key satellite systems at any one time to communicate with the outside world."

Bradd said, "What about fiber optics?"

"The government's already had total control of that for years. All of our digital optical traffic goes through four trunk lines to the Lower 48. They run for hundreds of miles under the Pacific Ocean to Seattle and Oregon. All civilian traffic goes through 'em. I don't know how much redundancy the military maintains. Maybe lots. But civilian traffic relies on just these four cables. The land portion of our network is a loop that follows the road system. You remember that statewide internet outage we had a couple of years ago? The official explanation was that two unrelated bozos with backhoes in different parts of the state accidentally cut the fiber-optic cables on the same day. Yeah, sure.

"The fact of the matter is, besides the satellites, Alaska stuffs all of its weather, navigation, government, business, entertainment — you name it — into four pipes, which they already have the kill switch to.

"So to answer your question, Governor — how hard would it be for Obama to cut us off? — the answer is: laughably easy."

Swayne finished his beer, and Bradd got up to fetch him another from the kitchen.

Vera said, "It may be laughable, Colonel, but you'll notice we're not laughing."

"Me neither."

"What can my government do about it?"

"Funny you should ask. That's the same question I put to my officers not two hours ago. I laid out the problem and gave them forty-eight hours to bring me solutions.

"I'm no expert in telecom," he continued, "but I believe there's enough ham radio capacity in our membership to bridge the gap and sustain a modicum of command and control throughout the state and across the border. There's probably some high-tech solutions too. Maybe we launch tethered weather balloons across British Columbia to act as relay stations, or we set up our own distributed networks, like they actually did in San Francisco where a few years back they made a civilian's network out of old Xboxes.

"I don't know what my men will come up with, but rest assured we have some of the best minds in the state wearing this uniform."

If only that uniform were more reassuring. "Will you share what you learn with me?" Vera said.

"It would be my honor, governor."

CA5 1.0

PARTLY OUT OF curiosity (or suspicion), partly for the novelty of riding the new Bearcat again, on Firstday morning Poppy returned to the ravine alone to see the effects of the flare. He left right after breakfast, before the sun was up.

The temperature had moderated, the trail they had broken was firm, and Poppy made good time to the overlook where they had kept vigil. He was shocked to see what the light of dawn revealed. The ravine below him was nothing but bare ground. The snow that had blanketed the forest was gone. The forest itself was gone. An irregular circle, perhaps three miles wide (4.8 km), was denuded of all trees, brush, and sedges. The thick muskeg mats of moss were missing, as well as the underlying layers of peat and the humus in the soil. In a word, all organic material, living and dead, had been stripped from the land. That included hibernating bears and ground squirrels, foraging rabbits and moose, lynx on the prowl, and any other living thing unfortunate enough to become entrapped by Hosea's "rattling trees." What was left was not just bare ground but dead ground — sterile silt, clay, and sand, and a minefield of scoured stones. If ever there was a land of scorched earth, this was it.

Poppy searched for the pillar with his binoculars. He couldn't see anything solid, but he caught the glint of sunlight bouncing off something suspended in the air. It was still there. The threads attached to it glinted in the dawn light as well, like strands of spider silk.

Poppy continued down the ravine, cautiously now, and halted at the borderline of teetering spruce and birch trees. He dismounted and stepped to the very edge of the wasteland. Hosea had spoken of sizzling slush, how stepping into it had cost him his boot and nearly his foot. There was no slush now, no sizzle, only a patch of desert.

Poppy picked up a handful of snow and tossed it over the line. It sprinkled the bare ground and did not melt. He found a fallen tree branch and scraped the dead ground with it. Then he brought the end to himself for a close-up look. The wood was not melting. He tossed the branch into the dead zone, intending to test the ground further inside. The branch tumbled end over end in a smooth arc, but before it hit the ground, it struck something invisible and was sliced in two.

He walked along the edge while watching the spot, and when the angle to the sun was right, he saw the glint of spider silk, or colored thread, or whatever it was.

Arming himself with another stout stick, Poppy said a little prayer and put one foot over the line. Immediately he raised the sole of his boot to check it. It wasn't melting, or at least not yet. He took another step into the dead zone, and another, all the while tapping the stick in front of himself like a blind man.

When he hit an invisible strand, it sliced through his stick. The severed end was glassy smooth. Slowly, cautiously, he made his way toward the glittering pillar. He had another mile to go when he heard the drone of an airplane in the distance. He turned around looking for it, but it was still too far away to see. It couldn't be the mail plane; today was Firstday, not Twosday.

Poppy continued on, but the engine noise grew louder, and he repeatedly glanced over his shoulder. Finally, when he saw a speck low on the horizon, he trained his binoculars on it. The small aircraft was still miles away, but it did seem to bear the familiar green color of Ned Nellis' Cessna. And then it occurred to him that Christmas fell on Mail Day this year, and Nellis had pushed the mail flight up a day to accommodate the holiday. Still, Nellis' usual route would turn him north before he got much closer to the bare patch of ground. And, in fact, as Poppy watched, the plane banked and headed toward McHardy.

Poppy offered a little prayer of thanksgiving and continued toward the pillar. Like the threads, it was invisible unless he kept it at a certain angle to the rising sun.

Before long, Poppy realized that the hum of the aircraft engine, instead of fading away, was increasing in volume again, and when he turned he saw that the plane was heading straight for him. Apparently, it was hard to miss a three-mile-wide bald spot from the air.

What to do? What *could* he do but pray? It was too late to pray that Nellis not see the dead zone, so he prayed that the man, a Christian of sorts and not an evil man, might keep the sighting to himself. *For the sake of Archangel Martha's mission, let Nellis never report what he has seen to the authorities.* That would be a miracle, but that was what Poppy prayed for.

Nellis was still up pretty high when he flew over. He banked hard to make another pass. The plane dropped lower as it went over a second time and rocked its wings in greeting. Poppy knew Nellis had spotted him. It would have been impossible for a person to hide in that bleak landscape.

"Go away, Ned," Poppy shouted at the receding airplane. "For your own sake, go away. Elder Brother Jesus, send him away."

But Nellis banked again and came back over, even lower, as low as the pillar, which he probably couldn't see. He passed so low that Poppy could make out his face in the cockpit and feel the thrum of the engine.

Fool.

And then it happened, the small airplane's left wing detached from the fuselage. It simply came off. The plane began to spin as it plummeted to the ground. It cartwheeled when it struck and caught on fire. Poppy began to jog toward the wreck but quickly remembered to slow down and wave his stick before him.

The fire was too hot for Poppy to approach. Nellis' bloody forehead was pressed against the glass on the pilot-side door, and flames engulfed the cockpit.

He's dead, isn't he? Dear Lord, let him be dead already.

No such providence. Nellis wasn't dead. He clawed at his chest, at the door, at the window. Poppy could do nothing but watch and pray. The pilot's agony was shocking but brief, and Poppy prayed for mercy on his soul.

When the fire had burned itself out, Poppy left the wreck and went to examine the fallen wing. The wing hadn't been torn off but sliced through cleanly. Like his stick, the edges had a glassy finish. As he trudged back to his sno-go, he heard a crashing sound behind him, like an avalanche of broken crystal, and when he turned, the central pillar was gone.

Poppy glanced at the broken airplane one last time. "I guess you won't be telling nobody. At least there's that. Amen."

CA6 1.0

IT SURPRISED JACE how indifferent the other overwintering McHardyites were about the problems with the phone and internet service. Of the small Mail Day crowd, only Kelly Cogwheel was moved to complain. He had a business to run, as he repeated *ad nauseam*, even though both his saloon and hotel were closed for the season. He, of course, blamed the unreliable service on over-regulation by the Obama administration (although it was the same administration that had extended service to McHardy in the first place).

For the most part, the technological difficulties with the wireless service only confirmed what most dyed-in-the-wool McHardyites had believed in their hearts all along — Maya Apocalypse or not, civilization was going down, brother, and you had better get used to it. It was the reason why many of them had come to McHardy in the first place. Also, they were already practiced in living off the grid; they even preferred it that way. Ed Sulzer, for example, dusted off his old 1990s-era radio transceiver, the one he had used to report his thrice-daily meteorological readings before the process was automated and his contract was allowed to expire.

Pre-Mail Day, as they dubbed Christmas week's early mail delivery, proceeded as usual with coffee and blueberry pie and overheated bombast from Cogwheel. Local anchorites got in their weekly dose of human contact. The one deviation from the script was the absence of the mail plane itself. Nine o'clock went by, ten o'clock, noon — the pie tins were empty, the coffee cold, and Nellis' Cessna was still a no-show.

Kelly Cogwheel said, "Maybe Ned forgot about the day change."

"That's not it," Sulzer said. "I just radioed his wife in Gulkana, and she says Ned left at his usual hour."

"Has he called in since?"

"Nope."

"Then what do you suppose . . . ?"

No one wanted to jinx Nellis by supposing that he had mechanical problems, or worse.

Ed said, "If she doesn't hear from him soon, she's sending a chase plane to go look for him."

After a moment of silence, Ginny Sulzer flicked cigarette ash on her own hardwood floor and said, "In the last thirty years, Ned's had trouble exactly twice. Both times were in the winter, and both times he simply set 'er down on a river or glacier and drank lukewarm coffee till help arrived. Don't worry about Ned. Ned knows what he's about."

By 1:00 P.M., still with no word from Nellis, people started leaving Pre-Mail Day for home without their last-minute Christmas cards, mail-order packages, and bills. Before they got away, Barbara Jean de Saul reminded everyone of the potluck Christmas dinner at her house the following day. She went out of her way to make sure Jace knew he was included. She told him to invite Ranger Masterson too.

"What should I bring?" Jace said.

"Bring anything you like, dear. Or just bring yourself."

"Good. Thanks. I'll be there." Jace had been wondering what he was going to do with the restaurant-size cans of sliced beets he'd purchased from the lodge. What a fine opportunity to put one of them to good use.

CA7 1.0

CHRISTMAS DAY 2012 was a bust. Without a Christmas tree (a pagan tradition) or exchange of gifts (every day is a gift), the Prophecy children had little to look forward to. The chores still needed doing, and work in the keep continued at breakneck speed.

Poppy spent the morning in the prayer cabin studying the Bible or sleeping in. When he came to the house for lunch, he seemed more irritable than usual, snapping at anyone who crossed his path. Outside, there seemed to be ten times more small aircraft traffic than usual, and every time a plane flew over the house, Poppy rushed to a window with his binoculars. Woe to the child who got in his way.

After lunch, before everyone returned to their chores, Deut organized the traditional Nativity Game. She set up the stable, star, and manger. Then she asked Bible questions, and the child who answered correctly was privileged to place a cow or Magus or angel into the scene. The child who scored the most points at the end won the honor of placing Baby Jesus in the manger. Little Uzzie won that honor, as he had every year since he could talk.

Then it was back to work. It was Sarai's turn to plan and prepare a special Christmas dinner, and she was hard-pressed to come up with a moose dish they hadn't eaten a million times before.

In the afternoon, Poppy went up to consult the angel. She already knew about Ned Nellis' accident. "It was unfortunate," Martha said, "but the pilot isn't the first casualty in the Final Battle. Nor will he be the last."

"Was it worth it?" Poppy said. "I mean, was the flare a success?"

Martha shrugged her tired shoulders. "We'll know soon enough."

"In the meantime," Poppy said, "there are planes buzzing around looking for Nellis' plane. With the size of that wasteland, they won't be able to miss it."

"Verily," Martha said. "Our peril has multiplied. Now will you drop the key into the cistern?"

He should have consented, but still he held back.

The angel said, "You fear this little ball is not the key to the pit, don't you, Master Prophecy? You still fear it's actually the star Wormwood. Allow me to reassure you, I am the Fifth Angel, not the Third."

Poppy did not feel reassured.

The angel said, "Machines will bear more men here. There is still time for Satan to snatch victory from us.

"And when the armies of Armageddon are camped outside your gate, who will be there to defend you if I am too weak? They will smash through the gate as though it were matchwood. They will cut down your sons like wheat in the field. They will smash through any door you brace against them. There is only one place in this fortress that will stymie them, only one place where we can keep this key safe. I give you my word, in Jesus' name, they will not find it there."

"I hear you, angel," Poppy replied, "and when they come, I may take your advice."

"You may . . . if you are inside the keep when they arrive. If you have time to act. If you are still alive."

CA8 1.0

CHRISTMAS DAY 2012 was a bust. The phone and internet were completely down, so Jace couldn't even email his sister.

This was how he spent his holiday: he caught up on long-deferred chores. He knocked down the large shitsicle about to poke up through the toilet seat in the outhouse. He hauled bathwater by sled from the dipping hole in the community stream (Beehymer had failed to mention that his hand pump would freeze up during the first cold snap unless he insulated it). He made a tour of his house and plugged drafts with bits of pink fiberglass insulation. He did maintenance on the snowmobile Elmer Gonzales had leased him. And other various odd jobs.

There'd been a lot of air traffic all day, and Jace was tempted to go to the airstrip to learn the latest about Nellis' fate, but he decided that bad news could wait until he joined the others at Christmas dinner.

When he did go out, it was only to discover that the potluck Christmas dinner had been cancelled. Or rather, it had transmogrified into a wake. They'd found Ned's charred body thirty-some miles (48 km) from town. Some of the men had gone out to retrieve it and were keeping it in a shed while they waited for some official or other to come out to claim it. The accident was a tragedy that seemed to touch the old-timers the hardest.

Jace had never been in Barbara Jean's house before. It was located on Main Street and was of the same vintage and architectural style as his own. It was a little bigger, though, with an extra bedroom and a walled-off kitchen, and it was in much better shape. A wood stove kept the place comfortably warm. Half of the entire wintertime population of McHardy was crowded into the living room discussing Ned's accident. The once-festive holiday potluck spread was laid out on the table. Jace added his bowl of sliced beets to it.

The fuselage of the Cessna had been incinerated in the accident. The cause of the crash was obvious — the port-side wing had come off and was lying some distance from the wreck. But airplane wings were not known to simply fall off, and no one could explain how it had happened. According to Kelly Cogwheel, who had snapped photos of it and was passing around his phone to anyone wanting to see them, the wing had been sheered off cleanly.

Harder to explain was the crash site itself. There was a rough circle of ravine and bottom land nearly three miles in diameter that was scraped bare of all snow and vegetation. Cogwheel had photos of that too, some of them taken from the air. No one had seen the likes of it, or even heard of anything so bizarre. The wreck was located near the center of this unnatural clearing.

"Before any more of you decide to go out there to rubberneck," Ed

Sulzer announced, "a guy from the NTSB radioed to say don't do it. They'll be out here tomorrow, and they don't want nobody mucking up their crime scene."

Interesting choice of words, Jace thought — crime scene. Surely he meant accident scene. After spending an hour at the wake, and despite Sulzer's warning, Jace did ride out to the scene. With all of the snowmobile traffic preceding him, it was not difficult to locate. He looked at the wreck and wing without touching anything. But it was the bare spot that caused him the most concern. It was miles away from where the alien snow circle and tulip had been, but it was a *circle* nevertheless.

On his way home, Jace found himself once again loitering at the end of the illegal Prophecy airstrip. The windows of the main house were bright with lamplight. Jace wondered what Deut's holiday was like with all the kids around. Christmas was a kid's holiday. The look of wonder (and greed) in their eyes. The squeals of delight as they tore colorful wrapping from their gifts. The carols under the Christmas tree.

"Merry Christmas, my love," he said as he restarted his engine.

A raven atop a spruce tree croaked a holiday greeting to him in reply.

CA9 1.0

WHEN PROVERBS OPENED the food slot, the powder room was dark. The camping buddy heater was not burning, and the air reeked of excrement. He'd have to empty the honey bucket, which meant he'd have to go in, which meant he'd have to have a girl to stand by when he did. Sue was in the keep. He could get her to help.

"Ginger, wake up," he said through the slot. "I got your lunch." When she didn't respond, he said, "You gotta eat. You gotta stay strong."

"Fuck you," she replied from the darkness.

"Watch your language, please."

"Fuck you, fuck you, fuck you."

"I know that's the demons talking, not you." He left the food tray outside the door and went to fetch Sue.

WITH SUE'S HELP Proverbs swapped out the honey bucket with a fresh one. He gathered the uneaten meals. All the while Ginger lay on the cot under sleeping bags and blankets. Proverbs tried to light the camp heater, but the propane bottle was empty. The two replacement bottles were empty as well.

"You're going through these pretty fast," he said.

"They're half gone when you bring them," Ginger replied. "What do you expect?"

"No, they're not. Don't lie. Leave the heater on medium. They'll last longer."

"I'm not lying!"

"Hello, demons. Don't make my girlfriend tell lies."

"I'm not your girlfriend. I hate you."

"But Elder Brother Jesus loves you anyway, and so do I."

Sue said, "Come on, Verbs. I have work to do."

"You're an accomplice, Sue," Ginger said. "You're going to prison for this too."

Sue said, "You can thank me later."

"You're as crazy as the rest of them, Sue."

Proverbs gathered up the empty propane bottles. "I'll fetch some fresh ones."

"Don't bother. Get me more clothes and blankets. I'm *freezing* in here."

HOSEA FOUND PROVERBS in the storeroom having a shit fit. He had overturned a whole row of supplies, undoing hours of Hosea's labor. He had torn open cartons of propane bottles and was slamming them against the stone floor with bellowing, unchristian oaths.

"What the heck, brother?" Hosea said.

Proverbs whipped around to confront him. "We been screwed, brother," he screamed in reply. "Screwed!"

Hosea knew better than to interrupt one of his brother's rants while he was wearing the eyepatch. Still, it pained him to stand by silently while the boy lay waste to his orderly aisles.

Proverbs pulled one fresh propane bottle after another from a carton, shook it, and then hurled it against the floor. Finally, Hosea stooped down to pick one up and shake it himself.

"Oh, my," he said.

"See?" Proverbs roared. "Now you see?"

The bottle, made from aluminum, should have contained sixteen fluid ounces of liquified propane gas (0.47 l). Even without the benefit of a scale, Hosea could tell that this one was seriously shy of that, practically empty. He lifted an unopened carton and weighed it in his hands. It weighed only a fraction of what it should.

"How could you?" Proverbs seethed.

"How could I what?"

"Let those bastards in Anchorage cheat us like this?"

Hosea set about checking the remainder of their stock. He lifted each unopened carton and put it in one of two piles. More than half of them were on the light side. "We're screwed," he said.

"I told you. Didn't I tell you?"

"And I agree with you, so why don't you settle down and let me think." Hosea eased himself onto a stack of cartons and called up his recollections of buying this lot of propane.

"No, you know what?" he said after a moment. "If these were light when I stacked them in the truck, I would'a known. They were good then. Which means they only started leaking afterwards." He popped a plastic cap off one bottle and sniffed the valve. "This much leakage and you should be able to smell it. I don't smell anything."

"So, you're saying they aren't light? Are you calling me a liar?"

"I said settle down. No one's calling nobody a liar."

"Who's gonna tell Poppy about this? You or me?"

Hosea said, "I'll tell Adam. Let him tell Poppy."

Proverbs grabbed a carton of full bottles and left Hosea to clean up his mess. Hosea heard him in another part of the storeroom chamber throwing more stuff around. When he was like this, it was best to just let him be.

PROVERBS STILL HAD the powder room key Poppy had loaned him, and he didn't bother fetching Sue this time to shadow for him. He set the carton of propane bottles next to the door and piled the new clothes, outerwear, and sleeping bags on top.

"It's me again," he called through the slot.

She was sitting on the cot when he entered. He brought the supplies in and set them in a corner, next to her untouched food tray. "Warm clothes," he said, "and good propane bottles."

She bolted for the door, but he was ready for her and grabbed her from behind. She struggled only a little and went limp in his arms. The heft of her, the shape of her hips, the funky odor of her unwashed hair — well, maybe it was the demons' influence, but holding her close felt so right.

"Don't you love me?" she said.

"You know I do."

"Then why do you torture me? I'll be good. I'll do what you say. But I'll die in here. I swear, I will."

"We won't let that happen." He gently brought her back to the cot and sat her down. "Everything will be okay, I promise you. We'll pop those demons out of you as soon as we can. Then you can come back to the house."

"Pop them out of me?"

"Yeah, you know, cast them out?"

She pulled him down to sit next to her on the cot and buried her head in his chest.

"Cast them out now. What are you waiting for?"

"Well, things are heating up out there. Obama's army is about to pounce on us. Even if you wanted to go back to Wallis, it might be too late. And what happens in the next few days will —"

"Did you ask him?" she said, cutting him off.

"Ask who?"

"Pastor Bunyan. About the girl angels? You didn't ask him, did you?" She pushed herself away (and he instantly ached for her touch). "You said you love me, but you don't. You don't want a real wife. You want a prisoner. Someone you can lock up and only see when you want to."

"That's not true! Ginger, please don't say that."

"And you're a coward who only does what his Poppy tells him to."

"It's not like that. Don't you see?"

"Of course it is. I've seen it from the start, way back in Wallis. It's all Yes, lord this and Yes, lord that, like you don't even have a will of your own."

"I'm only —"

"So, what are you going to say when Poppy tells you he wants to fuck me like he does your sister?"

Her words knocked the air out of him.

"You knew!" she said. She sprang from the cot and retreated to the far end of the cell. "I was praying it wasn't true, but you knew just like your brothers knew and you were all too cowardly to do anything about it. So you pretended you didn't know so you could live with yourself. You're as guilty as he is. Cowards! The lot of you! She's your own sister."

Proverbs rose to leave. "I don't know what you're talking about. That's not even you talking. I'll pray for you. We all will."

She followed him to the door but didn't attempt to escape again. "Your father rapes your sister; that's what I'm talking about. And you did nothing to stop him. Are you proud of yourself? You murder ravens and rape girls and call yourself blessed."

"Quiet, demons. Don't make my betrothed say such trash."

"I'm not your betrothed, and I never will be. I hate you. I hate all of you."

Proverbs' good eye burned in the lamplight. He gently shoved her away from the door so he could escape. The door clicked shut behind him, and he snapped the padlock on its hasp.

PROVERBS RAN INTO his father on the slide and asked him for a spark plug to go to his cabin on Trapper's Slough. At first Poppy reached into his bib pocket but then had second thoughts.

"Why aren't you up there helping your brothers?"

"Because I can't, lord!" he shouted. It startled his father. "I can't even see straight I hurt so bad! Lord!"

Poppy frowned and placed his hand on top of his son's head. "Dear Father," he said, "I ask You to ease my son's suffering in our time of need so that he may pull his weight around here. Amen." He removed his hand. "There. Is it any better?"

"No! No! No!"

"Well, give it a minute."

"I *hurt*, lord! I'll come back as soon as I can. I *promise*. I'm no good to you this way. Please, lord, let me go. *Amen! Amen! Amen!*"

But Poppy was unmoved. "We'll all pray over you tonight, son, but we can't let up on the work. It's life and death now. You know that. Take some extra of your pills and lie down for a little while. That'll help." And with that Poppy patted him on the shoulder and continued up the slide trail.

The Federal Dicks

FD1 1.0

THE KNOCKING ON his door was civil but insistent. Jace cracked an eyelid to look at his bedside clock — 4:23 A.M. He got up and threw on a robe and padded through the cold living room in his slippers.

"Who's there?" he yelled at the door.

"Federal agents," came the reply.

A storm of conflicting emotions coursed through Jace's sleepy brain. It was probably never a good thing to be rousted from one's bed by federal agents in the wee hours of the morning.

On the other hand, wasn't he a federal agent too?

Jace opened the door expecting to see men in black, but everything outside his door was black at this hour.

"I am Special Agent Nabor of the FIAS," said a shade standing on his porch, "and this is Special Agent Bertolli of the FBI. May we come in?"

"That's what I was thinking," Jace said, cinching his robe against the cold. "Come on in, guys." He ushered them in and asked them to wait a bit while he lit a couple of lamps. "Welcome to my humble abode."

Jace led the agents to the oil stove, which he cranked up, and cleared enough stuff from the couch for them to sit. Their gaze strayed all over the room, taking in his rustic decor. Then he excused himself to make coffee.

"So, how can I help you?" he said from the kitchen.

"We have a few questions for you. We're here with the NTSB team that's investigating the recent airplane crash," said one of them.

Jace set cups, sugar, and a jar of non-dairy creamer on the end table. They had already started recording with a video camera on a tiny tripod. Now that he could see them, he said, "You're the FBI agent, right?"

"That's right, Special Agent Bertolli."

"And you?"

"Special Agent Nabor."

"And what was the name of your agency again?"

"FIAS."

"Never heard of it. What does FIAS stand for?"

"You don't have the clearance to know that."

Jace thought he was making a joke, but the man seemed completely serious, and he let it drop. The FBI agent, Bertolli, was tall, lean, and square-jawed and looked the part of a G-man. But this Nabor fellow was of average height, average looks, and average weight. That is, slightly obese. He could have blended into any crowd of American adults. Yet he seemed to be the one in charge of this interview.

Jace set about laying a fire in the wood stove. "I knew Ned Nellis, the pilot, but I don't know anything about the accident except what I heard secondhand. I drove out to the crash site, but I didn't learn anything new."

Nabor asked Jace to recount that visit and then proceeded to walk him through everything he had heard in town about the crash, who said what, the timeline involved, anything he could remember. Then he walked him through it all again. Bertolli, meanwhile, took notes and operated the camera. Neither had asked for permission to record him, but Jace figured he didn't have anything to hide. It seemed to him they were mostly using him to confirm what others had already told them, and he wondered what time in the morning they'd knocked on Ed and Ginny's door.

But then, in true Hollywood police-procedural fashion, Nabor opened a folder and handed Jace a photo. "Tell me what this is."

Obviously, it was a satellite view of the bald spot, an irregular circle of bare ground between once-forested ridges. Near the center was the ruined airplane and the dismembered wing.

"That's the crash site. Weird, huh?"

Nabor handed him a second photo. "And this."

It was also shot from above and depicted snow-covered flatlands that could have been anywhere in South Central Alaska, except for a small odd structure that Jace recognized as the ruins of the rebuilt cabin on Trapper's Slough.

"Oh my god, somebody burned it down."

"Tell us what it is."

"It's a cabin — was a cabin — on park land near the Mizina."

"Do you know who burned it down?"

"Not a clue."

Whether or not the agents noticed Jace's lie, they continued with the interview.

Nabor pulled out a final photo, and this one got Jace's heart beating. It was his own snow circle, the satellite view he had tried and failed to find online. Printed in the margin were the GPS coordinates and the date. The picture had been taken the day after Jace saw the mysterious object fall to Earth.

"If I'm not mistaken," Nabor said, "you're an expert on this one."

"As much as anyone, I guess. How did you get this? How did you link it to me?"

Nabor ignored his questions and said, "Tell us about it."

Jace didn't know where to start. He wondered how much the government already knew or if this photo only came to light when the other circle, the bald spot several miles away, became a federal case.

"Gladly," he said. "Do you believe in aliens?"

"As in Mexicans."

"No, space aliens, like E.T."

JACE TOLD THEM everything, from the moment he saw the descending light and cone of welder's glass, and his days of searching for evidence, to meeting the soul-sucking giant tulip, the death march to the Bunyans', and meeting the Prophecy boys on the trail. When he finished, the agents asked him to start from the beginning and go through his account again, and then again. Unlike the earlier stuff, they really drilled down on his firsthand experience. With each iteration Jace remembered a few more details, such as the lack of any sound or odor associated with the artifact. They asked him to sketch its appearance, and he did so on a blank sheet of paper. They scratched their heads when they looked at the drawing, and Nabor held it up and said, "So, it's your assertion that this thing, this ten-foot-tall glass tulip thing, is still at this location."

"No, I asserted nothing of the sort. When I recovered my strength the next day, I went back out there with Ranger Masterson, but it was gone by then."

"Gone."

"Someone had chipped it out of the ice and removed it. And I think I know who."

"Who."

"Who else? The Prophecys." Jace told them about the airstrip showdown, the boundary survey standoff, the depleted mine and its newly fortified entrance, the scofflaw cabin, and everything else he could think of to shut down Poppy and his boys. Why not? Especially since it was all true.

Nabor said, "You saw the Prophecys remove the artifact, or you saw it in their possession."

Jace had to admit that he hadn't. "But I know they took it."

"How."

"Because . . ." Well, he didn't know for sure. For all he knew, someone from April Creek might have stumbled across it and taken it away. Maybe someone was lying in a remote cabin somewhere sucked dry of all life. None of the Prophecys had come to such an end, as far as he could tell.

It was nearly 10:00 A.M. when the agents got up to leave. They cautioned him to keep their visit confidential while they continued their investigation. Their outerwear, which Jace hadn't noticed when they arrived, was of arctic expedition grade and brand new.

Jace went back to bed, relieved to be finally free of his secret.

FD2 1.0

RORY LAWTHER CAME into the Greatland Action Sports office during one of his breaks. His dad was running fingers through his thinning hair while he talked on the phone, never a good sign.

"I see," Rex said into the mouthpiece, "and when do you think you'll be running regular . . . I see. No, I'm . . . yes. I see. Thank you. Good-bye."

Rex hung up the phone and mopped his face with his hands, another not-good sign.

"What?" Rory said, popping open a Dr. Pepper.

"Walthers called. There was an accident out near McHardy. The mail plane went down. Ned Nellis died in the crash."

Rory's heart stopped for an infinite moment. "Ginger?"

"What? No, thank God. She wasn't aboard. No one was except Ned."

Rory collapsed in a chair and breathed again. His sister was all right. "Do they know what happened?"

"Not yet. I just spoke to the mechanic in Gulkana, and he says the NTSB is on the scene. He says Nellis Air will be resuming operations in a week or two. Terry Nellis will be taking over for his dad. You remember Terry?"

A distant memory of a scrawny kid playing Mario Bros. with him came to mind, and he suddenly remembered father and son. Ned had been his Dad's friend from when he lived in Valdez, before Rory was born. The Nellises had come to visit them in Wallis when he was little. His dad's old friend had died; that was why he was so upset.

"They should be up and running when Ginger is due to fly out," Rex continued. "And Terry knows the area well. If he's half the pilot his dad was, I feel confident that she'll be in good hands." As though turning a page, Rex glanced at the clock and said, "Things slow down out there?"

"Yeah." Two days after Christmas, the showroom was dead.

"Then why don't you go home?"

"I need the hours."

"Suit yourself."

Rex returned to his paperwork, and Rory spent some time checking his phone, and then he set down his Dr. Pepper and said, "I got an idea. Why don't we drive out there and surprise her? We could take Mom and make a weekend out of it. Sadie can run the store. We had a good year, didn't we? We deserve it."

His dad didn't automatically say no, which was a good sign.

FD3 1.0

THERE WAS A soft knock on the prayer cabin door.

"What?" Poppy shouted.

"It's me, lord, Hosea. The angel wants to see you."

"What about?"

"I don't know, lord. She didn't say, but she said it was doubly urgent."

Hosea, whose foot was blistered but felt much better, limped up the tailings slide with his father. When they reached the ramp on the first level, Hosea told Poppy that the angel wasn't in the break room as before; she was in the cistern chamber.

The cistern chamber. Poppy knew where this was heading. He went to the break room anyway to check that the marble was still there. It was, on the table where they'd placed it. He returned to the ramp, and they climbed two levels. When they entered the cistern chamber, the archangel Martha was standing on the water's surface. The radiance of her body was much diminished, and her wings were charred sticks. As she walked across the water to them, she winced with each step. Her long mahogany hair hung limp and dull at her shoulders, and her halo was missing. Her once-sheer gown had turned coarse and grey. She clearly was not healing but only hanging on.

"Greetings, Master Prophecy," she said in a tired voice. "Thank you for coming without delay. There is news. My fear of Black Obama finding us had been justified. Three of his officers are even now charging across the landscape on their way here. They will arrive within the hour."

Like flipping a switch, Poppy was instantly on. "There's no time to lose!" he declared. "We're throwing the bolt! Son, go down to gather the family. Tell them to bring only what they can carry. Then collect your guns and loose ammo and —"

"I prithee stay!" Martha said, raising a once-resplendent arm. "And allow me to finish."

Hosea halted, and he and Poppy turned back to the angel.

"With the respect due you, Master Prophecy, as I've already told you, your redoubt, while effective against marauders and brigands, will be no obstacle to the powers of the Antichrist.

"You humans have advanced the machinery of war to such an extent that we angels can no longer watch when you take up arms against each other. We weep as your armies crush your enemies into bloody pulp. Much of your weaponry is immoral on its face and used in a cruel and ungodly manner.

"One small missile is all it would take to obliterate your gate and any of your sons guarding it.

"Nay, do not, as you say, throw the bolt, Master Prophecy. Not yet. It is premature."

"Then, what do you figure we should do? You said three of Obama's men are on their way."

"I propose that you do not resist these men, except to show your displeasure. Hide the key to the pit where they cannot find it and let them have the run of the keep, going wherever they want. Let them search until they are content, and they will leave you in peace. For now."

Poppy clearly was not sold on the idea.

Hosea said, "Lord, they won't be looking for the key."

"They won't?"

"No, lord. They don't even know about it. Remember, you and Adam dug the trumpet out of the ice. The rangers never even saw the marble."

"Your son is correct," Martha said. "They will seek only the trumpet. And they will not find it because it no longer exists."

Poppy smiled through his shaggy beard. "All right, we'll do it your way. I'll find a place to hide the key."

"But, lord," Hosea said, "what about Ginger? They'll discover her in the powder room and use her against us. They'll say we kidnapped her or something."

This too was true. Poppy looked to the angel for an answer.

"Worry not, Master Prophecy. There is still time for you to spirit her away somewhere for a few hours."

"Which trail are the feds using to come here?"

The angel glanced over her shoulder. "The one that hugs the skirts of the mountain."

Hosea said, "The Mizina spur."

"Good," Poppy said. "Find your brothers and spread the alarm." He removed the Bearcat key from his bib pocket. "Tell Proverbs to take his betrothed to his cabin for the rest of the day. Tell Deut to go along. Tell them not to come back till dinnertime. Then bring the angel's marble up here. Quick now. Then clean up the powder room. Get the cot and stuff out of there. Get the boys to help you."

When Poppy and the angel were alone, the angel said, "Where are you thinking of hiding the key?"

"I'll find some nook or cranny in one of the dead-end tunnels. It's small enough."

"You already know my choice for a hiding place, Master Prophecy, and I will not repeat my argument except to emphasize how ruinous it would be if Obama's men removed the key from this sanctuary."

"Duly noted."

"And to look forward to the aftermath of this crisis."

"Explain."

"I am convinced by now that my beacon has failed, and I believe I know why. It lacked the necessary fuel. On Earth, you cannot raise a signal fire without sufficient fuel. I pray we try again, send up a second flare, but this time tap into a much more heavenly energy source."

"I don't understand. What heavenly energy source?"

"The forces that the Father uses to glue together all of His creation down to its tiniest bits." When Poppy didn't immediately understand, the angel continued, "What you call atomic energy. In Heaven we have watched with alarm the unfolding disaster at the Fukushima-Daiichi nuclear power plant. Since its destruction last year, abundant energy escapes freely into the sea and sky. We could concentrate some of that energy to fuel our flare."

Poppy vaguely recalled news stories about this. A nuclear disaster in Korea or Japan or one of the other yellow nations. At the time, he'd taken it as divine retribution for the region's godlessness, and he had shed no tears for their misfortune (as long as their radioactive dust didn't drift over Alaska).

"That's a long ways away. How do you expect to get the flare over there?"

"One of your sons would need to take it there in person. I think Adam is competent to do so, and his love for the Father is strong. But the journey would not be without risk, and he might never return."

"You want me to sacrifice one of my sons for this?"

"Yes, but only if he is willing. Behold, Master Prophecy, much sacrifice is demanded from each of us in desperate times." Her own sacrifice was on open display in her suffering and weakness. "But there are worse fates than martyrdom. Martyrs to the Father's cause are exalted in Heaven for all time."

"WHAT TOOK YOU so long?" Poppy complained when Hosea returned, out of breath from pushing a hand truck up the ramp.

"Sorry, lord. I came as fast as I could."

"What's all this?" The golden marble lay in an old coffee can sitting in a wooden crate on the hand truck.

"It's heavy, lord, even for me."

The marble appeared to be the same size as before, but his son was right, and Poppy needed both hands to lift the coffee can. It must have weighed thirty pounds (14 kg).

"All right. Go now. There's plenty to do." He turned to the angel. "How do you explain this key getting so heavy?"

"Actually, it's not any heavier. The key seeks its appointed lock, which is located in the underworld, and strains toward it."

That made sense, of a sort. Poppy held the coffee can at the edge of the cistern and peered into the depths. "Say I drop this in. How deep is the bottom?"

"The key knows no bottom."

Well, that sounded profound, but unhelpful. How would they be able to get the marble out again?

Poppy decided against the cistern. He used the hand truck to take the key further up the third-level tunnel. Most of the excavation in this part of the mine had been exploratory in nature, and the tunnel and spurs were narrow and rough. The angel followed him well beyond the point he had ever explored on his own. From reports by his sons, Poppy knew of a particular excavation on the left side of the tunnel that had seemed promising to the miners of old. They had discovered a vein there that assayed eighty percent pure copper, richer than the ore in the main chamber on the second level. But it had been an anomaly, and the vein terminated only a few dozen yards in, so they backfilled the excavation and abandoned it. When Poppy found the site, his headlamp revealed a floor-to-ceiling jumble of broken limestone debris.

"There's a good spot," Poppy said to the angel, pointing at a large boulder sitting partway up the rock pile. He strained to haul the coffee can up to it.

The angel neither helped nor objected, and Poppy tipped the can and spilled the heavy marble into a dark crevice in the rocks. It might be difficult to ferret it out later, but not as hard as recovering it from the bottom of the cistern.

FD4 1.0

SOMEONE WAS ROUSING her from a long winter's nap. "Ginger, it's me, Deut. Wake up. We have to go."

"Deut?"

The cell was bright with the light of several LED lanterns.

"Yes, it's me." Deut kept her distance from her former friend so she wouldn't accidentally inhale a demon. "Get up. We're going."

"Going where?"

A boy outside the door said, "What's taking so long?"

"Proverbs?"

"No, it's Corny," Deut said. "We're leaving this place. Can you sit up?"

"Are you helping me escape?"

Deut didn't know how to answer truthfully and so said nothing.

"Are my parents here?"

"Just hurry, Ginger, please. Proverbs has a sno-go ready for us. Let's put your boots on, okay?"

Ginger sat up. She was already wearing her parka, hat, mittens, and every other stitch of clothing Proverbs had brought her.

"I have to pee," she said.

Deut told Corny to leave the doorway, and Ginger emptied her bladder in the honey bucket. When she was done, Deut called the boy to begin cleaning up. He, too, avoided getting too close to their guest.

Deut grabbed up an armful of sleeping bags and led Ginger out of the cell. Days of fasting and forced bed rest had weakened the once athletic girl, and she made slow progress down the tunnel and slide. Proverbs awaited them at the bottom with the family's new sno-go and a sled. Both girls got into the sled, and Proverbs covered them with the sleeping bags. Then he drove through the yard, past the house, and up the Stubborn Mine Trail. Ginger closed her eyes dreaming they were bouncing along to town and the community airstrip where her dad was waiting.

Proverbs drove at a modest speed and didn't stop until they reached the fork in the trail. To the left was the trail to Trapper's Slough and his cabin.

Straight ahead would take them to the Bunyan place, where Ginger probably preferred to go. He looked back at her in the sled. Her big, beautiful eyes were shut. She was asleep, and it was up to him to decide her future. It was his responsibility to do what was best for her.

So he turned left to his cabin. Someday, when she was restored to grace, she would thank him.

FD5 1.0

WHEN POPPY RETURNED to the big house, Adam and Hosea were waiting for him.

"Are we ready?" he asked them.

Adam said, "Yes, lord."

"The angel says to string them along."

"How do we do that, lord?"

"Refuse to cooperate at first and see what they do. Make 'em have to work for it, but eventually give in and bring 'em up to the keep. Let 'em have free run of the place. They'll be hunting for the trumpet because that's all they know about."

He glanced out the window. "Is Proverbs and the girl away?"

"Yes, lord, with Deut."

"Good. Now, where's breakfast?"

Sue, who was spoon-feeding Mama P in the warm corner, set the bowl down and went to the kitchen. The children had already eaten lunch, and they were silently skulking about. Even the two babies had the good sense to keep their big heads down.

POPPY SAT AT the head table eating a belated breakfast of scrambled eggs, bacon, and toasted buns, with half a grapefruit on the side, the last of their fresh fruit. Before he had a chance to finish, Hosea heard the whine of approaching sno-gos.

"I count two of them," Hosea said. "Coming by way of the airstrip, just like the angel said."

"Bunkrooms," Poppy said, mopping his empty plate with a crust of toasted bun. Sue and Sarai wordlessly herded the children to the girls' room and shut the door behind them. That left only Mama P with Poppy and the two boys in the common room. "Don't worry, Mother," Poppy told her. "I won't let nothing bad happen."

The two machines screamed into the yard and wound down to a rumbling idle but did not shut off. Boots climbed the steps and crunched across the porch. *Lord God, lend us the strength to defeat Your enemies. Amen.*

There were three booming thuds on the solid oak door. Adam rose to answer it, but Poppy tugged him by the sleeve and sat him back down.

More knocking, sharper this time, as though the caller had removed a glove to knock with bare knuckles.

Finally, at the third knocking, Poppy rose and ambled across the floorboards to the door. "Remember," he cautioned the boys, "let me do all the talking. Not a word, hear?"

Adam and Hosea nodded.

Two men filled the doorway. One was tall and handsome, and the other was about Poppy's own height and plain-looking. The angel warned of three dicks, and Poppy leaned out the door to see who else was there. The third man was waiting in the yard with the idling sno-gos. It was the chief ranger, Ranger Danger. When he saw Poppy, he gave him a mock salute.

Of the two men on the porch, the shorter one impressed Poppy as the man in charge, but it was the taller one who spoke. "I am Special Agent Bertolli of the FBI," he said, "and this is Special Agent Nabor of the FIAS. Mind if we come in?" They flashed their IDs.

Poppy pondered why every federal dick he'd ever tangled with was a *special* agent. What was so special if everyone was special?

"I reckon you'll come in one way or the other, if I minded or not," he said, stepping aside. He closed the door behind them.

The feds didn't have the common sense or the courtesy to knock the snow off their boots before entering. That and their suntanned faces marked them as Outsiders. When they opened their new-looking outerwear, they revealed body armor beneath. Their vests were emblazoned with the initials of their respective agencies in SWAT-sized capital letters. What was the FIAS anyway? Poppy knew who the FBI were. They were the godless brutes who had murdered his twin brother all those years ago. Ugly machine pistols hung in holsters at the their sides.

"What do you want?" Poppy said.

After gazing all around the room, especially at Mama P and the two boys, the tall one said, "Funny. I expected to see a whole lot of goldpan art." The purposeful remark put Poppy on notice that the agents had already interviewed Ed Sulzer.

The shorter agent, Nabor, said, "We have a few questions for you. You're the person known as Mr. Prophecy."

"*Pastor* Prophecy would be closer to the mark."

"You are also known as Marvin Johnson." If these were questions, they sounded more like statements of fact.

Poppy grunted.

"Tell you what," Nabor said. "Just for now we'll call you *Mr.* Prophecy. All right. I understand you have a third grown son and another in his teens. Tell us where those two are right now."

"Out doing chores."

"They're out of the house." The agent nodded his chubby chin toward the closed door of the girls' bunkroom. "Or they might be in one of the other rooms."

Poppy stepped between the agent and the door. "I'm not used to strangers I just met calling me a liar," he said. "My sons are out of the house, like I said. The kid is doing chores, and the older one ran into town on an errand."

The taller agent took over the interview. "On a snowmobile?"

"Of course on a snow-mo-bile. How else?"

"When did he leave?"

"Not long ago."

"How come we didn't see him on the trail?"

"Because you took the back way, and he went by the main trail. There's more than one trail out here, Mr. Agent Man."

"Fair enough. When do you expect him back?"

"What does fair have to do with it? He'll be back when he finishes his errands, I reckon."

The shorter one, Nabor, said, "Let me tell you why we're here, Mr. Prophecy. We came out with the NTSB team that's investigating the plane crash. You know about the plane crash."

Again with the statement of fact instead of a question.

"I heard about it."

"You didn't ride out there to look at it yourself."

"Why should I?"

"I'm not really interested in why you should or shouldn't do anything, Mr. Prophecy. I'm only interested in what you did do. You rode out there."

When Poppy made no reply, the agent went on, "You rode out there yourself or with one or more of your sons. Let me inform you that it's a crime to lie to a federal investigator. You understand what I said."

"Lying is a sin against Father God's law," Poppy replied simply. *Except, of course, when you're lying to the Devil.*

Nabor nodded and reached into an inner pocket of his parka and handed Poppy a sheet of paper. It was a pencil sketch by a dithering artist, more scratches than lines, that hacked out a semblance of the angel's trumpet. There were arrows with notations in large, loopy letters that read *purple glass, tiny pinwheels of threads, 10 ft. length.*

Nabor said, "Tell me what this looks like to you."

Poppy noted, with great and grateful relief, that the untalented artist had not even attempted to depict the mouthpiece end of the trumpet, with its golden key, but had left that end blank. Poppy handed the paper back.

"It looks to me like a child's drawing of a herald's trumpet. Why do you ask?"

The special agent scrutinized the drawing and said, "A trumpet. I suppose I can see a trumpet in it. It's long, and it has a bell at the end like a trumpet." He showed the picture to Prophecy's sons. "Either of you see this trumpet." Though they shook their heads no, they had guilty-as-charged written all over their faces.

"Just to be clear," Nabor said to Poppy, "you're telling me you've seen a ten-foot-long object that looks like a trumpet."

"I'm not telling you *nothing* except your *drawing* looks like a trumpet. That's what you asked me, isn't it?"

Nabor showed him the drawing again. "So you're saying you never saw anything like this around here."

"I said all I'm going to say on the matter."

"Then you don't mind if we take a look around."

"There you go again, putting words in my mouth. Of course I mind. If you got a warrant in your pocket, now's the time to show it to me."

"I agree," Nabor said. He took out a satellite phone and punched in a few digits, then looked at his partner.

Bertolli reached into the large pocket of his parka and pulled out a black plastic tube with knobs on it. And lo and behold, the tube started to hum and whir, and out of it came a shiny, narrow sheet of paper. The printer snipped off a two-page document, and Bertolli handed it to Nabor, who glanced at it, and handed it to Poppy saying, "Marvin Johnson, you are served."

Poppy took the document to the window to examine it under daylight. It granted the agents permission to enter and search his "domicile, outbuildings, cellars, and other structures, and the remains of a 1920s-era copper mine situated on the premises" for an "approximately 120-inch-long tubular implement associated with the unlawful downing of a federally registered aircraft used for official U.S.P.S. business."

Poppy folded up the warrant and tore it in half. "I have little kids in the house," he said. "Mess with them or harm them in any way and all bets are off. You understand?"

Special Agent Bertolli said, "Are you threatening us?"

"Call it the rules of engagement."

Special Agent Nabor said, "You don't have the privilege of dictating any rules of anything, Mr. Prophecy, as far as we're concerned. But you can relax; we're not interested in searching the house. At least not yet. We'll start up in the old mine."

"Of course you will."

BEFORE LEAVING THE house, the agents disarmed Poppy and the two boys. They searched them and their parkas and boots for additional weapons. When Bertolli discovered the leather holster on Poppy's belt, he said, "What's in there? A Claymore mine?"

"It's my Bible."

"In a holster?"

"It's so I can quick-draw a verse if the need arises." Poppy unsnapped the guard and showed them that indeed it was the Holy Book.

The agents laughed, and Nabor said, "Funny. You're a funny old coot. Now do us a favor and remove the book."

The agents made Poppy flip through the pages in case they were hollowed out to conceal a weapon. Poppy did as instructed and couldn't help but say, "Take a good look, Mr. Agent. It's probably the only time you ever seen the insides of one of these."

Nabor said, "You're barking up the wrong tree, preacher. We're not here to talk religion. All we want is the implement you found. If you tell us where it is, everything would be so much simpler and more pleasant for everyone. Now why don't we take this little get-together up to the mine." He went to the door and held it open.

Still on his snowmobile, LE Ranger Masterson watched them come out to the porch. Agent Nabor made a throat-slashing gesture, and Masterson turned off both snowmobile engines and pocketed the keys. He pulled his pump-action shotgun from its scabbard before joining them on the porch. None of the Prophecys acknowledged his presence.

"Mr. Prophecy declines to show us where the mine is located," Nabor said.

"No worries," Masterson replied. "Follow me."

The two federal agents, despite their training, were winded by the time they reached the top of the slide. They studied the fortified adit a longish while and unholstered their machine pistols before approaching the gate.

All of the sniper slots on both sides were shut, but the agents watched them closely as they herded their detainees to the sally door.

There was an iron D-ring fastened to the door to use as a handle, but when Bertolli tried to pull the door open, it was locked from within. "Someone must be inside," he said.

A moment later there was a scraping sound from the port-side gallery above them. The nearest sniper slot opened, and a teen-aged boy peered down at them.

Bertolli covered him with his pistol, and the ranger said, "That there's the seventeen-year-old. He's got a temper on him, but nothing like his brother. His name is First Corinthians."

"Hey, First," Bertolli called up to the boy. "Close the window. Do it now."

Corny looked at them stupidly, or defiantly. From below it was hard to tell which.

Nabor said to Poppy in a measured voice, "Tell your son to obey us. If we see a weapon, we will shoot to kill. And that's no lie."

Poppy craned his neck and shouted, "Shut the port, son. Come open the sally door. No guns, y'hear? Stow your guns away before you open the door."

The sniper slot shut with a bang.

A minute or so later, the sally door iron bolt slid in its track, and the heavy door creaked ponderously outward. Corny stood in the doorway, hands over his head, looking more defiant than stupid, it now seemed.

FD6 1.0

DEUT COULD SMELL the ashes before they reached the burned-out ruin. The cabin was gone, and in its place lay a rubble pile of charred logs. Only the sheet metal Yukon stove and stovepipe remained.

"Maybe it was an accident," Deut said to her brother. She stood next to him on a little rise next to the ruins. "Maybe it was some careless tourist."

Proverbs rocked back and forth on his heels and jogged in place in the snow to stay warm, but he said nothing.

It was no accident. The rangers had warned them to stay away from the cabin. And in defiance, Proverbs had used it for a picnic.

"What do we do now?" Deut said. "Poppy wants us to stay out here till dinnertime. How we gonna do that?"

Proverbs didn't reply to that question either, so after a few more minutes Deut left him and went, first to check on Ginger, who was still asleep in the sled, and then to the woodpile. There was less than half a rick of spruce and birch stacked far enough away from the cabin to have been spared the inferno. She levered the ax out of the stump and began to split a round of spruce into kindling. It was far too cold to simply stand around. At least they could have a camp fire. Or wade into the ashes and fish out the Yukon stove and a length of stovepipe and put it somewhere out of the breeze to huddle around. This could be an adventure, if it weren't for the demons.

But before Deut could split much wood, she noticed Ginger sitting up in the sled. She waved at her and yelled, "*Over here.*" Deut didn't want Ginger to wake up thinking she was alone. Ginger heard her and looked over at her, but instead of being reassured, she seemed to panic. She jumped from the sled to the sno-go in front of it and fiddled desperately with the controls.

It dawned on Deut that this was an escape attempt. "Look out!" she called to her brother. "She's getting away!"

Proverbs didn't so much as turn around to look, and Ginger quickly gave up trying to start the Bearcat. The new machine had a functioning ignition key, and he must have taken it. It was more convenient than removing spark plugs all the time.

Ginger, the person they were supposed to be protecting from the mischief of evil spirits, abandoned the sno-go altogether and bolted up the trail.

"She's getting away!" Deut shouted again. "On foot!"

This time her brother did respond. He glanced at Deut and gave her the stink eye. His expression said, *Really, sister, and how far is she going to get on foot?*

So Deut shrugged him a whatever and went back to swinging the old, rusty, double-bitted ax over her head. As chores went, the boys had it pretty easy with wood splitting. There was a fun element to it that, say, mopping a wood plank floor never achieved.

Deut couldn't tell what her brother was doing with all his communing with the ruins. Praying? That would be good. More likely he was soaking up the fire's residual heat to stoke his anger. There was no way Ranger Rick was involved in this. She was sure of it, and she prayed that it be true.

"Brother," she called. "Pray with me."

Slowly, he turned from the ashes to look at her again. This time his good eye was dismissive.

"Elder Brother Jesus," she intoned in her father's cadence, "we pray that our hearts are not consumed in the same fire as consumed this innocent little cabin. Amen."

It took a moment, but he said, "Amen." Then he turned abruptly and headed back to the sno-go.

"Wait for me" she called. She buried the ax in the stump and ran to join him.

Deut sat behind her brother on the seat and held on to him around his waist. She aimed little prayer bombs at the back of his beaver-trimmed hat. *It's not her fault. She's a good person inside. And Ranger Rick had nothing to do with this.*

They went slowly, tracking Ginger's bootprints. Her tracks stayed on the corrugated sno-go trail, which were firm enough to support her weight. But only after fifty yards (46 m), her footprints leaped off the trail into the loose snow of the woods, and Proverbs braked to a halt.

Ginger was too weak to run and had fled into the trees. But none of the trees were giants here, and there she was, comically trying to hide behind one that was skinnier than her bright red parka.

"Don't blame her," Deut said, out loud this time.

Her brother did not reply. Neither did he go after the girl. He simply idled the machine and waited. They all waited in the freaking cold. After a few minutes, Deut dismounted and brought a sleeping bag from the sled. She used it to cover her brother and herself as best she could. She shivered to get warm and stamped her feet on the running boards.

Ginger held out for as long as she was able. When she returned to the trail, stiff, lethargic, no one said a word. She simply climbed into the sled and covered up, and Proverbs put the machine into drive.

He drove fast, faster than the path was wide, and several times they had to swerve hard to avoid hitting a tree. The sled got knocked around a bit behind them. Deut leaned into the turns with her brother and kept her mouth shut. At the fork, Proverbs turned toward home without even slowing down.

A HISSING OLD pressure lantern, hanging from a nail, dimly illuminated the cavernous entrance area. The agents shut and bolted the sally door and lined the Prophecys up along the inner gate. Masterson covered them with his shotgun while the agents searched the entrance and gallery wings. They found a handgun and two rifles, but no "tubular instrument."

Nabor returned to Poppy and said, "You know, we can get a whole army of techs in here to search every nook and cranny of this place."

Poppy shrugged. "I guess you do what you have to."

"If we have to find it on our own, we'll charge you and these three nice young men with obstruction of justice."

"Nobody's obstructing your so-called justice because there's no trumpet, not here, not anywhere, except maybe in the throne room of Heaven. And that's Father God's own truth."

"Then you *do* know what I'm talking about."

"All I know is I seen your child's drawing of a trumpet. I know you come all this way to roust me and my family from our table, to threaten and abuse us over something that don't exist. That's what I know. That's the Obama government for you. Tell me, Mr. Agent, what does a glass trumpet have to do with an airplane crash? Was Nellis blowing it out his window when he went down?"

"So you *do* know something about the crash."

"I know a good man died delivering the U.S. Mail. A tragedy. A tragedy for his wife and children. And a tragedy for the community whose mail he faithfully delivered. But, to be honest, no worse than all the other tragedies that await the rest of us in these latter days. No one will escape untouched. Not you. Not me. Because men like you, marked with the sign of the Beast, will line up behind the Antichrist on his blood-drenched march across the sands of Israel. And across our own nation, butchering the faithful as you go, ripping babies from the womb and putting innocents to the sword.

"I bet you feel right proud of yourself, Mr. Agent Man. Don't you? Don't it give you a little thrill just to contemplate it? It's your kind of business."

Nabor threw up his hands. "Have it your way, Johnson." To the ranger he said, "Watch those men while we take the preacher farther in."

"You got it," Masterson said. He used his shotgun to nudge the Prophecy boys to the bench under the coat pegs. Adam and Hosea complied, but Corny held back and challenged the ranger's authority.

Nabor and Bertolli exchanged a glance, and Bertolli came over, producing plastic handcuffs from a pouch on his belt. "Let's make things easier," he said and cuffed the three men's hands behind their backs.

At the mouth of the dark tunnel, Nabor said to Poppy, "I don't suppose you'll be our tour guide." Before Poppy had a chance to refuse, he added, "Never mind. We'll just use this." He pulled an iPad from a pocket and brought up a diagram. It was a highly detailed floor plan of the mine. It laid out the tunnels, shafts, spurs, and ore chambers of the Stubborn Mountain Mine, circa 1929. It was from an insurance policy rider by a Boston underwriting firm and was dated 1973, a year when Beehymer was actively working the site. Satan's researchers were nothing if not thorough.

"I guess you don't need me then," Poppy said. "Why don't I just stay here with my boys."

Nabor said, "You'd give us free range of this place."

"I got nothing to hide."

"Ha ha," Bertolli said. "We still need you to show us where the booby traps are."

Nabor said, "We won't cuff you unless you give us reason to."

The agents put Poppy between them and let him lead the way. They had high-tech flashlights that were impressively brilliant. They could focus the beam of light in or out and illuminate whole sections of the tunnel at once.

"That third son of yours," Bertolli said as they went, "the hot-headed one. Is he in here too?"

"No," Poppy said. "I tole you he's on an errand into town."

"If he is in here, you'd best call out to him to give himself up, or I swear to you, if he pops up from behind some rock, we'll open fire on him. I promise you we will."

"I said he's not here. We're all alone except for the angels."

RANGER MASTERSON TURNED on all of the LED lanterns he could find in the entrance area, eight in all.

Sitting on the bench with his brothers, their hands bound behind their backs, Adam said, "You're wasting our supplies, ranger."

"The better to see you with, my dears."

IN THE FIRST chamber they explored, the machine room, the agents confronted the immensity of their task. With the piles, rows, shelves, and bins of obsolete equipment and supplies, and all of the possible hiding places they afforded, it was clear that a thorough search would take more time and manpower than they had available. No wonder the old coot seemed so smug.

The empty break room, with its overburden of dust, did not impress the agents, but the food slot, recently cut into the stout powder room door, did. Sawdust from the cut still lay on the stone floor beneath it. They opened the door and flooded the cell with light.

"Looks like you got yourselves your own little black site," Nabor said. "Recent too. Tell us who your guest was."

Poppy ignored the question. Nor did he speak when they asked what lay in the tunnel beyond the powder room. Their floor-plan map simply labeled it a closed area. They followed the tunnel until they were forced to crouch to proceed and decided to leave it till later. It was the second level tunnel that seemed to be calling them.

And it was on the second level that they witnessed the true scope of the Prophecy plan. Agent Bertolli whistled in admiration as they entered the storeroom chamber. The enormous space was a Sam's Club for preppers. There were aisles and shelves and bins all crammed with housewares, clothes, cleaning supplies, building material, tools, paints, fuel, and lubricants. The largest department, by far, was devoted to food: aisles of canned goods; pallets of grains, beans, rice, powdered milk, and sugar; drums of cooking oil. There were towers of green tubs containing staples sealed in nitrogen gas for long-term storage. There were walls of home-canned vegetables, jams, salmon, and moose.

While Nabor guarded Poppy, Bertolli made a quick pass up and down the aisles searching for the missing weapon.

"Looks like you got a lot invested in this," Nabor said to Poppy, but Poppy merely yawned.

"Over here," Bertolli called.

They joined him at the far side of the chamber where a side room was shut behind a solid, padlocked door.

Nabor said, "What's in here."

Poppy shrugged his shoulders.

"Open it."

"You're the dick with the warrant. You open it."

Nabor nodded to Bertolli, who pulled a pair of wire snips from a pouch on his belt. He turned a knob on one of the handles, and the tool emitted a high-pitched whine, like a dentist's drill. Then he wrapped the jaws around the padlock hook and clipped it as easily as trimming a fingernail. The ruined padlock fell to the floor, and Bertolli opened the hasp and pulled the door open.

It was the armory. The agents rummaged through the Prophecy collection of small arms and cartons of ammunition, but everything looked legal, and there was no sign of a trumpet, tulip, or glass bazooka.

In the next chamber, the agents laughed when they stumbled upon the windowless house. Spooky, they said. Hitchcockian. But it was the chamber itself that impressed them. The cottage chamber was so voluminous it swallowed up even their hi-tech searchlights. In a space so huge, the ten-foot-long weapon they sought might be lying openly on the ground several football-field lengths away and they'd never see it.

On their way out of the chamber, the agents found a water line near the tunnel opening. A garden spigot attached it to the chamber wall. There was a puddle of water under the spigot, and when Bertolli turned the valve, a torrent of water gushed out. He cupped his hand to capture some and taste it.

"Neat," he said, turning off the flow. "Appears you all solved your potable water problem. You tap into a spring or something?"

The sight of that man lapping that water from his hand and commenting on it like it was ordinary tap water, like you'd find in Detroit or Dallas, so disgusted Poppy that for a moment he felt too tired to go on, let alone follow the angel's instructions.

The agents had missed the black water pipe on the way in, but now they followed it down the tunnel past the ramp. They found dead-end spurs, open pits, loose rocks, and narrow passages. The tubular weapon might be anywhere. When they came upon a second ramp, this one leading to a third level, they consulted their floor plan again.

"Another closed area," Bertolli said.

The black PVC pipe continued upward, and so did they. The third level tunnel was clearly less developed than the lower two. There were few, small excavations along it and only one set of ore cart rails. The floor was wet. They continued following the PVC line until it terminated in a small collection basin chipped out of the rock and dammed with wooden planks.

"Neat," Bertolli said again.

The collection basin was fed by a small trickle of water that ran in a shallow stone channel along the base of one wall. They followed the channel to the only sizable chamber on that level. Even the air was moist.

"Nice. Very nice," Bertolli said when they entered the cistern chamber.

They stood on the edge and played their lights across the subterranean lake. Bertolli tossed a stone into the crystalline liquid and watched it flutter as it fell out of sight. It didn't seem to ever hit bottom. Again, Poppy felt violated by their attention to his water, as if they were fouling it.

"Seen enough yet?" he said, maybe a little too impatiently.

Nabor was watching him, had been watching him the whole time, and he, for one, wanted to see more. He gathered a handful of stones from the shore and began skipping them across the water's surface. In a little while, both agents were skipping stones. Each stone was another tiny insult. But that was their plan, to provoke him, so Poppy sucked in his breath and prayed for strength and forbearance.

"How long," Nabor asked his partner, "do you figure this water will last them."

"Assuming they don't exceed its refresh rate, I'd say it'll last indefinitely."

"So if their food supply holds out, they have it made in the shade."

"I'd say so. In medieval castles under siege, they sometimes drank their wells dry and lost the castle."

"But these folks won't have to worry about drinking this dry, will they?"

"I'd say they're pretty well covered in the water department."

Nabor dumped the rest of his stones into the water and brushed his hands on his pants. "Then it'd be a crying shame if something happened to this water so they couldn't drink it."

"That would suck," Bertolli agreed. "Like a plague right out of the Bible."

"Exactly. A disaster of biblical proportions."

"What are you thinking?"

"Nothing, except how when natural waterways get accidentally polluted with industrial waste and shit how everyone downstream suffers."

Bertolli shook his head. "It's a shame, but it happens all the time."

"I know. Coal ash spills, tanker cars, pipelines — You read about it all the time in the paper. Or actually, online. I get most of my news online these days."

"I still enjoy watching the CBS Evening News," Bertolli admitted. "I guess that dates me."

"Yeah. All those geriatric ads."

"I know. And boner ads."

"I was just wondering," Nabor said, circling back to his original threat, "how long this reservoir of spring water would take to clear itself if it got, you know, accidentally polluted."

"Polluted like how?" Bertolli obligingly asked.

"Oh, I don't know. You remember those storage batteries we saw in that machine shop down on the main level?"

"You mean the lead-acid ones? Nasty stuff — sulfuric acid. Probably take years to work that crap out of the water."

"Not to mention the lead."

"Lead, right. Bad stuff for growing children."

"Makes them retarded."

"Or that barrel of cleaning detergent we saw in the supply room."

"You wouldn't want the kiddies drinking crap like that. That's for sure."

"No, you wouldn't. Or those sacks of fertilizer."

"That would be totally fucked up."

The agents were on a roll, naming all of the possible polluting compounds they had noticed on their sweep of the keep. Finally, when they ran out of examples, Nabor said to Poppy, "It doesn't have to end that way, Mr. Johnson. We're not necessarily after you. We don't even know if it was you or somebody else who's responsible. Hell, we're not even sure what this is all about. But let me recap for you what we *do* know.

"We know that three weeks ago yesterday, something weird happened on the river near here. Big, bright light comes out of the sky. Ring a bell."

Poppy shrugged. He wasn't surprised they knew. The light was so intense he had wondered why everyone hadn't seen it.

"Whatever it was, it left behind an implement ten feet long like a glass trumpet. One of the rangers saw it, said that you stole it off park land. That's a federal offense all by itself, by the way.

"The next thing we know, you and your sons are in Anchorage spending wheelbarrows of cash. Most of which were marked bills, I might add, that ties you to some pretty nasty business down south."

"Nasty business," Bertolli agreed.

"As part of this shopping spree, you were observed meeting with Governor Tetlin, the sore loser rabble-rouser."

"Not a popular lady in DC right now, let me tell you," Bertolli added.

"Then, four days ago, there's a terrorist strike that disrupts our nation's eyes in the sky. Civilian and military satellites alike. And not only ours but China's too, and the Russians' — everybody's. It temporarily blinded the whole world and no one knows who did it, how they did it, or why."

"It's a mystery."

"And it gets even more mysterious because then two days later someone slices the wing off an airplane in mid-flight, and it crashes into your backyard. Hits the bullseye in a bald parcel of dirt that's miles in diameter where just last week there were trees and snowpack and all sorts of natural shit. Now there's nothing there but sterile sand. What causes that."

"Nobody knows," Bertolli said.

"Nobody knows. Not even our top scientists can explain it."

"Another mystery."

Nabor pulled the tablet out of his pocket again, not to check the map of the mine but to show Poppy a satellite image. "And this here's where the mystery comes crashing down on you, Mr. Marvin Johnson. There's a fresh snowmobile track that ties you to all of it."

In one corner of the satellite image was the large, bald crash area. In the opposite corner was the Prophecy compound. Someone had highlighted in yellow a snowmobile trail that connected the two locations.

"Take a look at the date in the margin," Nabor suggested, pointing to it. "December 23. That was the day before the crash. That puts you, or someone from this household, at the crime scene before it happened. There are no other tracks coming or going to this spot except yours, till later. We may not know what happened out there, but we do know that you're in the middle of it. Now, you may not have intended to take part in an attempt to overthrow our democracy. All you wanted to do was drop off the grid with your family and let the rest of the world go fuck itself. We can respect that, and you're off to a good start here. If that's the case, you need to get in front of this before it's too late. Things'll go a lot easier on you if you do. Who knows, your family might still be able to salvage this prepper's paradise of yours."

Nabor paused for Poppy to take it all in, but the old man remained resolutely silent.

"I see," Nabor continued. "You probably think you hid the weapon pretty good so we'll never find it. It could be here in the mine, in your house, in one of the outbuildings, or maybe you stashed it in the woods miles away. You're probably thinking to yourself it'll take a small army to turn over every rock. But guess what. We have the authority to call in a small army."

"I got the army on speed dial," Bertolli said.

"See. Men and dogs and special equipment are only a sat phone call away. Meanwhile, we award you and your adult children a free trip to a holding facility in Seattle while we tear this place apart. It could take months, years. So do yourself a solid, Marvin. Just show us where it is, and your family's life can go back to normal, however it is you define normal."

THERE WERE TWO strange sno-gos in the yard when they returned, a Kawasaki they'd never seen before, and a Ski-Doo with the satanic NPS arrowhead logo on its side. When Deut saw the logo she prayed it wasn't her ranger's ride. When Ginger saw the logo, she jumped out of the sled before it had come to a full stop and ran for the front door. When Proverbs saw it, he opened his parka and unsnapped his holster guard.

The children were sitting in a circle on the floor in the warm corner. They looked frightened. Sue and Sarai had been leading them in prayer, and when Ginger burst through the front door, they scurried into a knot and held each other tight. Sarai dashed to the stove and snatched up the fire poker.

"Where are they?" Ginger demanded.

"Stay away from us!" Sarai shouted. The poker was made from a length of iron rebar and had a wicked barb at the end. She waved it in front of her in a threatening manner.

"Are they up in the mine?"

"Begone unclean spirits. Leave this place. I command thee in Elder Brother Jesus name. Amen."

"Amen!" answered the children. "Amen!"

When Deut came in, she looked all around. Finding none of the visitors, she said, "Which one?"

"Which one what?" her twin replied.

"Which ranger?"

"Danger."

Deut collapsed into a chair. *Thank You, Elder Brother Jesus. Thank You, thank You, thank You.*

When Proverbs came in, the house fell silent. The older ones remembered what that face meant, and the little ones needed no explanation.

"Where?" he said.

"Up in the keep," Sue replied.

"How many?"

"Three. And they're heavily armed."

Proverbs left without another word, leaving the door hanging open behind him. He returned a moment later for the Winchester carbine mounted above the door.

Ginger went to the door and watched as he crossed the yard to the keep trail. Then she hurried out to the two snowmachines, praying that the rangers had left their keys in the ignition. No such luck. She looked around the yard for an idea, an answer, a miracle. She ran to the prayer cabin. Maybe it was open. Maybe the safe was open. Maybe there was a spark plug for one of the older machines. She prayed that it was so.

The door was padlocked.

Ginger hadn't eaten in days. She was still weak from her confinement. She was cold. There was nothing more she could do but wait for the rangers' return. They had to return eventually, didn't they? And when they did, she would be safe. They would take her back to town with them. They would call the Troopers. People would pay for their crimes. All of them. She would be safe.

But she couldn't wait outdoors. It was too cold. She was too weak. So she returned to the house.

The front door was shut and locked. This surprised her and made her more angry than afraid. She went around to the kitchen and tried the arctic entry.

It too was locked.

Unchristian rage filled Ginger's heart, but she damped it down. Rage made you stupid. They were trying to freeze her to death, and there was no margin for stupidity. She was scanning the snowy yard for something to break a window with when she saw the bathhouse. Of course.

The old, gasoline-powered washing machine stood on the bathhouse porch. A load of hastily abandoned laundry was slowly freezing in its tub. Ginger paused to open the drain. No sense allowing the old machine to be broken by freeze damage.

It was warm inside the bathhouse. Clean laundry sat in plastic baskets on the sorting table. There were embers in the barrel stove, and she coaxed them back to life with sticks of kindling. A window overlooked the yard. She pulled a chair next to it to shiver herself warm while she kept vigil for the return of her rescuers.

FD9 1.0

"TELL ME, BROTHER," Corny said, "why we don't just up and leave?"

Ranger Masterson was pacing back and forth, back and forth in the entrance area. He came close to their bench, made an about face, and continued in the other direction. Back and forth. Back and forth. This had been going on for two hours. In that time, three of the eight lanterns had dimmed and blinked out. The cavernous space was filling with shadows.

"See?" Hosea said to Adam. "The batteries are bad too."

"Now, brother?" Adam said. "You want to talk about that now?"

"Why don't we just get up and leave?" Corny asked again. "We're not under arrest, are we? We got constitutional rights or don't we?"

"Sit still," Adam said to him, "and shut up."

"I can't sit still." He strained against the plastic restraints. "If I don't move, my ass will fall off."

"Language, brother."

"Oh, bullshit."

On the ranger's next circuit, Corny stood up and silently followed in his wake halfway to the far wall before peeling off toward the gate. He moved swiftly and made it to the sally door before Masterson turned around. The ranger was startled to see him at the door. Corny fumbled with the bolt with hands bound behind his back. The bolt was difficult enough to open even when you could see what you were doing. He wiggled it as he pushed it with his thumbs, and it gave little by little — before going all at once.

"Halt!" Masterson shouted. He sprinted to the gate as Corny was pushing the armored door open with his shoulder. The ranger caught him by the arm and yanked him backward off his feet. The boy went sprawling, but he didn't stay down. Despite his bound hands, he sprang up and charged the ranger head first. Masterson changed his grip on the shotgun and struck the boy's skull with its maple stock. Corny's knees buckled, and he went down on the cold stone floor.

Masterson spun around. The other two Prophecys had catapulted themselves from their bench to charge him from behind. But he pumped a shell into the chamber of the gun and leveled it at them. Adam and Hosea slowed down and shuffled to a halt not ten feet away. Adam's whole body shook with fury. "You killed him!" he cried. "You killed my brother."

"He ain't dead."

Hosea pleaded, "Let me help him."

Bright blood was pooling on the floor of greenish stone beneath the unconscious boy's head. Masterson's action had been justified. Nevertheless . . .

"Turn around," he told Hosea, "and I'll remove your cuffs."

Masterson pulled a small pair of snips from his belt, but the big man, who only a moment before was desperate to aid his brother, now hung back and stared at the ranger with open mouth. Adam, too, was transfixed.

Masterson felt a draft of frigid air on his neck from the open door behind him. He glanced around and found Proverbs, armed with a carbine, coming in.

FD10 1.0

POPPY DID NOT doubt the agents' resolve to go through with their threat. He trusted in the evil that was lodged deeply in the hearts of men. He trusted the angel, too, to do everything necessary to protect the key. She had made it clear that everything Poppy had — even the lives of his children — was expendable in its defense. She had advised him to put up token resistance but to give the feds unfettered access to the keep. But she didn't say anything about letting them destroy it.

"Which one you prefer." Nabor asked Poppy, holding up two brightly labeled packages. Bertolli had commandeered a wheelbarrow on the second level and used it to schlep common household poisons he found in the storeroom up one level to the cistern. Now they were debating which ones to use.

"Suit yourself," Poppy said. "The power of the Lord will turn the bitter into sweet."

Bertolli asked Nabor, "Was that one of those quick-draw Bible verses?"

"It sure sounded like one."

"Excellent."

The agents settled on a foil bag of garden insecticide that Poppy had instructed Adam to buy on their supply run. There was certain to be an explosion of pests during the Last Days, and Poppy was anything but an organic gardener. Pests were to be massacred, not reasoned with.

"Let's see," Nabor said, reading the label. "Active Ingredients: Acephate [O,S – Dimethyl acetyl . . . acetyl . . ." He showed the package to Bertolli. "Read this."

"Sure. Acetylphosphoramidothiote 97.0%. Easy-peasy."

"Easy-peasy for a nerd." Nabor browsed the rest of the label. "'This product contains a cholinesterase inhibitor.' I don't know what that is, but it doesn't sound good."

"It's not. You never want to inhibit your cholinesterase. Period."

"Let's see. ' . . . may result in incontinence, unconsciousness, convulsions, and death.' Great. It not only kills you but makes you piss yourself first."

"That's pretty typical for any kind of poison."

"'Call a poison control center or doctor immediately for treatment advice.' That's always good advice — call an expert — but you can't call anyone when you don't have phone service this far out."

"Who you gonna call?"

"Nobody, I guess."

Nabor took out a jackknife and slit the top of the package, holding it away from his face. "Here," he said, handing it to Bertolli. "You do the honors."

Bertolli accepted the foil bag. He weighed it in his hand. Shook his head with regret. "Believe me, Marvin, when I say this: I get no pleasure out of doing this. I'd much rather just waterboard you, you know? But sadly the president has removed that tool from our kit." He extended his arm and held the bag of insecticide over the water. "Uh, last chance."

Poppy choked with anger.

"What was that? You say something?"

But Poppy calmed himself. The key to the bottomless pit was certainly more important than this water. Certainly, the angel would have the means to purify the cistern again, if not immediately, then after her host of angels arrived.

Bertolli began to tip the package, but he stopped. He just couldn't bring himself to do it, and he sheepishly handed the poison back to Nabor. Nabor replaced his partner at the water's edge and held the package out.

He locked eyes with Poppy and said, "My colleague here is a little soft-hearted, as you can see. But you know that I'm not similarly afflicted. You *know* that I can and will do this. I'll pour this in and chase it with everything else we got. This pool will be dead for a generation. That's what you want, Mr. Johnson; that's what you'll get. All right then, on three: One . . . Two . . ."

"Stop!"

"You want me to stop."

"I'll tell you what you want to know."

Nabor withdrew the poison. "You'll tell us where the trumpet is."

"I already told you it's gone. I had it, but it turned to dust."

Nabor held out the poison again.

"But it left something behind. It's what melted all those trees and brought down that airplane. It's not a weapon by design, but it's got tremendous power. If you wanted to use it as a weapon, there's probably no reason why you couldn't."

"Now we're talking," Nabor said, dropping the package of insecticide back into the wheelbarrow. "Take us to this thing."

WHEN PROVERBS COMES through the sally door, the ranger is standing on his right side, in the blind spot of his eyepatch. It's all the advantage Masterson needs to swat aside the short barrel of the Winchester and jam his own shotgun into the boy's gut.

"Drop the weapon!" Masterson screams in his face. "Drop the fucking weapon!"

Proverbs rears back in surprise, but, instead of dropping his weapon, he swings it around to aim at the ranger.

Masterson braces himself as he pulls the trigger. The firing pin strikes the primer with a hopeful click, but the expected, satisfying jolt never comes. *Misfire!*

Now Proverbs has the advantage. "Stop!" he shouts at the ranger. "Don't move!" But in the time it takes him to say this, Masterson has pumped his gun, ejecting the bad round and chambering a new one. *Fuck you!*

Both men pull their triggers at the same moment, but only the boy's Winchester barks. Masterson staggers backward off his feet. He lands next to Corny in shock and disbelief and with a .30-30 slug buried in his armored vest. He struggles to clear his head. What are the odds of two bad rounds in a row? Men are shouting, but he can't altogether follow their meaning. The shotgun is still clutched in his right hand, but when he tries to raise it, a boot pins it to the floor. He lets go of the shotgun and reaches for the pistol at his side. But as he wraps laggard fingers around its grip, the Winchester pokes him between the eyes.

Do I have any regrets? Yes, quite a few, actually. Was it a happy life? Not particularly. More lonesome than anything else.

And then it's over.

ADAM WAS SHOUTING, "Cut us loose. Proverbs, cut us loose." Over and over again until Proverbs looked up from the ranger's ruined face.

"*What?*" he said.

Adam turned around and showed him his bound hands. Proverbs reached into his parka, searching for a knife, but Adam told him to use the ranger's snips. They were lying on the floor where the ranger had dropped them. Proverbs used them to free his brothers' hands, including Corny's. The boy was coming around and trying to sit up, but Hosea ordered him to stay down while he tended to his head.

Adam, meanwhile, picked up the ranger's shotgun and ejected the dud cartridge and two more, emptying the magazine. He weighed the cartridges in his hand. The ranger's ammo was light, just like their fuel supply, just like everything was coming up light these days. On a hunch, Adam retrieved the ranger's Super Redhawk Alaskan. Now here was a man's pistol. Its hard rubber, finger-grooved grip fit his hand perfectly. He cocked the hammer, pointed it into the far corner of the entrance, braced for a powerful recoil, and pulled the trigger.

Click.

He pulled the trigger again.

Click.

Six pulls, no joy. Adam opened the cylinder and extracted the bum rounds for later examination. He collected the shotgun rounds too and dropped them into his pocket.

Hosea said, "Search him for the sno-go keys."

Meanwhile, Proverbs shucked off his heavy parka and leggings. He took a hard hat from a peg and picked up the Winchester. "Where's Poppy?" he said.

Adam said, "Wait. I'll go with you." Quickly, Adam stashed the ranger's guns out of sight in one of the galleries. When he returned to the entrance, Proverbs had already gone without him.

"Stay with Corny," Adam told Hosea. "And be ready in case the feds come out before we do."

FD13 1.0

"WHAT WAS THAT?" Bertolli said, pausing to listen down tunnel. They were still on the third level, beyond the cistern chamber.

"I don't hear anything," Nabor said.

"Could'a been a gunshot."

"Let's hope those young men aren't giving the ranger a bad time. That one's got a short fuse, I'm told." He said this to his partner, though it was intended for Poppy.

But Poppy was too busy listening to his conscience to pay much attention to the agents. It wasn't too late to turn back; they hadn't reached the rock pile yet where he'd hidden the key. But if he changed course now, the soulless bastards would only go back to poisoning his cistern. Where was that pesky angel when he needed her? He thought she had said she could take on an entire army of men.

When they came to the backfilled excavation, Poppy stopped. It was decision time, but the decision was already made. "Up there," he said, pointing.

"Uh," Bertolli said. "Where exactly?"

"See that boulder up there?" The agents raked the rock pile with their searchlights until they found it.

Nabor laughed. "You're fucking with us, old man."

"That's where I put it."

"Show us."

The three men climbed the rock pile to the boulder, and Poppy located the crevice into which he'd dropped the golden marble.

"This weapon of yours must be kinda little to fit in there. A hand grenade wouldn't fit."

"It *is* small. It's a marble, but heavy, like a sack of cement."

That gave the agents pause. Bertolli pulled out a small digital instrument and passed it back and forth over the area. He checked the display and said, "It's not hot, but give me a sec." He fiddled with the controls, swiping pages, checking boxes, and passed the phone over the crevice again. He and Nabor switched off their searchlights, throwing the alcove into total darkness.

Gradually, as their eyes adjusted, the crevice began to glow with an eerie purplish radiance, the same weird color Poppy had first seen on the river flats.

"Well, I'll be," Nabor said. "There *is* something down there after all. Any reason we don't dig it out."

"None I can see."

They switched on their lights again and began to pull the rock cover away by hand. Poppy's legs were shaky on the uneven surface, and he sat down nearby to watch. The agents wouldn't have to actually move the boulder, but they did have to pry loose rocks wedged beneath it to reach the key. There was one large stone in particular that would not budge. They decided to leave it and try to dig around it. After ten minutes of finger-stubbing labor, the two agents paused to straighten their backs and shuck off their heavy parkas. They piled them out of Poppy's reach. Their machine pistols hung at their sides.

"We should get those boys to come do this for us," Bertolli joked.

Poppy said, "You want me to fetch the boys?"

The agents ignored the question, and Nabor tipped his searchlight to look at its display. "You bring spare batteries for this."

"Yeah, back with the snowmobile."

"That's a fine place to keep them."

"Why? These had a ten-hour charge when we started."

"Mine's at thirty percent, and we haven't been here all that long."

Bertolli checked his own searchlight. "So's mine. I don't know what to tell you. I'll conserve mine." He turned it off. "We only need one."

They resumed digging, and when they cleared all but the large stone wedged under the boulder, they took another breather, and Nabor said, "You bring anything to snack on."

"Only just a candy bar. You want it?"

"Yeah. I could use a boost."

Bertolli checked his pockets but found only empty wrappers. Odd.

When they resumed work, they crouched behind the stone to give it a final push. Straining, farting, swearing, they managed to tip it slightly out of the way.

"Hold it there," Nabor said. "I can see it. You got this."

"Yeah, but hurry."

With Bertolli supporting the stone, Nabor tried to let go of it, but his hands wouldn't come free. His fingers and palms were stuck to bare rock.

"The fuck," he said.

"What's wrong?"

"Let it down a sec."

"Just grab it if you can see it. I got this."

"No, no. I said let it down."

They allowed the rock to settle into its previous spot and quickly discovered that neither of them could let go of it. The flesh of their hands seemed welded to the stone surface.

"Booby trap," Nabor said. "Superglue of some sort. Where'd he get that from." To Poppy he said, "Well played, Marvin, but this is no game. Release us from this rock immediately, or you won't like what happens to you."

Poppy was just as stunned as they at the suddenness of their setback.

"Now how'm I supposed to release you?"

"Whatever you used on us has a releasing agent. Use it to release us."

"Releasing agent?" Poppy drawled. "All I see are special agents. Did another agent sneak into the picture while I wasn't looking?" Poppy had a mad urge to gloat in righteousness, but he stifled it. The wisdom of Obadiah: never get ahead of yourself.

"Cut the crap. You can't win this."

Poppy got up to assess the situation. The key to the pit was buried again, and the agents' hands did appear to be held firmly in the angel's grip. So he reached for Nabor's machine pistol. But the agent was still able to use his legs and shoulders to block him.

"I swear you don't want to do this," Nabor said. "They'll find us no matter what you do, and you'll get a dose of lethal injection. Your whole family will suffer. That's what you're asking for. Release us this instant."

"It's not me holding you but the angel."

"Angel? What angel? What are you talking about?"

"I told you, when you asked about my son, that we were alone here except for the angels. Well, one angel anyway. Her name is Martha.

"Watch this," Poppy said, leaning over to place his hand between theirs on the stone. After a moment, he removed his hand just as easily. "See? No glue. Only angel spit or something."

With this, the agents seemed to sag with sudden exhaustion. They sat down as best they could with the stone between them, and Bertolli said, "What's happening? Are you drugging me?"

"I'm not doing nothing. Like I said, the angel . . ."

"Listen," Nabor said, wheezing a little and resting his head on his outstretched arms. "I'm a Catholic. That means I'm a Christian too. I believe in angels, and I have no beef with any of them. Least of all any angel named Martha. That was my sister-in-law's name before she passed. Angels are good folks. They're guardians and warriors for good, not evil. Call your angel. Call Martha so we can talk to her."

Poppy didn't believe a word of it. Catholics weren't Christians, not real ones anyway. The agent was simply angling for any advantage, any fingernail of an advantage, to extricate himself and his partner from this, their sudden comeuppance. Not two minutes ago they were in charge; they were the wise-cracking masters of the universe, willing to destroy his family's life in Obama's name. Now they were dog meat, and he longed to see their expressions upon confronting an actual angel.

"You really want to talk to Martha? Be my guest." He turned and shouted down the tunnel, "Martha! Seraph of the Ninth Order! Someone wants to talk to you." But she didn't show, and he called her again. "I guess she don't want to talk to you. Can't say I blame her."

There were sounds down tunnel, and light, but not heavenly light. In a moment, Proverbs appeared. He was armed, and he crouched behind the rock wall and peered around it before coming out into the open. Poppy was surprised to see him.

"You're back."

Proverbs didn't reply, only waved his father to come down to him, and as Poppy made his shaky way down the loose rocks, the boy never took his eyes or his gun off the agents.

"Are they really bound to the rock, lord?"

"Yes, it seems so. How did you know?"

"Martha told us. She's dying, lord. Adam is with her. She wants to speak to you."

"Where is she?"

"In the cistern chamber."

The agents, bound to the stone, watched the Prophecys even as Proverbs watched them. "She says to hurry, lord."

"Yes, yes, we'll hurry, but while they're bound, you need to go up there and take their guns away from them."

"Martha says there's no need, lord. She says she made their guns impotent."

"What does that mean?"

"I don't know except that they won't fire."

"What about yours?"

"Mine fires good enough."

ADAM HAD GATHERED up all the poisons into the wheelbarrow and removed them from the chamber. He was just as protective of the water as his father.

"Did they contaminate it?" he asked when Poppy and Proverbs arrived.

"No, praise Him," Poppy said. He entered the chamber and looked around. "Where is she?"

At first he couldn't see the angel because she had no radiance to spare and was laid out on the rocky shore and cloaked in darkness. Adam led him to her. If she had looked ragged before, now she was shattered.

"Master Prophecy," she gasped when he knelt beside her. "You have failed me."

"I failed *you*? You would have them destroy the keep?" He already knew her answer to that, but he couldn't help asking.

"Yes, if it was necessary, but it wouldn't have come to that. I was right here, ready to catch the poison before it could reach the water and to fling it back into their faces."

"You should have communicated that to me."

"You should have trusted me. But let's not pick at bones while the battle rages. I am holding those two henchmen down, but I won't be able to continue for long, and when I let go, they will destroy you."

"Proverbs says you messed with their guns."

"Yes, but they carry other, just-as-lethal weapons, not the least of which are their satellite telephones."

"What should we do?"

"Isn't it plain, Master Prophecy? Put an end to them before they have another chance to put an end to you."

Adam, who had been listening, said, "What? But that would be murder."

"Killing one's enemy in time of war is not murder," Martha said, "if the war is just."

"I hear you, Angel Martha, but can't we lock 'em up in the powder room or something? Use 'em for — I don't know — hostages?"

"There are no hostages in the Final Battle, only the victors and the vanquished. Decide which you would be, Adam the Firstborn, before my strength fails me. These agents of Darkness will show you no mercy if they escape."

"She's right," Poppy said. "You saw the poisons they brung into this chamber. Take your brother's gun and send them to their judgement."

But Adam was not convinced. "Why's it up to us to do it, lord? She's the angel; it's her key; it's her battle. She should leave us out of it."

"Does it look to you like she's fit to fight?"

"Oh, I don't know, lord. Looks can be deceiving. She's fit enough to hold those men down all the way from here. She can make their guns misfire. That seems pretty powerful to me. Why don't she just choke them to death from here while she's at it?"

"Son . . ."

"No, lord, I mean it. Are you telling me that Father God wants *me* to go up there and execute those two men?"

Poppy stifled his anger — and embarrassment — over his son's display in front of the angel. "No, He's not," he said. "It was me who asked you, and now I'm un-asking you, so settle down and shut up. I'll do it."

"Lord?"

"I thought you wanted to step up around here. You wanted a wife, you said. You wanted to give me grandchildren, you said. Boy, you had me fooled. So sit tight and suck your thumb while I do it."

Poppy reached for the Winchester. Proverbs, who had been silently observing them, at first lifted the gun to his father, but then withdrew it.

"You too?" Poppy said. "Give it to me!"

"No, lord, I'll do it."

"You'll put those dogs down?"

"Yes, lord. I already put down one of 'em today. I can probably handle two more." He said this with the cool self-assurance of a born-again psychopath.

"Then go in haste," Angel Martha said, resting her pale cheek on the cold stone shore. "With the Father's blessing."

THE AGENTS' ONCE powerful searchlight had glimmered its last by the time Poppy and Proverbs returned to the rock pile. But there was enough heavenly light from the buried key to make out the captured agents. They lay on either side of the stone like exhausted marathon contestants unwilling to let go of the prize. Proverbs handed the rifle to Poppy and began to climb the pile alone.

"What's this?" Poppy said. "Don't you need it?"

But Proverbs never looked back.

Agent Nabor's head snapped to attention when he heard Proverbs approaching. The agent struggled to his knees and pulled and tugged his hands, but the stone held them fast. Finally, he let out a low howl that rose in intensity and ended in a fierce shriek as he jerked his right hand and tore it free. He left behind the pads of his fingers and palm of his hand.

Freed of his restraint, the agent drew his machine pistol from its holster, bare tendons on blued steel, and brandished it at Proverbs.

"Halt!" he cried.

Proverbs paused only for a moment.

"Have it your way," Nabor said and opened fire on him. But his weapon misfired, and he struggled to eject the bad round with only one free hand. He raised the gun again and pulled the trigger, only to misfire a second time. Desperate, he hurled the bulky pistol at Proverbs' head. Proverbs ducked, and the gun clattered on the rocks below. The agent tried to wrest his other hand free, but he lacked the strength or the resolve this time. So instead he picked up a sizable rock and flung it at his approaching, patch-eyed killer. But the rock stuck to the agent's raw hand, and its inertia pulled him off balance. He toppled awkwardly, and his captured arm twisted until it snapped. He scrabbled on the rocks frantically trying to relieve the pain.

Proverbs calmly searched for a suitable rock of his own and found one the size of a watermelon.

"Don't do it, son," Nabor gasped. "You know it's wrong."

"I'm not your son," Proverbs said, taking a position over the man's head.

The other agent, Bertolli, said, "You can't murder federal agents and get away with it. We'll hunt you down."

"You shut up and wait your turn," Proverbs scolded. "You should be spending your time asking for the Father's forgiveness."

Nabor said, "Give me a moment to make my peace."

"All right, but hurry. This stone weighs a ton."

"Then put it down!" Bertolli pleaded.

"Heavenly Father," Nabor prayed, "I implore You to send wisdom to this young man before he does something he'll regret the rest of his life. Let him see that we are Christians too, just trying to serve Your will —"

"Liar!" Proverbs said. "You're not real Christians." He strained to raise the rock over his head. Balancing it there only a moment, he slammed it down on the injured man with enough force to crush his skull. The rock tumbled down the pile with a strip of scalp stuck to it. Nabor spasmed violently, but only once, and lay still.

Bertolli was already on his knees furiously trying to yank his hands free. He cursed with each pull and managed to tear away one palm. But before he could get any fingers free, Proverbs picked up a small rock, the first one at hand, and whacked him on the side of the head. The blow stunned Bertolli, and the rock stuck to his scalp. Proverbs picked up another rock and hit him again. It stuck too, and it slowed the FBI agent down enough to give Proverbs a chance to find a proper killing stone.

"Pray," Proverbs advised. "Pray fast."

The Bringer of Sorrow

BS1 1.0

GINGER SHOOK OFF her fatigue and sat up straight. She had no way of telling the time, but she'd been in the bathhouse for hours, and still the rangers had not returned. She prayed for their safety as she tossed more firewood into the barrel stove.

The short winter's day was spent, and the long subarctic twilight was turning the whole world outside the window gray. Lights came on in the big house. Maybe she should forget about the rangers and try to make it to the Bunyans' on her own. She was dressed for the cold, and eight miles was not that far. But she doubted she'd make it; she was still too wobbly on her feet.

There was the sound of a door shutting, and she looked out the window to see Deut coming across the yard with a covered tray and LED lantern. The dog Chrissy Lou came with her. They tramped across the porch and came in without knocking.

Chrissy Lou bounded to the window to greet Ginger, and Deut said, "I'm sorry you were locked out. My sister locked all the doors, and I didn't even know it until a few minutes ago."

She shut the door with her hip and set the lantern and tray on the sorting table. She'd brought Ginger a bowl of soup and a large moose roast sandwich. The meat oozed with ketchup and was topped with home-fried onion rings between two thick slices of white bread baked just that morning.

"I thought you might be hungry."

Ginger *was* hungry. Still . . . "Aren't you afraid of me?"

Deut gave a nervous laugh. "Actually, I am."

"Yet here you are."

"Yet here I am."

"Why?"

Deut glanced all over the room. "I guess because you used to be my friend."

"Used to be? I'm not your friend anymore?"

"I don't know. You changed."

"I didn't change, Deut. The situation changed. Do you know what the situation is?"

"The demons got you."

Ginger laughed bitterly. "No, Deut, the demons didn't get me. Let me tell you what the situation is. It involves your father and your twin. You won't want to hear it, but you have to because it's true."

ADAM HAD STAYED behind with the angel in the cistern chamber. "It's done," she told him after a while. "We're safe, for now." The angel seemed to gain renewed strength and sat up against a rock ledge.

"My brother killed them agents?"

"Verily."

Adam didn't know what to think about this. His little brother had taken the lives of three men in the span of an hour. Did he even know who Proverbs was anymore?

A short time later, his brother and father entered the chamber in silence, heads down, solemn. Martha struggled to boost herself to the rock ledge where she sat hunched over. She was faintly glowing again.

"No blame," she said. "It needed to be done."

"We know that!" Poppy snapped.

"It's begun, the Final Battle."

"We know that too!" To Adam, Poppy said, "Go help your brother move the bodies and clean up the mess. Take them and the ranger to the river and cut a hole in the ice. Get rid of everything they brought with them: their sno-gos, their guns, flashlights, phones. Burn what papers they have on 'em."

"Even their guns?" Proverbs said. "Can't we at least keep those? We could hide them in the woods."

"I agree," Adam said in brotherly solidarity. He favored the dead ranger's six-gun.

"Everything means everything. Get rid of every trace those men were ever here."

"Master Prophecy is correct," Martha said, "Scour every trace from these walls, but not yet. Deal with the dead tomorrow. A more urgent matter clamors for our attention at this hour."

"This seems pretty urgent to me," Poppy said. "What if more come looking for these ones?"

"More will come, but not today. And when they do come, the key must be in a place they cannot find. Let us secure the key before we deal with any other matter."

Poppy didn't have to ask what place she had in mind for it. "All right," he said. "We'll try it your way. Adam, go bring the key here. Proverbs, show him where it's at."

ADAM SWEPT HIS gaze back and forth, lighting the execution scene with his headlamp, trying to piece together how it had all gone down. The bodies of the two agents lay sprawled on their backs, released from the bondage of the stone. Their bloody heads were weirdly misshapen, and the torn finger pads and palms of their hands still lay on the stone. Proverbs collected the bits of flesh and tucked them into one of the agents' pockets.

"We'll never mop up all this mess," he said, meaning the blood and brains coating the rock pile.

"We can burn it off or something," Adam said.

They moved the agents aside and used an iron pry bar to lift the stone and retrieve the golden marble. It glowed of fairy light.

"How come you didn't just shoot them?" Adam said, dropping the marble into the coffee can. "Your ammo go bad too?"

"No, I don't think so."

"Then why?"

Proverbs removed his eyepatch, for the first time in weeks. He wound the leather cord around it and stuffed it into his pocket. His eye was bleary-looking, and he rubbed it and said, "Because I loaned them my headache and sent it straight to Hell."

HOSEA AND CORNY were in the cistern chamber when they returned. Corny wore a bandage on his head and seemed a little dopey.

Adam set the coffee can down on the shore in front of the angel. "Now what?"

Poppy said, "Now I drop it into the lake."

"But how will you ever get it up again?"

"I won't; the angels will, when they come."

"And what if they don't come?"

"Then all is lost and nothing matters," the angel interjected. "Have faith, Son of Abraham. "My cohort will surely come if we launch another flare, a more powerful beacon than the last."

"And how we gonna do that?"

Poppy said, "She wants you to go to Korea."

"Japan," the angel corrected. "And I have changed my mind as to the courier. Proverbs has proven his warrior's spirit today; he should be the one to deliver the flare."

"What?" Proverbs said. He looked oddly boyish without the patch.

The angel explained the mission of delivering the flare to the ruined Fukushima nuclear reactor, the danger involved, and the low probability of returning alive.

Adam said, "But my brother doesn't speak Japanese. Neither do I. He doesn't have a passport. None of us do. We don't have any Japanese money or even know where this reactor thing is or how to get there."

"Courage," Martha said. "I will make the way smooth."

Poppy said, "I need to pray over this first."

Proverbs said, "I'll go. If that's what it takes, then I want to go."

"Brave lad," Martha said. "Then it's settled."

"Nothing's settled!" Poppy said. "I *said* I need to pray on it first."

"Yes, pray on it," the angel all but purred. "Go, and take your fine sons for a break. Join the others in your household for Worship and dinner. The day has been overfilled with terrors; relax a little. Take as much time you need, Master Prophecy, to pray on it.

"But before you do, please finish securing the key."

The can with the marble sat on the shore. All the angel needed to do was lift one foot and knock it over, and gravity would do the rest. And yet she expected him to do it for her. At least that was what he thought until he came over to do just that and she stopped him.

"Think, Master Prophecy," she said. "You need to remove the flap, as you did the first one, *before* sinking the key."

Well, that made sense, though Poppy didn't appreciate be lectured to by anyone, even an angel. He removed the heavy marble from the can. The flap was more like a skin tag now than the mouse ear the earlier one had been.

"Remember to let go of it," Martha said.

Poppy pulled the flap from the marble and dropped it on the ground. It skittered about as it coalesced.

The thing that Poppy didn't understand: If the Final Battle had truly begun here in the keep, or even if this was only a minor opening skirmish, wouldn't the bleachers of Heaven be straining as all the saints and angels leaned forward to watch them? Shouldn't he be able to wave his arms to get Heaven's attention? What need did Martha have of a flare?

Without the skin tag, the key was now a perfect, mirror-surfaced sphere.

It was heavier than a cannonball and impossible for Poppy to shot put far into the lake. So he simply stood at the edge of the shore and dropped it in. The marble did not flutter as it sank but plummeted straight down into the depths.

"Thank you," Martha said. "It was the correct thing to do."

When the flap, now a golden pea, had cooled, Proverbs came over to pick it up.

"Leave it," Poppy said.

"I can keep ahold of it while you pray, lord."

"I said leave it."

If the flare was so essential to the success of the angel's mission, maybe Proverbs wasn't its best courier, in spite of his warrior's spirit. Just the other day the boy's head hurt so bad he couldn't see straight. Now he crushes men's skulls.

Who then? Who should he send on a one-way trip to Japan? It was one more thing to pray over.

"We'll be taking that break now," Poppy said, turning toward the tunnel. His boys followed in his wake. Their lights lurched down the tunnel and faded from sight.

Do pray, Master Prophecy, but pray fast.

BS3 1.0

THE FIVE PROPHECY men paused at the gate to regard the dead ranger lying in a pool of his own blood.

"He would'a killed me," Proverbs said.

"I don't doubt it," Poppy replied. "He was a violent man."

They left the keep, and Poppy padlocked the sally door from the outside. Hosea and Proverbs escorted Corny down the slide. As soon as they reached the bottom, Adam started talking.

"I couldn't say this in the keep, lord, because she's always watching. She might be watching now, but I gotta say it."

"Enough with the windup!" Poppy snapped. "If you got something to say, Adam, just *say it.*"

"Yes, lord, sorry, but Martha has been pilfering our supplies."

"What? What supplies?"

"I don't know. Maybe all of them."

"You don't know?"

"I know how she made their guns 'impotent.'"

When they got to the yard, Poppy sent Corny into the house to go lie down and took the others to the prayer cabin with him. Adam dropped a handful of .44 Magnum rounds on Poppy's desk.

"These are from Ranger Danger's handgun," he said. He used pliers to remove the lead slug from one of them and tipped the brass case upside down. No gunpowder fell out. "A dud. They're all duds."

Poppy examined the empty brass. "How did she get the powder out?"

"How did she melt trees?"

Poppy returned the case to Adam. "So what? She disarmed the feds, not us. Proverbs' gun fired, didn't it?"

"Yes, lord, except it came from the house, not the keep. I'd bet the ammo that's been sitting in our armory is bad."

"That's insane. Why would she do that?"

Hosea said, "I don't know why she would, lord, but she already done it to our propane canisters."

"What are you talking about?"

Adam said, "I tried telling you about it last week, lord."

Adam related Proverbs' discovery that half of their newly purchased propane stock had inexplicably leaked away. And not only their propane but their firewood too. About six cords of what Hosea had stacked was missing.

"And remember how it took a whole forest to fuel her flare?" Hosea said. "She can burn wood, but maybe she prefers stronger stuff. Maybe that's why she wants to send Proverbs to go get himself killed by radiation."

"If that's true," Poppy said, "I can't help but wonder if all of Father God's angels are as incompetent as this one."

"Maybe they're not," Proverbs said. "Maybe she's no angel in the first place."

"Don't talk stupid. She may not be in the first rank of angels, I'll grant you that, and she's clearly unqualified to hold the key to the bottomless pit, but she's still an angel and a warrior of the Father. She thinks like a warrior; it's all about her mission. If she took stuff from us, it was in the name of her mission. That's how soldiers think."

"That's not what I meant, lord," Proverbs said. "I meant she can't be an angel because there are no girl angels in the Bible."

"Of course there are. Are you a Bible expert now? What kind of bullshit is this? There's lots of them." But as soon as the words left his mouth, they sounded false.

"Name one, lord."

"Well, there's . . ." Though there were many mentions of angels in Scripture, only two of them were actually named — Michael and Gabriel — and three more fallen angels: Satan, Abaddon, and Beelzebul. Nevertheless, unnamed angels abounded in both Testaments and were referred to by their pronouns. Poppy pulled his Bible from the holster and began to flip through to notable angel passages to look for an angelic *she* or *her*.

"You just need one, lord," Proverbs said, repeating his father's own logic with Ginger.

"I know that!" Poppy said, slapping the book shut. "This might take some study. Why don't we go inside and eat. Then you can take care of the bodies while I pray on this and everything else."

The boys got up and put on their parkas.

"What's that?" Adam said. The dog was in the yard, barking his head off.

Hosea went to the window to look out.

"Holy crap."

BS4 1.0

GINGER HAD GIVEN Deut a lot to think about. None of it was true; it couldn't be. But if it was, it would explain a lot of things about her sister. Deut had wondered, for example, why Sarai's corrections always took place in the prayer cabin and not at Worship Time like everybody else's. Or why she seemed to change so much after Mama went away on vacation. They all missed Mama, but only Sarai seemed to turn away from the family, and from her, her own twin.

Still, the devil was a master in concocting believable lies, and that was all it was, a believable lie. Anything else was unthinkable. Still, Deut wanted to go inside and confront her sister about it that very moment, except that she couldn't imagine how to ask her if their father had — what? — what was it he was supposed to have done? She could never utter the words Ginger had used to describe it. Language.

So rather than go to the house, she stayed out in the bathhouse with Ginger and finished the laundry. She pulled the washing machine inside to thaw the clothes that were frozen in its tub. While they thawed, she hung, sorted, and folded the earlier loads. After a while, Ginger came over to help, and they worked in companionable silence on opposite sides of the table.

Crissy Lou had curled up near the barrel stove and gone to sleep. Every little while Ginger went to the window to check the yard. Deut fed the stove. At one point, Crissy Lou picked up her head to listen to something, and both Ginger and Deut went to the window. It was Poppy and the boys finally returning from the keep. But where were the rangers?

Poppy sent Corny to the house while he and the rest went to the prayer cabin and stomped their boots on the porch before they went inside. The prayer cabin window lit up.

The nearly full moon bathed the yard in cold, grey light. But where were the rangers? Where were they?

CRISSY LOU LEAPED to her feet and commenced to barking most furiously. She ran around the bathhouse whining to be let out. She bolted through the door the moment Deut cracked it open.

"They're back. They're back," Ginger sang, dashing from the window to the clothes pegs where she had hung her outerwear. Deut went to the window to look. Three men shuffled through the snow to the two sno-gos that were still parked in the yard.

"I'm sorry, but I have to go now," Ginger said, pulling up her snow pants and slipping into her parka. "I can't stay, but I promise I won't say anything about your brother. I'll find a place where everyone can live together, if it comes to that." She continued talking, apologizing, and promising as she pulled on her gloves and hat and headed for the door.

"Wait!" Deut said. "Look!"

"What? I can't. They'll leave without me."

"No, they won't. Something's wrong. Come here and look."

"I can't."

Crissy Lou started barking insanely outside the window, and Ginger came over to look. The three men stood in the moonlight on either side of the sno-gos with their arms dangling at their sides. The dog was barking at them from inches away, but they didn't even seem to notice her.

"What are they doing?"

"Nothing, so far as I can tell."

"I have to go. They'll take me to town."

"No, look at them first. Two of them are in their shirtsleeves. Look. They should be freezing themselves dressed like that."

It was true. As they watched, one of the men, Ranger Danger, sat astride one of the sno-gos, but he sat facing the rear of the machine. The other two piled on the same machine, also backward.

"This is not good," Ginger said.

There were shouts and the slam of a door, and Poppy and the boys spilled out of the prayer cabin into the yard. They shined lights on the men, who dismounted the machine and fled. They men didn't run but toddled, like babies, toward the Stubborn Mountain Trail, falling and picking themselves up again, with the dog snapping at their heels.

BS5 1.0

THE SALLY DOOR was still padlocked from the outside, the way Poppy and the boys had left it. But the larger portal, the gate itself, was open. It had been opened from the inside.

Adam, Proverbs, Cora, and Sarai accompanied their father. Hosea, Deut, and Sue were left behind to guard Ginger and watch over Corny and the household.

After removing their outerwear and donning hardhats, the holy posse proceeded to the main tunnel, but Adam told everyone to stop.

"This is where Ranger Danger beaned Corny," he said, pointing to blood stains on the floor. "But where's the ranger's blood? There used to be a pool of it right over here. Now it's gone along with his body. Did he collect his blood before he left?"

They walked up the tunnel in silence. Proverbs split off from the group at the machine room. On the second level, Adam and Cora went to the storeroom chamber while Poppy and Sarai continued to the cistern on the third level. The angel wasn't there, so they waited for the others.

Proverbs came first. "Two of our barrels of motor oil and all of our gasoline barrels are empty," he reported. "One of the acetylene tanks is empty too."

When Adam and Cora arrived, Adam reported, "About a third of the ammo I checked is no good, and the rest is iffy. Much of our high-energy food is gone — whole cases of cooking oil, bacon, nuts, corn syrup. The cans and jars are unopened but empty. Same with the sacks of beans, rice, and sugar. We didn't have time to check everything, but almost all the rolls of visquene, vinyl flooring, tarpaper, paint, varnish, and adhesives are missing too."

Poppy led the group up the tunnel to the rock pile. There they found the angel. Her inner light was completely extinguished. Her last remaining wing had been hacked off and was lying nearby. Her once-powerful arms were slashed to the bone. Her porcelain skin was scorched and blistered. She lay absolutely still.

"Is she dead?" Sarai asked, horrified. To her, Martha was still an angel.

Martha stirred and turned her head toward them. "The Father's grace be upon you," she said. "Greetings, special daughter. Do not be troubled by my appearance. I am not dead. Angels are not alive in an earthly sense, so we can't die. The damaged body you see before you is but an outward manifestation of the injury to my celestial being."

"Which means your celestial being is hurt!"

"Enough!" Poppy said. "What happened here, angel? Where are the dead men?" He tipped his headlamp to illuminate the boulder and large stone where the agents had fallen but were no longer lying. Gone too was their gore from the rocks. "I would'a never left them with you if I thought you'd turn around and resurrect them."

"The men were not resurrected."

"They were! I *saw* them."

"You saw puppets dangling from the devil's strings."

"Explain."

"The tone of your voice is offensive, Master Prophecy, but I will answer your question because you have a right to know. Shortly after you and your sons departed, I felt the presence of a powerful spirit, and I came here to investigate. I was ambushed by Camael, the Bringer of Destruction, an old foe of mine. He had been riding one of Obama's men but had kept his presence hidden from me until that moment. When your son dispatched the agents, Camael was forced to reanimate them because of their usefulness to him in the fallen world. They, especially the man called Nabor, are well placed in the ranks of the Antichrist, and it would have taken too long for Lucifer to groom their replacements."

Poppy scratched his chin. He had to admit it sounded plausible. "And the key? Did they take the key with them?"

"Nay, I am pleased to say. Nay, thank the Father, they did not. Much of the credit for that goes to you, Master Prophecy, for hiding it where you did. I cannot begin to think of the damage to the Father's plan its loss would have caused.

"Yet now that Camael has found me, he will be back with legions of devils and men. Your son's journey to Japan is more critical than ever. If he is ready to depart, I will give him instructions. I have made all his travel arrangements."

Poppy said, "That brings up another matter. I can understand why you would need to consume a forest to fuel your flare, but why steal from me?"

The angel raised herself on her elbow. "Steal is a strong word, Master Prophecy. Think twice before accusing an angel of stealing. Angels do not steal, lie, or fall victim to any of the other vices of men, but one. Pride is our weakness. Pride banished Lucifer from Heaven, not larceny."

Poppy continued, "Then what do *you* call taking the very fuel and food we rely on for our survival?"

"I think the word you're seeking is 'borrow.' Fear not, when this battle is concluded, the angels will replenish your stores seven times over. You shall not want for anything. That is a promise. And if we don't win, no one will survive long enough to care."

Despite everything, Poppy wanted to believe her.

"Is there some reason why you didn't tell me about all of this *borrowing* sooner?"

"Verily, I didn't think it was necessary. But now I see that men and angels have grown apart for too long, and men have forgotten how to trust in the nature of angels."

"Is that so? Then why don't you refresh this man's memory. What is the nature of angels I should trust in?"

"Gladly. As you know, angels are creatures made of pure spirit, whereas men are spirits clothed in matter. Your spirits are bedazzled by all of the wonders of the physical world that surrounds you, and so you cannot easily see spirits with your earthly eyes. Therefore, when we angels manifest ourselves to you, as I am now doing, we must, perforce, borrow a little matter from your world to become visible. I have been forced to borrow even more matter to counteract the evil that has befallen me and to stand guard over the key. Believe me when I say I have used the bare minimum of your stores.

"And believe when I say that all will be restored in due time — with interest."

Poppy spat on the ground.

Martha said, "That appears to be a gesture of disrespect, Master Prophecy. Do you mind explaining why you behave in this manner?"

"You're good, Martha. I'll give you that. You had me fooled. So tell me: how come there are no female angels named in the Bible? How is it that you're the only girl angel in Heaven?"

"But I'm not. That is, I am neither a female angel nor a male angel. Again, allow me to remind you, angels are pure spirit with no need for gender. Only when we manifest to *you humans*, who are consumed with sex, are we compelled to choose one or the other. In biblical times, men had authority, and women did not. Is it, therefore, any wonder why we chose to appear solely as males in those days? Today's society is more diverse, and we are competing for your children's attention with princesses and robots. Therefore, in the modern era, we angels are just as inclined to appear as female angels as male ones. But in truth, it is all, as they say, window dressing. For I am neither male nor female nor anything in between."

"Also in biblical times," Poppy added, "before the Flood, angels slept with human women and begat the race of giants. That requires something more than flim-flam 'manifesting,' you can be sure. It requires male seed, and you can't make jism out of acetylene gas and gunpowder. Or can you?"

Gathering new strength, Martha rose to her feet and towered over the humans. "Just what are you implying, Master Prophecy?" The angel didn't seem so ragged as she had a moment before. Her wounds had vanished, and fire blazed in her eyes.

If she meant to intimidate Poppy, she failed (though his offspring clung to each other behind his back). Poppy took a step forward and said, "Go ahead and insult my intelligence again."

"Know this," Martha said. "I'm getting a little tired of your doubting nature. Your parents should have named you Thomas instead of Marvin. I understand that the task ahead is frightening and that you may be reluctant to undertake it, but that's no excuse to heap insult upon this servant of God."

"Bullshit!" Poppy said. "Go ahead and pretend I'm insulting you. Listen to me, angel. I'm not *insulting* you; I'm *rebuking* you."

"Careful, mortal. Think about what you're saying, for your life and your family's life depend on it. I am no devil, but if I were, would you really want to be pissing me off? I don't think so. It makes me wonder if you truly read the Book of Job."

"I read it every year."

"Then you know that devils are a touchy lot and you don't want to be on their bad side. God has granted Satan and his cohort the special privilege of testing men's faith. This is a concession that Satan has won in battles past. If I were a devil, which I'm not, I would have God's own blessing to torment you in this life until I broke you into pieces. Think about it. Is that the fate you desire?"

But Poppy took another step forward and bellowed, "Begone, devil. I rebuke thee in Christ Jesus name!"

"Silence!" the angel roared back at him. "Or suffer the consequences." She pointed at Poppy's children behind him. "The Prince of Darkness will claim the lives of all your children. You will cry out to God for relief, just as Job did, but He will not hear you. That is, if I were a devil, which I am not."

"Eat shit, Satan, and begone." Poppy gestured for his reluctant sons and daughters to join in: "We rebuke thee in Christ Jesus name."

"We rebuke thee in Christ Jesus name."

"Cease this. I'm warning you."

In a tremulous chorus, the prayer warriors exhorted Martha to depart. Again and again they rebuked her in the Savior's name, and with each repetition their courage rebounded and her heavenly facade splintered and fell away. Her skin became the scaly skin of a serpent. The sandals on her feet became cloven hooves, and her legs the haunches of an ass. Horns protruded from her forehead, and her handsome face grew hideous with hooked nose, iron nails for teeth, and beady little pig eyes full of hate, hate, hate. And, because all angels, fallen or otherwise, were male, from between her legs sprouted a cock as long as a man is tall and capped with a shiny crimson head.

"We rebuke thee in Christ Jesus name."

And still the devil withstood the authority of their faith, though it plainly caused him misery. With each repetition, the Prophecy siblings became more strident in their courage.

"Begone, devil, in Christ Jesus name."

Finally, the devil lifted a leg and, with a sharp cry that echoed up and down the length of the tunnel, stomped his hoof on the floor, striking sparks and opening a fissure. A curtain of flames sprang up from the depths of Hell, along with the ceaseless screams and howls of the damned. The stench of sulfur and of searing flesh befouled the air of the tunnel.

"Begone, devil, in Christ Jesus name."

"Marvin Johnson," the devil declared, "you will curse this day, for you have sorely displeased me. Therefore, I shall prepare a trial of faith for you to test your devotion to the Creator. We shall see how true you remain while standing on the bloated bodies of your family, with your house on fire, and your wealth trampled into the mud. We shall listen for your hosannahs when your health and dignity are broken and your reputation is stripped from you. You imagine you are stalwart, but you are weak. You imagine you are righteous, but you are a hypocrite. Let us see how faithful you remain when God is deaf to your prayers."

The devil turned to the siblings. "And you, Adam the Firstborn, you will not live to enjoy your birthright, and your betrothed will betray you with another man. You, Cora, will die without ever loving a man or having a room of your own. You, Proverbs, well, you are my pet, aren't you? I have a special place for you right here at my side."

"Begone, devil, in Christ Jesus name."

The devil made to leap into the fissure of flames but held back for one final curse. "I almost forgot about you, Sarai, because you are so forgettable. Special daughter? Don't make me laugh. Oh, you're special all right. A special strumpet for the incestuous pleasuring of your unholy lord.

"So says, I, Beezus, brother of Lucifer and the Bringer of Sorrow."

And with that, the devil leaped into the crack of Hell. The entire mountain groaned as the fissure closed over him and the flames and cries of agony were cut off.

The Prophecys reeled from the encounter. After a long moment, Poppy reached out his hand, and Cora gave him the bottle of olive oil from the kitchen. Poppy spilled some of it on his fingers and sprinkled it on the floor where the fissure had been.

"And stay out," he said, "in Christ Jesus name. Amen."

BS6 1.0

THEY RETURNED TO the cistern chamber in silence. Poppy stopped there and said, "Go on home, all of you. You did good. Hide the agents' sno-gos for now and tomorrow dump them in the river. Now go."

But none of them went.

"What's this?" Poppy said. "Do as I say."

Adam said, "Lord, we killed those agents on the *devil's* say-so."

"We were tricked."

"Is that what we're gonna say to the next ones who come looking for the last ones? Sorry, we were tricked?"

"We don't have to say nothing, not if we get rid of their stuff like I told you. The devil, Beezus, already took care of the hardest part for us; every scrap of their bodies is gone. You said so yourself.

"Listen, all of you, get it through your skulls: these aren't normal times. The war has begun. Terrible things happen in wars. Those men were our enemy no matter who told us to kill them. They were scouts in the Antichrist's army. They were the devil's own soldiers. That's why he took them away, to use them again. Don't go feeling sorry or guilty about them. They're his men.

"What's important is to finish cleaning up. Make it like they were never here. And if you can't do that now, you can wait until tomorrow to get started. A few hours probably won't matter."

Adam turned his father's words over in his mind. "All right," he said. "I'll get Hosea to help me. We'll do it tonight." He left down tunnel, and Cora went with him.

Then it was Sarai's turn. The tear tracks on her cheeks glistened in Poppy's headlamp.

"Well?" he said.

"I need to know, lord, if what the angel said was true."

"That was no angel! Didn't you notice that, you idiot girl? That was the devil! He has a name — Beezus!"

"Yes, lord, sorry. Is what Beezus said true?"

"Beezus said a lot of things."

"What he said about me."

"What about you?"

"That I'm . . . That you . . ."

Poppy waited with mounting fury for the girl to ask her question, daring her to ask it.

"Forget it," she said at last and turned to go.

Proverbs, who had been waiting with his own question, looked away in shame. Now that he knew.

When Sarai was gone, Poppy turned to him. "What about you? What's your problem?"

"I don't have a problem," Proverbs said. "But what about Ginger?"

"What about her?"

"She don't need to be locked up anymore."

"Are you asking me or telling me?"

The boy took the question seriously. "I was gonna ask you, but now I guess I'm telling you."

Poppy struggled to control his temper. "How do you figure?"

"Because she's not infested with demons. Probably never was. Her accuser was the devil."

"That logic is ass-backwards, son. Who better to see lurking demons than a devil? That girl's infested. I have no doubt about it, and I won't allow her near the children."

Proverbs nodded and rubbed his eye. "Then we cast the demons out."

"Maybe."

"Not maybe; right now. Didn't we just cast out the devil himself?"

Poppy didn't enjoy being ordered about by this boy. He had already come to the conclusion that, demons or no demons, that girl wasn't daughter-in-law material. But then he flashed on the image of this same boy standing on the rock pile not two hours ago, hoisting a large stone over his head.

"Tomorrow, first thing," Poppy conceded.

"Good," Proverbs said. "Thank you, lord."

BS7 1.0

THE GOLDEN PEA still lay on the shore of the underground lake where Poppy had left it. No longer was there an angel or devil guarding it while secretly stealing their supplies. Poppy sat on the rock ledge and turned off his headlamp to let his eyes adjust to the darkness. He prayed to the Holy Spirit for some insight into the bizarre events of the day. He thanked the Father for the strength to banish the devil from the keep, and he beseeched Him not to grant Beezus the power of Job's curse. After all, the coming time of Trouble would be test enough of any man's faith, wouldn't it?

Finally, Poppy peered into the darkness at his feet, looking for the golden pea. But unlike the marble from which it sprang, the tiny orb didn't seem to possess any inner light of its own.

Which led to the question: just what was the golden marble that now lay at the bottom of his lake? Maybe the devil had told the truth and it was the key to the bottomless pit. Maybe it was a key to something else, or not a key at all. Clearly, it was of heavenly origin: the devil himself was unable to touch it. Whatever it was, it seemed to be extremely valuable, so valuable that even Satan coveted it and needed to summon help from Hell to steal it from the keep.

But why didn't Beezus use Obama's men to recover it for him? Weren't they on the same side? Why did he conspire instead to kill them? Was it possible that the golden marble could give the Antichrist power over Satan?

Did that mean by extension that Poppy now had power over Satan?

Poppy switched on his headlamp and knelt at the shore. He scooped up a handful of water. It was intensely cold. He brought it to his nose. There was no foul odor: wormwood, brimstone, pestilence or pesticide. He brought it to his lips. It tasted fresh and sweet. Whatever the marble was, it was not poison. It would not harm his family. *Though being in possession of it might.*

> *Heavenly Father, You know that we have this little ball bearing here, right, Lord? You dropped it in our backyard so we could safeguard it for You. And we will. Only tell us how. Amen.*

There, message sent, and no need for a flare.

Poppy rose from his creaky knees and straightened his back. He regarded the golden pea lying at his feet. He couldn't just leave it there, could he? Especially if it truly was a beacon tuned to demon frequencies.

But where to hide it? Somewhere within the keep for sure.

In the end, Poppy could think of no better vault to safeguard it than the watery one where lay the marble. So he picked up the heavy smidgen and dropped it into the lake.

Down it went straight.

Watching the unearthly thing disappear, Poppy heard the familiar voice of the Holy Spirit. It had been a long while since that particular godhead had offered Poppy any insight, and he had sorely missed it. Now the Holy Spirit said, *Time to wrap things up.*

BS8 1.0

PROVERBS APPEARED AT the bathhouse door bearing a mattress. Deut let him in. Behind him Solly lugged another mattress, and Ithy and Uzzie brought extra lanterns, bedding, and food. The younger boys set down their burdens and left as fast as they could.

"You need to shadow Ginger out here tonight," Proverbs told Deut. "Unless Ginger wants to spend one last night in the powder room." Ginger watched him from the opposite end of the room but said nothing.

"What happened to them feds?" Deut said. "What happened in the keep?"

There was something weird about her brother, besides the fact that he wasn't wearing his eyepatch. He seemed at peace with himself, even light-hearted for a change.

"Let's just say a glorious victory was won today in Father God's name and leave it at that for now."

"What's that supposed to mean?"

"It means our God is a mighty God."

"It means," Ginger said, crossing the room, "that I was right all along, wasn't I? She wasn't an angel, was she?"

"Hello Rath," Proverbs said, calling her the name Martha had used in the tunnel. "Hello, Zorn and Tork and the rest of the gang." He smiled charmingly as he spoke. "Don't get too comfortable there inside my sweetie because you're not staying."

"What's that supposed to mean?" both girls said. But Proverbs only wished them a pleasant night and left the bathhouse. As soon as his footfalls faded, Ginger went to the clothes pegs and began putting on her outerwear and boots again.

"You're not going?" Deut said.

"I feel stronger now. I'm sure I can make it to the Bunyans." She glanced at Deut. "Promise me you won't tell till morning?"

"You can't go."

"I can't stay."

"But the feds we saw. They weren't moving all that fast. You'll run into them on the trail for sure."

It was true, and it gave Ginger chills, but she picked up one of the LED lanterns and said, "Can I borrow this?"

Deut began to cry.

"Don't cry, Deut. I can make it. I can outrun those guys. And I'm sure Crissy Lou will be there to protect me." Ginger approached Deut. "Can I hug you? I promise I don't have demons."

Deut opened her arms, and they hugged for a while. Then Ginger went to the door. But they heard footsteps again, and something heavy clattered on the porch.

"I brought you more firewood," Proverbs said through the door.

Deut said, "Thank you, brother. Good-night."

"You're welcome, sister. If you need anything else, just holler."

Deut and Ginger looked at each other, and Deut said, "And then what?"

"And then I'll fetch it for you."

Ginger opened the door. Her tireless suitor was bathed in moonlight. "You're planning to stand out there all night?"

"Yes'm."

"To keep me prisoner?"

"No, to protect you."

"I don't want your protection."

"Yes, you do, only you don't know it. You'll know tomorrow."

"Why? What happens tomorrow?"

"You'll have your own mind back."

"What are you talking about?"

"First thing in the morning," Proverbs explained, "we're gonna drive out all the evil spirits that's got into you. Then you'll see everything with new eyes, and you'll be able to decide your fate with *your own free will*. Then if you want to go home and take your chances with the Antichrist, that's up to you. If you want to stay here safe in the keep as my betrothed, tomorrow you'll be free to choose. In the meantime, you're under my personal protection. I am at your service."

Social Media

SM1 1.0

MEANWHILE, ACROSS THE state in Wallis, Bradd Tetlin was in the kitchen grating cheese for a platter of nachos. The governor sat beside him on a barstool drafting a Facebook post on her laptop. She read the latest draft under her breath and said, "Done."

"Want me to read it?" Bradd said.

"Would'ja?" She turned the laptop toward him.

> *OBAMA IS A SPECIAL KIND OF STUPID*
>
> *We've had about enough of you, Mr. President. Pulling sick stunts like this frees us of any obligation to show you respect. You say you went to Newtown to comfort grieving parents after the horrible crime against innocents there? But what you really did was use their bleeding bodies as a platform to spew your asinine, ideological-driven garbage about Americans who value their 2nd Amendment rights. Shame on you. You disrespect your office.*
>
> *And if that isn't bad enough, after every one of these terrible shootings,*

316   David Marusek

you try to put the blame on law-abiding American gun owners, millions of us, who are not terrorists. When nothing you and the Dems propose would have prevented this or any of the earlier massacres.

Yes, it's a special kind of stupid to blame the victims, Mr. President, but then you probably already know that. God help America if we have to stomach another four years of you.
—*Vera Tetlin*

"Well?" Vera said.

"It reads fine to me," Bradd said. "It's strong."

"I was going for strong. Are you saying it's too strong?"

"No, I'm not. When you're looking down the wrong end of the barrel for four more years, then, no, it's not too strong. The opposite, maybe — a little too constrained."

"Thank you." Vera kissed his cheek. She reached over and clicked the button to send the post to her thirteen million friends.

When the nachos were done, Bradd removed the platter from the oven and brought it and a couple of Buds to the living room where Vera was watching *The Good Wife*.

She said, "Any word back from Beaver Swayne?"

"Not yet."

"It's been almost a week already. Before you get too comfortable, Bradd, give him a call, will ya? See where he's at on the telecom thing."

"All right."

"And tell him to come see us again. There's more we need to discuss."

"Such as?"

"It's like you said; we're staring down the barrel of a gun. More and more, we Alaskans are sitting ducks up here. Maybe we need to discuss contingencies."

SM2 1.0

THAT SAME EVENING, Jace's phone and internet service returned for a few hours. He had just enjoyed a hearty meal of Dinty Moore stew and French-style green beans from cans and was debating how to wind down the day. The return of the internet was a perfect occasion to spark up a bedtime blunt from his dwindling stash and spend a pleasant evening catching up on family, friends, and the news of the day.

There was plenty of news for him to catch up on at the end of December, 2012. The Maya Apocalypse, as he already knew, was a no-show, but no one had really taken it seriously anyway, except for a bunch of wackos in the French village of Bugarach. Another no-show was the all-important Christmas shopping season, according to early sales numbers. In other news: the Muslim Brotherhood had rammed a partisan constitution down Egypt's throat, setting the stage for years of civil strife; the last of the slaughtered Newtown first-graders and teachers were laid to rest; the VP of the National Rifle Association proposed installing armed guards in every school in America; psychiatrists affirmed that people with Asperger's Syndrome were not prone to becoming mass murderers; Nelson Mandela and the first George Bush were both hospitalized for old age; Russia passed a law prohibiting the adoption of Russian children by Americans; Secretary of State Hillary Clinton fainted, hit her head, and got a nasty blood clot on her brain; the U.S. economy fell off the fiscal cliff — again; President Obama gave away the store — again; Congress kicked the can down the road — again; and Alaska governor Vera Tetlin posted another Facebook rant calling Obama a "special kind of stupid."

In other words: same old same old.

Among the nearly five hundred email messages waiting in Jace's mailbox was a notification of a friend request on Facebook from someone named Crissy Lou. Who was Crissy Lou? The name rang a bell, but he couldn't place it. The tiny profile photo didn't help. It depicted a mountain scene, not a person's face.

Then it struck him — he knew that mountain. It was the iconic Stubborn Mountain.

So Jace clicked through to the Crissy Lou profile, where he found precious little additional information. No About or Likes. A timeline that began that very day. The few photos showed only unpeopled winter landscapes from around the Stubborn Mountain Mine site and Prophecy compound. Crissy Lou wanted to be friends. He didn't know the names of all the young people in the family, but he couldn't see how Crissy Lou was of biblical origin the way the other names seemed to be.

Something was fishy. Even if the old patriarch permitted his children to browse the internet, which Jace doubted, they didn't have service out there, let alone computers. Did they?

Was this a trick? Was someone pranking him? But prank or not, there was no scenario in which Jace could ignore this friend request. So he swallowed his doubts and tapped *Accept*.

Before Jace could surf away from the profile, the little chat window popped up:

u there ranger?

Crissy Lou was online and logged in and wanted to chat with him. Jace began to freak. Could this possibly be her? With equal measures of excitement and doubt, he typed, "Hi."

hi yerself ranger. are u saved?

Whoa, talk about getting right down to business. This could be the shortest chat ever. "Maybe. Who's Crissy Lou?"

dog barked at you near rabbit hutch wehn surveyers were here.

Well, as far as he knew, Deut was the only person who had witnessed that encounter. "Okay. And who are you?"

who u think?

"Deuteronomy?"

woof!

"Prove it."

how?

"How do I know this isn't one of your crazy brothers?"

arf arf my crazy bros would sooner shoot u than chat with u : O)

That was true, and they probably wouldn't use emoticons. "So how come you have internet out there? The mountain must block it?"

same way 2-way radio back when mine operation long copper cable antena through tunnel and out vent hole on town side. reception fine but only near antena

"You got a cell?"

no only poppy

"But you have a computer?"

no its my bros

"And they let you use it?"

no : O)

"How do I know you're not one of your sisters?"

because they think your the devil. are you the devil?

"I can honestly say I'm not the devil."

prove it

"Is that an order?"

yes

Back to the matter of faith and his total lack thereof. Could they get beyond it? "Sorry, I can't prove I'm not a devil because you can't prove a negative."

?????

"I'd love to discuss my faith with you sometime in person."

ME TOO!!!

Reading this, Jace let out a whoop and jumped off the couch. This wasn't happening. This was unreal. "Can you come into town? I live on Lucky Strike Lane."

are u crazy ranger?

"Then where? When?"
    : O)

[Crissy Lou has logged off chat.]

Jace stared at the screen. She'd logged off before arranging a time or place to meet. Had he scared her away with his enthusiasm? Was she toying with him? Or maybe someone had interrupted her? It didn't matter. What mattered was that she obviously liked him! This was the start of something big!

Caw Caw

CC1 1.0

[Following is a storyboard script for an animated epilog.]

Panel 1: The silhouette of a young man in the window of a small dilapidated house at night during winter.

Panel 2: Our POV rises to take in the roof of the house and neighboring houses on an empty, snow-covered street.

Panel 3: POV rises high enough to encompass all of McHardy, its surrounding countryside, and the peak of Stubborn Mountain.

Panels 4-5: We continue to zoom out, see the outline of Alaska and the Pacific Arctic.

Panel 6: We see the whole Earth, moon, and sun.

Panel 7: We see the entire Solar system.

Panel 8: An alien planet suddenly pops into existence on the far side of Neptune.

—End of Book 1—

Sidebar: Ghost Town with Footbridge
GT1 1.0

MCHARDY AND ITS sister town of Caldecott had both sprung up overnight in 1910. Located five miles (8 km) apart, they were cultural symbiotes. That is, Caldecott was the copper syndicate's company town: prim, sober, and virtuous by decree. McHardy, on the other hand, was whorish, boozy, and predatory. They were born together, and they perished together on the same day in 1938, when monied interests in far-off New York and Chicago, having exhausted the copper deposits, ordered the mines to close. Trains that over the course of a quarter century had transported six hundred tons of copper (544 metric tonnes) and nine million ounces of silver (255 metric tonnes) suddenly stopped running. The last train to depart transported only people and what they could carry in their arms. Residents were forced to abandon their clothes, furniture, machinery, cutlery, tools, toys, books, gramophone recordings, hand-crank telephones, automobiles, and everything else they possessed.

A handful of oddballs missed the last train out. They rather preferred living where they were and saw no need to leave just because society did. For the next thirty years, they and a few newcomers had the entire region to themselves. They scratched out meager lives in total oblivion, which was how they liked it. Some of them worked small placer gold claims on outlying creeks or, like Dupré, trapped fur-bearing animals. Most of them were fugitives from something or other, at least in their own minds.

The Caldecott River served as the town's moat against the world. Back in 1942, the Alaska territorial government commissioned a project to salvage the iron rails of the abandoned railway to help in the war effort. Salvagers started at the mill in Caldecott and worked backward one hundred twenty miles (193 km) to the deepwater docks of Cordova, lifting rails as they went. The operation left behind a bare wooden trestle over the Caldecott River as the only overland means of reaching McHardy and Caldecott.

The few stragglers haunting the towns at the time disapproved of the trestle. They could have paved its surface with boards, making an automobile bridge out of it, but they were afraid that a bridge might be an open invitation to curious motorists on the territory's primitive road system. So they cut up the trestle and hauled it away for building material and firewood, further isolating themselves.

For their own access, McHardy residents scrounged wire cable, pulleys, and scrap iron from the mine and constructed a hand-operated tramway system. If you wanted to get into town, you had to pull the two-passenger tram car across the river by hand, risking crushed fingers and steel splinters and the possibility of not being able to muscle the tram out of the sag in the middle. McHardyites kept their own highway vehicles on a rocky parking lot on the Chitina side of the river and used them only once or twice a year on supply runs to Anchorage. Everything they brought to McHardy had to fit in the tram car. Otherwise, they left it with the vehicles until winter when they could drive the last mile into town over the frozen river. (The town's civic motto: "You can't get here from there.")

McHardy suffered a revival of sorts in the 1970s when it was rediscovered by a new generation of social misfits who were drawn north by the construction of the Trans-Alaska Pipeline. They bought up town lots and launched the decades-long task of restoring the town. This was when Orion Beehymer, flush with pipeline wages, began his climb to the status of local land baron. And one of his first purchases was the rocky lot next to the river where everyone parked their vehicles.

In the 1970s, the state Department of Transportation was lousy with oil money, and it turned its attention to the McHardy Road, the fifty-nine-mile (95 km) single-lane pioneer road built on top of the old gravel railbed. DOT proposed tearing down the treacherous McHardy tramway and replacing it with a steel bridge. McHardy residents, old timers and recent arrivals alike, took up their pitchforks to shout down the plan.

Then, one morning in December, 1980, McHardyites woke up to discover that they were living smack dab in the middle of the newest and largest National Park and Preserve in the United States. They became prisoners of the very bureaucracy they had worked so hard to escape.

The first thing the National Park Service wanted to do in its new domain was to buy up the mill town of Caldecott, restore it, and turn it into a National Historical Landmark and first-class tourist destination. Naturally, the success of the plan relied on tourists not having to risk losing fingers on a tramway. But despite the emergence of a pro-bridge faction in town, McHardy residents stubbornly thwarted the government's plans and stymied progress for another decade.

Eventually, the government won out, as it always did, and before the new millennium arrived, the state finalized plans to condemn the tramway as a public safety hazard.

Still, the isolationist community fought on, with itself as much as with state and federal agencies. Out of the turmoil, a compromise with modernity emerged: there would be a bridge, but it would be a *footbridge*, a bridge too narrow to permit any vehicle wider than an ATV to cross. No cars, trucks, vans, RVs, campers, or buses allowed. McHardy Road terminated abruptly at its abutment. You could drive to McHardy, but you had to hike the final mile.

Sidebar: Sex on a Glacier

SG1 1.0

JACE FILLED OUT the paperwork for submitting his newly purchased McHardy property to the National Registry of Historic Places and looked into the state restoration grant. He maybe should have done these things before forking over the money to Beehymer. It was a much more complicated and much less automatic process than the old shark had made it out to be. Moreover, Jace had never built a structure bigger than a birdhouse before, let alone restore a historical building that needed to stay true to its 1910 floorpan, materials, and character.

Jace abandoned the historic landmark project and moved into the shed for the rest of the season. There he successfully bedded a shuttle van driver from Albuquerque, an interpretive ranger from Philadelphia, and a lodge hostess from Topeka. In October, when tourism dried up and Jace's park service contract ended for the year, he locked up the shed, drove to Anchorage, and caught a flight to Menominee, Michigan. That fall and winter he held down two jobs for two different uncles in order to begin paying back his house loan.

In December, while assembling Christmas bicycles at the Menominee Sports Emporium, Jace received an unexpected email from Danielle in Paris. She briefly reminisced about their meeting and asked if his chalet invitation was still open. She said she was trying to decide whether or not to take an offer she'd received to join an international NGO doing humanitarian work in Niger. Or another from a women's collective in Indonesia where she would foster the use of birth control in Muslim communities. If his invitation was still open, she had two weeks free in June she'd love to spend with him in his "chalet in the park," as long as he promised to keep the bears at bay.

"That would be très cool," he emailed right back, meanwhile asking himself, What chalet? He'd forgotten he'd made such an offer. Still, if that was what it took to entice Danielle to McHardy, a chalet it would be. The following spring he convinced his cousin, a master carpenter, to return to Alaska with him. Together they brought up a trailer load of building material and spent four weeks fixing the worst of the structure's flaws. By the time his cousin returned to Michigan in May, the Lucky Strike Lane house was as inhabitable as it would ever be.

SG2 1.0

DANIELLE ARRIVED ON time at Ted Stevens Anchorage International after an exhausting twenty-four-plus hours of travel with multiple layovers. She and Jace spent the night at the home of one of Jace's Anchorage friends and set out early the next morning on the day-long drive to McHardy. Jace was due back at work the following day.

Danielle ooh-la-la'ed at the epic scenery for the first couple of hours. The Glenn Highway followed the Matanuska River between two spectacular ranges of mountains. When they passed the grand Matanuska Glacier, glittering in the sun, Danielle asked him to pull over.

They used the public telescopes at the Mile 101 rest area to gaze at the ancient blue ice. Danielle so effused about the beauty, the splendor, and the grandeur of the sight that Jace said, "If you like that one, just wait till you see Caldecott Glacier. This one's nothing compared to the Caldecott."

He didn't want to tell her yet, but ever since their memorable hookup at the Captain Cook Hotel last year, he'd been entertaining a little fantasy in his head in which she played a central role. It was called "Sex on a Glacier."

Jace gassed up in Glennallen and turned south. The Wrangell Mountains were out, but Danielle had fallen asleep and missed one of the most spectacular parts of the trip, their descent into the grand Copper River Valley.

She awoke seventy miles (113 km) later in Chitina, another ghost town resurrected by historical preservation (civic motto: "Where the Hell is Chitina?"). There they bid adieu to blacktop, crossed the Copper River, and began the final leg of their journey, the 59-mile (95-km) McHardy Road to the heart of the park.

Despite her nap, Danielle seemed less and less enthusiastic with each passing mile. She didn't complain exactly, but she set her jaw in a grim look of forbearance, as though counting the minutes till the ride was over. She looked straight ahead, not turning to look even when he pointed out astonishing views and vistas.

After ten weary hours of travel, they arrived at the private parking lot at the end of the McHardy Road. To Jace's surprise and relief, the parking booth was manned by Drew Reed, a local man. The odd pioneer family and their encampment were gone. Good riddance. Their school bus was still parked in the lot, but it seemed to be vacant. Drew told him that Orion Beehymer had offered the family another of his lots to camp out on until they found something more permanent.

"More permanent?" Jace said. "They're planning on staying in the area?"

"I guess. Pappy Prophecy — that's the old dude — says that God sent them here to multiply and prosper."

"But haven't they multiplied enough already?"

Danielle asked Jace if something was wrong. Jace parked in his old spot at the end of the lot and replied, "No worries." Danielle drew a blank, and he rephrased, "There's nothing wrong. Everything is good."

He shouldered his duffel and hoisted two of her suitcases.

"We walk?" she said, looking around the stony lot.

"Yes, a little ways."

They set off for McHardy, and when they reached the footbridge, Danielle stopped short, appalled by what lay before her. Or rather, by what sprawled beneath her feet — the churning, foaming, thundering Caldecott River, which was swollen with the summer melt of three separate glaciers. Jace tried to reassure her. The bridge is sound. The bridge is strong. An army tank could drive across it, if it was a particularly narrow tank. He demonstrated by jumping up and down on the steel grating.

Then Danielle asked an odd question, one that must have been on her mind for a while: how far away was the nearest hospital? Confused by the question, Jace had to admit that the nearest medical facility of any kind was the urgent care clinic located in Glennallen, where they had gassed up four and a half hours earlier. The nearest hospital was the Providence Valdez Medical Center, even further away. "But don't worry," he said, trying to reassure her, "if there's an emergency, we can always medevac out."

"What is this medevac?"

When at last they'd hiked through town and turned the corner onto Lucky Strike Lane, Jace thought they were home free. He was wrong. The vacant lot that Beehymer had loaned the Prophecy clan turned out to be the brush-choked one next to his own. The crazy family had become his new next door neighbors! And like a family of land beavers, they had already cleared the lot of willow and aspen brush and piled it next to the street. The pile was so large it spilled over into Jace's driveway. In the center of the lot, tents and lean-tos surrounded an open fire pit. Dozens of children played in a yard already worn down to bare dirt. Older children tended goats in a makeshift pen or hauled water in plastic jerry jugs or helped prepare dinner at the fire pit. Woodsmoke permeated the area. They might have been camping there for weeks instead of just the two days he'd been away.

Danielle, in her gorgeous accent, asked, "What does it mean?"

"It means we have neighbors," Jace said.

Danielle slapped the back of her bare neck, and when she removed her hand, there were five bloody smears on her palm. He'd forgotten to warn her about Alaska mosquitos.

Then Danielle turned her attention to his "chalet." Jace looked at it too and saw his house for what it really was: a tiny, century-old, unpainted shack half hidden by weeds. He had tried to prepare her for rustic accommodations, but as she followed him through the warped doorway, he wondered if he had prepared her enough.

She wandered through the tilting rooms in silence and then turned to him with a look of hope in her pretty French eyes and said, "You are joking me, yes?"

Jace dropped their baggage on the living room floor. He wanted to fetch the rest of her stuff from the pickup before some bandit walked off with it, but the aroma of grilled meat coming from his new neighbors reminded him how hungry he was. So he led Danielle to the kitchen area to show her how to light the propane camping stove that served as his range. Of all the rooms, he had spent the most time and effort fixing up the kitchen area, installing shelves and a wash basin, a dish rack, and floral print curtains. He had debated with himself whether his attention to the kitchen was in any way sexist, but she was the one who had told him how much she enjoyed gourmet cooking. He surveyed his stock of canned goods and asked her if she liked beef stew and green beans. He laid the can opener on the countertop and pulled a skillet from a hook.

"I gotta go get the rest of your stuff," he said and headed for the door. "I'll be back in about forty-five minutes."

An hour and a half later, when he returned, Danielle was standing in the same spot, and dinner was still in the cans. "I look," she said, "and I cannot find the toilet room."

"Ah, the toilet room," he replied. He'd forgotten to tell her about the outhouse.

THEY SLEPT TOGETHER chastely, both of them too tired and stressed out to attempt lovemaking (though Jace was briefly up for it as he spooned against her silk-clad French hotness). He had stapled cardboard over the bedroom window to block out the midnight sunshine, and the neighbors graciously kept their noise level down.

Jace slept soundly and awoke in the cool hush of early morning to find Danielle still beside him. Her pretty face seemed completely relaxed. Her pretty breasts pressed against the sheer fabric of her chemise. Intermingling fragrances of unbathed bodies seeped from under the covers.

But Jace resisted the tug of his desire and slipped out of bed. Poor baby, she needed her rest. He eased the door shut behind him and tip-toed to the kitchen area to make a hearty breakfast of flapjacks, maple (flavored, high fructose corn) syrup, cantaloupe, and French Roast (instant) coffee. The Prophecy camp outside the kitchen window was stirring. One of the boys was heating water over the fire pit while older girls prepared to feed their little army.

Danielle was awake when he carried the breakfast tray (a scrap of plywood) to the bed (a queen size mattress on the floor). She was listening to the increasing commotion next door but seemed refreshed, and she smiled warmly when he entered. They discussed the day ahead while they ate. It was a work day for Jace. He supposed she'd appreciate a day to herself to settle in and unwind. If she wanted to stretch her legs, there were plenty of things to see in the little tourist town. He drew her a map and highlighted points of interest. There was the saloon, now part of the hotel, the mining-era museum, gift shops, and the St. Elias Mountain Center. The Mountain Center was a popular destination for culturally and ecologically sensitive young people and, if he wasn't mistaken, its annual nature writing seminar was underway. Perhaps she'd like to go over there and write a poem?

Jace donned his ranger uniform, collected his gear, and kissed Danielle good-bye. He fetched his dirt bike from behind the shed, but before starting it, he decided to pay his new neighbors a friendly visit to talk about the brush pile in his drive. He found the old patriarch seated at a picnic table serenely sipping coffee as his noisy brood swirled around him. The children stopped in their tracks to stare at Jace. Jace politely introduced himself and wished Prophecy and his family a pleasant day. Prophecy nodded in response.

"Say, I wonder," Jace went on, "could you tell your sons to kindly move that brush pile off my driveway?" As he waited for a reply, Jace uncrossed his arms so as not to appear hostile or overly aggressive.

After glancing at the brush pile, sipping his coffee, and glancing again at the brush pile, Poppy Prophecy raised unblinking grey eyes to Jace and said, "Hain't on your property."

Jace practically fell over in surprise. "What do you mean it *hain't* on my property? Of course it's on my property." And he pointed to the large rock next to the driveway that marked the corner of his lot.

Prophecy only shook his head and pointed to a second rock. "Orion tol' me that rock yonder is the corner. He says your driveway encroaches on his lot and he wants you to move it."

"Move my driveway?" Jace said, stunned by the absurdity of the idea. "That's crazy. My drive is certainly not encroaching. That's the legal corner, and that —" he said, pointing to a tree at the rear of the lot — "is the . . . is the . . ." The tree was gone, cut down with the rest. Anger flared in him. "You fuckin' cut down my tree!"

In an instant, the three older boys were surrounding him. The eldest, the one who had bedeviled the motorcoach driver, was tall and dark. The middle one was heavyset and gentle looking. And the fiery youngest one was wearing a patch over his right eye. If Ben Cartwright of the Ponderosa and his sons had evil twins, these Prophecys could be them. Jace waved his arm at his corner rock and loudly asserted his ownership. Then he said, "I have to go now, but you'd better rectify the situation before I return." He stalked back to his bike and started it. *Rectify*, he thought. *Did I just use a ten-dollar word with that old hillbilly?*

Jace spent the day inspecting a beaver dam that threatened to undo a couple of summers' worth of salmon stream restoration work near Round Lake. He was well out of cell phone range and unable to call Beehymer. When he returned to the ranger station at Caldecott, he learned that Beehymer had left town that morning, and no one knew when he'd return. After work, Jace wanted to check on Danielle to see how she was doing, but he couldn't stop stewing over that big pile of brush next to his drive, and he rode out Stubborn Mountain Trail to Dell Bunyan's place. Pastor Bunyan was a resident of long tenure and one of the most level-headed locals Jace had met (though Bunyan believed in miracles and preached from the pulpit that President Obama was a crypto-Muslim). Bunyan welcomed him inside and listened sympathetically to his story. When Jace was finished, Bunyan told him that, with the recorder's office fire, everyone in McHardy was pretty much in the same boat.

"Wait. What?" Jace said. "Fire?"

"Chitina used to have the recorder's office for this district, but it burned to the ground in 1961, and all property records of the original town were lost. Add to that the sloppy way they laid out McHardy in 1910, and no one's really sure where all the boundaries are. Or, for that matter, who the legal owners are. When the copper mine closed in 1938, people just kinda pulled up stakes and left everything behind. Do you have a warranty or a quit claim deed to that lot?"

"I'm not sure. What's the difference?"

"I'll bet it's a quit claim deed. That means Beehymer's selling you his interest in the property, if he has any, but he's not guaranteeing anything. Some other person might show up and claim he's the owner."

"Huh?"

"The town's been trying for decades to scrape up the money to have the entire townsite re-platted, but Orion's against it, so nothing's happened yet. But don't be too concerned. Odds are no one else has a better legal claim to your lot than you do, wherever your lot actually is."

No wonder Beehymer hadn't been able to find another buyer.

As they talked, Bunyan's eyes seemed to mist up, and he had to blow his nose. "In the end," Bunyan concluded, "we must fall back on the Bible's admonition to love our neighbors in order to keep the peace in McHardy. And frankly, you have nothing to worry about. Mr. Prophecy is a Christian man; he'll do the right thing. And just consider his position for a moment. With all those mouths to feed and no roof over their heads, he's in a pickle. Cut him a little slack, ranger, and God will reward you for your patience." He wiped a tear from his eye.

When Jace arrived home, he found his drive now completely blocked with brush. If it even was his drive, or his lot, or his house. As he detoured his bike around the brush to the shed, something inside him snapped. Leaping off his bike, he started at one end of the pile and began flinging the brush back into Prophecy's yard. He worked up a sweat in no time, and the three evil Cartwright twins came over. They didn't speak or interfere but only watched with smug expressions on their dopey faces. Before long, Danielle came out of the house to watch too. To Jace's surprise she was still wearing her skimpy bathrobe from the morning, and to his delight the boys were scandalized enough to avoid looking at her. When she came off the porch to speak to him, they left.

"Hi, honey," he said, tossing a young aspen across the line. "How was your day?"

"Okay," she said in a small voice. She didn't seem okay. Her hair was a mess, and it looked as though she'd been crying.

"Did you see the town?"

"*Non.*"

"Check out the Mountain Center?"

"*Non.*"

"The museum?"

"*Non.*"

It occurred to Jace that she'd spent the entire day in bed. "Go inside and get dressed, and I'll take you for a ride, okay?"

She shrugged her delicate shoulders and shuffled back inside.

Jace took her to the Caldecott Glacier Lodge in the mill town to sample the finest dining in a thousand square miles (2,590 sq. km). Then he took her to a lookout above the town where a breeze kept the mosquitos away. He pointed out two bald eagles riding updrafts next to Eureka Ridge. Bald eagles, of course, did not resonate in the European's imagination, and Jace explained to her their significance to Americans and the threat of their extinction in the last century due to poaching and DDT use. He told her the names of the mountain peaks and glaciers surrounding them. He talked about the geology, wildlife (but not bears!) and human history of the area. He explained the purpose of the fourteen-story ore concentration mill beneath them that the park service was restoring. Jace was a backcountry ranger, not an interpretive one, but he had soaked up enough local lore to impress a visitor. Danielle's spirits lifted a bit, and by the time they returned home she was smiling again. The brush Jace had flung across the property line had not been re-stacked on his drive, and so he was smiling too.

That evening, after sharing a bottle of wine, Jace heated up many gallons of water so that they could each bathe in the galvanized basin he used for a tub. One thing led to another, and soon they were in bed making love. It started out tender and exploratory but gradually grew louder and more frenzied. Loud and frenzied enough, Jace hoped, to reach the Prophecy camp. And, in fact, as he brayed the arrival of his climax, a couple of fiddles next door struck up a bluegrass tune. Afterward, as they lay in each other's arms, they listened to the music and agreed that those people were quite fine folk musicians.

THE NEXT DAY Jace took Danielle back to Caldecott where he set her up with a computer in the ranger office while he worked, and she spent the day catching up with her friends on Facebook and skyping with her son in Toulouse. After work, Jace took her to the lodge again for dinner, and things were looking so promising that he broached the idea of camping that night on the glacier. She agreed to go along though she didn't seem too enthused by the idea. After dinner he borrowed camping and hiking gear from the backcountry storeroom. They hiked up to Bough Glacier where it collided and merged with the Caldecott Glacier. Although it was after midnight, the sky was as bright as noon. They crossed a little open ice with crampons on their boots and skirted a gaping crevasse, pausing to peer down its cyan-blue throat. He chose a campsite on top of gravel-encrusted ice and pitched the tent. He had packed in a few pieces of firewood, and in no time at all he had a cheery little campfire going. They sat side by side on a ground pad next to the fire and draped a sleeping bag over their shoulders. The honeyed fragrance of wildflowers drifted over the ice. The natural world in all its primordial glory stretched out below them. There were no buildings or roads in sight. No power lines, airplanes, or radio towers. No sign of humanity whatsoever. It was just them and the unsullied Earth.

It was the perfect occasion for a joint, so Jace pulled one out of his pocket and offered it to Danielle. He lit it for her, and she took two tiny sips before passing it back to him. A couple of minutes later, she scrambled to her feet and went into the tent.

Yes! Sex on a glacier.

But when he joined her in the tent, she was wrapped up and trembling in a fetal position.

"What's wrong?" he said, alarmed. She told him what was wrong in rapid-fire French, of which he understood not a word. So he covered her with her sleeping bag and lay next to her. In a little while she switched to English.

"It is too much."

"What's too much?"

She waved her hand at the world beyond the tent flap. "Too much crazy people. Too much mountains! Too much . . . *outside*."

It was the dope. She was a little freaked.

"Well, then, it's a good thing we have a tent," he said, "so we can stay *inside*." He took off his boots and helped her with hers. He placed the boots outside the tent and zipped up the flap, shutting out all that overwhelming space. She removed her trousers and slid into her bag and zipped it up to her chin. He undressed and got into his own bag next to hers. The midnight sun, shining through the thin tent fabric, turned everything orange.

"Don't worry, Danielle. We're perfectly safe here."

"*Merci,*" she said.

"*De nada.*"

He gazed at the back of her head for a long time. A breeze rose to gently buffet the side of the tent. They were both too wide-awake to sleep. Eventually, she unzipped her bag and said, "You like to come here?"

She didn't need to ask twice. Sex on a glacier! Sex on a glacier! He unzipped his bag and draped it over the both of them. He helped her off with her shirt and bra. Gaa, he loved her breasts. Firm little handfuls. Her nipples swelled when he teased them, and her breath deepened. She seemed to especially like stroking his cock, and he was out of his undies before she was out of hers. The dope intensified every touch. He had a log between his legs, and she was scooting her hips beneath him to receive it when there was a sound like a rifle shot. It was distant but sharp.

She froze. "What was that?"

"Nothing. Just the ice buckling."

"A crevasse opens?"

"No, no. The glacier moves about a half meter a day, so it grinds and bends, and cracks all the time. Nothing to worry about."

Easier said than done. He entered her at last, but she no longer seemed to be interested. He tried to rekindle the mood, but she said, "Just hurry."

He was at the point of no return anyway, so he came, but it was a fizzle and a disappointment, and she immediately slipped him out of her. She retrieved her clothes and began to dress.

"What's going on?" he said.

"Take me away from this place."

"Right now?"

SG4 1.0

IT WAS NEARLY 3:00 A.M. by the time they returned to the house on Lucky Strike Lane. He thought they could still salvage the warm feelings of the day, but she said she wanted to sleep alone, so he slept on the couch in the living room. Not three hours later he was awakened by the sound of digging outside the house. He went to the kitchen window but couldn't find the source. He peeked into the bedroom and saw that the noise had awakened Danielle as well. It sounded louder in the bedroom, in fact. He pulled cardboard from the window, and right outside was the eldest Prophecy boy digging a pit. Jace's anger flared, and he tried opening the window. But the sash was glued shut with a century's worth of dried paint. So Jace threw on some pants and boots and stormed out and around the side of the house.

"What the *fuck* you think you're doing?" he demanded of the man.

In a flawless imitation of his father, the man looked at the pit under his feet and then at the shovel in his hand and then at the pit again before looking at Jace and saying, "Why, I'm digging a hole."

"I can see you're digging a hole, you ape."

"Then why'd you ask?"

Jace trembled with fury. "Get off my land this instant! You're trespassing."

"You're the one doing the trespassing, son. Like Poppy tole you yesterday, the property line goes right through here. This is our land. We need a latrine, and Poppy says this is a good spot for it."

"I don't give a *fuck* what Poppy says." Jace tried to snatch the shovel out of the evil Cartwright twin's hand but he tossed it to evil twin Hoss, who had materialized at his side. Evil twin Little Joe was there too. Jace didn't waste his breath on them but marched to his shed and retrieved his own shovel. He backfilled the pit while they watched. They laughed and went back to their camp.

DANIELLE DIDN'T LEAVE the house for the next three days, not even to visit the outhouse. Jace couldn't entice her outdoors at all, not to go to dinner or take a walk or visit the mill town. He put together a honey bucket arrangement with a plastic pail and old toilet seat in her bedroom, and he dutifully emptied it each morning and evening. He spent as much time with her as he could manage. He left her his iPad, and she whiled away her days on it. She allowed him to sleep with her, but she was in no mood for sex, and he didn't push it.

Meanwhile, Jace deployed shark repellent against the neighbors by frequently urinating next to the side of his house. He kept his back to the camp, and he wasn't visible from either the bedroom or kitchen window, so it wasn't as if he was exposing himself. He just spread his legs, unzipped, and let it splash, and that seemed to be enough. The Prophecys rearranged their tarps and tents to create a wall of privacy between him and themselves. Score one for Ranger Rick.

On Jace's first day off from work, Danielle woke him as she crawled over him to get out of bed. He dozed again but awoke when he heard her busy in the kitchen. In a little while he could smell bacon frying. She was making breakfast. Perhaps the worst was over. She was settling in at last, giving Alaska a second chance. He lay in bed with his morning chubby and dared to feel optimistic about the remainder of her visit.

A moment later she shrieked and screamed, and Jace was on his feet and in the kitchen in an instant. Ashen-faced, she pointed to the window. He approached it carefully and looked out. A tripod made from spruce poles stood right outside. Hanging from the tripod by its hamstrings was a goat that the boys had slaughtered and bled and were presently gutting and skinning. Without its hide, the goat might have been a gutted child hanging upside down.

A WOMAN WHO worked for one of the guiding companies was leaving that morning to pick up supplies in Anchorage, and she agreed to take Danielle to the airport. Jace helped carry Danielle's things across the footbridge to the van. They embraced and kissed good-bye. He never expected to hear from her again, and he never did.

The following evening, when he returned home from the ranger office, Jace was surprised to discover that the Prophecy camp next door was abandoned. All the tents, tarps, and belongings were gone. The family had left behind only trampled ground, a fire pit, and the cleared brush. Good riddance. He hoped that they too had left the park.

He wasn't so lucky, as he later learned. Beehymer had returned from wherever he'd gone and agreed to lease them his old mine site out at Stubborn Mountain. Well, at least they were sixteen miles away (26 km); they probably wouldn't bother Jace again.

Sidebar: A Herd of Picnic Tables

HP1 1.0

IN ORDER TO meet the Monday flight at the Anchorage airport, Jace had to leave McHardy on Sunday afternoon after work. His pickup was parked on the other side of the footbridge, so the first mile of his three-hundred-mile trip (483 km) was on foot. It was high summer, and tourists owned the ghost town. They strolled its dusty streets or waited at the air-taxi office for a flightseeing tour. They crowded the deck of the saloon drinking microbrews and dining on mooseburgers with cheechako fries. They snapped selfies at the People's Museum.

When Jace reached the footbridge, a string of tourists was coming over, having just been disgorged from a luxury motorcoach. He welcomed the visitors to the park, though he was off-duty and out of uniform.

The parking lot on the other side of the footbridge was its usual summertime circus of cars, busses, and RVs. Jace made his way to the end where he kept his Toyota. A slip of paper was tucked under the windshield wiper. In a childish scrawl it read, *Atension! You are in violation of parking regs! See atendent or risk towing ASAP!!!*

Jace puzzled over the message. The parking lot was on private land, and he concluded that the owner must have hired a new lot attendant to collect parking fees. Jace got into his pickup and crossed the rocky terrain to the entrance.

The weathered wedding canopy that served as the attendant's booth was still there, and it was joined by other slapdash structures — tents, a herd of picnic tables, an old yellow school bus — in what resembled a nomadic encampment. About a million children of all ages dressed in vintage pioneer costumes seemingly cut from the same bolt of blue gingham were running around and playing games. The girls wore bonnets and long dresses and the boys bibbed trousers with suspenders. Only their swooshed athletic shoes broke the spell.

Jace couldn't figure out who or what these costumed people were. A children's choir? A traveling Gold Rush act? (Years later, when he thought about this encounter, he realized that Deuteronomy must have been there too with her family, but he had no recollection of seeing her. Maybe she was in the bus behind the curtains.)

Jace approached the booth. The attendant was a paunchy old fellow with long, grey hair and beard. He had a Father Time air about him. That is, he was not only ancient but worn down. Shambling. World weary. His hair and beard were untrimmed and untamed. Moist eyes lurked under bushy eyebrows. He slumped in his lawn chair and watched Jace's arrival without a shred of interest.

Next to Father Time sat an incredibly tired-looking woman nursing a gingham-clad baby under a shawl. Arrayed on the table before them were Christian-themed tchotchkes for sale: wooden crosses, praying hands, angel dolls, cross pendants. The pieces ranged in quality from crude to master-craftsman and were decorated with spruce cones, moss, birch bark, moose nuggets, and bits of fur.

"Hi," Jace said, placing the scrap of paper on the table in front of Father Time. "It seems I got this by mistake."

The old man didn't even look at the paper. He only needed to glance at Jace's pickup to say, "Weren't no mistake. You owe five days at five dollars per. Comes to twenty-five bucks."

"You don't understand. I'm a local. Beehymer doesn't charge us locals."

"We have the parking franchise now, and things are changed. Everyone pays the day rate. That'll be $25.00. Cash."

To park his vehicle at $5.00 per day for the rest of the season would cost Jace $500 for something that had always been free. And it wasn't even a paved lot but only an expanse of glacial detritus left over from the last Ice Age. While Jace was considering his options, he noticed the new district ranger coming across the footbridge. Ethan Parkhurst Masterson was a Law Enforcement Ranger who had been in the park less than a week and had a reputation, both within the service and on the internet, for being something of a bad apple. Jace was still trying to separate the legend from the man.

Meanwhile, the large tourist motorcoach that had been idling on the road began backing into the lot entrance. McHardy Road itself was only one lane wide, too narrow to turn around in, and had no shoulders or cul-de-sac. So this was the only way for the driver to turn his ungainly bus around. But a man appeared out of nowhere and dragged a wooden barrier across the entrance, blocking the motorcoach. The man was about Jace's age, and judging from his suspenders and full brown beard, he belonged to the same pioneer troupe as Father Time and the children.

The motorcoach driver locked his brakes and leaned out his window. "Hey, move that outta the way."

But pioneer man crossed his arms and stood his ground. So the driver, a balding, pear-shaped man, emerged from the motorcoach to confront him.

"What's your problem, Jack? I'm trying to turn around here."

Pioneer man, at six foot three (2 m), towered over the driver and said, "You wanta use our lot, you gotta pay the parking fee."

"I'm not parking," the driver shot back. "All I want to do is turn my rig around."

"Turn around in Chitina."

"Bullshit. They always let me turn around here."

"That was then. This is now."

The two men went back and forth for a little while before the exasperated driver lost his cool and tried to move the barrier away. Immediately, two more bearded pioneers joined the first to surround the driver. One was tall and fat, and the other handsome and slim. All three pioneers appeared to be in their twenties. They shouldered the driver away from the barrier and backed him against his motorcoach. By now, tourists were turning their phones from the glaciers and mountains to the more tweet-worthy shouting match.

Jace debated with himself whether or not to intervene. The road was under State of Alaska jurisdiction, not park service, and the parking lot was private property. Before he could make up his mind, his fellow ranger strode into the scene. Attired in his NPS uniform — heavy-soled boots; armored vest; a Batman belt studded with handcuffs, radio, pepper spray, telescoping baton; and .44 Magnum snubnosed leg cannon — Law Enforcement Ranger Masterson looked more suited for urban warfare than nature walks. "Break it up. Break it up," he bellowed.

The pioneer brothers stepped away from the driver, who was dripping with sweat and gasping for breath. Masterson placed a hand on his shoulder and said, "Why don't you go sit down, sir, until you recover." But the man shook his head emphatically and hunched forward with his hands on his knees.

The eldest of the brothers, the one who had started the confrontation, said, "This is a state highway, Ranger Danger. You don't have no authority here."

Jace was astonished. Based on what he'd heard about Masterson, it was probably not a good idea to challenge his authority. Now Jace was tempted to take out his own phone and start recording.

LE Ranger Masterson had the distinction of racking up the highest number of public complaints against an individual ranger in NPS history. Yet his career had started on a high note. In 1999, the son of a U.S. senator crashed a private airplane during a snowstorm in the Klamath Mountains in Northern California. It was Masterson, new on the job, who led the rescue mission that found the plane and successfully evacuated its passengers. The incident made national news, and for a while Masterson was the park service's golden boy. But his behavior soon changed, and he began to fixate on minor park regulations, such as the noise curfew and leash laws. He patrolled parking lots at park concessions and wrote traffic citations for cracked windshields or burned-out tail lights. He seemed to want to instill fear in every park visitor he encountered, even children. To ask him where the porta-johns were located was to risk a public haranguing.

As complaints about Masterson mounted, his NPS superiors transferred him from park to park like a pederast priest. Then came the notorious "Kitten

Incident," after which only the influence of the senator whose aviator son Masterson had rescued could save his career. Or so went the rumor.

This is a state highway, Ranger Danger. You don't have no authority here.

Despite his reputation for abuse, Masterson replied in a respectful manner. "Ordinarily you'd be correct, sir," he said, "but the law gives me authority to intervene when I see a felony assault in progress."

"Felony assault?" the pioneer said with a laugh. "Don't worry; I won't press charges."

At that the driver straightened up and cursed out loud. He jabbed a finger at the pioneer and said, "Assault and robbery! Assault and robbery! Arrest this man."

"He tried to rob you?" Masterson said.

"Yes! He wants fifty dollars just to turn my rig around."

"Is that true?" Masterson asked the pioneer.

"That's our hourly rate for a bus to use our lot." The young man pointed to a sign on a post next to the attendant's booth. A zero had been added to the old bus rate of $5/hr.

"I don't want to park in your lot!" the driver screamed. "I just want to turn the fuck around!"

"Then turn around somewheres else. Here you pay a fee. Keep swearing and the fee will double."

"If that's not robbery," the driver complained to Masterson, "what is it?"

"The cost of doing business," said the pioneer.

Masterson looked at the driver, the pioneers, and then, turning halfway around, at Jace. To the driver he said, "This man appears to be in the right. The owner of this property has a concession permit to run a parking lot. If this man is his agent, he can set any price he sees fit. If you don't like it, make some other arrangements for your bus."

"I want to press charges for assault."

"That's your right, but you'll need to press them with the Alaska State Troopers, not with me." He turned to pioneer man and said, "I suggest you modify your business plan."

"Or what?"

"Or I'll make it my mission in life to put your business in the ground."

THAT WAS IT. No riot. No flying fists or abuse of police power. The tourists put away their phones. This video would not show up on YouTube tonight. Even Jace felt a little let down. Masterson left the motorcoach and joined him at the booth. He scowled at the pioneer encampment — the yellow school bus, tents, and tarps — that was set up just a few yards outside his jurisdiction. He picked up several of the handicrafts the family offered for sale and examined them with a critical eye. He held an angel figurine in front of Father Time and pointed at its wings, which were glued together from real bird feathers, and said, "It's against federal regulations to harvest natural products on park lands without a permit."

Father Time replied, "It's a good law. Otherwise, man might take it upon himself to make use of Father God's bounty without permission from the government."

Masterson let the remark pass without comment.

"Until you obtain a permit, don't let me catch you or your daycare center here out harvesting. I won't hesitate to fine you."

The old man yawned, exposing yellow stumps of teeth. "Go with Satan, my son," he said cordially, "for you suckle at his putrid teat."

Masterson shook his head in wonder and simply walked away, gesturing for Jace to follow. They strolled side by side in silence down the gravel road. Jace sneaked a few glances at his new park service colleague. The man was still a cypher.

They walked a quarter mile without speaking. Dozens of homemade signs lined both sides of the road, nailed to trees and stakes, all located on private land:

TIRE REPAIR
ICE
GLACIER VIEW B&B
BASE CAMP HQ
CUSTOM KNIVES
COPPER NUGGETS
FLIGHT-SEEING

Beehymer wasn't the only land-owning entrepreneur operating within the park at the end of McHardy Road. Masterson halted suddenly and said, "Hear that?"

Jace listened. He didn't hear anything except the sound of a small gasoline engine off in the distance somewhere running a generator or compressor or something. Which was probably Masterson's point — noise pollution.

"Our institution's mission is a contradiction in terms," Masterson said. "It's downright schizoid. You can't both preserve a wilderness in perpetuity while at the same time making it easy for every half-crippled, obese, smog-sucking touron to see it from a bus window. It's one or the other; you can't have it both ways. You have to decide which one is important and let the other one go." He locked eyes with Jace as he said this. "As a ranger for the National Park Service, you shouldn't make the situation worse than how you found it."

He was probably referring to Jace's private residence in McHardy.

"Do you know why I came up to Alaska in the first place, Kuliak?" Masterson went on.

Jace shook his head no. *Because it was the last place they could reassign you?*

"Because someone told me that Alaska is a state that bans highway billboards and signs. Doesn't matter if they're on private land; they're against the law, even in towns. Nature trumps Commerce. Imagine that, a state with balls enough to ban private signs. And yet . . ." He spread his arms to take in the haphazard signs littering both sides of the road. "Here we have a state road with signs sprouting up like dandelions. Why do you suppose that is?"

Jace paused to see if this was a rhetorical question. Apparently not. So he said, "Signs are sprouting up like dandelions because the nearest state trooper post is 130 miles (209 km) away by road in Glennallen, where they are perennially understaffed and have more important things to do with limited resources than chase down signage scofflaws at the end of McHardy Road."

"Bingo," Masterson said. "Allowing a state road to penetrate so deep into a protected federal reserve is insane. McHardy and its road is an abomination. Which brings me to you."

"What about me?"

"I don't mind the college-boy attitude. I don't mind the ponytail. Hell, I don't even mind the drugs. Live and let live is what I say. But sooner or later you're going to have to decide which side you're on."

Drugs? That was probably a lucky guess; Jace kept his tooting to himself. "Which side of what?" he said.

"Whether you value wilderness or you value access. You gotta choose one or the other. There's no such thing as an inholder in a wilderness. It's a contradiction in terms."

Sidebar: Tour of the Mine

TM1 1.0

AN OUT-OF-CONTROL Oxicontin habit, a costly medical procedure beyond the scope of Medicare, breaking his great grandnephew out of prison, a gambling debt to the mob, a new condo in Orlando, a young girlfriend with expensive tastes, blackmail payments, or all of the above: these were the most popular explanations floating around McHardy in the summer of 2010 when Orion Beehymer announced he was finally selling off Stubborn Mountain Mine. The sale would include: three hundred forty federally patented acres (138 ha), including subsurface mineral rights; the hard rock mine itself with over five miles of shafts and tunnels, mining machinery, and chattels; an operational Caterpillar D6 bulldozer; and a main house and six outbuildings.

The Stubborn Mountain Copper Company dated to 1909 when it was established by a group of East-Coast investors who were not aligned to the Guggenheim syndicate. The Stubborn ore deposit wasn't as extensive or rich as the Caldecott, and its owners struggled for eight years before declaring bankruptcy. A Boston bank held the property on its books for forty-five years and sold it at a loss to Beehymer in 1962.

For the next twenty summers (except during the Pipeline years) Beehymer and Salame, his common-law wife, worked the mine and its extensive tailings for gold. The mine provided them a decent living and, during its heyday, employed about a dozen seasonal workers. After Salame died of breast cancer in 1982, Orion lost heart and shut down operations permanently.

The gate to the mine remained padlocked until July, 2010, when Beehymer gave Poppy Prophecy a guided tour. Beehymer had recently rented him the property, and he was showing him around.

"Watch your step, pastor," Beehymer said, dusting off an old, tin miner's helmet for his guest. "The floor is uneven."

Beyond the gate, the mine entrance was shaped like a hangar, about twenty feet high (6 m) and fifty across (15 m). The tunnel itself was wide enough for two ore cars to pass each other on parallel tracks, plus a catwalk along both walls. The air was chilly and damp. Fifteen or so yards in (14 m), a section of ceiling was braced with treated timbers. Beehymer shined his flashlight along it.

"There's only a few spots that need cribbing on account of loose rock. This mountain is basalt, Chististone limestone, and Triassic Nikolai Greenstone, so the tunnels hold up pretty well on their own."

Beehymer played his light along bare copper wires hanging from the ceiling. "I wired the place for power. We passed by the generator on our way in, but it looks pretty shot." He wet his index finger with spit and raised it over his head. "Feel that breeze? There's ventilation shafts throughout the levels and a main air shaft that goes all the way through to the other side high on the mountain. Air flows through here continuously by convection, so I never had to worry about foul air."

An alcove on the left opened to a large, warehouse-sized chamber carved out of the rock. "This used to be a full machine shop when it was a copper mine. There's still some machines that work, or worked the last time I was here, but I mostly used the room as a graveyard to park old, useless stuff." He swept the space with the beam of his light, momentarily illuminating a clutter of steam drills, pipes, a portable boiler, compressors, a forge, and other metallic hulks of unknown purpose. "It was all coal and steam in those days."

At a wide spot further along the tunnel, a second tunnel branched off and climbed a shallow gradient. "There's three levels all told. We're on the main one, which goes on for another half mile or so. Powder storage room and mess hall are that way. Up this ramp are the other levels."

Beehymer led the way up the ramp, which doubled back in a broad curve. "Summer and winter, the air temperature stays pretty constant at thirty-eight degrees (3 C). I suppose if the government ever gets its claws on it, they'll want to store cheese here."

They visited a chamber on the second level that was so large that it dwarfed the machine room. It was so broad and so high that their puny flashlights couldn't reach the walls or ceiling. "This is where they found their mother lode. After it petered out, it was pretty much all over for them."

After exploring the second level, Beehymer led Poppy to the third. "Plenty of dead-end shafts and tunnels and pits hereabouts. Some are unstable. This ain't no place to let kids run around in, but I wanted to show you one more thing. I think you'll be impressed."

The tunnel floor was wet there, and a little rivulet of spring water ran in a culvert chipped along one wall. Throughout the tour Poppy had let his host do all the talking, but when they entered the final chamber, he gasped and exclaimed, "Father God Almighty, all praise to You."

"It's something, ain't it?" Beehymer said. "Over seven million gallons, as best I can calculate, of the sweetest, cleanest, coolest spring water you ever tasted. Go ahead, try it."

Poppy knelt down on the rocky lip of an underground lake. He dipped his hand into the water, not to taste it, but to bless himself in thanksgiving.

THE PROPHECY FAMILY journey had been long, and every member had borne hardships and doubts with a trusting heart. Poppy had almost lost faith along the way, but Father God had come through in the end, as He always did. Although they were only renters, there was no doubt in any Prophecy mind that Father God intended for them to take dominion over the mine.

And so, when Beehymer returned unexpectedly less than a month later with the news that he had decided to sell the mine and that they might soon have to vacate the premises, they took it surprisingly well.

"Not right away," Beehymer added, afraid they'd misunderstood him. "And the new owners might let you stay on anyway, as caretakers or something. So there's no cause to panic just yet."

"We're not panicking," Poppy said. "We're giving praise."

"Uh, what for?" Beehymer asked, truly puzzled.

"We've been praying that you'd sell us the mine, and Father God answered our prayer."

"Now just hold on there, pastor," Beehymer said. "I'd gladly sell you the mine, but I doubt you can meet my asking price."

"Which is?"

"One million dollars. With ten percent down."

The astronomical figure didn't faze Poppy. A number ten times as high wouldn't have either. Their God was a mighty God. What was mere money to Him?

BY THE SUMMER of 2010, the world had endured two and a half years of the Great Recession, and though Beehymer advertised far and wide, few prospective buyers expressed any interest in a played-out copper mine. Unlike the town lots Beehymer owned, the mine property came with a U.S.

mining patent, recorded in Washington, D.C., not Chitina, Alaska, and the title was solid enough to qualify for bank financing. At least it would have been in pre-recession times. Nevertheless, the only qualified buyer in the game was the National Park Service.

When the park superintendent heard about Beehymer's intention to sell, she fired off letters, phone calls, and emails to her bosses in D.C., who lobbied Congress, which sat on its hands. The Secretary of the Interior testified about the rarity of such opportunities to reclaim large inholding tracts from private hands while at the same time extinguishing mining rights within a national park. Park Superintendent Rodgers enlisted the support of the Alaska delegation and conservancy groups alike in her campaign.

After much back-room dickering and arm twisting, the government encumbered enough money to at least partially meet Beehymer's asking price. Superintendent Rodgers was cagey enough not to try to approach the land baron directly. Beehymer's hatred for the park service was legendary, and Rodgers felt an indirect approach would have a greater chance of success. So she and headquarters worked out a secret deal with a major land conservancy organization, the Wild Lands Trust to act as an intermediary.

Orion Beehymer had no love for do-gooder, anti-development organizations like the WLT either, but at least they weren't the government, and so he held his nose and looked at their offer, unaware that a sale to them would, after a bit of paper shuffling, turn his mine over to the feds. Meanwhile, whatever was compelling him to sell the mine in the first place was increasing in urgency, and though the WLT offer fell short of his expectations, all indications were that he would eventually ink the WLT deal.

However, Superintendent Rodgers had neglected to factor into her scheme the awesome power of prayer. The entire Prophecy family was on its knees day and night throughout the first week of Eighthmonth beseeching their Creator for the keys to Stubborn Keep.

On the ninth day of the month, the miracle happened. Alaska Governor Vera Tetlin announced a one-time Heating Cost Equalization payment to every resident of the state. The price of heating oil in Alaska had reached an all-time high the previous winter, exceeding $4.50 a gallon in urban areas and double that in the bush. Ironic for a state whose dominant source of revenue was from oil. Tetlin hoped to ease the pain on average Alaskans by paying every man, woman, and child a cool $2000. In addition, she combined this heating relief with the annual Permanent Fund Dividend payment, which was disbursed in October. The PFD was the portion of state oil revenues that then-Governor Jay Hammond decreed in 1976 should be shared directly with Alaska residents.

And so it transpired that on the morning of Firstday, the 25th of Tenthmonth, Mama and Poppy Prophecy showed up unannounced on the back porch of Orion Beehymer's McHardy residence. They each bore a bundle. Orion invited them into the kitchen and made a fresh pot of coffee. Mama P's bundle contained a platter of still-warm cinnamon rolls glazed with maple icing and sprinkled with chopped pecans.

They enjoyed an hour of small talk over their coffee and rolls. Then Mama P removed plates and platter, and Poppy lifted his bundle, a child's backpack, to the table. Without a word he unzipped it, reached in, and pulled out a wrapped $5000 bundle of hundred-dollar bills. He placed the money in front of Beehymer, reached in again, pulled out a second bundle, and stacked it on top of the first. He repeated this action until a tower of three hundred Benjamin Franklins teetered on the table.

Poppy paused to take a sip of coffee. The final state payout that year of the combined Heating Cost Equalization and PFD had totaled $3751 per resident. Multiply that by sixteen children and two adults, and Poppy continued stacking money until he had built two identical towers. Then he took another sip of coffee and a gander at Beehymer's reaction.

Poppy started a third tower but built it only a third as high as the first two. He turned the backpack over and shook it out. It was empty. Seventy thousand cash dollars now stood on the breakfast table. Beehymer gazed at it for a long time. Eventually he tore his eyes away and said, "This is almost a down payment. But what about the rest of it? A million dollars; that's my price. I'd rather sell it to you than anyone else I can think of. It would make me feel good to know that you and your precious family were out there. But there won't be another PFD payout as rich as this year again. You can count on that. Where will my mortgage payments come from then?"

"Don't worry about that," Poppy said as though it were a trivial matter.

"Why shouldn't I worry?" Beehymer insisted.

"Because it's in Father God's hands. It's always been in His hands, from sending us up here to your taking us to the mine. Even this money is all part of His plan. He wants us to possess the mine. Why would He change course now? Have a little faith."

"Excuse me if my own faith requires verification. But I'll tell you what. I will take this as down payment, and I will work out a private mortgage arrangement, but only on one condition — you agree to an iron-clad reversion clause. If you fall behind in your payments, I have the option to summarily repossess the property, keep all your payments to date, and evict you. No foreclosure procedure, no court case, no muss or fuss. Fall behind and you're out, and I'm back in."

"Deal," Poppy said, and they shook on it.

ON THE WAY home, flush with success, Poppy wondered out loud, "Just who is this governor, this Tetlin?" Until then, neither he nor Mama had paid much attention to politics. Now they made room in their prayers for a state governor.

Sidebar: The Kitten of Our Discontent

KD1 1.0

Excerpted from the *Liberty Frog Blog*

ANOTHER REPORT FROM the Bizarro File about that government assault on innocent campers at Big Pine National Park with more details and perps' names. The perps are E.P. Masterson, a ranger for the NPS, and Deputy Sheriff Lloyd Pattison from Apgar County Sheriff's Department (although he says he was acting as a civilian and not in any official capacity). Seems that these two heroes of the nanny state took it upon themselves to stamp out a flagrant violation of the park's strict nuisance pet rule. The pet in question was a 3-month-old calico kitten, whose name we have yet to uncover. The instigating incident, according to reliable witnesses in neighboring campsites, occurred at approximately 2 A.M. when two young campers, J.A. and J.J., both from Portland, were making sweet love in their tent. Though they took great effort to muffle their lusty cries of hot-blooded ecstasy, the frenzied rubbing together of their nylon sleeping bags broadcast their activity to the whole campground and was probably what set their kitten off in the first place mewing like a house on fire.

We don't know if anyone climaxed before Masterson and Patterson launched the raid with ear-piercing blasts from a marine horn and blinding lights from their 4-wheelers. They rousted the couple from the tent with nightsticks — Show me your hands! Show me your hands! — and forced them to lie face down in the dirt. The boy was completely naked except for a condom dangling from his limp organ. The girl wore a cotton t-shirt but was bottomless. The boy was screaming too — Show me your badge! Show me your badge!

But witnesses say there were no badges in sight. The two officers had entered the campground in plain clothes and failed to identify themselves as law enforcement. And they were driving non-official 4-wheelers. The only answer the boy got to his demand was a swift kick to the kidney and zip cuffs. The girl went berserk and started wailing for help. Masterson crouched down to scream in her face to shut the blank up, you sick blank. When that and cuffs didn't calm her down, he maced her at point-blank range in the eyes and mouth.

Deputy Patterson reportedly stood to the side during much of this and let his partner do the peacekeeping, but he did jump in to help when Ranger Masterson arrested the kids on charges of public indecency, disorderly conduct, and resisting arrest, as well as the original charge of violation of being in possession of a nuisance pet.

Here is the regulation in question taken from the NPS website:

> — *Allowing a pet to make noise that is unreasonable considering location, time of day or night, impact on park users or frightens wildlife by barking, howling, or making other noise is prohibited.*

This last charge had to be dropped when further investigation of the tent failed to produce the kitten, who had wisely fled during the melee.

The rest of the charges were dropped the next day and the miscreants released with a warning. They immediately launched a lawsuit against the Sheriff's dept. and the NPS. We wish them well in this.

But there's a happy ending. Someone recovered the missing kitten and returned her to her owners. Saucers of milk all around!

Sidebar: The Man in the Skiff

MS1 1.0

An American Maverick
Copyright © 2009 by Vera Tetlin
Little Brown Jug Publishers
New York

Chapter Six — The Way Forward (excerpt)

WHEN I RETURNED to Alaska in November 2008, after John's and my "thumpin' at the polls," I was exhausted, depressed, and confused. It was more than losing the White House to the Democrat party that got me down. Golly, I know how to lose with grace. That's one of the lessons that school athletics will teach you. No, it was more than that; I was experiencing a full-on crisis of faith. And I was angry too. As self-centered as it may sound, I felt like God had set me up to knock me down. "Why, Lord," I would pray, "if You didn't intend for me to be vice president, why did You open that door if You didn't want me to charge through it?"

Bradd understood my pain, but he chalked it up to the stress of the national campaign. "You've been going non-stop since September," he told me. "No wonder you're worn out. Take a breather. People will understand, and you earned it."

Good advice, but not very practical when you're the sitting governor of a state as dynamic as Alaska. In fact, my detractors in Juneau were already complaining that I had been away on the campaign trail for too long and had left the state "rudderless."

Here was something else I didn't understand. When I accepted the VP nod at the Republican National Convention in Minneapolis only a few month earlier, my voter approval rating in Alaska was at a staggering 85%. It meant that Alaskans from all political persuasions approved of the changes I spearheaded in the first year of my administration. And what was not to love? In that short amount of time we crushed the good-ol'-boy Republican Corrupt Bastards Club and ushered in a new era of bipartisan ethics reform. We broke the chokehold that Big Oil has had on our state politics since the first well was drilled in Prudhoe Bay, and we replaced its sweetheart tax structure with a clear and equitable formula for maximizing Alaska's share of the returns. It's *our* oil, after all; the oil giants might pump it, but they don't own it. We also hammered out a framework for bringing North Slope natural gas south to energize the economies of both our state and the nation. We privatized the state-run dairy and put it on sound financial footing. And we broke ground for the new, privately owned state prison.

These were major accomplishments, and I was justifiably proud of them.

Yet, when I returned after the election, it was as though all of it had been forgotten. During the heat of the campaign, the national lamestream media had hurled buckets of hyper-partisan mud at me. Had my fellow Alaskans taken their lies for fact? The usually cordial Alaska press corps grew confrontational. My return also spurred the haters to spread new lies about me and my family. They took advantage of our reformed ethics laws to file a string of bogus ethics complaints against *me*. Some of these complaints were laughable, and all of them were false, false, false. Without exception they were tossed out of court, but in the meantime they compounded the stress I was under. And because the law required me to mount my own legal defense, my family was drowning in attorney fees. By June 2009, we were over a half-million dollars in hock to the lawyers. This bloodletting could not continue.

Things came to a head one day when my closest advisor, Kris Derry, made an offhand remark to me during a teleconference. She said, "At least we don't have to worry about another campaign till you run for re-election."

I was puzzled. We had never talked about taking another swing at national office. But then I realized she was talking about the next gubernatorial election.

But a second term as Alaska's governor was the last thing on my mind. I wasn't even sure I was capable of making it through my first term, which was less than half over at that point.

Kris' innocent remark threw me into a tailspin, and for the next several weeks it was all I could do to get out of bed in the morning, let alone fire up enough enthusiasm to run a state.

I prayed, of course. Boy, did I pray. But looking back, I'm sure it sounded to the saints more like a three-year-old whining, "Why? Why? Why?" Finally, it got to be too much, and all I wanted was the whole mess to go away. Bradd knew what I was going through as much as anyone could, and he promised to stand by any decision I made, but even he was surprised on July 1, when I told him I was going to resign my office as governor. He insisted I give it some more time and offered to pray with me, but my mind was made up, and that very evening we broke the news to Taiga. She was as surprised and upset as her father. But it was my decision to make, and I made it. End of story.

We called a lakeside news conference for July 3. It might have been better to wait till after the Independence Day weekend, but all I could think of was getting it over with. We were keeping it a secret, even from my closest advisors, and I didn't want to take a chance that something one of us said or did might spill the beans.

So on Friday morning, Bradd wheeled the lectern with the official seal of the state of Alaska down the back yard slope to the water's edge. Our living room was too small to accommodate many camera crews, and we used Lake Lola as a backdrop for news conferences when the weather was fine. While Bradd was setting things up, the first news trucks with satellite dishes on their roofs began to show up from Anchorage. Reporters asked him what the big announcement was all about, but he only smiled and shook his head.

At 11:00 A.M., Bradd, Taiga, and I emerged from the house and walked hand in hand down to the lake. While I attempted to show my game face to the photographers, I think it was the most wretched stroll of my life. When we got to the lectern, I noticed that there was a lone fisherman in an aluminum skiff on the lake not far from shore. He was casting his line into the water again and again. I remember thinking, that old boy is going to photobomb my press conference, and I wondered why Bradd hadn't chased him away.

Ever since the unfortunate turkey slaughtering fiasco during my first year, I have been extra careful to pay attention to what is going on in the background of my interviews. At first I was annoyed by the fisherman, but then I thought, So what? At least he's starting out his holiday weekend on a high note. Let him fish.

As I composed myself at the lectern, I nodded greetings to the reporters, several of whom had once been fair and friendly toward me but who now had joined the ranks of the haters. I was just about to begin speaking when I heard the ploink of a fishing lure hitting the water behind me, and I wondered if anyone ever told this angler that Lake Lola was a dead lake. Years of toxic runoff from the Parks Highway and the miles of parking lots on its shore had poisoned the lake and killed off its population of rainbow trout and coho salmon. Algae blooms suffocated the rest. It was an unfortunate side effect of the rapid growth of our community that I worked diligently to correct.

Then I heard a splash, and I glanced over my shoulder in time to see the fisherman reeling in a rainbow trout. Its iridescent scales flashed in the sunlight as it broke the surface of the water. It was at least twenty inches long, a real trophy. But as remarkable as the fish was, the real shocker came when the fisherman looked up at me. Moments before, he had been just some balding sportsman in an Old Navy sweatshirt. But now the man in the skiff was young and fit. He wore a resplendent white robe, almost too bright to look at, with a purple sash. He had a full beard and flowing chestnut locks. He was beautiful. He didn't smile but gave me a stern, loving look, like a dad who must discipline a willful child. I could hear His gentle voice as though He was standing right next to me. "Didn't I make you a fisher of men? Why do you forsake me, daughter, before my work is done? You must prepare your people for what is to come."

Well, as you can imagine, my mind was blown. Meanwhile, the TV cameras were rolling, and Bradd edged closer to the lectern and whispered, "Are you all right?"

"That fisherman," was all I could say.

"What fisherman?"

And wouldn't you know it, when I looked again the fish and fisher, skiff and kicker, hook, line, and sinker were gone, vanished as though they'd never been.

Bradd said, "We can postpone this."

Postpone what? My resignation? Too late for that. Resigning my office was clearly off the table now. Jesus had just seen to that. Postpone the press conference? Again, too late. Our back yard was teeming with reporters who were already put out because their governor had forced them to come in during the Independence Day weekend for an important announcement. And then she freezes up like a deer caught in the headlights?

"No, I'm all right," I told Bradd.

"You sure?"

"You betcha." I folded my sheet of notes and handed it to him. "I have a different announcement, though." I gave him a confident wink, and his face lit up with a surprised grin.

"Give 'em hell, Vera."

I turned to the reporters before I had any idea of what I would say to them. All I knew at that moment was what the fisherman had told me, to prepare my people. I took a deep breath and began to speak, as curious as anyone to hear what I would say.

> *Hi, Alaska. I appreciate this opportunity to speak directly to you without the media filter, the people I serve as your governor. People who know me know that serving her people, our beloved state of Alaska, besides my family and my faith in the God of our fathers, there's nothing more important to me.*
>
> *Some of you with cynical hearts might ask then why did I leave Alaska to run for national office in the first place if Alaska means so much to me. Good question.*
>
> *Some in Juneau keep asking when am I coming back! Another good question.*

That last one got a laugh from the press corps.

> *Let me take a crack at answering the first question. Did you know that men and women serving in our nation's armed forces are not allowed to pray in public while wearing their uniforms? It's a federal law. Can you believe a government would pass such a law to push God away? What kind of longterm survival strategy is that? Sorry, God, we don't need You anymore. We'll just handle national security on our own.*
>
> *That's just one example. There are thousands of federal laws on the books that are sapping our beloved country of its moral strength, that are robbing our beloved country of its moral authority around the world. People of good conscience cannot allow that to stand, especially in these turbulent times.*
>
> *That's why I left my home in Alaska for a shot at taking our country back, putting America at the top of the charts again, preparing the nation for whatever may befall her. It was a worthy cause, and I gave it everything I had, and just because we lost doesn't mean we have to abandon our dream of a godly nation.*
>
> *Not at all. In fact, let's redouble our efforts and our prayers and make Alaska a shining beacon of traditional values for the rest of the country to follow. We may be the smallest state in terms of population, but we can be the leader in restoring the union to the faith of its founders, who we celebrate tomorrow on Independence Day.*
>
> *As to the second question — hey, give me a break, will ya? It's only been a month since the election; I need to catch my breath. Tell Juneau that I'll be back in the office on Monday with new initiatives in hand. Tell 'em to quit worrying about me and to get their own wagons in gear. Recess is over. It's time to knuckle down and move Alaska forward.*

I ended it there. Hands shot up all across the yard. The reporters wanted to know what new initiatives I'd be proposing on Monday, something I wanted to know myself. It seemed I had a busy weekend ahead of me, so I waved away their questions and hustled back to the house with Bradd and Taiga.

Later, Bradd dubbed the encounter with the fisherman my "burning fish" moment. I doubt it's in the same class as Moses' vision, but it has served as a bright demarkation in my life. There's my life before the fisherman and my life after. My governorship before and after. My dedication to God's plan. My purpose for being alive.

Sidebar: A Taste of Wormwood

TW1 1.0

TRUMPETS FIGURED LARGE in the Bible. You could scarcely smite your enemies without one.

> *My bowels, my bowels! I am pained at my very heart; my heart maketh a noise in me; I cannot hold my peace, because thou hast heard, O my soul, the sound of the trumpet, the alarm of war. (Jeremiah 4:19)*

Except for the rams-horn variety, Poppy couldn't find anything in either testament to inform him what biblical trumpets were made of. He presumed that earthly trumpets were made of brass. But he was interested in heavenly trumpets, especially those recorded in Revelation. Yet those lacked descriptive detail of any sort. At least the Bible didn't rule out heavenly glass.

Of all the many trumpets mentioned in Revelation, the two that caught his attention were those associated with stars falling to Earth. Surely, what was the blinding light that had knocked him off his iron steed if not a falling star?

The problem was that both of these trumpets spelled major trouble, and you didn't want either of their associated stars to fall in your back yard.

His trumpet might have belonged to the Third Angel:

> *And the third angel sounded, and there fell a great star from heaven, burning as it were a lamp, and it fell upon the third part of the rivers, and upon the fountain of waters;*
> *And the name of the star is called Wormwood: and the third part of the waters became wormwood; and many men died of the waters, because they were made bitter. (Rev 8:10, 11)*

If the falling star Poppy encountered was, in fact, the one known as Wormwood, the waters of Alaska and the Pacific Northwest were doomed. True, the pond the star fell into was frozen, but those ponds never froze completely. A trickle of water flowed even in the coldest weather. The road glaciers on the McHardy Road were proof enough of that. Eventually, the wormwood poison would seep into the Mizina River, which joined the Chitina, which flowed into the Copper, which emptied into the Gulf of Alaska at the northernmost corner of the Pacific Ocean.

The Copper River watershed drained one sixth of Alaska's land mass, and since Alaska was equal to one sixth the area of the Lower 48 states, that meant that one sixth of one sixth of America's freshwater reserves would soon turn poisonous. Poppy had never been a star pupil in math, but even he knew that 1/6 + 1/6 = 1/3. The "third part of the rivers."

Fortunately, his family was safe. They possessed seven million gallons of the freshest, sweetest water in the world. Moreover, their water was sheltered and secure in the bowels of a mountain. Pity everyone else downstream of them, saint and sinner alike. This was one more proof of Father God's plan in bringing his family to this Promised Land.

That is, if the fallen star was indeed the one known as Wormwood. By Father God's grace, he could test whether or not it was so (whoever said a Christian man couldn't be a scientist?) because Poppy actually knew how Wormwood tasted.

Wormwood was an ingredient in absinthe, that foul, sea-serpent-green, hallucinogenic liquor that he and his first wife, Abbie, scored while in Paris on holiday when they couldn't find any acid or mescaline. (This was, of course, before Poppy took Elder Brother Jesus as his personal savior.)

Absinthe was nasty, nasty stuff. Vile and more bitter than even peyote buttons. And the quality of the high it engendered was downright hellish. Ecstasy it was not. Mellow Yellow it did not make you, nor Lucy-in-the-Sky-with Diamonds. More like a hot poker stabbing you in the eye, with venomous snakes dripping from the rafters, and every crack in the sidewalk an open wound. Wet death on the breath of his beloved. All hope lost.

Nasty stuff, but Abbie said she liked it fine, and when a guy she met the following week offered her more — Gilles was his name, a thug and petty thief from Algiers — they had a party in Gilles's room without Poppy. Wormwood, then, was the beginning of the end of Poppy's first marriage.

And now millions of American men, women, and children were about to be treated to a taste of the same medicine — that is, if the star was the one known as Wormwood.

THE THIRD ANGEL was bad enough to deal with, but he was child's play compared to the Fifth Angel.

> And the fifth angel sounded, and I saw a star fall from heaven unto the earth: and to him was given the key of the bottomless pit. (Rev 9:1)

If the golden marble plugging the mouthpiece of the trumpet was the key to the bottomless pit, it would jeopardize Father God's whole plan of salvation.

The bottomless pit was the subterranean prison into which Elder Brother Jesus would banish Satan at the end of the Apocalypse and where He would bind him for a thousand years. Elder Brother Jesus would reign over a New Earth during that time in an unprecedented era of universal peace and harmony.

But without the key to the pit, Satan could not be bound, the war in Heaven and on Earth would never end, and there would be no New Earth or New Jerusalem. Judgment Day itself would have to be postponed or cancelled. Losing the key turned the promise of salvation on its head. The saved would not be saved, and sinners would not be punished eternally in the lake of fire as was their due.

A more immediate threat caused by a fumbling Fifth Angel would be the widespread effort to recover the key. Everyone in Heaven and Hell would be searching for it. Angels, devils, saints, and demons. And the combined armies of Gog and Magog would soon be beating a path to Poppy's door.

How could Father God tolerate such a clumsy angel? That angel deserved to have his wings clipped, or worse.

Unlike the Wormwood star, Poppy could think of no way to test whether the golden marble was a key to the pit or to anything else. *Grant me the wisdom, Holy Spirit, to know what to do. Amen.*

Sidebar: So He Masturbated

SH1 1.0

SINCE THE END of tourist season and the absence of horny girls from Outside, Jace had been doing a lot of it. Usually in bed, assisted by a dollop of Vaseline and a couple of facial tissues. He was a skilled masturbator. The trick was in the quality of his imagination, the inventiveness of the sex scenarios he could conjure up, and the bootylisciousness of his fantasy partners.

Though thoughts of Deuteronomy Prophecy ruled Jace's waking hours, he never allowed himself to fantasize about her while spanking the monkey. It was a matter of honor for him. He respected her too much to use her for sex without her permission, not even in his imagination. Even mental rape was rape. When they eventually did make sweet, hot love in reality, if they ever did, his heart would be pure.

> *Deut Prophecy looked up at his entrance into the bathhouse. She suppressed a smile and went back to the business of folding the family's laundry on the long, wooden table. Only the pink flush of her cheeks revealed her interest. Her eyebrows were so fair as to be all but invisible on her brow — until she blushed!*

> *She was, he told himself all over again, the most unlikely young woman a powerful and god-hating governmental employee could ever expect to make himself a fool over. She was Christian Taliban. She had a heavily armed posse of older brothers who hated his guts and a father who would gladly pitchfork him in the throat.*

No, that would not do.

Instead, Jace usually chose one of the girls of summer for his partner, a real girl he'd actually boinked or wanted to boink but never got the chance. And always waiting at the front of the queue was the French girl. Danielle was the hottest girl he'd ever made love to, and she had given herself to him wet and eager that first time in Anchorage. There was still a lot of good masturbatory material to mine from that encounter, but most of Jace's fantasies sprang from her brief visit to his McHardy "chalet."

In a way, these sessions with Danielle followed a "do-over" script. And they were much bloodier than his usual erotic reveries. They began with some fresh insult from the Prophecy clan, over which Jace would confront the cowardly bastards and trade them blow for blow. Sometimes he delivered nothing more than a drubbing, a bloody nose, or a broken bone with witty riposte: *Who's your savior now?* Usually, the target of Jace's retribution was the surly one, Proverbs, and the confrontation escalated from fisticuffs to bodily dismemberment. Knives, axes, chainsaws — that sort of thing. Whenever Jace killed off Proverbs, Danielle was right there, an eager witness. The brutish callousness with which he butchered the boy never failed to arouse her. Often she became so hot that he had to break off the fight to fuck her on the spot, even as Proverbs' arterial blood squirted from his body. Yes. Yes. Yes.

SH2 1.0

FOR DEUT'S PART, she never did it, not once. If pressed on the matter, blushing fiercely, she wouldn't even know what the word masturbation meant. Except that, whatever it was, it was a devastating sin and Satan's tool to lead young Christians away from Father God. Deut didn't need to know more than that, and frankly, with Mama P on vacation in Heaven, she didn't have anyone she could ask. (Not that Mama P had ever discussed sex with her anyway.)

Actually, it was impossible to grow up in the country and not witness Father God's creatures engaging in procreation. Goats, horses, donkeys all did it no matter who was watching. The rabbit bucks they raised were especially randy little beasts, and a dog they once owned tried to mate with anyone or anything, even your leg, once even with a chicken. (Poppy got rid of him soon after.) But as Mama told them, it didn't mean you had to watch.

The few times Deut had brought up the subject of sex, Mama told her to wait. When the time came — meaning when she was betrothed to marry — they would have a talk and all would be explained. Exactly where Deut would find a suitable mate while locked up in a cave for seven years was a mystery. But Father God was sure to provide. After all, didn't He find matches for Adam and Proverbs?

Now that Mama was on vacation, there really wasn't anyone to ask about these things. For a while Deut considered broaching the subject of masturbation with Ginger. Ginger lived in the fallen world, but she was still godly and faith-filled. She even went out on dates with boys. She would have a wholesome take on the matter. Still, masturbation was not something Deut would bring up on her own.

All of which was not to suggest that Deut was carved from a block of wood. No, she was a healthy, fit, young human with a responsive body that was swimming in a sea of God-given sensations. Sometimes, as she lay in a tub of warm water, bathing herself *down there* through the cotton fabric of her undergarments, well, the warmth would spread throughout her body in a most delicious way. And sometimes, with her legs straddling the cushiony seat of a sno-go, she could feel the deep vibrations of the engine *down there*, and lots of bumps in the trail would make for a fun ride. Surely, that was a gift and not a sin.

The odd thing was that thinking about the ranger sometimes stirred those same sensations. Now *that* was troubling, especially since, short of a miraculous rebirth on his part, Jace Kuliak was doomed to burn in eternal torment and was not someone Poppy would ever allow in the keep.

None of which prevented her from dreaming about him once. Or more than once, actually. They were weird dreams. He was both piloting the Mail Day plane overhead while at the same time helping her carry jugs of hot soup from a clearwater creek. Odd. She was making fun of his ponytail, though in truth she really liked it.

Sidebar: Raven Song

May they always dwell
in purple beds on mountain crags.
May they always dwell
in purple beds on barren ice.
May they always dwell
on plastic mats on ocean gyres.
Caw! Caw!

Acknowledgements

Much thanks to **Deb Vanasse** and **Elyse Guttenberg**, each of whom collaborated with me on trying to write a book about our celebrity governor. Neither project got off the ground, but working on them helped me shape the parody character who eventually became Vera Tetlin.

Thanks to **Ramey Wood** for the loan of the eyepatch.

Beta Readers
Thanks to **Sandra Boatwright, Terry Boren, Kay Kenyon, Deb Vanasse,** and **Gary Wolfe** for reading and commenting on the early drafts of this book. Their feedback has been essential to its development.

Thanks, too, to **Sarah Campbell** for editing the manuscript and to **Don Pendergrast** for his insights into NPS culture. Of course, I am solely responsible for the portrayal of the park service and its personnel. Thanks to **KJ Kirby** and **Sharron Albert** for proofreading the completed manuscript.

Patrons of the Arts
No public tax dollars or foundation money has gone into the creation of this work. Individual contributions, however, have helped keep me in the writer's seat through the lean times, and I would like to thank **Ruth Nicolas**, O.D. and **Kimberly Sherrill**, M.D. especially for their patronage.

Reading List

A Land Gone Lonesome, Dan O'Neill, Counterpoint, New York, 2006

Chapter 18, Are ETs & UFOs Real?, Dr. Jason Lisle, Answers in Genesis, December 6, 2007, <https://answersingenesis.org/astronomy/alien-life/are-ets-ufos-real/>

The Belief Instinct, Jesse Bering, WW Norton & Co., New York, 2011

The Copper Spike, Lone E. Janson, Alaska Northwest Publishing Company, Anchorage, 1976

"DNA is Not Destiny: The New Science of Epigenetics Rewrites the Rules of Disease, Heredity, and Identity," Ethan Watters, *Discover Magazine*, November 22, 2006

Going Rogue: An American Life, Sarah Palin, Harper, New York, 2009

Last Ape Standing: The Seven-Million-Year Story of How and Why We Survived, Chip Walter. Walker & Company, January 29, 2013. Copyright © William J. (Chip) Walter, Jr.

Millions Disappear: Fact or Fiction?, by P. S. R. BB Bookstore, Copyright © 1989 by P. S. R.

Pilgrim's Wilderness: A True Story of Faith and Madness on the Alaska Frontier, Tom Kizzia, Crown, New York, 2013

Errors and Whatnot

Writing, even writing fiction, requires a great deal of knowledge about the world. There's a near certainty that one of more errors of fact are lurking somewhere in this book, despite the author's Herculean effort to root them out. If you, the reader, come across a genuine error and are the first person to alert the author at <utr@marusek.com>, your contribution to accuracy will be acknowledged in subsequent, corrected editions. Please note, however, that this offer applies only to errors of fact, not differences of opinion, taste, or belief. Also note that the needs of the plot may sometimes supersede the desire for factual accuracy.

You are welcome to share your opinions too, and if you succeed in convincing the author to alter the text as a consequence (possible but not likely), your input will also be acknowledged.

For purposes of easy reference, each scene sequence in the text is labeled along the right margin. Please use these labels when reporting errors or whatnot.

Book 2

You can receive occasional updates on the progress and release of the second book in this series, *Upon This Rock: Book 2 — A Little Nudge,* by asking to join the "Novel Update" list at utr@marusek.com.